"Bianca Zander's *The Predictions* is ... plunge into a fringe community—so alive with smells, sounds, and textures that you forget you are reading at all. An unforgettable novel about breaking away from others' doctrines in order to discover what you truly believe and desire. Absorbing, compassionate, and filled with gloriously flawed characters that are sure to set off book club fireworks!"

—Susan Henderson, author of *Up from the Blue*

"In *The Predictions* Bianca Zander creates pure magic in a nostalgic tale of the seventies and eighties with a twist. Life on a commune might be all about free love and free will, but for Poppy and Lukas, this life creates difficulties after a startling announcement rocks their idyllic world. When an alluring, mysterious visitor to the commune grants each of the children predictions for the future, and one of their own goes missing, Poppy and Lukas abandon the shelter of the commune and attempt to outrun their destinies by escaping into eighties heavy metal London. *The Predictions* is a wild and exhilarating ride, and Zander has created an otherworld where destiny collides with life and reality, where lust and love complicate and heal, and where fate and faith triumph."

—Robin Antalek, author of *The Grown Ups* and
  The Summer We Fell Apart

"A richly atmospheric, rollicking journey through two of our most socially controversial—and entertaining—decades. As tender as it is gripping, *The Predictions* is an unforgettable coming-of-age story that beautifully addresses what it means to move beyond the youthful winds of influence and into the hard-won rewards of mature love."

—Elizabeth Percer

"So funny and smart, so sharp and artful. In every sense, Bianca Zander is a fantastic writer."

—Curtis Sittenfeld, *New York Times* bestselling
    author of *Prep* and *American Wife*

"Zander shows novels can embody truth—in the dialogue that hits the perfect pitch, in the emotional span from glee to guts to grief."

—*New Zealand Herald*

THE PREDICTIONS

ALSO BY BIANCA ZANDER

The Girl Below

THE PREDICTIONS

Bianca Zander

WILLIAM MORROW

An Imprint of HarperCollins*Publishers*

P.S.™ is a trademark of HarperCollins Publishers.

HarperCollins books may be purchased for educational, business, or sales promotional use. For information please e-mail the Special Markets Department at SPsales@harpercollins.com.

FIRST EDITION

Illustrations from the Aquarian Tarot Deck® reproduced by permission of U.S. Games Systems, Inc., Stamford, CT 06902 USA. Copyright ©1993 by U.S. Games Systems, Inc. Further reproduction prohibited.

Designed by Lisa Stokes

Library of Congress Cataloging-in-Publication Data has been applied for.

ISBN 978-0-06-210818-0

15 16 17 18 19   OV/RRD   10 9 8 7 6 5 4 3 2 1

For Matthew, Rafael, and Hector—

all parenting is an experiment. Sorry!

And for Azedear—

with gratitude and love.

THE PREDICTIONS

PART I

CHAPTER 1

Gaialands
1978

WE WERE RAISED AT Gaialands to believe in freedom—personal, societal, spiritual—but in the years after I left the commune not a single day passed when I did not feel tightly bound by the fate laid down for me there.

Conditions on the commune were harsh. No electricity or flushing toilets or hot running water in the long winter months, and in the summer, no way to keep a beer cold, or even any beer. Despite all legends of hippie excess, no one on the commune was allowed to drink or smoke or take LSD or sleep with their mother. And then there was the groovy outdoor lifestyle. Each December we were hit with summer storms, days of lightning strikes and torrential rains that took out trees and burst the creek, drowning animals and flooding the surrounding paddocks, and that was in a good year. In the bad years we had to evacuate, returning when the valley had drained of water and our belongings were covered in silt.

But it wasn't the weather or the basic facilities that made

living at Gaialands a trial. It was philosophy. The commune
was never what anyone expected it to be—and nobody could
stand it for long. People who had heard about us, hippies
mostly, arrived at our gate with big, wonky ideas about dropping out of society and living where no one expected them
to lift a finger unless it was to roll a joint. They wanted yoga
and meditation and a smattering of Zen Buddhism and whole
foods, but had no concept of how hard it was to grow all your
food from scratch and how little time it left for other pursuits.

We didn't welcome the hippies with open arms but we
allowed them to stay a few days, feeding them up on nut
roast and alfalfa sprouts and letting them sleep in the tepee
down by the creek, which leaked when it rained and was
too hot, during the day, to hang out in. If they lasted a week,
the hippies were given chores: picking apples, chopping fire-
wood, scrubbing pots; and if that didn't make them leave,
there was one task that always broke them.

Early in the morning, before the heat of the sun triggered the high-noon stench of feces, Hunter woke up the hippies and handed them a long-handled spade with which to
dig out the long drops. These were six-feet-deep holes filled
with communal excrement, and that was on a day when it
hadn't rained, when the shit hadn't spread to the paddock. As
one by one the hippies laid down their spades and refused to
go on, Hunter, our self-appointed leader, rubbed his hands
together with glee. He loathed hippies and nothing pleased
him more than proving they were a no-good breed of dirty,
privileged layabouts.

He drove them to the end of our driveway in his ute, and

there he gave them his farewell speech, so well rehearsed he could say it in his sleep. The climax, which followed a bunch of Marxist stuff about the cooperative labor ethics of a working organic farm, was an idiosyncratic take on an old Zen proverb. "Before enlightenment: chopping wood, shoveling shit," he would say, waiting for his audience to grow agitated before delivering the punch line: "After enlightenment: chopping wood, shoveling shit."

And then, one fine day in the spring of 1978, a woman turned up on the commune who single-handedly reinstated the hippie reputation we had worked so hard to destroy.

The afternoon she arrived, I was on pig duty with Fritz. The two of us shoveled pig shit into a wheelbarrow, trying to get the job done as quickly and as badly as possible. As the oldest, I was supposed to supervise. Fritz had just tried to run away from the commune again, and I had been told to keep an eye on him. To this end, I had so far handed out only one instruction, and that was to at least try to look as though we were doing what we had been asked to do. Just because we had grown up at Gaialands, and were stuck there, did not mean we shared our leader's work ethic.

"Do you think," said Fritz, leaning on his spade, "we could get away with rinsing the rest of the yard with a bucket of water? I don't see why we have to get every last bit of crap—it only gets dirty again."

"I don't make up the rules," I said. "I only know what happens if we don't follow them."

"You're such a goody-goody," said Fritz. "I can't believe we're related."

"We weren't—until a few months ago."

"Can we change it back?"

"Nah. You're stuck with me until one of us carks it."

Brother-sister teasing was new to us, risky and untried. Barely a few months had passed since we had found out we shared a set of parents. Before that we had been forbidden to speak of such things or even to speculate. But I think I had always known Fritz was my kin. He had been born with a clubfoot, never treated, and though the other kids had teased him about it, made fun of his lopsided walk, I never had. Instead I had felt protective, as though his clubfoot was *my* clubfoot. There were other things too that made me suspect. Sometimes I heard him talking when he wasn't, or I knew what he was going to say before he said it. When we were alone together we barely spoke, not because we had nothing to say, but because we didn't need to talk.

I watched him shuffle over to the water trough with an empty bucket and return with it full, at which point he flung water at the yard, standing back to survey the results.

"Bugger," he said, throwing the pail aside. "I've made it worse."

He had. Propelled by the force of his sluicing, the water from the pail had briefly flowed uphill, and then, according to the laws of physics, flowed downhill again, bringing with it all the shit we had scraped up that morning.

I didn't have the heart to tell Fritz off. Better to lean on my own spade and laugh at the inanity of being made to shovel the same shit twice.

We were easily distracted after that, looking out for

trouble. The sound of an engine straining to climb the loose gravel on the last stretch of road before the commune was all the encouragement we needed to abandon our task. We stood, hands on hips, waiting to see who would appear over the hill. I expected a car but the first thing that came into view was the yellow roof of a gingerbread house, like something out of "Hansel and Gretel." The car that towed it was a thing so rusted and barnacled that it might have been a fishing trawler.

Fritz scratched his head. "What is that?"

"Some sort of caravan?"

At the crest of the hill, gravity took over. The car swooped forward, out of control, propelled by the weight of the gingerbread house behind it. Missing the curve at the bottom of the driveway, the car then fishtailed through a pile of rotten avocados, picked up speed, and set off on a direct collision course with the pigpen. And in the pigpen, my brother.

"Fritz!" I called out, and he turned and looked in my direction instead of moving out of the way.

The pigpen fence gave way like paper. The car was seconds from impact. Seemingly in slow motion, his head swiveled back toward the oncoming car and stayed there. With not a moment to spare, I leapt out of my gumboots and across the pig shit toward him. Here the slipperiness worked in my favor, and I skated the last few feet in time to grab him around the waist and fling both of us out of harm's way.

Squeals and oinks filled the air, along with the sound of metal grinding against metal, and then a loud bang as the car slammed into the stump of an old oak tree. This stopped the car, but not the carriage behind it, which shunted forward, driving a long metal tow bar clean through the vehicle's boot. The car made an awful splitting sound while the caravan, which I now saw was painted midnight blue under its yellow roof, swayed from side to side before settling intact on its wheelbase.

Over by the water trough, the pigs snuffled around, unharmed, and my gaze returned to the car, whose windscreen had shattered in its frame, concealing the driver. For a few ugly seconds, I feared we would have to retrieve a corpse. But then, the driver's door swung open, and a woman exclaimed joyfully, "Wow, what a ride!"

I still could not see her, but below the driver's door, a bare foot and an ankle festooned with silver bells peeped out. When it encountered pig shit, this foot retreated, and the door closed.

In slow and jerky increments, as though the glass had come out of its hinges, the driver's-door window lowered to reveal a living mirage.

I was used to the commune women: plain and hearty; milk-washed or sunburned, depending on the season; and sturdy as livestock, built for work. But this woman was the human equivalent of a Fabergé egg, existing only to charm and beguile. Beside me, Fritz gasped.

"Oh my lord! I seem to be stranded," she exclaimed, and the two of us stepped forward, eager to assist but mute.

The woman laughed openly at our efforts. "You're very sweet but I think what we need is a man—don't you?" Her accent was American and soft like waves lapping at a beach.

Valiantly, Fritz held out his hand. "I'm strong for my age."

"I'm sure you are," she said, stroking the offered hand, then rejecting it, "but I doubt you could lift me an inch off the ground."

She sat resolutely in the car, while Fritz tried his best not to look crestfallen.

"Oh look," she said, pointing out the window, "one is coming!"

From far away across the paddock, Hunter strode in our direction, arms waving. Halfway to us he broke into a run— something I hadn't seen him do since we were kids. Behind him, at a slower pace, others followed.

"Hunter," said the woman. "I'd recognize that beard anywhere."

"You know Hunter?" I was taken aback.

"Oh yes," she said. "We share a deep connection."

"I'm Poppy. And this here's Fritz."

"Shakti," she said. "Pleased to meet you."

A couple of pigs had strolled over to sniff the car, perhaps eager to meet her too, and I tried to shoo them away. "Come on, girls, leave the lady alone."

"I thought Gaialands was vegetarian," said Shakti, eyeing the pigs with pity.

"It is," I said. "They're more like pets. They eat our scraps and turn it into manure."

"Of course," said Shakti. "How silly of me."

One of the pigs, Doris, who thought she was human, wandered back to the car and head-butted it repeatedly.

"Would you look at that?" Shakti reached out and tentatively scratched the pig's head. "She's welcoming me. Telling me I've come to the right place."

"She does that to everything," said Fritz, slapping Doris's huge hairy backside to get her to move. "She'll get bored in a minute."

"Never ignore a sign," said Shakti. "No matter how humble the messenger."

"Shakti!" called Hunter, reaching the pigpen and skidding across the last stretch of filth. "You made it. Are you all right?"

"Never been better. Though I am sorry about the pig house. I lost control coming over the hill."

Hunter surveyed the damage, then waved it away. "We were thinking of building a new one anyway. Maybe now we'll actually get around to it."

If there were plans to build a new pigpen, this was the first I'd heard of it.

Hunter leaned in through the open car door, and Shakti reached up and put her arms around his neck. He carried her, bridelike, across the mud and settled her gently down on a patch of grass. She wore a flimsy sarong, tied in a knot at the nape of her neck. The hem flitted up, revealing a thatch of black hair.

I pretended not to have seen and tried not to blush. When I looked at Fritz, his eyes were popping out of his head. A second later, he turned on his heel and sprinted across the paddock.

No sooner had he left than the twins, Nelly and Ned,

made it to the crash site. Nelly was the girl I was closest to, and we told each other everything, or had done so before the business with Timon. She was still cut up over that.

"Where's Fritz off to in such a hurry?" she said.

"He's gone to wash his eyeballs in the river."

"What did he see?"

I nodded in Shakti's direction. She was deep in conversation with Hunter, her back turned on the wreckage.

"Who's she?" asked Nelly.

"A whole lot of trouble," said Ned, surveying the damage. "If that's who was behind the wheel."

"She lost control coming over the hill," I explained. "It wasn't her fault."

"That thing shouldn't even be on the road—it's a wreck." Ned was obsessed with cars and couldn't resist trying to lift the front bonnet to inspect the engine.

"I wouldn't touch that if I were you," said Paul, one of the fathers, who had arrived from his workshop, still in his overalls, a wrench in one hand and a grease-splattered towel in the other. "You don't want to blow up the commune." He shook his head. "That thing's a goner."

He walked over to Shakti and introduced himself, wiping his hands on his overalls first. I heard him say, "Well, love, you won't be leaving here in a hurry," and Shakti replied, "Oh, that's quite all right, I hadn't planned to."

"Poppy," said Hunter, waving to me. "Why don't you take Shakti to the mess hut and fix her a cuppa? Get out the honey. She's had a bit of a fright."

We kept beehives and harvested honey made from the

nectar of manuka bushes, prized for its medicinal qualities. But we also weren't allowed to eat it. We bottled the stuff and sent it to Auckland, where it fetched a tidy price before being sent overseas. It was one of the few products we sold to the outside world, one of the few exchanges we made that resulted in money. Hunter's idea was to live a cash-free existence, but we couldn't barter for engine parts, or farming tools, or the sacks of grain that we needed to get through the winter.

I clomped over to Shakti in my gumboots. The pig shit inside them was starting to dry. They'd be hell to clean out.

"This way," I said.

We set off in the direction of the mess hut, Shakti gliding next to me, with Nelly and Ned trailing behind. I told Shakti who they were but didn't properly introduce them.

"And you're Poppy?" said Shakti, with another one of her smiles that felt like a kiss. "What a pretty name."

"You think so?"

"The poppy is a beautiful flower—and it gives us opium, one of the most powerful narcotics known to man."

"You mean a drug? Drugs aren't allowed on the commune."

Shakti considered this for a moment. "Well," she said, playfully, "maybe you'll grow up to be an intoxicating woman?"

Somehow, I doubted it. Shakti followed me down a dirt path that ran between the chook house and a hay barn, the bells on her ankles tinkling as she walked. *She* was certainly intoxicating. Next to her I felt like a troll. We passed by the orchards, where a couple of the boys were up in the avocado trees, whooping and hollering as they picked ripe fruit. Lukas climbed halfway down his ladder and wolf-whistled. I waved back. Then he climbed back up the ladder, no doubt to speculate with Timon about who the pretty visitor was.

"Who was that?" said Shakti, when he had disappeared.

"Just Lukas."

"*Just Lukas?*" she repeated. "I'd call that a handsome young fellow."

"He's the oldest of us kids—and boy does he like to remind us."

"And he's how old?"

"Seventeen."

"Seventeen," repeated Shakti. "The perfect age."

She didn't say what for. Behind us, Nelly and Ned peeled away. They were supposed to be picking avocados too.

Shakti turned around and watched them go. "Are they twins?"

"Yes."

"And are there more of you? More kids?"

"Seven in all. After Lukas comes Timon. I come next, followed by the twins, Nelly and Ned. The youngest are Meg and Fritz. You met him too." I paused, adding, "He's my . . . brother," to see if saying it out loud still felt strange, which it did.

"You all have quite straight names for a commune. The one I've just come from, there were kids called Astral and Rainbow and Star."

"Is your name from a commune?"

"No," said Shakti. "It's a name I have earned."

In the mess hall Elisabeth was in the process of setting the table for dinner. She was in charge of the kitchen, making up menus and rosters and supervising whoever was on cooking duty. We ate dinner early, when the heat had gone out of the day—or in winter, the light—then went to bed early and rose not long after dawn. We had to. Sunlight ruled the length of our days. The commune had no electricity, only candles, kerosene lamps, and a diesel-powered generator for emergencies.

I was surprised to have to introduce Elisabeth to Shakti. Elisabeth was Hunter's life mate, and I had assumed she and Shakti would know each other. Hunter and Elisabeth had been married once, before they realized marriage was a capitalist construct.

Elisabeth was her usual prickly self. Instead of welcoming Shakti, she said, "You're our first visitor. It always starts this time of year, in the spring. Hippies mostly. They think they can come here and sit around getting high. They don't want to lift a finger." She was setting out chairs, and as she spoke, she moved an enormous stack of them from one side of the room to the other, showing off her strength.

"We work hard at Gaialands." She put her hands on her hips and looked squarely at Shakti. "Hippies don't last long around here."

"Oh, I'm used to hard work!" said Shakti. "I've been living on an *ohu*. You've heard of those, right?"

Elisabeth nodded. "We met some folk from the one near Wanganui."

"That's the one I've been living on," said Shakti. "Ahu Ahu."

"Across the river from Jerusalem?" Elisabeth was more interested now.

Shakti nodded. "We had to do everything from scratch. It was like a frontier settlement."

I had heard of the place too, and the ohu scheme. Prime Minister Norman Kirk had leased shitty pieces of land to groups of young people for next to nothing to build communes. Most of them had lasted five minutes but the people who had started Ahu Ahu were made of hardier stuff.

"Just getting to it was a mission," said Shakti. "There's no road access so the only way in was to cross the river. It was all right in the summer but in the winter"—she whistled— "boy, you took your life into your own hands. They had this basket, attached to a rope, operated by a set of pulleys. It was basically just a flying fox."

"Cool!" I said. We kids had been trying for years to build a flying fox across the stream, but the trees on either side were too low and we could never get the wire tight enough.

"Nuh-uh," said Shakti. "Not cool at all. A death trap."

I had heard of Jerusalem too, not the Holy City but its namesake, a small settlement up the Wanganui River. A famous poet started a spiritual commune there with a bunch of his followers but the newspapers were filled with reports of squalor and drugs and children with head lice. Then the poet died. It was one of the stories Hunter loved to tell to remind us of the difference between our commune and the ones started by "bandwagon jumpers and filthy bloody hippies." Hunter and Elisabeth had started Gaialands in the early sixties, long before anyone in New Zealand had even heard of communes. They had gone on an overseas experience as undergraduate students and spent a long, hot summer on a kibbutz, returning to New Zealand eager to start one of their own.

Shakti drank her tea and I sat next to her while mine went cold. I liked tea well enough, but I was too mesmerized to drink it. Two of the other women, Susie and Katrina, a couple, had come into the mess hut, and listened quietly to the end of Shakti's tale about the ohu. "All winter it rained and rained," she told us. "All of the buildings were makeshift and leaked like nobody's business. The place was like a swimming pool; all the food got wet, ruined. I had to leave, before my caravan floated down the river."

"How did you get it across to the ohu?" I asked.

"I didn't," said Shakti. "It was waiting for me on the other side."

I wondered what had happened to the other people living there, if they had stuck it out, eating ruined food and wearing soggy clothes. But Shakti didn't say.

"Anyway," she said, "already I can see Gaialands is nothing like that place. I've dreamt of coming here ever since I met Hunter at the Nambassa Festival last year. It's so good to have finally made it!"

We had all gone to Nambassa the year before but it seemed only Hunter had met this dazzling woman, about whom he had said absolutely nothing in the months since. We were going to the festival again this year. Paul had built a wood-powered combustion engine, and he and Hunter were going to demonstrate how it worked.

"What part of America are you from?" asked Katrina.

"Berkeley," said Shakti. "My parents were professors."

We looked at her blankly. No one knew where this was.

"The Bay Area—near San Francisco."

"I went there once," said Elisabeth. "Everyone was so stoned. Tripping on acid. No one washed. You could see fleas jumping off their skin. I couldn't leave fast enough."

"That must have been a while ago," said Shakti, laughing. "Things have really changed. Everyone's into disco, and all the men are gay. Before I left I was the spiritual adviser at a self-help clinic for women."

"What's a self-help clinic?" asked Susie.

"We helped desperate women find men that aren't gay."

"Really?" said Katrina, who was a lesbian. "What for?"

"I'm joking," said Shakti, adding in a serious voice, "it's a health clinic. We helped women find their cervix—and in a surprising number of cases, their clitoris."

"Oh," said Elisabeth, reddening, and looking in my direction. "I'm not sure we need to mention that in front of Poppy."

"Are you kidding?" said Shakti. "Every woman needs to know how to find her clitoris."

"She's still a girl," said Elisabeth.

"What's a clitoris?" I said, then wished I hadn't when the women around me all laughed.

Shakti looked with curiosity from me to Elisabeth and back again. "Only the most important part of your anatomy," she said, addressing me. "But I'll leave the details to your mother."

"I'm not her mother," said Elisabeth, sharply, while I backed this up with a shake of my head.

"I'm sorry," said Shakti, perplexed. "It's just that you two look so much alike."

Elisabeth said, "What a person looks like is of little concern."

Shakti said nothing.

"We do things a little differently around here," said Susie, trying to patch things up. "You'll get used to it."

"I guess I'll have to," said Shakti, her smile broader than ever.

Elisabeth began to clear away the teacups and wipe the table clean.

Footsteps sounded on the porch of the mess hall, and then in walked Paul and Hunter, sheened in grease and sweat.

"I was right about the car," said Paul. "It's rooted. But we've moved the bloody thing to where it won't cause any more trouble. And the caravan—"

"Under a willow tree down by the river," said Hunter. "We thought it would be nice and quiet for you there."

"Thank you," said Shakti. "That's kind."

Katrina offered to show Shakti the way to her caravan.

"I'll take her," I said, my heart beating faster at the tiny lie I was about to tell. "I'm going down to the river anyway—to clean off this pig shit."

IT HAD RAINED SO much that spring that the area down by the river was a bog, and we made our way cautiously around it on narrow mounds of dry earth. I kept apologizing for the terrain and once or twice thought of offering Shakti a piggy-back, as though she was some kind of princess, and I was . . . what? Her manservant?

The caravan had sunk about a foot into the soft, buttery mud. Shakti was thoughtful on the walk and had barely spoken, but now she turned to me and said, "Elisabeth—she *is* your mother, isn't she?"

"She birthed me, yes."

"She gave birth to you. Then why did she deny it?"

"Because we don't say 'mother' and 'father.' We call the adults by their names. They raised us in a group."

"Of course. It's a commune. They brought you up together."

She hadn't exactly understood my meaning but I was reluctant to explain. The few times I had explained to outsiders that we were raised without knowing who our parents were, they had reacted with shock or disapproval, and I had learned to keep quiet about it, to let people assume whatever they wanted.

Shakti walked around her caravan as best she could, inspecting it for damage, while I studied the symbols painted on the side. Next to the moon, there was Saturn, and one of the blue planets; I didn't know its name. Signs of the zodiac were dotted about, a few constellations, and some symbols that looked like letters of a foreign alphabet.

"She's a beauty, huh?" said Shakti, completing her circuit and climbing the steps at the front to stand on a little wooden porch. "Whenever I find symbols that mean something to me, I paint them on the outside—kind of like a patchwork quilt for the soul." When she opened the door, an upside-down stool and a stack of other items blocked the way. "Oh dear," she said, stepping over them. "Everything must have moved around in the crash."

I craned my neck to see inside the caravan, drinking in the potpourri of books and macrame and sculptures of dripping candle wax.

Shakti deftly positioned herself in the doorway, blocking my view. "I'd invite you in but I need to sort out this mess before I have visitors." She smiled, then closed the door emphatically.

I stood in the mud, not moving, wanting to get back the feeling I'd had a few minutes earlier, when I was with Shakti. In something of a daze, I climbed the porch steps and stood dumbly in front of her door.

"Dinner is at sundown!" I called out. "There's a cowbell, but you might not hear it from here!"

When there was no reply, I wondered if I should knock on the door and hesitated a moment too long. Something at my feet caught my eye, a playing card of some sort, and I bent to pick it up. On closer inspection, it turned out to be not a playing card but one from a deck of tarot. Some of the women had tarot cards, but they hadn't got them out for a while. This one showed a picture of a man and a woman gazing dreamily at each other, below which was printed "The Lovers." I was studying it intently when Shakti flung the door open, giving me a fright.

"What was that about a cowbell?"

"It—it rings," I said, stammering. "To let you know when it's dinnertime."

I had foolishly tried to hide the card behind my back, but of course Shakti had seen it. "What's that in your hand?" she said.

Embarrassed, I handed it over.

Shakti examined the picture. "Very interesting," she said, with a look that was filled with meaning. "Very interesting indeed." She held the card to face me. "The Lovers," she said. "Do you know what this means?"

"No," I said. "I mean, not really."

"Well, it can mean you're going to be faced with a huge decision about an existing relationship—or that maybe you'll face a temptation of the heart."

At the word "temptation," a hot patch flared on my neck.

"Or," said Shakti, "it can signify the thing that drives us out of the garden—like Eve when she bit the apple."

"We're atheists," I said.

"The card doesn't care what you believe," said Shakti. "The important thing is that you picked it up."

"Only so I could give it back. I wasn't going to keep it."

"I know," she said, smiling. "But there's no such thing as coincidence." She held the card to her chest and glanced above her, sweeping her free arm across the vast, empty sky. "The map is up there—written in the stars." She fixed me with a cosmically charged stare. "All we have to do is follow it."

CHAPTER 2

Gaialands
1978

LESS THAN A MONTH after her arrival Shakti had won over almost every individual on the commune. Not only had she charmed us, but she was made to do barely any chores, or only the ones she found pleasant and rewarding. I never once saw her with dirt-covered hands.

As far as the men were concerned, she needed to do no more than flutter her eyelids or glide by in a flimsy sarong, or better still, glide by in nothing at all, and they were bewitched. She was so startling to look at that even Paul, who was notably devoted to his life mate, Sigi, grew flushed and starry eyed whenever she was nearby.

Winning over the women required a little more time and attention, but at this she was no less skilled. Within a week or two, she had Katrina and Susie getting up with her at dawn to practice yoga by the creek, naked, the three of them lifting their buttocks high in the air for downward dog, oblivious to the huddle of teenage boys stationed close by behind a large boulder. I hadn't seen this with my own eyes, but I had heard the boys whispering late at night in the sleeping hut. That is, until Lukas told them to quit their gas-bagging and go to sleep. I took this to mean Lukas was not a part of their spying, a fact I noted with a strange satisfaction.

When she was on the roster to help in the communal kitchen, Shakti was meek and subservient, which eventually got her on Elisabeth's good side (or as close to it as was possible with Elisabeth). In the schoolhouse, which was Sigi's domain, Shakti taught bits and pieces of American history as well as rudimentary Spanish she had learned from a Latino grandmother on her father's side. But she always worked under Sigi's direction, and never in a way that was showy or took away from Sigi's lessons. Compared to Elisa-beth, Loretta was a walk in the park, as easily won over as the men. She had always been into astrology and palmistry, which Shakti practiced, along with tarot and runes and just about every system of divination known to humanity. In fact, the two of them were soon in cahoots, planning some kind of mass astrology chart that encompassed every inhab-itant of Gaialands, and probably some of the animals too.

One Sunday afternoon, after she had been with us about a month, Shakti spread the word that the women were to gather that night for a secret meeting—no men allowed. Along with Nelly (but not Meg, who was only fourteen), I was surprised and flattered to be included. Our instructions were to remain behind in the mess hut after dinner until all the males had left.

When they were gone, Shakti closed all the doors and lit

candles and incense that infused the room with the falsely sweet smell of flowers. It was a warm night. Many of the women had been hard at work all day, and beneath the floral scent was a punch of underarm odor.

"Next time, we'll fashion some curtains," Shakti said. "But this should do for tonight." She cleared a space on one side of the room, scattering cushions in a random formation on the floor, and instructed us to sit or lie in whatever position we found most comfortable.

"It's important to feel relaxed," she said. "Because tonight is all about sharing."

Rather than relaxed, a few of the women looked more uptight than usual. We sat about as we had been told, some cross-legged or with knees folded underneath, trying very hard to impersonate a chilled-out vibe.

Someone triggered a round of nervous laughter and over the top of it, Shakti said, "I can't believe you've never done consciousness raising before."

"We've heard of it," said Katrina, "but I guess we never felt the need."

"We're hardly oppressed housewives," added Susie.

At this statement, Shakti raised her eyebrows in surprise. "Well," she said, after a long pause. "In that case, it might be a good place to start the discussion."

Katrina said, "You want us to talk about housewives?"

"Sure, why not?" said Shakti. "What does the idea of a housewife mean to you?" She fixed her gaze on Loretta, who was trying to be invisible. "Loretta—do you want to start?"

Loretta looked around the room at the doors and windows, trying to find an escape route, before saying in a quiet voice: "Someone who stays at home, who looks after the children and does all the chores—the housework."

"Anyone else?" Shakti studied the gathered women.

I put up my hand, unsure if it was okay to speak.

"Go ahead, Poppy—your opinion counts as much as any other."

"A housewife doesn't go out to work," I said. "So she doesn't have her own money. She's dependent on her husband for everything."

"The only bargaining tool she has is sex," said Susie. "So she has to use that to get what she wants."

"These are all great points," said Shakti. "But instead of describing this other woman, this 'she,' I want us to relate things back to our own experiences." She rubbed her hands together. "Ladies, let's get personal."

"We're lesbians," said Katrina, gesturing to Susie at her side. "So we don't have to put up with any of that bullshit."

To everyone's surprise, it was Elisabeth who piped up next.

"I don't put up with any of that bullshit either. I refuse to use sex to get what I want."

"I do," said Sigi, and we all looked at her, shocked. "If I want to ask Paul to do something, I make sure to have sex with him first."

"Really?" said Susie. "You actually do that?"

"Sure," said Sigi, shrugging. "Men are simple creatures. It makes life easier."

I was unsure if I wanted to hear any of this—if I was

ready to hear it—but at the same time, I was hungry for these insights into the strange world of grown-ups. It was like an initiation, or a warning as to what lay ahead.

"Let me ask you a question," said Shakti, addressing the group. "All of you have fairly specific roles on the commune. How was it decided who does what?"

"It wasn't," said Susie. "We just started doing what we were good at—and I guess we got better at those things, and stopped doing the things we weren't good at."

"And what things were those?"

"I've always tended to the vegetable gardens," Susie said proudly. "I love watching things grow from tiny seeds into flourishing plants and legumes that you can eat."

Sigi said, "I run the school. I love teaching. The children are like my plants."

Everyone nodded approvingly and said, "Right on."

"I do all the cooking," said Elisabeth, also with pride.

"Loretta, what about you?" said Shakti, singling her out yet again.

"I like sewing—and I also run the laundry. We don't have an automatic washing machine, no electricity, so that keeps me busy. I don't have time for much else."

Katrina said, "I used to be in charge of the nursery. I was really good at that. Since then, well, there's still plenty to do—cleaning and organizing and helping the other women—but I miss having small children around."

Susie squeezed Katrina's arm and smiled. "Don't you worry, there'll be littlies around again one day." She glanced at Nelly and me and winked.

"You say 'helping the other women'—don't you ever help the men?"

"Not really," said Katrina. "I guess they don't need it."

Shakti narrowed her eyes and nodded, processing this information. "And the men, do they ever help out with what I'd call the domestic chores—cooking, cleaning, washing, that sort of thing?"

It was Sigi who said, "They would if we asked them to."

Shakti replied, "And have you?"

Sigi shook her head. "It's like what Susie said. Things work best when we stick to what we're good at."

"But how do you know?" said Shakti. "You haven't tried it any other way."

Sigi laughed. "We don't need to try it to know Paul or any of the other men would be hopeless at washing clothes. Can you imagine it? All the muddy clothes mixed together with our underwear?"

Loretta laughed loudest. "We'd have to wash everything twice!"

Shakti listened to all this, let the women have their joke. But when the laughter had died down, she cleared her throat. "I just wonder if women are naturally better at washing and cleaning, or if men do it badly because they don't want to do it." She paused. "I mean, I'm no good at it—and I don't try to *get* good at it."

Shakti's words hung in the air while no one said anything. Nobody spoke, but the room was thick with the collective dawning of a realization, a thing so palpable that you could almost see it, even if no one was prepared to say it out loud.

When the silence became too uncomfortable for anyone to tolerate, Shakti spoke.

"Well, I think that's enough for tonight, don't you?"

Several of the women hastily agreed.

"For our next session, I want you all to wear loose-fitting clothing and bring a hand mirror."

Someone gasped.

"What about the girls?" said Elisabeth, under her breath. "Surely they won't need to bring one of those?"

Nelly and I looked at each other, utterly bewildered.

"No, I suppose not," said Shakti. "They'll be fine to just watch."

"And will it be all right," said Loretta, discreetly raising her hand, "if some others among us don't bring mirrors either?"

Shakti frowned, or as close to that as her exquisite features would allow. "No one can force you to do anything you don't want to do, but shared experience is one of the foundations of consciousness raising. We learn through taking part."

THAT NIGHT, NELLY AND I were too worked up to sleep. Our beds were next to each other in the sleeping hut, but still we had to whisper very quietly so as not to be heard by the other kids.

"What do you think the hand mirrors are for?" said Nelly, squeaking with excitement.

"I don't know," I said. "But whatever it is, I'm glad we don't have to do it."

"Don't have to do what?" said Timon, from one of the other bunks.

"None of your beeswax," I said.

"We heard all about your secret meeting," he continued. "In fact, we had a grandstand view."

"You creep." I picked a book up off the floor and hurled it into the darkness around his bed.

"Ouch," said Fritz. "You missed!"

"Sorry, Fritz."

Timon snorted with laughter. "You all looked so serious, like somebody had died. Were you having a séance?"

"Rack off, dickhead."

"Poppy!" said Nelly, close by. "You don't need to swear."

"Oooooh!" said Timon, imitating a girl's voice, which always made me want to murder him. *We had an itty bitty séance and talked about our titties.*"

"Timon," said Lukas. "That's enough."

But it wasn't enough for Timon—not even close. He could keep this going for hours unless somebody physically stopped him. I had a glass of water by my bed, and as he launched into what he thought was a hilarious monologue about periods and fannies and how girl farts smelled like flowers—all in that same high, grating voice—I picked it up, crossed the room, and poured it over his head.

Timon batted at the wet bedclothes. "Fucking hell, Poppy! You're going to pay for that!"

He didn't need to remind me. Halfway over to his bunk bed with the glass of water, I had, in fact, imagined the revenge he would take and had almost turned back. The last time I'd picked on him, about two years earlier, Timon had spent a week collecting native cockroaches, which grew to about two inches long, and had filled my bed with half a dozen of them. Sometimes, even now, when I climbed into bed in the dark, I recalled them scuttling against my skin, and my legs kicked out in fearful response. But then I had thought, *At least the worst thing has been done.*

The following Sunday, after the evening meal, Shakti unfolded several large swathes of Indian batik fabric and began to drape them over the half dozen windows of the mess hut. The joinery had been salvaged from old houses and churches and some of the windows were oddly shaped, bowed, arched, even circular, and defied the hanging of curtains. The gaps around the edges troubled me, and I remembered what Timon, the peeping rat, had said about his grandstand view.

As before, Shakti laid out cushions, but this time they formed a more defined circle with an empty space in the middle. "Don't be shy," she said, before placing the plumpest cushion in the center of the circle and seating herself upon it. Slowly and hesitantly, the women took their places around her, with Nelly and me hovering at the edge of the group. Each woman took out the small mirror she had brought and placed it beside her, every last one with the glass facing down. Most had brought plain squares of mirrored glass, like the ones we had tacked to the walls of the communal bathroom.

Shakti, in the middle, removed a series of items from an orange string bag. The first was a small bottle of oil with a cork stopper; the second was a hand mirror, a professional-looking thing that propped upright on its own metal stand; the third was a flashlight; and the last was a book, which she held up so we all could read the title. *"Our Bodies, Ourselves,"* she said. "The foundation of the women's self-help movement. Make sure you all take a look afterward."

"I've read that," said Susie. "It sure is an eye-opener."

"Is that the one with all the drawings?" asked Sigi.

"Yes," said Shakti. "Drawings of women's bodies as they really are—not as they appear in medical textbooks." She took the last item out of her bag and it was unlike any object I had ever seen before. It looked, at first glance, like a pair of plastic salad tongs, joined together at one end in a beak, like you might find on a sea bird, a gannet or shag. Shakti propped the mirror on its legs in front of her and reclined on the cushion, gathering up the folds of her long Indian cotton skirt and hitching it above her waist. She was not wearing underpants. Her legs she bent to form two triangles. I was behind her, to the left, and stuck with a bad view. But then she adjusted the mirror, tilting it up, and I saw everything, magnified and framed.

The room fell very quiet; all rustling and moving ceased.

"This is my vagina," said Shakti, matter-of-factly, as though describing the contents of a kitchen cupboard. "At the top, under here, is the top of my clitoris, and these are my labia majora." She drew a line down, nearly to the crack between her butt cheeks. "The muscles of the clitoris go right down to here. It's much larger than everyone thinks."

At the mention of the clitoris, I had strained to get a better look, but either I had missed the revealing moment, or there was nothing to see. Frustrated, I turned to Nelly. She was biting her lip, maintaining a neutral expression, which I tried to copy, but my face grew warm and then prickly, like I was coming up in a heat rash. When I turned back to Shakti, she had picked up the salad tongs and was slicking them with an oily substance from the small, stoppered bottle. Then she leaned forward and inserted the beak end into her vagina, fiddled with a screw on the side, and readjusted the mirror. "Can everyone see properly?"

There was murmured assent, then an even deeper silence than before, as though every last bit of air had been sucked out of the room. All eyes were fixed on the mirror in front of Shakti, and I swallowed my embarrassment and looked.

"In the center here is my cervix," she said. "It's the pink mound with the dot in the middle. There's also some scar tissue on one side from an old surgery. It was at the hands of a male gynecologist—I prefer to think of him as a butcher." Someone made a tsk-tsk sound of solidarity. "Otherwise, everything is healthy, the flora and fauna normal. Any questions?"

Elisabeth said, "Why are you showing us your cervix?"

"Have you ever seen one before?"

"Yes, in a medical diagram—a cross section of the female reproductive organs."

"Exactly," said Shakti, gently removing the salad tongs and returning to a cross-legged position. "But I bet you've never seen one up close, in the flesh—not even your own. Don't you think that's weird?"

Elisabeth shrugged. "Not really."

"Well, I do," said Shakti. "We women have no idea what we look like down there—let alone what's normal. We can't just flop it out like men do so we rely on doctors—most of them male—to take care of our sexual health and deliver our babies." She observed the group to make sure everyone was listening. "We have given away control of our bodies and we need to take it back. The first step is to share knowledge, to learn how our bodies work. Self-examination is a political act."

"I'll go next," said Susie. "You haven't lived until you've seen a lesbian's vagina."

The women laughed, earthy and full.

"You got it," said Shakti, delighted. "The more we look at, the more we learn. The next step after this will be to teach you a few simple techniques for self-care."

The salad tongs were washed in a bucket of soapy water that someone had fetched from the kitchen and then dried on a tea towel that said "Welcome to Waihi." With a little help from Shakti and a gasp of mild discomfort, Susie inserted the salad tongs, and everyone peered at her anatomy.

"You see how it's the same but different?" Shakti said, encouragingly, to a chorus of agreement.

"That's more what I look like down there," said Sigi, chuckling. "Things move around a little when you have children."

"They sure do," agreed Katrina. "I hardly even need a mirror to see my cervix."

A couple of the women laughed, but not Shakti. She had been, and remained, steadfastly earnest all evening.

"I want to go next," said Loretta, taking everyone by surprise. "It'll be a good comparison."

I had rarely seen the women so fired up about anything, and the spirit was contagious. The only one seemingly not caught up in this energy was Elisabeth. She hung back for most of the evening and was the only woman to abstain from self-examination.

Filing out of the mess hut afterward, Nelly and I broke away from the other women and sprinted arm in arm across the dark field, so exhilarated I thought we might at any moment break out in song. There was something I wanted to ask Nelly, but I waited until I was sure we were alone before I stopped her. Breathlessly, I whispered in her ear, "Did you see a clitoris?"

"I think so," said Nelly.

"What did it look like?"

"Hairy."

We both laughed and carried on walking, navigating blindly through the pitch-black darkness. When the faint lights of the sleeping hut appeared in the distance, so did the outlines of two scurrying figures. Whoever it was, they had been traveling in the same direction we had but reached the hut before us. I halted in my tracks and tugged on Nelly's arm.

"Did you see that?"

"What?"

"I think we were followed."

"By who?"

Kerosene lamps flickered in the windows of the sleeping hut, casting pockets of light onto the porch. We pushed open the door and were immediately greeted by the smirking faces of Ned and Timon, both flushed with excitement and in the process of describing something to the other boys, one of whom was Lukas. Poor Meg, tucked up in bed on the other side of the room, was either asleep or, more likely, feigning it.

"Good night, was it, ladies?" said Timon, with a shit-eating grin.

I couldn't resist giving him the finger.

Timon held up his own middle finger and put it in his mouth, before languidly drawing it out, taking great care to make sure it was coated in saliva.

I was about to run at him, to do what exactly, I wasn't sure, but Nelly held me back. Timon looked to the other boys for support, but instead of giving it, they one by one wandered off to their beds, either too traumatized, or too embarrassed by Timon's lewd gesture, to do anything else.

Lukas, on the way to his bunk, fixed me with an intense look that I took to be sympathetic, until I smiled back, to reassure him I was fine, and he turned away, self-conscious.

In the usual underpants and T-shirt we all wore to bed, I climbed beneath the covers, my mind whirring with the knowledge I'd gained that night, and listened for the reassuring sounds of everyone around me nodding off. After sharing a dormitory our entire lives, I knew intimately the shifts in breathing and tiny sighs that signaled each individual was drifting off to sleep. But that night, the sleeping hut pitched with restless energy. My bunkmates fidgeted and tossed in their beds, releasing audible sighs of frustration. No one spoke but a thrilling new current charged the room, and I wondered if the others heard it too.

CHAPTER 3

Gaialands
1978

O UT OF THE YOUNGSTERS, only Lukas failed to warm to
Shakti at all. At first he had been just as curious about
her as the other boys, but once she had been on the commune
a few months, I noticed he had developed an aversion. Had
she insulted him? But then I decided the main reason had to
be what he called "that witchy-poo stuff." Whenever Shakti
got out her tarot cards, or offered to read someone's palm, he
would cast a disdainful eye over the proceedings or would
simply get up and leave. One night after dinner and sing-
along, when she had, in front of half a dozen people, offered
him a reading, he had told her openly that he thought it was
"a bunch of bullcrap." Shakti's response had been simply to
laugh, which impressed me as a highly effective way of both
belittling and dismissing his opinion.

Shortly after their exchange, Meg piped up with, "Please
read mine instead." She had been watching eagerly from the
sidelines, waiting for her turn. "I believe in it."

"Precious child," said Shakti. "You're too young to have your fortune told. Your personality isn't formed yet."

"I'm not!" said Meg. "I'm almost fifteen."

"Then fifteen is when I'll do your first reading. It will be your birthday present."

Meg counted on her fingers how long she'd have to wait. Her birthday was two or three months away, and I wondered how Meg's entire personality could form in such a short amount of time.

"I'll go next," said Sigi, positioning herself across the table from Shakti and rubbing her hands together in anticipation. "And, Meg, you come and sit next to me to give your good vibes to the cards."

Meg was delighted and nestled in next to Sigi. A few months into being a daughter, she was the only one who was beginning to get the hang of it. Sigi would often stroke the hair out of Meg's eyes, for no reason other than to touch her, and the two of them would look at each other in a wistful way that was also somehow greedy and exclusive. Their interactions mesmerized me, but I was glad I didn't have to go through that myself. Since I'd found out Elisabeth had birthed me, she hadn't changed her attitude toward me at all. She was still cool, businesslike, practical—constantly preoccupied by all the mouths she had to feed—and I couldn't imagine her behaving any other way. To see her behave like Sigi would have been disconcerting. But still, I sometimes thought it was strange that she hadn't acknowledged our connection at all.

While Shakti shuffled her deck of cards, Lukas got up

from the table and stalked off to the orchard by himself. In addition to avoiding Shakti, he had been doing that a lot lately—trying to find places where he could be alone. I thought just this once I might go after him to see if I could draw him out of his sulk.

I found him under one of the plum trees, stripping the bark off a sapling branch with his pocketknife. It was something the boys had done compulsively when they were younger but now they only did it when they were in a funk. By the time I got to him, Lukas had been going at the branch so aggressively that there wasn't much of it left. His expression, by the moonlight, brewed with dark thoughts.

"That was pretty harsh," I said, standing above him.

He didn't look up, but continued to slice at the sapling. "She's a goddamn phony. She talks total horseshit but nobody sees it because they're all trying to get into her pants." Lately, Lukas had been reading a stash of pulp novels we had found in a junk shop in Coromandel town and talking as though he was a hardboiled American detective, an affectation that I hoped would soon wear off.

"Not everyone," I said.

"No. You're not, but you still fawn all over her."

"You have to admit that she's livened things up around here."

Lukas scoffed. "A talking monkey would have done that. Living here is like being buried alive."

"But that's what I mean. It isn't—not anymore." I wanted to tell him about the consciousness raising, how it had opened my eyes to a whole new world, but I was too embarrassed to go into detail. "She's given us so much," I said lamely.

"She doesn't care about any of us. We're just playthings to her."

"Playthings? What do you mean?"

Lukas reddened slightly as he said, "Do I really have to spell it out?"

I didn't give him the chance.

"She can't help it if she's prettier than everyone else."

Still flushed, Lukas said, "Forget it, Poppy. The minute I turn eighteen, I'm leaving this loony bin behind."

He had been saying that a lot lately, and each time he did, I wanted to shake him. There were seven of us kids at Gaialands, and even though I knew it was silly, I felt strongly that if we could just stick together, we would be okay. "Where will you go?"

"Auckland, probably. That's where all the bands are."

Lukas played guitar, self-taught, and even though he sounded okay to my ears, I wasn't sure he was good enough to join a city band. "But you don't have any money. Stuff isn't free like it is here."

"I'll get a job," he said. "Like everyone else."

I was shocked. "You'd work for the man?"

Lukas snorted. "There is no man. That's just some communist claptrap Hunter made up to scare us."

"What about the rat race? That's real."

"Only to hippies. To everyone else, that's just progress. I don't want to live in the dark ages for the rest of my life."

Lukas gently poked my leg with the stick he had sharpened. When I grabbed the end of it to stop him, he pulled me down next to him on the ground and pummeled my shoulders and back. We had been roughhousing since we were little, but this time when he started wrestling with me, I had an involuntary urge to submit to his physical strength, to let him win. Only when I offered no resistance we butted heads, our skulls knocking together like a couple of hollow coconuts.

The sound of it was worse than the pain, but I cried out anyway.

"Poppy?" said Lukas, springing apart, confused. "Did I hurt you?"

"No." Whatever the submissive urge had been, it was gone, and I wished I had fought back when I had the chance. I got to my feet. "Last one to the mess hut is a big fat moron."

"Don't be an egg," said Lukas, not moving.

He had never refused to race before, and it threw me, so I called him a dick and took off for the mess hut, trying to run off all these odd new sensations.

Rumors had been going around that in addition to doing tarot-card spreads, Shakti had been slowly and methodically compiling the astrology charts of everyone who lived at Gaialands. I was not sure what this entailed, but I was certain that if everyone else was getting one then I wanted one too. Weeks went by while I waited to be asked. Then Nelly had hers read and I could no longer bear it. On the pretext of delivering Shakti some coconut oil she had ordered from Auckland to smooth her hair, I made my way across the field to her caravan. A couple of the tires had gone completely

flat, giving it a tilted appearance, and I wondered if it bothered her to go about her business on a lean.

Halfway to the caravan I paused to consider something
that had never occurred to me before. Did my outfit look
okay? We shared clothes and lived in the sticks. Other than
checking if what I was wearing was warm enough or too hot,
I had never given clothes a second thought, but lately I had
decided that I wanted to look more like a girl and less like a
Coromandel bushman. But as for how to go about this, I was
stumped. Boys and girls on the commune dressed the same.
In the summer we wore running shorts and faded T-shirts
with slogans for tractors or sports teams, and in the winter,
dungarees or cords with a Swanndri or woolen jumper.
Susie knitted all these jumpers to the same pattern, and they
were stored in a trunk in our sleeping hut. We all wore
them, moaning all day long about the coarse, scratchy wool.
Sigi and Elisabeth occasionally wore faded shift dresses or
sarongs, but nothing of the sort had found its way into our
communal clothing trunk. We couldn't just go out and buy
anything new—we didn't have money. I sometimes handled
it when I worked in the Gaialands veggie shop, but other
than that it never passed through my hands.

That day, I doubled back to our sleeping hut, found nothing except more shorts and more threadbare T-shirts, then
made my way to the washing line and helped myself to a flowing Indian skirt I had seen Elisabeth wearing once or twice.
It was a commune. We shared everything. Didn't the skirt
belong to me as much as it belonged to anyone else? It was
the first time in my life I had worn anything other than pants.

Eagerly, I rapped on the door of Shakti's caravan and waited, adjusting the ties of the skirt one more time. After a short interval, the door opened—she hadn't asked who was there—and she stood in front of me naked.

"Poppy!" she said. "Nice skirt."

"I brought you this," I said, thrusting the coconut oil into Shakti's hands and wishing I hadn't changed. I didn't feel like myself and was unsure how this new version of me ought to behave.

"You look pretty," said Shakti, holding out her hand. "I've been wondering when you would visit."

I took her small, agile hand and was pulled into the caravan, where Shakti had candles and incense burning, the air so thick with fragrance it was hard to breathe. My eyes darted about, greedily taking everything in. It was dark inside but the space was bigger than I thought it would be, with the bed tucked away on a platform at one end. This left enough room for a small round table and chairs, plus a kitchen area, shelves, and bench seats. Every surface was covered with batik cloths, shawls, cushions, lace, and on top of these were stacks of books, potions, candlesticks, trinkets, a lunarscape of carved boxes, copper vials, divining instruments, and fertility dolls. Shakti caught me drinking it all in and laughed. "I collect things," she said. "As if you couldn't guess."

She picked up a fringed shawl and tied it in a knot around her waist—hardly covering anything, but modest compared to nothing at all. Then she cleared objects off the table, a set of watercolors and a stack of thick pieces of cardstock. The card on top was painted with strange hieroglyphics, almost recognizable as an alphabet but not quite.

"What are those?" I asked, pointing at the symbols.

"Runes," said Shakti, shuffling them into a pile and putting them away. "Would you like some tea? I have chamomile, peppermint, or nettle."

"Peppermint, please."

She balanced a small orange cast-iron kettle on top of a portable gas burner and shook out some leaves into a red enamel teapot. Then she reached into an earthenware jar and pulled out something that was banned from the commune, a large bar of supermarket chocolate. She broke off a square and handed it to me, holding a finger to her lips to let me know it was our secret. I wasn't sure whether to eat it or save it, and settled on both, nibbling off a section and letting it melt on my tongue. God, it was delicious. She poured the tea into cups the size of thimbles.

"Those are tiny," I said.

"Japanese," she explained. "Given to me by my first lover. An older man. He really knew how to make love to a woman."

"Oh," I said, scandalized, bringing the tiny cup to my lips, then yanking it away when I realized the liquid was piping hot. I spilled some on my T-shirt and clumsily tried to wipe it off. "Sorry."

"It's your birthday next week, isn't it?" Shakti said.

"November eighteenth."

"Ooh la la—a Scorpio."

"Is that bad?"

"It's intense. Scorpios are deeply emotional—and elemental. They're drawn to matters of life and death—almost to the point of obsession."

"Oh," I said. "Are we all like that? The twins and Fritz were born the same month."

"They're a week or two after you though, so they fall in the next sign. Sagittarius is a different breed altogether, much lighter of heart. How funny that you were all born so close together though, almost like someone planned it."

"They did plan it. I mean, all the babies were born within two years of one another, then they stopped having any. I'm not sure why. Maybe seven was enough."

"That's so fascinating." Shakti blew on her tea, then carefully took a sip. "I've been watching how you all behave around one another, and I have to say, some of the stuff I've seen is, well—it's a little messed up."

"That's because the way we were raised was . . . unusual." I had just opened the door to more questions, I realized, but I couldn't think how to turn back without offending Shakti.

"You told me you were raised in a group. Does that mean you lived with your mom and dad until a certain age, then you were all lumped together?"

"No," I said. "It doesn't mean that." I wasn't sure how to continue. This was the part that always freaked everyone out. "It means we were raised in a group from day one."

"From birth?"

"From birth."

Shakti let out a whistle and shook her head. "That's

even more nuts than I thought." She looked at me with a sad expression. "You poor, poor creatures."

I had known this would be her reaction, but coming from her, the pity was strangely gratifying. I wanted more. I found myself adding, "We didn't even know who our parents were until earlier this year."

"Holy smokes!" she exclaimed, and her shock was like a drug. "How did you find out?"

"They called us all in for a meeting," I began, wanting to tell her everything—to have her listen to me all day. "We had no idea what it was going to be about." Once I was sure I had Shakti's rapt attention, I continued, going back a little way to the end of summer, when Nelly had first confessed to me that she had fallen passionately in love with Timon. For as long as possible, I tried to prevent Nelly from saying anything, but as summer rolled into autumn, she only grew more determined to tell him how she felt. Nelly was too bold and too lovesick to wait any longer. She was convinced he felt the same way she did, and because she was so sure of it, the next thing I knew she had me helping her to write a love note.

"That's so sweet," said Shakti.

"It could have been—but things didn't work out exactly as she'd planned."

Late one night, Nelly and I crept out to the orchard armed with a pencil and a stack of brown paper bags taken from the Gaialands fruit stall. Not the most romantic of notepaper, but it was either that or rip a page out of one of the novels on the schoolhouse bookshelf. Paper, like everything else that had to be bought from the outside world, was in short supply on the commune.

Nelly was so wound up that she couldn't hold the pencil steady. She told me she'd had a crush on Timon for as long as she could remember—since she was four or five years old. "You write it," she said, handing me the pencil.

"I can't. I don't even like him."

"All that teasing—you know it's just a front, eh? Underneath it, he's a sweetheart."

"He is?"

Nelly dictated, "Start with 'Dear Timon' . . ."

"This is weird."

"You are."

I wrote down the words.

"Put that you think he's good at woodwork. That *I* think he is," she said.

"But he's hopeless at it. Remember that three-legged chair?"

"That's not the point. He *wants* to be good at it."

I was alarmed. "You're going to lie?"

"Flattering a man is how you make him love you."

"How do you know?"

"It's obvious."

It wasn't obvious to me but I did as I was told and wrote it down, making sure my handwriting was neat but also a little different from how it usually was. "Do you want me to write that you love him?"

"Shit no," Nelly said. "He'd run a mile."

The next day, after breakfast, Nelly had posted the note

in Timon's gumboot, one of dozens lined up in pairs along the porch. We were not allowed to wear them inside, eating barefoot, or in hand-knitted loose-fitting socks, one of the only items of clothing that wasn't shared. The adults had, in the early days, shared socks, but in the wet winter months, foot fungus grew quicker than field mushrooms. For the same reason, no one shared gumboots either—or we tried not to. Most gumboots looked the same, and pairs often got mixed up by mistake, which is exactly what happened when Nelly tried to pick Timon's out of the lineup. Several minutes later, she watched Hunter come out of the mess hut and push his big hairy foot into the gumboot with the note in it.

"Now what do I do?" asked Nelly, panic stricken.

"Nothing. With a bit of luck he won't even find it."

Days of dread followed. Nelly was sure everyone was looking at her, that everyone knew about the note, not just Hunter but Timon as well. I promised her that wasn't the case.

"And was it the case?" said Shakti, interrupting.

"Not quite," I said. "We were both wrong."

"But the note triggered the meeting?"

I was enjoying her impatience, the power it gave me. "Yes," I said. "But we didn't find that out until right at the end. First, we had to sit through a sermon. You know what Hunter's like."

Shakti nodded. "I do."

The meeting was in the chapel, a scrappy tin-roofed barn at the end of the chook run. We called it that because the seats in there were pews that had been salvaged from a derelict church in Coromandel town. I liked the pews. They were

solid, finely hewed, and had arrived on the commune with
Bibles still slotted in the back, the first I'd ever seen. I had
admired the fine vellum paper and marveled at how much
text was squeezed onto each page. But after hippies and the
nuclear family, the thing Hunter hated most in the world was
religion. He ordered us to tear off the spines and use the soft
vellum as toilet paper, which we did, without argument.

Hunter opened the meeting the way he opened every
meeting, with a speech that went on for twenty-nine years.
Lately these had been about oil shock and getting prepared for
an economic collapse the following year, but on this occasion
he went all the way back to Gaialands's founding philosophy.
He talked about how they had wanted to break away from
mainstream society, the stifling conventions of the suburbs,
white picket fences, meat and potatoes for dinner followed by
cricket commentary on the wireless. Then he got around to
the seven of us, how we were the first generation to be born
at Gaialands and how special that made us. "You alone are
unique among men—and women, of course," he added.

"You have grown up with an unrivaled spirit of freedom
that we have instilled in you from birth. To grow up outside
the constraints of conventional society, liberated from the
shackles of the nuclear family, well"—he paused for effect
and looked at each of us in turn—"I don't need to remind
you how privileged that makes you."

He was right that he didn't need to remind us. We'd
heard this speech so many times before that I sometimes fell
asleep with his mantra ringing in my ears. We were privileged. The hope for the future! The chosen ones who would

lead humanity into a New Age of enlightenment. The Age of Aquarius is nigh!

I didn't tell Shakti that at this point in the meeting, I had glanced over at Lukas, and he had done something he never had before: he rolled his eyes at me and mimed a yawn. It wasn't his reaction that surprised me—we were all bored to death—but the fact that he had directed it at me, and not his best friend, Timon, who sat next to him, and with whom he most often shared his asides. I had smiled back to let him know I agreed with him and then I felt warm all over, as though I had moved out of the shade.

When I tuned in again to Hunter, he was still going strong. "You won't have to unlearn bad habits, like we've had to. You'll be free to love everybody the same—to give to your community, your planet, without putting your immediate family first. I believe this detachment will lead to a higher consciousness that will benefit the whole of mankind. The Aquarian Age is coming, and you are the ones who will lead us to a new world order." He put his hand on his heart and took a deep breath. "What we're about to reveal to the seven of you is something we swore we never would, but in light of recent events, we realize that we have to. My only hope is that the work we have done here has created a foundation that cannot be undone—that the seeds we have sown will bear fruit."

Hunter stopped at this point and looked around the room again and I could have sworn he was nervous. "Stone the crows, this is difficult," he said, looking down at his notes.

"Go on," said Paul. "It's now or never."

"You're right. Let's get it over with, shall we?" In a loud voice, Hunter called out the names of the adults, one couple at a time, and asked them to stand in separate groupings along the low wooden platform. First, Susie and Katrina, then Tom and Loretta, then Paul and Sigi, and finally he called to Elisabeth to join him. When everyone was in place, he signaled to Tom and Loretta to shuffle closer to Susie and Katrina, forming a group of four. Tom, in this grouping, appeared content, almost smug, an expression that was ill matched by his wife's one of discomfort.

For a few minutes they stood in silence.

"Oh my word," Nelly whispered, "this is it."

She had guessed but I hadn't, not yet. Then Hunter called out my name and Fritz's, and told us to come and stand next to him, and I did what I was told, stumbling up the short climb to the podium. When I turned around, I saw Fritz hadn't followed me. He stood in his pew looking as defiant as ever. "Come on, Fritz, this is important," said Hunter, summoning him with his hand.

"If it was so important, why didn't you tell us ten years ago, or better still, when we were born?" Fritz had already guessed too; I felt so dense.

Hunter grimaced. He looked like he wanted to punch Fritz. "I acknowledge and honor your feelings, Fritz, but I'd like us to save any discussion until the end of the meeting."

Fritz didn't move. He did obstinate better than anyone else.

An edge crept into Hunter's voice as he said, "Fritz. Get up here, now."

I caught Fritz's eye and silently pleaded with him. *C'mon. Don't make me stand up here by myself.* This did the trick, and an audible sigh of relief went around the chapel when he shuffled to the podium. *This is bullshit,* his expression said as he quietly took his place.

Hunter called out to Lukas and Meg, the second youngest, to stand next to Sigi and Paul, and they did so obediently, Lukas with an air of resigned boredom. Sigi beamed at Meg, and then at Lukas, as though she had just won them in a raffle, and I noticed for the first time that Lukas and Meg's sandy hair and freckled skin were identical to Sigi's.

Next Hunter asked Timon, Nelly, and Ned to join the group of four that included Susie and Katrina. "Are you okay with this?" he said, directing his question at Tom and Loretta, the other couple with them.

"We don't have any choice," said Loretta, looking pale. "Just get it over with."

Listening to Hunter call out names and watching everyone move to their places, I felt seasick, like I might fall over. We were about to find out who our parents were—were in fact already standing next to them—but instead of anticipation, joy, or excitement, I felt dread, as though we were all on a train that was about to go off the rails. Why were they doing this now? Had something gone wrong?

When I looked at Nelly, I knew what it was. She was white knuckled, staring at Timon. Had she fallen in love with her brother? He was part of her group, along with Ned, her twin, but it didn't make sense that they were grouped with two couples—three women and Tom.

It was Tom who said, "For goddess's sake, Hunter, get on with it!" He put his arm staunchly around Loretta. She was tight-mouthed, frozen.

Hunter was grave. "The people standing with you are your next of kin—your parents, your brothers and sisters, your children." He paused, for effect, and grinned at me. "Hello, daughter."

He pronounced the word "daughter" as though it were in a foreign language, and my first instinct was to flinch. This was horrible, a cruel joke. For seventeen years the adults had kept our parentage a secret. For as long as we could talk, we had been forbidden even from speculating and now they were undoing all that because they had changed their minds? I glared at the man who'd just told me he was my father, and I didn't think I trusted a word that came out of his mouth.

I wasn't the only one floundering to make sense of it all. Timon, who had been silent up to now, piped up. "What about us?" He swiveled to face Susie and Katrina and Loretta. "Which of these women is my mother?"

"I'm your father," said Tom, proudly, "and your mother is"—he squeezed Loretta, who stood rigid by his side—"your mother is Katrina."

Katrina smiled, sheepishly, and everyone stared at her, and then at Loretta because it didn't make sense that Tom had fathered children with Katrina and not with his wife.

"Loretta can't have children," said Tom, as Loretta burst into tears. Everyone avoided looking at her, although she tried to smile bravely and said, "At least I've had a taste of what it's like to be a mother. That wouldn't have happened outside the commune."

Upon hearing of Loretta's infertility, Shakti actually gasped. "That poor woman," she said solemnly, placing her hand over her heart. "Imagine her pain."

"I guess," I said, though truthfully I couldn't. The cause of Loretta's pain was outside my realm of experience; at that point in the proceedings I had been more consumed with my own—and with Nelly's. "Here's where it gets really weird," I said, enjoying Shakti's spellbound expression.

Throughout the meeting, Nelly had been very quiet, but she was unable to contain herself any longer. "Timon can't be my brother," she burst out. "He looks nothing like me— or Ned!"

"That's because he's your half brother," Susie had said calmly. "I gave birth to you and Ned."

"My *half* brother?" repeated Nelly. "I don't understand."

"You and Timon have the same father," said Tom, standing a few inches taller and grinning like a fool. "Me. We could scarcely believe it when Susie fell pregnant with twins." For a moment he flushed with pride at having fathered a miracle, before remembering the poor barren woman standing next to him. Loretta had by this time stopped crying and was doing her best to appear not to care.

"I think you can guess why we had to tell you," Hunter said, fishing a piece of paper out of his pocket and handing it to Nelly. "I believe this belongs to you."

It was the love note.

"Oh, wow," said Shakti. "That's so dramatic. How did Nelly react?"

"She ran crying from the barn."

"Poor girl." Shakti shook her head. "I don't understand how they could have been so naïve."

"Who?"

"Your parents. I mean, what did they think would happen when you all hit puberty? That you'd just carry on playing cowboys and Indians and not try to have sex with each other?"

"No one's done that."

"Not yet."

She was right. Our parents had been naïve. Even before the love note, things had been slowly changing, and the adults should have noticed sooner. We hadn't, for example, showered together since we were about thirteen, when the gaze of one of the boys had lingered a little too long on the newly formed bumps on Nelly's chest, and the tiny curls sprouting between her legs, and she had seen them looking and covered herself up for good. I was older than her but a late bloomer and even though I had nothing to cover up, I did the same. As did Meg, and then the boys, bringing to an abrupt end the rowdy soap and water fights we had enjoyed since we were little.

"Was that the end of the meeting?" Shakti asked. "Or was there more?"

"Hunter tried to tell us that nothing would change because they didn't want it to. He thought we could all just carry on as before, as though we hadn't just found out they had been lying to us for seventeen years. He said to try and remember our beliefs—"

"You mean *his* beliefs," said Shakti.

"Yes," I said, with dawning recognition, though I wasn't quite sure yet of what. "*His* beliefs."

"What about the other adults? How did they behave?"

I opened my mouth to speak and found myself choking up. "Some of the parents, like Sigi, tried to turn back the clock. Now that her children knew she was their mother, she expected to have a special bond with them. She wanted to be close. Meg was okay with that for a while but Lukas went the other way—he didn't want anything to do with her."

"Ah, Lukas," said Shakti. "Doomed to fall in love with unavailable women."

I wondered how she could have drawn that conclusion about Lukas from what I had told her, but she didn't explain, and I didn't ask.

"As far as I know, he's never had a girlfriend."

Shakti smiled, beguilingly, and got up to boil the kettle for a second pot of tea, refreshing the tea leaves with scalding water. "I don't suppose Elisabeth was all over you and Fritz," she said, settling across the table from me again. "But I could be wrong."

"She wasn't." In fact, if anything, Elisabeth had been even more aloof than usual, barricading herself in the kitchen and bottling enough fruit to last through half a dozen winters. "And Hunter stuck to his word, too."

Shakti shook her head and sighed. "That must have been a confusing time for everyone."

Confusing and raw. That night, after the meeting, was the only time in the history of Gaialands that anyone forgot to sound the cowbell for dinner. But the worst part had been the crying that came at night from the adults' huts. There were loud male voices, slamming doors, and at breakfast the next morning, red eyes and silence. In the daytime, the women neglected their chores or went about them at a slower pace than usual. Over in the workshop, the men shouted and cursed at their machinery. When the combustion engine that Hunter had been working on failed, he exploded in a fit of rage.

None of this was talked about openly among the seven of us kids, but it was silently agreed upon that we would not allow ourselves to be drawn into whatever catastrophe had overcome the adults. We achieved this by spending more time on our own, taking tents and camping at the base of Mount Aroha for several nights, inventing reasons to hitch, in groups of two or three, into Coromandel town. We grew even closer than we had been before.

Then one day, to our relief, it all stopped. Normality was restored. The majority of the adults ceased trying to be mothers and fathers and went back to behaving like the group of caring but slightly detached parents they had always been. They must have had some sort of discussion among themselves but if they did, we were not party to it. We experienced this as a kind of victory. By getting the adults to back off, we had won, and I thought it served them right. We had become the thing they had engineered us to be: a generation of kids who loved everyone the same, who had no favorites among the men and women who had raised them.

I didn't say any of this to Shakti, but in my opinion if the adults didn't like the way we had turned out, that wasn't our fault. It was theirs.

From off in the distance, the cowbell sounded for dinner. I hadn't realized it but for the last few minutes, I had been staring out the window of Shakti's caravan, lost in thought, and only dimly aware of what she had been doing. I saw now that she had gathered up the cards with the strange hieroglyphics. She was shuffling through them, studying what she had drawn. Seeing her do that reminded me that I had forgotten to ask for the thing I had come here to request.

"You know how you've been compiling everyone's astrology charts?" I began.

"I was," said Shakti. "But I'm starting to think you folks might need something stronger."

"Stronger?"

"To shift the energy around here."

I had no idea what she meant.

"Whatever it is, it's going to have to involve all of you— the adults, but also the kids. Maybe a . . . *ritual* of some sort." At the word "ritual" her eyes lit up. "Yes, a cleansing ritual," she repeated. "Or a rite of passage." She had risen from her seat and was busy going through a set of drawers that were built under the kitchen bench. "Or maybe something that combines the two." She pulled out folders tied with string and sheaves of loose paper, and a few well-worn hardback books.

"Tell the others I'll be late for dinner," she said.

"Sure," I said. "I'll get Elisabeth to keep a plate warm for you."

Much as I wanted to stay, I knew I had been dismissed. I had been in Shakti's caravan for hours, and I was exhausted and hungry after so much talking. It had been a relief to unburden myself, but as I wandered away from the stand of willows where her caravan was parked, I also had the uneasy feeling that I had gotten caught up in the moment and said too much.

On my way to the mess hut for dinner, I passed the ruins of an old wooden fence that had once functioned as a kind of playpen when the seven of us were little. The space it enclosed was large and grassy and shaded by trees, and there had always been two or three adults stationed inside it with us. They had built it, I supposed, to shield us from the many hazards to be found on a working farm—silage pits and machinery and exuberant bulls—but also to prevent us from wandering into the creek.

Inevitably, the day arrived that we were more interested in climbing out of the enclosure than staying inside it, and it was a memory from this era that assaulted me on my way to dinner that night.

I would have been about three or four. I had climbed to the top of the wooden fence post, whereupon I stood up and turned around and proudly waved to the other children. One of the women shrieked and ran toward me, shouting. The noise and the expression on her face frightened me and I tried to shuffle away from her, toppling backward—or maybe it was forward—and nitting the ground with a crunch.

The next din came from me, screaming and yelling and tears. One of the women picked me up and comforted me, folding her arms around me and drying my eyes with the hem of her dress. She did this to soothing effect, but only for a moment before I was prized out of her arms by one of the other women. The faces of these women have blended together to form a single motherly presence, and the same is true of all my early childhood memories. What I remember most clearly is the first woman's tears and the firm voice of the other woman as she said, "You can't do that—it isn't your turn."

After the conversation with Shakti, the memory took on a note of desolation. I had always thought the adults were united in the way they had brought us up in a litter, like puppies, but that wasn't the case, not even close. At every stage, there had been disagreements and doubts and at least one of the women had tried to buck the rules.

CHAPTER 4

Gaialands
1978

I VISITED SHAKTI'S CARAVAN on my own one last time that
spring. I was still disappointed that she hadn't offered to
do my astrology chart, and when I finally summoned the
courage to ask her outright, she refused.

"All that is irrelevant now," she said, gathering up the
growing pile of cards she had been embellishing with ink
and watercolor. "I'm working on something bigger. It's really
going to shift a few paradigms—yours included."

"Is that what the cards are for?"

"Eventually."

"Can I see one?"

Shakti hesitated. "You can look at this one, but the drawing isn't finished and I haven't written the words to go with
it." She handed me a card festooned with symbols around
the central figure of a woman. "This prediction is for a girl,"
she said. "These symbols here represent fertility, and these
ones here mean love."

"Why are there so many of them?"

"Because the girl is destined to have many children and always be loved. She's very fortunate. I see great harmony in her future."

The woman in the card was little more than a stick figure in a dress, and a bright childlike sun shone down on her. I hoped it was my prediction but the fact that she'd let me see it meant it was more likely to be for someone else. "Do we all get one of those?"

Shakti took the card from my hand and shuffled it back into the pile. "All will be revealed."

She poured me a thimble of tea, which tasted bitter, as though it had brewed for too long. Across the table, I noticed Shakti had half a dozen long hairs growing around her nipples and tufts of kinky hair sprouting from her armpits. I didn't have that yet, and thought how strange and furry that must feel.

Shakti caught me studying her and said, "Have you ever gone nude? It's so freeing to be in the world in your natural state."

The question alone made the skin on my neck grow hot. "Not since I was a child."

"It could be good for you to do it again. Empowering."

"You mean embarrassing."

"Embarrassment is just another name for fear. What are you afraid of?"

I felt put on the spot. "I don't know."

"Trust me," she said. "You will feel so liberated. Think of it as a rite of passage to womanhood. You don't want to be stuck in childhood forever do you?"

"I guess not."

I had not, in my mind, agreed to anything, but Shakti seemed to think I had, and proceeded to come up with a plan that involved a dawn meditation the very next morning, before anyone else on the commune was up. I tried telling her that someone on the commune was always up before you were, but she thought I'd meant it as a joke and didn't realize I was genuinely worried about being seen.

I did not sleep much that night, but none of my fretting and worrying resulted in a watertight excuse to withdraw. At dawn, Cowboy the rooster crowed his daily lament, and I climbed out of bed, resigned to my fate.

We had arranged to meet at the far edge of the forest just before sunrise and I was already late. Shakti had suggested coming to our sleeping hut to wake me, but I had told her not to because I didn't want any of the others to notice I had gone. Even before I went into the orchard, I looked behind me to make sure no one was following. Tiptoeing through the woods, I tried to psych myself up for what was in store by remembering I had run around naked as a child all the time. Before the age of thirteen, the seven of us had stripped off in front of one another without a second thought, had spent whole summers bare-bummed and carefree on the beach. All I had to do was channel that same nonchalance and I would be fine. But cutting through the woods, following a path so familiar that I could navigate it in the dark, I couldn't do it. I felt as though every tree, every blade of grass, every bird, was looking at me and getting ready to laugh. Then I remembered what Shakti had said, about how doing this would make me a woman, and that if I didn't go through with it, I would be stalled, forever a girl.

I came to the end of the woods, and there was Shakti, sitting cross-legged in a skimpy Indian sari, facing the sea and the rising sun, her hands resting on her knees, finger and thumb pinched together to form a tiny oval. When I got closer, I saw that she had her eyes closed in meditation, and I sat down next to her and imitated her pose. For a couple of minutes, she didn't register my presence, and then she whispered, "Are your eyes shut?"

They weren't—but I quickly closed them. "Yes."

"It's just us here," said Shakti. "Just us and the sun."

I heard her whip off her sari and opened my eyes a fraction to confirm it.

"That feels better," she said with a sigh.

Below the thin fabric of my T-shirt and shorts, my skin tightened, as though I had shrunk a little bit in size.

"Take your time," said Shakti. "Wait until it feels right."

She was waiting for me to take off my clothes but I wasn't sure how to go about it without first standing up. "I'm wearing shorts," I whispered. "I didn't really think this through."

"No matter," said Shakti. "Start with the T-shirt. One thing at a time."

I pulled the T-shirt over my head and crossed my arms to cover what wasn't there. Perhaps above all, I didn't want Shakti to see how flat chested I was.

"Ommm," she said next to me. "Om shanti om."

I had heard these chants before, when the women practiced yoga, and wasn't sure if I was meant to join in, like the other women did, or to stay quiet. I whispered, "Do you want me to say that too?"

Less patiently than before, Shakti said, "Up to you, honey."

I decided not to. I still had not taken off my shorts, but uncrossed my arms and moved my hands to the ends of my knees, where I pinched my thumb and forefinger together. A cool breeze tickled my chest, a sensation that was not unpleasant, but that also felt wholly inappropriate, given that we were supposed to be meditating.

"How are you doing with those shorts?" whispered Shakti. She had apparently changed her mind about letting me do things on my own schedule. "Let me know when you're done. I won't start the meditation proper until then."

I was holding things up. Very quickly, as though it was no big deal and I was just about to take a shower, I stepped out of my shorts and underpants and hurriedly sat cross-legged on the grass. Bits of it were spiky, and I discovered why sitting bare-arsed on kikuyu grass is a terrible idea. Shakti, when I looked over at her, was sitting on her sari, and I quickly did the same with my discarded shorts.

"I'm ready," I said, and closed my eyes.

"Great," said Shakti. "I'll start us off with a chant for peace."

The sun was coming up fast, turning the backs of my eyelids orange and warming my skin all over. I must have been sitting in a slumped position, which wasn't unusual for me, because the next thing I knew, Shakti had placed one hand in the small of my back and another on my shoulder, and pushed them in opposite directions to straighten my spine. She had strong hands, like a man's.

My chest was thrust forward at an alarming angle—like I was trying to make more of what little was there—but I didn't dare move in case she tried to correct me again.

"It's a beautiful sunrise," Shakti said softly. "Let's chant."

She started out quietly, her voice gradually building in intensity until it was booming and deep, almost a growl. I joined in with a weaker sound of my own. For a few seconds I forgot my nakedness. But then the fact of it came back to me in the points of my skin that were most exposed to the sun. Bits of me were warm, too warm, and other parts tingled in response. I recognized the sensation, though I had no experience of where it was going, or knowledge of how to control it. As best I could, I carried on chanting, and dug my bottom into the hard earth, which seemed to help. The feeling didn't go away, but nor did it get any stronger.

I risked opening my eyes a little, to see if Shakti was looking my way or had noticed. Her chants seemed to be reaching a crescendo, and she looked completely out of it, eyes tight shut, her skin flushed and glistening with sweat. She even seemed to be straining against something, as though an unseen force was pushing against her. At the height of the chanting, her voice faltered for a second, and she paused to catch her breath before carrying on in a more subdued fashion. This was unlike any meditation I had ever been a part of, and I shut my eyes, quite bewildered.

When it was over, and by over I mean that Shakti fell silent, I reached for my T-shirt, which I pulled over my head, and then my underpants and shorts, which I stood up to put on. Even fully clothed, my heart was pounding as though I had been caught doing something I shouldn't, and I shook out my arms and legs to try to make it stop.

Shakti opened her eyes. "Wow. That was intense. It must have been our combined energies." She stretched her arms above her head and stood up. "How was it for you?"

I was not sure what she was asking me, or what the correct response was, so in as neutral a voice as possible, I said, "Okay, I guess."

"Okay?" Shakti laughed. "Just 'okay'? Well, I guess it was your first time, so we shouldn't expect too much."

We did not say much on the way back to the commune. Breakfast was already under way, the mess hall jammed with hungry teenagers and adults, the rise and fall of conversation, and the clunking of spoons and bowls like an out-of-tune orchestra. I deliberately did not sit next to Shakti, but squeezed in next to Nelly, who asked me where I had been all morning. "Shakti and I went for a walk," I said, and she replied, "Not in the nude, I hope."

For the rest of the day, Shakti was missing from the commune, along with one of the shared cars, but she reappeared in the evening with a box of half-melted Pinky bars she had bought in Coromandel town. The others pounced on the chocolate bars but I held back, feeling strange about what had happened that morning. I still couldn't say one way or the other if something was wrong, but every time she came near me, my body pulled away from her.

Shakti was her normal genial self, perhaps even more

full of smiles than usual. Later on, after we'd had our customary post-dinner sing-along of folk hits, accompanied by Paul and Lukas on the guitar, she took me aside, holding me by the arm so I couldn't squirm away, and presented me with a gift wrapped in tissue paper. "Go ahead," she said. "Open it."

I did as I was told. Inside the paper was a leather necklace, the attached metal pendant a cross hanging from a circle. It was ugly, a symbol of some kind, but I didn't know what it meant. "Thank you," I said, as she took the pendant from my hands and hung it around my neck, standing back to admire it, then coming in close to whisper in my ear, "I'm so proud of you. Today's the day you became a woman."

BETWEEN SEPTEMBER AND DECEMBER each year was birthday season at Gaialands. In the space of those four months, six out of the seven of us had birthdays. At the close of 1978, Timon turned seventeen, the twins and I turned sixteen, and the younger ones—Meg and Fritz—turned fifteen. The odd one out was Lukas, who had turned seventeen the previous May, and had cultivated a crop of fuzzy hair on his upper lip to prove it.

We were used to the eccentric cluster of our birthdays, but Shakti seized upon it as hugely significant, a sequence that could only have been divinely ordained. "Everything in nature happens for a reason," she said. "There are no accidents." And so it was decided that in the month of December, after the last birthday had been celebrated, she would hold her ritual, a ceremony called the Predictions. "Think of it as a rite of passage," said Shakti, when she announced the date. "A ritual to seal your seven destinies."

As December drew to a close, momentum gathered, and an air of anticipation overtook the commune. The adults held secret planning meetings and went to Whitianga for supplies. Shakti's caravan was a hive of activity, day and night. The seven of us, however, were kept in the dark. This secrecy, so we were told, would result in a more powerful outcome.

Some preparations were stranger than others. A few days before the ritual was due to take place, a noise woke me early one morning. I was tired, and it was still dark in the hut, so I didn't open my eyes. Assuming it was one of the others getting up to pee, or an animal scratching in the dirt outside, I drifted back into a half sleep. The noise went on, punctuated by snipping sounds, which blended into a dream in which a woman was making a dress and cutting off threads as she sewed. It was only when I heard the door to the sleeping hut click shut that I opened my eyes and realized that the snipping sound had been real, not part of the dream at all. Why had I heard scissors, of all things? I sat up and looked out the window, the ledge of which was right by my bed. In the soft early light, I made out the figure of a woman in a billowing caftan crossing the field, heading away from our hut. She walked purposefully and, halfway there, stopped to examine or adjust whatever she held in her hand. For a second or two, scissor blades glinted in the day's first sun, and then she carried on walking. It was only when

she veered off in the direction of the willow trees, where her
caravan was parked, that I realized it was Shakti. She did not
normally wear caftans, and it had been the presence of this
garment, more than anything, that had confused me.

Despite my reservations about Shakti, I was excited to
take part in the Predictions and eager to find out what my
future held. Most of the other kids shared my enthusiasm.
Only Lukas had doubts. Several times in the lead-up to the
ceremony, he had told me how silly he thought it all was.

The day of the ceremony, timed to coincide with the summer solstice, dawned bright and loud with chirping cicadas.
By eight in the morning their chorus was deafening, herald-
ing a scorching day and a balmy night to follow. Conditions
couldn't have been more perfect. But at half past eight, we
discovered Lukas had gotten up early and disappeared, leaving the remaining six of us to try to figure out where he was.
Everyone was in agreement that we had to find him.

Sheepishly, the six of us went to see Shakti and confessed
to her that Lukas had split. She asked us to sit with her in a circle under the trees by her caravan, a space she had hung with
dream catchers, talismans, and crystals to enhance its sacred
vibe. "You do realize," she said, after some consideration,
"that without Lukas we can't go ahead with the ceremony?"

I felt deflated, and so did the others. "That's not fair,"
said Meg. "He can't ruin it for the rest of us."

Shakti said, "The universe has made it quite clear to me
that for the ritual to work, the seven of you must form an
unbroken circle. Take any one of you away and that magic
is lost."

"Can't we just do it another day?" said Timon.

"Timon," said Shakti gravely. "There *is* no other day. I have been summoned to heal Gaialands on the summer solstice in the year 1978. I didn't choose that date. The universe chose it. Just like it chose me to be the instrument of your destiny."

The six of us fell silent, overwhelmed by the gravity of her words.

"I want to do it," said Fritz. "It's Lukas who's stuffing everything up."

"I know, darling Fritz. It isn't fair." Shakti focused her amber-flecked eyes on me. "Poppy," she said. "You have the power to turn this around."

"How?"

"You can change Lukas's mind."

Six pairs of eyes turned my way.

"Me? But I don't even know where he is . . ."

Shakti sighed dramatically. Her eyes had filled with tears. "I don't think any of you understand how important this is—how many preparations have taken place. The fate of the commune is at stake."

"I'll try," I said, feeling suddenly responsible for everyone's future. "I'll do my best to find him."

Timon had a hunch that Lukas had gone into Coromandel to replace the transistor radio, so I hitched in the same direction, hoping to find him. It wasn't easy to get a ride, but eventually an elderly couple stopped to pick me up, and I sat in the back of their dusty car, next to a picnic basket full of delicious-smelling ham sandwiches.

In town, I asked around. Had anyone had seen a boy fitting Lukas's description? Someone said they had spotted him hanging out with the Maori boys at the end of the wharf. Everybody knew everybody in this town, and if you weren't from around here, then you stood out even more.

I recognized Lukas from a long way off, his lean torso and the flared jeans that ended too far above his ankles. He had grown taller, suddenly, but we did not have any new clothes. The guys he was with seemed older, more like men, but then, when I got closer, I realized Lukas was the same age, that he was no longer the boy I thought of him as. Approaching the group, my confidence stalled. In my plain, boyish clothes, and despite Shakti's declaration otherwise, I still felt very much like a child.

One of the boys must have seen me approaching and alerted Lukas, because he turned around before I reached the group. He looked baffled, but also pleased, to see me.

"What are you doing here?"

"You have to come back to Gaialands." In front of these boys, I was reluctant to say what for. "If we leave now, we can be back before it starts."

Lukas felt no such reluctance. "I don't want anything to do with her fortune-telling bullcrap."

"But Shakti says . . . She says the fate of the commune is at stake."

"The fate of the commune my arse." Lukas laughed, and the other boys joined in. He was showing off for them, using dirty words. "It's a power trip. I'm telling you, she's a witch."

One of the boys said, "Oooooooh," like he was a ghost,

and another said, "Don't do it, bro. What if she chops off your old fella?"

They hooted with laughter, Lukas loudest of all. Had he been telling them stories about us, how crazy and weird we all were? I bit my lip, not knowing what to say. One of the guys, wearing a Coromandel school T-shirt a few sizes too small for him, had been looking me up and down, and now he caught my eye and tilted his eyebrows and chin in a way that was definitely flirtatious but also mocking.

I scowled at him, as much to stop myself from crying as to show disapproval. "Please come back," I said to Lukas, in a plaintive and pathetic voice. "You're ruining it for the others."

Lukas wasn't laughing anymore, but he was still smiling—not taking any of this seriously—and rather than humiliate myself by crying in front of all these boys, I turned on my heel and scurried away. The tears that came were blinding, and I stumbled once or twice before making it to the road.

I was almost there when, behind me, Lukas called out: "Poppy, wait!"

I wiped my eyes with the sleeve of my T-shirt but didn't stop.

Lukas caught up to me and gently grabbed my shoulder. "Don't bugger off yet. Stick around. I'll get you a milkshake or something."

"So you can make fun of me?" I shook off his hand. "No thanks."

"I was just kidding around. You know I didn't mean anything by it."

I burst into tears again. "You don't get it," I said, sobbing. "We can't do it without you."

He tried, more gently, to put his hand on my shoulder again, and I let him. "Does it mean that much to you?"

"Not just to me. To everyone."

"I don't give a shit about the others," he said, brushing the hair out of my eyes and putting it behind my ear, something I did a hundred times a day but no one else had ever done for me. When he realized what he had done, Lukas quickly withdrew his hand and shoved it in his pocket.

"Okay," he said.

"Okay, what?"

"I'll do it."

"You will?" The despair lifted so suddenly that without thinking, I threw my arms around him and squeezed.

He hugged me back, saying, "Steady on," in such a prim way that I laughed.

"I can't believe you ran away," I said, punching his arm. "You're such a dork."

"*I'm* a dork?" he said. "What about you? Crying like a baby in front of all those boys."

Normality had been restored, or so I thought, but as we walked back to the main road and stuck out our thumbs to hitch, Shakti's words echoed in my ear. She was right. I had been able to change Lukas's mind. But how had she known?

A ute picked us up at the start of the 309 Road, and we climbed into the backseat, which was narrow with very little legroom. Even so, Lukas managed to shuffle into a position, hard up against the opposite window, where there was no danger of our arms or legs accidentally touching. He didn't speak once the whole way back to the commune, not even when the ute almost skidded off the road and into a ravine. Worse than that, he was broody, deep in thought. Going to fetch him had been a mistake. He was mad with me.

A cheer went around the mess hall when I returned to Gaialands with Lukas in tow, but I couldn't join in. I was worried that saving the day had come at a price. We ate early, a light supper of dal and brown rice, followed by bottled peaches and thin, sour yogurt for dessert. While we ate, Shakti gave each of us our tasks. Nelly and I were to gather up candles, one for each person, plus a couple of spares. To this we were to add a box of matches and a kerosene lamp, in case it rained or was windy on top of Mount Aroha. Sigi had put together what looked like a first aid kit, but when I asked if that was what it was, she said it was more of a just-in-case kit. "Things could get messy, but I don't think anyone will get hurt," she said ominously. We had been told not to ask questions, that we should trust in the universe's plan.

The base of Mount Aroha lay just beyond the boundary fence of the commune, on Maori land. The lower slopes were covered with wild manuka bushes, home to swarms of honey-making bees. As children we had called it Buzzy Mountain.

In the twilight, the bush-clad peak was already in silhouette, a blue-black slab, giving away nothing of its difficult terrain, the bracken so dense that climbing through it would be like trying to unpick knitting. Despite the status of the land as Maori owned, we wouldn't be trespassing. Local *iwi* had given us permission to go up there, but still I worried we might disturb something, an ancestral spirit or a long-forgotten curse. Not to mention the bees. We kept hives on the commune, but these ones were wild and didn't like humans.

Wide tracts of sunlight broke through the clouds. "You see?" said Shakti, pointing skyward. "The cosmos has blessed our little gathering."

Shakti had timed our ascent so that we would reach the peak when there was still light in the sky. It was the summer solstice, which coincided this year with a full moon, and she reassured us, even though it was cloudy, that there would be plenty of light by which to navigate our way down.

On past ascents, it had taken hours to reach the peak of Mount Aroha, but on this occasion, we arrived near the top, fresh and giddy, after what felt like no time at all. In a clearing of flat stones, we sat down to catch our breath, and none of us could fathom how we had climbed up so quickly, stomping through the thick, tangled bush as though it was a smattering of weeds. "Another blessing!" said Katrina, throwing her hands in the air.

Before we climbed the final section, Sigi retrieved a large earthenware jar from her knapsack and passed it to Shakti, who then passed it to Lukas. "I'd like each of the seven of you to take a long drink," said Shakti. "It's to open your chakras." She watched us drink the bitter liquid, but she herself abstained. "The unusual taste comes from a rare and sacred herb," she explained.

A few meters below the rocky peak there was a broad

circle of earth where nothing grew, not even weeds. It was perfect for our ceremony. Shakti instructed Paul and Hunter to dig a pit for a small fire, and the rest of us set about collecting as much dry kindling and heavier branches as we could find. Most of it was too damp to use, and we were grateful for the stuff we had carried up in slings on our backs. Once the fire was lit, Shakti told us where to stand, the adults to one side of the clearing and the seven of us in a circle around the fire. Because the fire was the only light source, the adults fell into shadow and after a while I forgot they were there. I stood with Fritz on one side and Ned on the other, with Lukas directly opposite me, his face licked with gold from the flames. He was the first one Shakti went over to, whispering something in his ear. He turned to her, mystified, but then nodded.

From the adults, cloaked in darkness, came chanting—an unfamiliar language, mouthed with hesitation. Shakti held Lukas by the arm and guided his hand toward the fire. She moved her grip to his palm and held it over a small metal bowl. She had something in her hand, a sharp tool of some sort, and she pushed it into his thumb. Lukas winced, and in response, I felt a nervous spasm in my own chest. Was that his blood dripping into the bowl? Shakti next approached Timon, who offered up his hand and bit his lip when the tool pierced his skin. Nelly, who was standing alongside him, reached out to touch his arm, then retreated. When her turn came, she yelped in pain.

Soon, Shakti stood in front of me, her skin glowing in the firelight. She smiled at me elatedly, then pricked the cushion of my thumb with the pointed end of the blade. It didn't hurt. The anticipation had been worse than the pain itself, but looking into the blood-spattered bowl, my insides churned.

Once Shakti had collected blood from the seven of us, she pushed the blade into her own thumb and squeezed a few drops into the bowl. This she mixed with a series of powders and liquids from vials she had carried up the hill in her knapsack. The resulting liquid was thinner and bluer than the blood had been, and she wiped some on her arm to test the color. She placed the bowl next to the fire, and came and stood with us in the circle.

"Join hands with me," she said. "And we will say the invocation."

Fritz, who stood next to me, folded his arms so no one could take his hands, but then, when he saw that he was the only one not joining in, he reluctantly took mine. His hand felt cold and sticky with his own blood, and I felt the familiar surge of tenderness toward him. On the other side of me was Ned, calm and inscrutable and sturdy. You could plant Ned in the middle of a hurricane and he wouldn't blow away.

"I call on the power of the beloved I Am," said Shakti, "to bind us and protect us in spirit and in body." She signaled for us to echo her, and obediently we chanted, "We call on the power of the beloved I Am to bind us and protect us in spirit and in body."

I was starting to feel woozy, light-headed. Around me the others mumbled incoherently, their eyes shining blankly in the dim light.

"I call on the great spirit of the beloved I Am to heal what was broken, to bind this circle together with love for eternity. Tonight each one of these seven gathered souls will receive the blessing of your guidance in the form of a prediction. We recite for you now our prayer of devotion to the goddess Shakti, the source of all things."

Had Shakti just referred to herself as a goddess? The thought zoomed across my temples, then was gone. I had trouble remembering where we were. In the flickering light, I caught Lukas's eye and I thought he mouthed something to me but I couldn't be certain.

Shakti finished her prayer, then instructed us to join in the chant the adults had been keeping up. At first, I was self-conscious and hesitant, but before long, the sound of my voice had merged with the others, and soon, it was no longer a human voice but part of a hum that was already in the air and I was merely tuning into. It went on and on, this drone, until it was the only thing holding me upright, and I worried I'd collapse if it stopped. For a few seconds, the air in front of me swarmed with tiny pale stars, and I thought I saw the outline of a dancing woman, her hair and skin white to match her dress. She flashed luminous for a second, this ghostly dancer, and then was gone.

Shakti picked up the metal bowl and dipped in her forefinger. She went first to Lukas, then to each of us in turn, dabbed a streak of the blood mixture across our foreheads. Some of it rolled down my nose and a small droplet trickled into the corner of my eye, where it burned like acid.

When she had been around to everyone in the group, Shakti told us to stop chanting and to sit on the ground. The sudden silence was deafening, like being plunged underwater. The fire had been slowly gathering in heat and size—the men had been feeding it logs—and all I could see were flames, orange, red, and fierce, and beyond them, nothing but blackness.

Shakti flitted between us, handing each person a black felt package tied with ribbon. She placed one in my hand and whispered for me not to open it yet, adding, "It's bad luck." When she had given a package to everyone in the group, she stood to one side and raised her arms to the sky. "I present you each with a prediction—a glimpse into the future from the highest order of the sacred realms. In this task, I am merely a messenger." She bowed her head and held her hands in prayer position. "Om shanti om. You may look at your predictions."

I unfolded the piece of felt in my hand. Inside was a rectangle of cardboard, and on it was an ink drawing, the lines heavy, not at all like the delicate one Shakti had shown me in her caravan.

I squinted to make out the drawing, of a woman standing next to a man. The man was a king of some sort—he wore armor and a crown, and carried a shield and a sword. Above them was a giant heart, cartoon red, and at their feet an empty cradle. The woman had a big blue tear running down her cheek, a blob that was larger than her mouth. On the back of the card Shakti had written

In a faraway land your true love waits . . .
But your womb shall bear only sorrow.

The first part of the prediction thrilled me. Somewhere in the world, my true love was waiting. All I had to do was to find him. The cryptic words leapt off the page and straight into the ironclad part of my brain, where memories lived that I'd never forget, even if I wanted to. The second part barely registered. I was not planning on bearing anything with my womb, an organ that seemed wholly abstract to me.

Fritz stood next to me, studying his card. Even in the firelight, I could see it was wildly different from mine in one important aspect—the bright color. Almost the entire card was green, a riot of leaves and the trunk of a tree, colored brown. Inside this trunk crouched a boy. The tree sheltered the boy but he was also part of it, his feet mingling with the root system. Fritz had always been crazy about climbing trees, had from a young age tried to scale everything from the smallest sapling to the giant kauri that stood at the base of Mount Aroha. It was a way to give his clubfoot the finger, and his card made perfect sense.

Everyone crowded around, showing each other their predictions, and I let them see mine, but not for too long. I worried that sharing it would take away its power. For the same reason I tried not to be nosy about what the others got despite how curious I was. I saw flashes of this and that—a dagger of some sort on Timon's card, and a wizard on Ned's; on Meg's a woman looking at her reflection in the mirror—but I did not stop to consider what their symbols meant.

The mood was celebratory, and the adults came forward and embraced us, passing around a few bottles of homemade pear wine that we were allowed to try. Lukas hung back, taking no interest in anyone's prediction, only in the booze. Wine was a rare privilege, and he and Timon guzzled as much as they could, trying to get drunk.

Nelly linked her arm through mine and squeezed it. She was fizzing with excitement and held out her prediction for me to see. Sure enough it was a version of the one Shakti had shown me in her caravan, the woman surrounded by love and happiness and children. It was even more colorful than I remembered, and Shakti had added the stick figure of a man, holding the woman's hand.

"There he is," she said, pointing to the stick man. "My husband! I wonder what these are?" She caressed the little symbols with her index finger.

"Your kids," I said. "You're going to have heaps of them."

"How do you know?"

"Shakti told me."

"Wow!" Nelly laughed. "What about you?"

Reluctantly, I showed her my prediction. She examined the front, then turned it over. "Crikey," she said. "A fellow with a sword—and he lives in a faraway land." She ran her finger over the handsome king. "That's odd. I always thought you'd end up with Lukas."

"Really?"

She nodded. "You guys always seemed made for each

other." She ran her finger over the writing. "This other bit is weird. 'Your womb shall bear only sorrow.' What does that mean?"

"Nothing," I said, feeling defensive. "I don't even want to have kids."

"Of course you don't now." Nelly looked again at the card. "But what about when you're older?"

I took back my card. "I can live with that if it means I get him." Then I vowed not to show it to anyone else.

Across the fire, Lukas was kidding around with the other boys, but he caught my eye and smiled. I hoped he hadn't heard my conversation with Nelly.

It was time to go. Paul and Hunter had been flinging wet logs on the fire, and it hissed with steam as the flames extinguished. I hadn't noticed until then that it was the only source of light, and as the fire went out, we were plunged into shadow. A couple of the adults lit kerosene lamps to light the way down the hillside, and Hunter split us into walking groups, two lamps apiece. Nelly and Meg had congregated around Hunter and Shakti and a few of the women, who were laughing and talking excitedly, but I didn't feel like joining in and found myself bringing up the rear with Paul and the boys. Feeling tired after so much excitement, I mechanically followed the footsteps of the person in front of me and barely noticed Lukas walking next to me until his hand found mine in the dark. The feeling of it there was so natural, as if we had been holding hands all along, and after only the briefest glance into each other's eyes, we went back to looking straight ahead.

I had pushed the felt-wrapped prediction to the bottom of my shorts pocket, but knowing it was there, while holding Lukas's hand, felt treacherous. Perhaps that feeling would go once he had shown me his prediction. "What did you get?" I said, turning to him in the dark and trying to make out his expression.

"No idea," he said. "I threw it away."

"You didn't even look at it?"

"What for? It's a load of crap."

"What if it isn't?" I said. "What if it's true?"

I stopped walking, as did he.

"Please don't tell me you believe in it." His eyes were pleading, but his mouth was a smirk.

When I didn't respond, we both knew what that meant.

I let go of his hand, and we continued on, the silence between us masked by the crunch of twigs underfoot.

Maybe Lukas felt bad about what he'd said because after a time, he added, "Anyway, who cares what I think. What'd you get?"

"You're right," I said, suddenly aware that I ought not to show him. "It's silly."

"So silly you can't show me?" Now he sounded bruised.

Reluctantly, I handed him the prediction, hoping he wouldn't be able to see it in the dark. He glanced at it for a few seconds, then handed it back, saying nothing.

"Well?" I said.

"Well, what? I've told you what I think."

We couldn't see two feet in front of us on the dark hillside, but the first part of the descent went off without a hitch. We followed the same route we had taken on the way up, sticking to the tracks we had hacked out of the bracken. But about a third of the way down, the party at the front came to a halt, and word filtered back that they had lost the path—our tracks had disappeared. They were going to start forging their way through virgin bush, cutting new tracks.

The group I was with thought that was a crazy idea. "Why don't we backtrack?" suggested Timon. "See if we can find the original path? We'll be up here all night if we have to cut a new one."

"Good idea," said Paul. "Lukas, you tell the others and I'll go back with Tom and Timon."

Lukas called out to the group ahead of us to stop and wait. When there was no response, he walked up the path toward them and called out again. But still they ignored him. "Wait here," he said, and disappeared down the dark track, while at the same time, Paul and Timon, with the other lamp, clambered up the hill in the opposite direction.

Seconds later, I stood in the pitch dark on my own, barely able to see my hand in front of my face. "Guys?" I called out. "Can someone come back?" I tried to walk in the direction Lukas had gone, but with no light to guide me, it was impossible to see where to put my feet. The ground was uneven, crisscrossed with branches, and fell away sharply to one side. The only way I could make anything out was to look above my head, where small patches of moonlight filtered through the trees.

I sat down on the path and waited. Sooner or later, I reasoned, either Lukas would return, or Paul and Timon would come back for me. I could hear them scratching through the undergrowth somewhere behind me. And if I squinted, I could even see the head of a tiny, bobbing lamp. No reason to panic, not yet.

Sure enough, I had not been waiting long when from somewhere not far away, Lukas called out, "Poppy? Where are you?"

"Over here," I replied as loudly as I could. "Only I don't know where that is."

"Stay put," he said. "I'll come to you."

"Okay."

He called out: "Keep talking. So I can hear where you are."

I stood up, so my voice would carry further. "What should I say?"

"Anything. My name will do." His voice had already grown louder; he was getting close.

"Lukas?"

"Say it again. I'm almost there."

"Lukas." A twig snapped nearby, and I turned my head in the direction of the noise. "Lukas, is that you?"

"Poppy," he said, beside my ear—so close I could hear him breathing. His fingers brushed my arm, warm air hit my face, and I froze. Aside from my own pulse, all noise had drained from the world. I was sure that if I moved so much as an inch to one side, our bodies would collide, but when I did dare to move, we didn't meet. I reached my hands out where I thought he was, but nothing was there. How could he have been standing right next to me, then disappeared?

Seconds passed while I waited for him to loom out of the bush, but the more I tried to see into the shadows, the darker they became. "Lukas?" I whispered, hearing panic in my voice. "Are you there?" But there was no response.

For a few seconds the silence ticked with the sound of my own heartbeat, then somewhere up ahead a branch snapped, triggering a landslide of soil and leaves. There was a bloom of light, and as the forest around me lit up, I saw that I was alone. Lukas was heading toward me with a lamp, but he was not by my side as I had thought.

"Poppy!" he said when he saw me. "Are you okay?"

I couldn't speak. I was too stunned.

"What happened?" He rushed to my side. "You look like you saw a ghost."

"I thought . . . I thought someone was standing next to me."

"I'm here now." He put his arms around me, and I sank into his chest. Some people, when you hugged them, were lighter than you expected, filled with air, but not Lukas. He was more solid than he looked, radiating a steady, comforting heat. In that moment, I didn't ever want to let go of him.

"I stopped the others," Lukas said, "but it took some bloody convincing."

Before we pulled apart, I stood on my tiptoes and sought out his mouth, wanting to taste his warmth with an eagerness that amazed me. Everything about Lukas was so familiar that I had expected kissing him would be like going into a room I had been in before. And in some ways it was. I knew the scent of his breath, what the small of his back would feel like when I put my hand there, how his skin would be firm yet soft. But I was ill prepared for my response. When I kissed Lukas, I wanted to consume him. I wasn't ready for the strength of my desire and pulled away, astonished.

Afterward, we said nothing. Lukas seemed just as unable to comprehend what had happened as I did, but I took his hand, like before, and we searched around for the others.

Paul, Tom, and Timon had set off up the hill behind us, but we soon heard their voices coming from a position parallel to us on the hillside. At first they weren't loud enough for us to be able to make out what they were saying, but then we heard "Over here! We've found the path." It was unclear quite where "over here" was, but Lukas suggested we go back for the others and then retrace Paul and Timon's steps up the hill. The process was more complicated than it needed to be—some stragglers had insisted on continuing to hack their way down through the undergrowth—but eventually all sixteen of us stood in single file on the same part of the slope, the number confirmed by a head count, and ready to commence our descent.

Paul and Timon led the way down from there and were much more cautious to not lose the path again. Even so, progress was painstaking, and several hours passed before we finally reached the lower slopes, where thick native bush gave way to meadows that were dotted with wildflowers during the day. My sandaled feet were black with forest mulch and my legs were covered in scratches. It was the chilliest part of the night, the air like a cold bath, and in the silvery light of the meadow, I felt tired. The descent had taken so long that we had lost faith, and it showed on our gloomy faces. Even Shakti looked spent, as if she had left her magic power on the mountaintop, and now she was mortal like the rest of us. I remembered the phantom on the hillside, the one I had thought was Lukas, and realized it hadn't been him at all but the man in my prediction, the one I hadn't met yet. He was there still, had followed us down the mountain, shadowing us, a few paces behind, even as I held on tightly to Lukas's hand.

CHAPTER 5

Nambassa
1979

FOR THE LAST FEW summers we had traveled to the Nambassa music festival near Waikino, at the bottom of the Coromandel Peninsula. There wasn't only music at the festival, but also workshops on yoga, whole foods, meditation, rammed-earth housing, and recycling for biogas fuel—all the stuff that we had been doing for years but others still thought of as alternative. The guy who ran it was a friend of Hunter's and a regular visitor at Gaialands. He was trying to raise money to build an eco village where he could ride out the social and economic collapse that was coming, in 1980 or perhaps 1981, that would destroy the world order they loathed so much. On one of these visits, he and Hunter had stayed up late into the night talking about it, and they were still talking about it the next morning when we met in the mess hall for breakfast. Paul and Hunter were going to the festival to demonstrate a wood-fired tractor, and the women were selling vegetables and fruit, but the seven of us were going for the rock bands and not much else. We had been talking about it for months.

We set off the day before the festival in a convoy of utes and Land Rovers, packed to the roof racks with people, produce, and canvas tents. Lukas had his acoustic guitar. He was hoping to find some dudes there he could jam with, or better still, a band he could join. I was holding his hand, which I had done nonstop since the night of the predictions, and speculating, which I had also been doing nonstop, as to whether his hand, or my hand, would ever wander anywhere else. The desire to touch him was strong and constant, but I wasn't sure it was right to lead him on if I was going to spend my life with someone else.

We had not gone very far past the turnoff to the festival site when we were forced to get out of the Land Rover and walk the rest of the way. Half of New Zealand was on their way to Waikino for the weekend, and the road was backed up with cars and house trucks almost as far as the turnoff to Thames. The closer we got to the festival site, the less clothes people wore, and by the time we had passed through the entrance gate and made our way across the paddocks to the festival village, I was starting to feel like a prude in my crocheted bikini top and running shorts. It was hard not to stare at all the bare breasts, comparing the different shapes and sizes.

The boys—Lukas, Ned, and Timon—tore off straightaway to find the bands, but Nelly had promised to attend Shakti's yoga workshop, and she persuaded me to come with her. I was reluctant to go in search of Shakti but went for Nelly's sake. Since Lukas had been taking up more of my time, I had been feeling guilty about neglecting her, my best friend. We found the yoga workshop on the hill above the village, where someone had built a mandala decorated with multicolored flags. Underneath it a half dozen people creaked from mountain pose to downward dog and back again. Shakti stood at the front, guiding and demonstrating in loose Indian pants, her voice slow and mesmerizing, as though trying to hypnotize her followers into a deep sleep. When the session finished, everyone bowed, then Shakti went and stood by a tent pole and got undressed.

We went over to join her.

"Isn't this just the most wonderful place?" she said, introducing us to her friend Johannes, who had sailed all the way from Holland on a ketch. This boat was moored off the beach, and Shakti told us she was planning to swim out there later to meet some other friends. Johannes was tall and blond, with a long shaggy beard, and he was about to do a Reiki demonstration under the mandala.

"As a matter of fact, I need a volunteer," he said, looking hopefully at Nelly, and then at me.

A few minutes later, I lay under the flags on a folding massage table, eyes shut, my body covered with a yellow blanket, while Johannes hovered his arms slowly up and down my torso. He had warned me that I might feel strange sensations in my belly while he performed his spiritual surgery, but despite my best efforts to surrender to the experience, to feel what he said I would feel, the only thing I was aware of was the displacement of air as he flapped his arms above me. I tried very hard not to nod off, but at this too I failed. Johannes woke me up with a persistent prod to the shoulder.

When I went to stand up, he said, "Don't forget to drink plenty of water. It helps your body to release all the toxins." He warned me that I might feel dizzy for a few hours while the surgery healed. "The energy around your heart chakra was very blocked," he added. "I had a hard time shifting it."

Shakti, who had been listening in, said, "Really?"

"Yes," he said. "You were right."

I was annoyed that Shakti had talked about me to her friend, but I said nothing.

The boys were at the Aerial Railway, but it took us a long time to find this oddly named stage, and so many people were crowded near it that I worried we wouldn't see them at all. Then I heard someone singing very fast and very out of tune, beating out a rhythm on the side of his guitar. Some of the lyrics were familiar but the melody was mangled beyond recognition. Then the person playing it came into view. It was Lukas, head down, strumming furiously.

I felt so embarrassed. What was he doing up there, playing so badly in front of people we didn't know? We had joked about it on the way to Nambassa, all the hippies, bonged out of their trees, trying to play Dylan. Now Lukas was one of them. It took all my self-control not to run up and stop him.

But when I looked at the faces around me I was startled to find they weren't cringing. People were nodding in appreciation. Some were guys with short, spiky hair, but most near the front were girls. A few had their eyes closed in rapture. One woman, very pretty, licked her lips. Whenever Lukas glanced up from his guitar, he appeared scared, not from stage fright but from something else, and it took me a while to work out what that was. There was something predatory about these women, and they weren't embarrassed about his playing. In fact, they wanted to fuck him.

I had multiple reactions at once. First, to laugh out loud. How absurd! Then I panicked, because these women wanted something that was rightfully mine. I had never known such possessiveness, and the force of it made me giddy. A hectic few minutes followed, and by the time Lukas reached the end of his song, my view of him had utterly changed. On the final strum, I rushed to him.

"There you are," he said, looking triumphant but also wanting something from me, which I guessed was approval.

"You did great," I said. "Really great."

"Thanks, Poppy." He grinned and bent to put away his guitar. Most of the women had dispersed, but a few stuck around, checking out Lukas but also waiting for a sign from me. I understood what was expected, what I had to do. While Lukas fiddled with his guitar, oblivious, I put my arm around his shoulder, claiming him.

Sure enough, within seconds, the few remaining women had lost interest and walked away. Lukas stood up and smiled at me. "Shall we go?"

"Yes," I said, and leaned in to kiss him, not in the usual timid way but with purpose. When I let him go, Lukas was dazed.

"Crikey, Poppy, what happened?"

"Like I said, you were great."

We made our way in a group to the main stage, a gargantuan wooden structure in the bottom of a natural amphi-
theater. The arch above was painted with cosmic symbols
and a giant eagle beneath an exploding sun. Thousands of
people danced in front of the stage, their bare feet stomping
up clouds of dust from the bone-dry earth.

"Come on," said Lukas, grabbing my hand. "Let's go
right to the front!"

Near the stage, the crowd was denser, the air thick with
perspiration and marijuana smoke, the yeasty smell of beer
and tobacco. Men in leather vests were arriving with wooden
crates of booze, loading empties into the slots vacated by
full ones, and wrenching off bottle caps with their teeth.
Someone passed Lukas a beer and after he had swigged on
it, he passed it to me.

The next thing I knew I was drunk. We had come
down here with Nelly and Timon, but now I didn't care
where they were. The crowd around us chanted "sex and
drugs and rock 'n' roll!" and the frenzied energy was contagious. Lukas craned his neck toward the stage, then
turned to me and yelled, "Look! Split Enz are on!" and
even though I had only a vague idea who they were, a wave
of excitement rose in my chest. A cheer went up—"Split
Enz! Split Enz!"—followed by a powerful surge toward the
stage. Lukas grabbed me around the waist and together we
were pulled into a riptide. Every now and then I caught a
glimpse of the band—a handful of men in checkerboard
pajamas, their faces painted geisha white under stiff peaks
of cartoon hair. As the rolling, heaving crowd pushed and

pulled my body from all angles, their guitar riffs pinged in my ears. By my side, Lukas was having a religious experience, his body leaning toward the music, playing an imaginary guitar, and I realized how badly he wanted it to be him up there onstage.

At the end of their set, we stumbled into the dark, wooded area behind the stage. The forest there was cool and welcoming and quiet. A whining noise filled my ears, and my voice, when I tried to speak, sounded like it belonged to someone else. I decided not to try anymore, and Lukas did the same, guiding me silently through the trees with one arm around my shoulders. We stumbled along, until we found ourselves climbing a mound and reaching a boulder, where there was a flat spot, invisible from below and shielded from above by trees. Still without words passing between us, we started kissing, and before long, the hands that had always been so respectful, that had never wandered off course, were all over the place. Our clothes flew off and I was stretched out naked on the warm stone next to a body that I had not seen in its entirety for several years, during which time it had become lean and muscular and in certain places thick with dark, wiry hair. It was the hair that scandalized me most. How had Lukas grown it, this manly pelt, when his chin and upper lip bore only fluff? He climbed on top of me, and even though we were about to do something neither of us had done before, we did not, as I had often feared we might, need instructions. His penis, which had grown vastly in size—a feat that was somehow exciting and off-putting at the same time—was nudging between my legs when Lukas suddenly pulled back. "Are you sure you want to do this?" He stared into my eyes. "Because we can wait."

Breathlessly, I said, "Wait for what?"

"I don't know. It just feels sudden, like you've changed your mind." His erection hovered between us, a third party with a mind and a plan of its own, and I adjusted my hips to meet it, to take it in—a move that Lukas stopped with his hand. "You never wanted to do this before."

He was right. I had never wanted to do this before, and the difference was that I had realized his value. He was a prize, and if I didn't claim him, someone else would. Unable to explain any of this without coming over as a scoundrel, I said, "We've known each other forever. Why not?"

He shook his head, frustrated, and his voice turned hoarse with emotion. "It's more than that for me. I've wanted to do this for so long—as long as I can remember. Night after night, lying across from you in the dark, I've imagined what it would be like to climb into your bed and—"

"Wait," I said, interrupting him. "You've wanted to do this since we were kids?"

"Haven't you?"

"Not really," I said truthfully. "Before that night on the mountain, I thought of you more like a brother."

Lukas rolled off me, and I realized I had hurt his feelings after all.

"But that night, something changed. I can't explain it but I really want to do this."

"But are you sure it's me you want to do it with?"

The question floated between us. Was he wondering,

like I had, if he was only a stopover on the way to my true love? "I do," I whispered, pushing those thoughts away. "I want this more than anything."

Lukas didn't respond with words, but propped himself up on one elbow and leaned over me, staring into my face, then pressed his free hand solemnly over my heart, as if it would tell him the truth. I felt tested by him and didn't trust myself to move or speak. Against his palm, my heart thumped wildly, so wildly that his expression became curious and then faintly amused. He moved his hand away from my heart and ran it down my belly and over my pubic bone, where he pushed his fingers carefully, but decisively, into the hot, wet cleft between my legs. I bucked underneath him, an intense spasm that caused me to gasp and made Lukas laugh out loud.

"I believe you," he said, and for a few seconds, I was mortified, before Lukas plunged his mouth to mine, driving himself into me with such force that I was the one who felt claimed, and there was nothing to do but surrender to a bond that had been growing since the day we were born.

CHAPTER 6

**Gaialands
1979**

AFTER THAT EVENTFUL NAMBASSA Festival, Shakti did not
return with us to live at Gaialands. On the final day of
the festival she wandered into our campsite just as we were
dismantling tents and cleaning up three days' worth of rubbish. She was covered from head to toe in paint the color
of egg yolks, her lips and eyes outlined in thick black lines.
Only her hair was natural, and stood out in tufts between
her legs, under her arms, and on her head. She was with
another woman, similarly painted, whom she introduced as
Marcia, one of the backup singers from the Plague. Lukas
and I had seen the band earlier that day. The lead singer had
been cobalt blue, the guitarist red, and both had painted
their genitals. I had idly wondered, while they played, if they
had dabbed at their penises with a brush or dipped them in
a jar of paint.

After Shakti had introduced us to her friend, she collected
a few of her belongings in a string bag, then waltzed off, not

saying where she was going or helping to dismantle the wind-blown canvas tents. Less than a week later, she turned up briefly on the commune with Marcia. They were driving to Auckland that day in Marcia's car, a rusty beige station wagon with strips of peeling wood veneer down the sides, and stayed long enough to go for a swim in the creek, drink a cup of tea, and walk around the orchards, filling a basket with fruit. While Paul and Tom struggled under the willow tree to hitch the caravan to the back of the car, they watched. After months of not moving, it was wedged into the dried mud. When they were finally able to roll the caravan forward, something deep in its bowels made a snapping sound, but no one could find what had broken.

"That tow bar's rooted," Paul said. "You'll be lucky to get over the first hill. I could fix it but you'd have to stay here for the night."

The two women conferred. "We can't," said Marcia. "I have a gig tonight. There isn't time."

Against Paul's advice, they attached the caravan via the rooted tow bar to the car, waved breezily good-bye, then drove off.

Tom shook his head. "Those birds will never make it to Auckland."

"No shit," said Paul. "But buggered if anyone could have stopped them."

Three short months, almost to the day, since she had arrived on the commune and turned all our lives upside down, Shakti was gone.

I barely noticed her absence. In the days and weeks following the festival, it was not an exaggeration to say that Lukas and I went at it day and night, as if we were the first people in the world to discover sex. What we lacked in skill we made up for with enthusiasm—and months and months went by before I wondered if there might be more to sex than the frenzied humping we engaged in. The best part was the anticipation of his entering me, and the moment he did, but everything after that was an exercise in frustration as I chased down a sensation that seemed hell-bent on running away. I felt a growing sense of disappointment and blamed it on my own faulty anatomy. I wanted to talk to Lukas about it, but early on, and despite the fact that we knew each other so well, a precedence of silence had been set. There had been one night, not long after Nambassa, when I had worked up the courage to ask him if he knew how to find my clitoris. When he replied, "What's that?" I had been too shy to show him what I didn't exactly know how to locate, and the subject was buried, perhaps forever. I still enjoyed what we did, was even addicted to doing it, but it was like scratching at an itch that flared up every night without ever locating the source of irritation.

We shared a sleeping hut with five other teenagers, some of whom, like Timon, were bloodhounds when it came to any hint of sexual activity, and the rest of the time we were rarely alone. To get any privacy, if you could call it that, we had to roam to the far edges of the commune, late at night, or before dawn, to make love under the cover of darkness, and even then, there was no guarantee we were alone. Every snapping twig or rustling leaf made me pull away from Lukas and glance, possumlike, into the shadows.

One particularly clear and starry night, we had gone as
far as the beach, where we made love under the lone pohutukawa tree that grew sideways out of the cliff. Afterward, we
went for a swim to get the sand out of our bums, and Lukas
told me about his plans to leave the commune. He had mentioned before that he wanted to leave, but I didn't know how
serious he was. Auckland was the first stop, he said, where
he would form his own band. But as soon as he had saved
enough money, he wanted to go to London.

"London?" I said, hearing in the word how far away
that was. "Why not Australia? Isn't that where everyone goes
to make it big?"

"It's only a stepping stone," he said. "And I don't want to
be in a Kiwi or Aussie band that goes to London and tries to
make it. I want to be in an English band."

The scale of his ambition awed me. The fire lit under
him at Nambassa had grown into a furnace. From that
moment on Lukas devoted all his free time to music, at
the expense of all other interests. At the breakfast table,
he strummed his latest song, writing down lyrics on any
scrap we had on hand, even toilet paper. At night we talked
across the guitar, which was always in his lap or swinging from his back. Often there was no talking, only Lukas
singing, and me listening, or pretending to. A couple of
times, early on, I had made the mistake of thinking it was a
sing-along, and I had tried to join in with harmonies, until
Lukas had reminded me that I couldn't listen to him and
sing at the same time, and that what he needed most was
an audience. So I got better at listening, even when it bored

me and I couldn't pick out anything that sounded like a tune. He wrote a lot of lyrics about women, about their cunts, reassuring me that he was singing about a feeling or an idea and not about an actual woman, especially not me. The Lukas who made up songs, who belted them out in a clearing in the forest, was so much angrier than the boy I had grown up with, but if ever I mentioned this to him, he denied there was a split. "The songs tell me what they want to be," he explained. "I just write them down."

That same night on the beach, lying on our clothes, drying off after our swim, Lukas asked me to go with him to Auckland. I wasn't surprised by the request—in fact I had been waiting for it and dreading it and planning what I would say in response. But until now, I hadn't known Auckland was only the first stop, that he was going on to London as well. I thought about my prediction, of the true love waiting for me on the other side of the world, and even though I knew it was deceitful, and worse, to think like this, I said, "I'll go overseas with you."

"All the way to London?"

"Sure, if that's what you want."

He didn't answer straightaway, and I thought he was working out how to say that he wanted to go without me, and I was gutted, even though I had no right to be.

But then he said, "Of course that's what I want. I was afraid to ask because I thought you'd say no."

I wasn't ready to be apart from Lukas, and now that it wasn't going to happen for at least another couple of years, I felt a huge weight lifted.

All around us, though, commune life was unraveling, and fast. We had started out the summer, as always, a tight group of seven. We planned our days together, did everything in a group, and were so used to deciding things by consensus that we didn't even know we were doing it. Then, slowly, toward the end of that summer, some of us, the older ones, became bored by the activities we had filled our free days with as kids. Climbing trees and making forts seemed pointless. But Meg and Fritz still wanted to play those games. Fritz, in particular, was very much still a child. Increasingly, he was left out of our conversations, which often revolved around rock concerts and booze—things he knew nothing about. And when he couldn't get anyone to roam with him in the forest, to trap possums or tip empty birds' nests off their branches, he would stalk off on his own, determined to dam the stream with twigs or make bivouacs by himself.

One scorching-hot day near the end of what had been a particularly dry summer, we set out for the orchards as a group, running for a stretch to make it more quickly to the beach, then dawdling for a spell because it was just too darn hot. It must have been a Sunday, the only day of the week we did not have to do chores. I had been stopping now and then to canoodle with Lukas. After persuading Fritz to come with us, I had been paying him scant attention, and I recall feeling bad about that briefly, and calling out to him to wait up. He turned and stared at me for a moment, and I walked faster, trying to catch up to him, then just as I was making ground, his expression changed. I thought he might cry. "Fritz," I said. "What is it? What's wrong?" Then he turned on his heel and sprinted in the opposite direction, yelling out to everyone that the last person to the other side of the forest was a rotten egg.

"Rotten egg" was a game we had played for as long as anyone could remember. If he had called out anything else, no one would have followed him, but the threat of being crowned rotten egg was a challenge that still held sway, even in this heat, and before Fritz had the chance to grab much of a lead, Lukas and I had taken off after him, and the others were legging it too.

Within seconds, I had lost sight of Lukas, who was faster than me at running and fiendishly competitive with the other boys. Sprinting through the dense avenues of macrocarpa pine, I remembered how frightened we had been, as children, to run through here alone. Even now, the closeness of the trees and their sameness made me think of an army that might at any moment turn on us.

To run from one side of the wood to the other took about seven minutes. We had timed it once, with an old stopwatch of Tom's. It was a far enough distance to get lost or disoriented in but we knew the path so well that none of us ever had. On this particular day, in an effort to be more sophisticated, I had worn flip-flops, and about halfway across, where there was a gentle slope, I tripped on a tree root and stubbed my toe. I stopped just long enough to rub the toe and find my errant shoe, before setting off again, but it was enough to send me permanently to the rear. For the last half of the race, I couldn't see or hear anyone, and I was sure that when I reached the other side of the forest I would be the rotten egg.

But when I popped out into the clearing no one jeered or called it out. Instead they scanned the forest behind me, waiting for someone else to appear. I did a quick head count. Six of us had made it through but one was missing. Ned said, "Where's Fritz?"

"He wasn't behind me," I said, doubling over to catch my breath. "No one was."

Lukas wiped the sweat off his face with a towel. "It's not like him to call a race, then lose it. I reckon he's playing a trick on us."

"He'll be out in a jiffy," said Meg.

For a few minutes, all six of us peered into the forest, expecting at any moment for Fritz to appear, and then, when he didn't, Timon said, "You lot can wait for him. I'm going for a swim." He sauntered in the direction of the cliff edge, where a path ran precariously down to the beach. "Last one in the water is a bloody idiot."

Even though I was worried about Fritz, when Lukas followed him, I did the same, thinking only of how refreshed I would feel after diving into the surf at the bottom of the cliff. Relief from this heat was only a scramble away, and I couldn't get down the hill fast enough. Once in the water, I forgot about Fritz altogether.

We horsed around in the waves for a long time, treading water and dunking each other and body surfing, until every muscle in my body felt battered and wrung out. Nelly had brought a bag of apples, and we shared them around, wishing we had thought to bring a drink. All that salt water had made us thirsty. Then the six of us lay on the sand and dozed in the breeze, rousing only when a fly ticked our skin or a loud set of waves crashed ashore.

We had been out in the sun all summer long, and every summer before it, adding sunburn to sunburn, and except where it had peeled off and was pink, the skin on our backs was a deep chestnut brown. Out of all of us, Meg was the brownest, and I had been studying her lovely tanned shoulders when I noticed Ned and Timon doing the same thing, only more furtively. There was no doubt about it, she was turning into a beauty, but I was still astonished when she looked back over her shoulder and smiled at the boys. She liked the attention, encouraged it.

Hours and hours passed and the shade from the pohutukawa moved down our bodies and reached the water's edge, bringing with it a chill. When someone suggested it was time to go back, I groaned at the thought of trekking up the hill and perspiring all over again.

We got back to the commune just as the cowbell sounded for dinner, and the six of us made a beeline for the mess hut, trying not to look like we were rushing.

I was halfway through my second bowl of spinach and chickpea curry when across the table Nelly caught my eye. "Where's Fritz?" she said with alarm. "He should be back by now."

"He'll be up a tree somewhere," said Ned, "eating berries, pretending to be a possum."

"He's never missed dinner before. Not even that time he ran away." My stomach clenched with dread. "What if something's happened to him?"

"Don't worry," said Lukas. "He can't have gone far."

The adults did not seem to have noticed Fritz was missing and we decided to search for him on our own before alerting them. Looking back, I can see this was an unspoken acknowledgment of guilt. We had left him alone in the forest. We hadn't been looking out for the youngest in the group. The burden of guilt I carried was heavier still. He had run off in the first place because I had been ignoring him.

We took kerosene lamps and an emergency battery-powered flashlight and combed the surrounding orchards and forests in pairs. When we found no trace of him, we searched further afield, and long into the night, before heading back to the sleeping hut to regroup. Some of the others thought Fritz had run away again, but I was adamant he hadn't. "He had nothing with him. Those other times he was prepared. He planned it." I didn't tell them about the sad look he had given me just before he ran off. I felt too bad about it.

"We'll have to tell the adults," said Lukas. "Who's going to come with me?"

None of us wanted to. We looked at our feet.

"I'll do it, mate," said Timon.

We hated it when the oldest boys took charge, but the other side of this was that they sometimes acted heroically.

At first light the next morning, Lukas and Timon, wearing solemn expressions, knocked on the door of Hunter and Elisabeth's hut and were ushered in, while the rest of us huddled in the bushes nearby to wait. A haze of fine droplets hung in the air, waiting to evaporate or turn into rain and making it harder to see what was going on.

Hunter came out first and saw us straightaway but didn't speak. Behind him, Lukas and Timon emerged, their faces downcast with shame. They must have been given a grilling.

All that day, search parties went out from the commune and came back without Fritz. Tom drove the old Land Rover up the access road, as far as he thought Fritz might have made it on foot, but he came back with nothing but an empty gas tank. We followed any orders we were given to the letter but otherwise kept quiet. In the evening, Hunter and Tom drove reluctantly to Whitianga to notify the police, an organization they neither respected nor had any trust in. A couple of times a year, going back at least a decade, the cops had turned up at Gaialands to bust us for growing marijuana. Each time Hunter informed them drugs were banned from the commune, but they didn't believe him and kept coming back with their dogs. He had even once given them some pamphlets, outlining the philosophy behind his antidrug stance, but we had found those a few days later in a bush at the side of the road.

No one on the commune had much time for the pigs, as we called them, even though it was an insult to our animals, but on this occasion we had no choice but to ask for their help. To their credit, and to Hunter's surprise, they came through. At seven the next morning, a dozen men in uniforms arrived with flashlights and sniffer dogs. They cast an ever so slightly distasteful eye over the wild chooks and composting toilets, then set off into the forest. One of the cops remained behind to question us, and we told him what we could remember of the events leading up to Fritz's disappearance. They wanted so many details. What had he been wearing, not just "shorts and a T-shirt," but what style, what color, what shop it was from. The questions baffled us, and our answers—"Whatever was in the box that morning," "We share all our clothes," "They're mostly homemade"— utterly bewildered the cops. Only Nelly seemed able to answer with any certainty. "It was a green tank top with the number three on it," she said. "I remember thinking it was getting tight, that it wouldn't fit him much longer. He must have grown over the summer."

"What sort of green?" the cop asked.

"Bright green," said Nelly. "The color of new spring grass. The three on it was white."

We told him about playing rotten egg in the forest, how Fritz had started the race but hadn't come out the other side in the clearing, and the cop had said, "Aren't you a bit old to be playing those sorts of games?"

The cops didn't ask if Fritz had ever tried to run away before, and none of us mentioned it, though I worried that was vital information that ought not to be omitted. Then the policeman made us sign a joint statement, and right before he handed Lukas a pen, he said, "Can you lot even read or write?" and I was glad we hadn't told him.

I signed on the dotted line at the bottom of the police document and stared at the letterhead, at our six names in a row. Six, not seven. Fritz was missing. Gone. Here was an official document to prove it.

After the police found nothing, the wider community joined in the search, looking for Fritz in nearby towns and in remote stretches of the Coromandel ranges. They showed his photograph on the six o'clock news, though we didn't see it because we had no television set. The week after Fritz went missing was the closest I think Hunter ever came to buying one.

In his search for Fritz, Hunter was relentless—and secretive. He roamed the hills, around the clock, and would often show up haggard at the breakfast table, not saying where he had been, but the red eyes and flashlight giving him away. We overheard the other adults whispering about him. Was he too proud, someone wondered, to admit he was falling to pieces?

Meanwhile, Elisabeth, Fritz's mother—my mother—let nothing show, and I saw this as ultimate proof she was cold and uncaring. It hardened me against her for good.

While Hunter roamed the surrounding bush, looking for Fritz, I searched for clues closer to home. I climbed to the top of all his favorite lookouts, searched his bed, and walked through the macrocarpa forest a thousand times, retracing his final movements, trying to imagine what had been going through his head and what might have happened to him. Despite my intuitive feelings about him when he was around, I could not tune into his absence.

One awful consequence of our communal life, the fact that we shared everything, was that Fritz had left behind nothing to remind us of him. Not one scrap of clothing or book or toy had been uniquely his. The only thing he alone used was his bed, and that sat unmade, stripped bare, a gaping wound in the sleeping hut.

Three weeks after Fritz disappeared, the police scaled down their search operation, and the sniffer dogs were sent back to Auckland to root out a new missing person. The sergeant who spoke to us said he didn't like to leave an open case, he was usually a finisher, but he had been given his orders and they were to move on. None of us liked the way he spoke about Fritz as a case and not a person, but it was worse once the pigs had gone because then he wasn't even an open case. He was nothing.

The weeks of missing turned into months and at some point, though he didn't talk about it with any of us, even Hunter stopped searching for Fritz. Even I stopped searching. We thought there was nowhere we hadn't looked.

We went about our routines, carried out our chores, grew vegetables, chopped wood, shoveled shit, but it was as though the lot of us were trapped in tar. We couldn't move forward, and we couldn't go back. Without a body there could be no funeral, but to hold out hope against hope was to welcome in never-ending misery.

ONE MORNING, AFTER HE had been missing a few weeks, I recalled the image on Fritz's prediction: a boy entwined in a tree, with roots for legs and branches for arms. At the time of the ceremony I had thought it funny Fritz would end up with a tree, not a wife. But now that same image was a sinister prophecy. Fritz hadn't married a tree, but the forest army had taken him and was not going to give him back. Those trees that had always seemed so threatening had finally lived up to their promise, and so had Shakti's card. His prediction had come true, just like mine would. Just as, one by one, they all would.

PART II

CHAPTER 7

Auckland
1980

O UR FINAL YEAR ON the commune was one that I tried to forget. Fritz had never struck me, out of the seven of us, as the linchpin. But without him the group quickly came unstuck. Perhaps it was only coincidence but when friendships and alliances that had been so solid fell apart, I couldn't help tracing it back to Fritz's disappearance. For starters, he and Ned had been tight, but without Fritz around, Ned focused all of his energy on Meg. Timon had a crush on her too, and what had started on the beach that afternoon as shared admiration soon mushroomed into a bitter rivalry between the two boys. They scrapped openly, fistfights at the dinner table and refusing to share the few possessions we owned. Lukas tried to play peacemaker but his unwillingness to take sides only soured his relationship with Timon, who thought his best friend ought to fight in his corner.

Meg wasn't overly interested in either of the boys but

gave just enough encouragement to each of them to stoke both their fires.

And Nelly, because of her history with Timon, couldn't stand to be in the same room as Meg, which made it awkward for everyone else. When I tried talking to her about it she said I couldn't possibly understand because I had snared Lukas without even trying, and what did I know about heartbreak?

I mourned my lost friendship with Nelly. I loved being intimate with Lukas, but there was so much I couldn't share with him, my feelings not just about the prediction, but about plenty of other stuff too. Having sex with him had made us closer in some ways but also more distant. I had to be careful not to say things that would hurt his feelings, and the list of those things seemed to grow day by day. He had never been this sensitive before. For large parts of that year, I felt lonely.

As 1979 became 1980, the six of us limped on, still sharing sweaters and sleeping quarters and our parents, but the old joy of togetherness was gone. A few days after Lukas turned nineteen, he announced he was out of there. He couldn't stand it a minute longer. Auckland beckoned. I was only seventeen, too young, but he had waited for me as long as he could and there was no way I was going to let him leave without me. And then, at the back of my mind—but way, way back where I was barely conscious of it—was the thought that I was taking my first steps toward fulfilling my prediction. The adults tried to talk us out of leaving, but our minds were made up, and though they had forced many things upon us in the course of our short lives, in this instance they were philosophically bound to grant us our freedom. Hadn't they, after all, raised us to refuse the shackles of the nuclear family? Having done so, they couldn't very well insist we remain with them forever.

What began with Lukas's announcing his departure quickly turned into an exodus. Despite the fracture in their friendship, Timon followed Lukas and me to Auckland, where he soon discovered Meg wasn't the only girl in the world with lovely shoulders. Within six months, he had slept with every waitress in the central suburbs and saved enough for a one-way ticket to Melbourne, Australia, where he planned to do more of the same.

Ned chaperoned Meg to Wellington, where she intended to become an actor on the stage. She had so far applied for drama school, and was hopeful she would be accepted. In letters, Ned sounded still very much in love with her, but reading between the lines, it seemed she did not reciprocate.

Nelly stuck around on the commune for the longest, but even she met a boy at the Sweetwaters festival the following year, a boat builder from the Bay of Islands, and not long after her eighteenth birthday, she was pregnant with the first of their children. She sent me a postcard, a peace offering, when their baby girl was born. The following summer, we went to their wedding on a Northland beach not far from Opua, where they lived, and Nelly, already four months pregnant with her second child, seemed well on her way to fulfilling her prediction. Nelly didn't invite any of the adults to the wedding, so Ned gave her away, and Lukas and I signed the register to witness the union.

We lived in Auckland for more than three years, dossing at first on couches in various slum villas in Freemans Bay and Grey Lynn, before moving into a slum of our own, a half-converted basement on the slopes of Arch Hill. We paid ten dollars a week for the indignity, enough to cover the power and phone bill of the students living upstairs. Our hovel was so damp that a variety of translucent fleshy pink mushrooms grew in the corners of our bedroom ceiling, and so cold that an entire winter passed without either of us getting completely undressed. We had sex in the woolly jumpers and hand-knitted socks we had brought with us from the commune, and in the scummy, lopsided bathroom sink, we doused either from the waist up or waist down, but never both at the same time. When we weren't dying of bronchitis or gastroenteritis or stumbling home drunk, we were saving like crazy for our airfares to London. We never ate more than once a day. Beer was considered a meal. Add a meat pie and that was a banquet. In photographs from that time, despite the starvation, I am pudgy, a raccoon-eyed, pasty punk beneath a scrum of dyed black hair. We smoked a lot of roll-your-owns, crammed with cheap Fisherman's tobacco, and what we didn't save went into slowly paying off a magnificent red Fender Stratocaster that Lukas had put on lay-by—a guitar so tenderly saved for and anticipated it may as well have been our first child.

Irrespective of the squalor, we were never happier. We had grown up not being allowed to drink, smoke, eat meat, wear leather, believe in god, or love our parents in the normal way. Every pie, every roll-your-own, every secondhand biker jacket and pint of beer before lunchtime, was a strike against our puritanical upbringing. The night Lukas paid off the last ten bucks and finally brought home his baby, he placed it in the living room on a throne he had built out of cushions. When the Fender Strat wasn't being played, it was proudly displayed, the only gleaming thing in our sordid, fungus-ridden world. In Lukas's mind that guitar *was* his future, his ticket to a better life. His ambition was enough for both of us. I was just grateful to be included in his plans. He was different from other boys in bands. Some of them were in it for the perks or the groupies, and drank their way to oblivion eight nights a week. But not Lukas. He considered all that a distraction. He was too ambitious to have anything other than a steady girlfriend. Those early band names, when Lukas was still trying to be a punk, were designed to revolt: the Rioters, Vulture Culture, Urban Parasites, Reject Street, Arch Hill Rats. My job was to put up posters in coffee shops and Laundromats, anywhere with a blank wall and an owner who wasn't too squeamish. The band lineups were a revolving door of bassists, drummers, lead guitarists, and even synth players, depending on whatever sound variation Lukas was trying on at the time. He moved on quickly from punk, which had fallen out of favor, to a style of music that was more friendly on the ears, if you liked synthesizers, but still rebellious in spirit. He tried on vocal styles like new hats. The band names cycled on: Candyhead, the Clownz, Blister Sister, Cherry Rope. I went through all these iterations with him, trying to make sense of what I heard, until at some point the sounds fell into place and I wrote gig reviews, which we sent in to *Rip It Up, Cracuum,* and *Inner City News.* The rest of the time I was at university, not very studious but going on protest marches and debating feminism with lesbians in the student union Women's Space. It was something to do while Lukas gigged and gigged, playing in any venue that would have him, from the suburban RSA clubs to local pubs and beery student parties. If they made it to the end of the set without being bottled offstage or the amp blowing up, the gig was considered a success. Not many were. Most gigs ended in a fight, with either band or patrons thrown out of the venue, sometimes both. No one ever got paid. We shared a job washing dishes in a Parnell restaurant. I was better at it than Lukas but got paid fifty cents less an hour.

At the end of three years, I had a B.A. in women's studies (useless) and Lukas was no more successful or well known than he had been at the start, but he knew what a pop hook was, how to hold together a rhythm section, and who not to be in a band with. Lukas wanted us to move to London before a little bit of success tempted him to stay. He wanted to be fresh when he got there, to be ready for the climb. "I need to be hungry," he explained. "I need to have a fire in my belly."

To make what little money we had saved go further, we sailed to London, via the Panama Canal, on a cargo ship carrying frozen spring lamb to the supermarkets of Europe. The crossing was diabolical. Rolling seas, prison slop, and a cramped, stuffy cabin thick with diesel fumes. Every dollar we saved on the crossing we paid for in puke. We disembarked in Southampton as pale and thin as junkies, not a good omen, but an apt one. Just over three years had passed since our last day at Gaialands, and four since Fritz had disappeared. But we still were not adults, and nothing had prepared us for the scale and assault of London.

The first few days, we cowered in pubs and in Tube station foyers, too scared to set foot on streets that seethed with speeding vehicles and mobs of unruly, shouting people. We had believed rustic Auckland, with its wide avenues and seven-car traffic jams, was the big smoke, but it was little more than a village. We didn't know where to stay, what to eat, who to trust, and all within the first week, we demonstrated our greenness by getting lost, mugged, and on one occasion, peed on, when a tramp relieved himself uphill from where we had flopped down for a rest in an underpass near Marble Arch.

A passerby, dressed no less shabbily than we were, took pity on us and guided us to a semi-derelict squat, at the seedy end of Edgware Road, that he shared with a dozen other emaciated kids. The place seemed all right the night we moved in, or at least warm and dry, and best of all it was free. But we soon discovered the catch. Everything that wasn't on our person got stolen while we slept, including, one dismal night, the shared toothbrush we had left in a scummy tin mug by the kitchen sink. Calling it a kitchen sink implies that the room it was in was used as a kitchen, and maybe once it had been, but it was now a storehouse for used hypodermic needles, and the only thing cooking, not on the stove but in blackened teaspoons over naked lighter flames, was a crumbly brown powder that came wrapped in white paper

squares. To eat there risked hepatitis or accidental overdose, so we ate on the street or at a greasy spoon, toast with
jam, or baked beans if we had enough coins. At night we
huddled together on the heavy wool coats we had brought
with us from New Zealand and tried to ignore the stench.

Not a day went by when I didn't miss the serenity and
ease of Gaialands, where we had eaten fresh food and bathed
every day in a river as clear as glass. At night, I dreamt I was
back there, running through the forest with the scent of pine
needles in my nostrils or lying on the beach with the sun
warming my skin.

After a month had gone by, we stopped ever mention-
ing the reason we had come to London, especially after
Lukas's beautiful red Fender Stratocaster had been stolen
from him in broad daylight at a Tube station. A string bean
of a kid, a Gypsy, had come up and asked Lukas for directions, shoving a map in his face. While Lukas squinted at
the map, he put his guitar case down for a second, and the
kid ran off with it. Lukas leapt over the barrier after him,
but the kid had timed his theft to perfection and squeezed
onto a Circle Line train just as its doors were closing. From
the other side of the barrier, I watched Lukas punch the
moving train with his fists, then chase it the length of the
platform, shouting abuse and mowing down anyone who
got in his way. He was escorted from the station by a guard,
told off for causing a ruckus and for trying to board a train
without a ticket.

Lukas vowed to rip "that little wanker's head off" if he
ever set eyes on him a second time, but even as he was saying

it, we both knew he would never see the boy, or his guitar, again.

Walking back to the squat, wanting something else to feel as broken as he did, Lukas destroyed a steel and concrete rubbish bin. I tried to lead him away from it, to calm him down, but he shook me off and went back to finish what he had started, removing the metal canister and hurling it across the pavement, strewing rubbish everywhere, then picking it up again and throwing it into the middle of the road. It was broad daylight; he was lucky not to get arrested, just stared at by a few passersby, who, like me, were too afraid to stop him.

From that day on, Lukas was like a loaded pistol, and I never knew when he would go off. One night we walked several miles to see a band in a Camden pub, and the band was good, really tight, but Lukas started heckling, yelling out that the music was shit. He was thrown out of the pub, and afterward, standing on the pavement, I asked him what the fuck he thought he was doing.

"That was the worst band I've ever seen," he raged. "Someone had to tell them how shit they were!"

"How could you do that to another band?"

"Did you see the lead singer? What a cunt."

"They were good, and you know it."

"I could play better than that with my arms cut off."

I laughed. "You're just jealous." I knew I shouldn't have said it but it was too late to take it back. Off he went, a tirade against not just the singer but the drummer and guitarist too. For half an hour, I tried to talk sense into him, tried to placate him; I even tried agreeing with him, but that only made him more mad, so that in the end I gave up, and we walked the rest of the way to the squat in silence.

That night, as we lay on the coats, shivering, I tried to think of a day since we had arrived in London that we hadn't argued, but there wasn't one. The disagreements had started off small but were getting bigger, and in between explosions, I had tiptoed on eggshells, held my breath. A week or so later we reached our lowest ebb, in an alleyway behind a Chinese restaurant, where we had gone to scour the dustbins for discarded takeaway containers of food. We were starving, hadn't eaten since the night before. Sometimes, if a wrong order got made, they would throw the whole lot out, and you would find it, cold but untouched, in the dustbin. At the exact same moment, we spotted a full container of fried rice and both lunged for it, spraying the contents across the ground like confetti, losing it all. I sprang back from the evidence, ashamed, while Lukas slid down the graffitied brick wall of the stinking alley and buried his head in his hands. "We can't go on like this," he said.

"I know."

"We should go home."

"Back to New Zealand?" I couldn't believe it. "You're going to give up?"

"It's time to face reality."

"But you haven't even tried to start a band."

Lukas sighed, utterly defeated. "What's the point? London already has thousands of them. I don't have a guitar. And I can't afford to buy one."

"Not now you don't. But if you get a job . . ."

"Why don't *you* get a job?"

This was the worst thing he could have said. I had been looking nonstop for a salaried job but so far had only been able to pick up casual work in restaurants, washing dishes and waiting tables, which I was spectacularly bad at. Most Kiwis who came to London got work in pubs, living upstairs as part of their wage, but Lukas had decided early on that we weren't going to do anything that would lump us together with other New Zealanders, otherwise we would never assimilate. We were not allowed, for the same reason, to go and live in one of those flats in Finchley, with eight or ten Kiwis in each room, one couple dossing on the couch and another behind it, bodies in sleeping bags everywhere, splitting the rent seventeen ways. Lukas would rather have lived with Scottish and English junkies, he would rather have starved than pull pints, and so, after six months in London, that's exactly what we were doing.

"We can't just leave," I said. "We came here to follow your dream."

"That isn't why *you* came to London."

He had never expressed this before, and because he hadn't, I had assumed he didn't know. But the truth was, I had deceived him. When I did not immediately respond, Lukas laughed bitterly and said, "You can't even admit it to yourself," which had been true up until that moment.

I turned away.

Lukas stood and brushed the rice off his trousers, then buttoned up his coat. "Don't you have anything to say?"

I shook my head. I wanted to say something that would give me another chance, but I also knew that I didn't deserve one.

Lukas walked out of the alley, and I watched him go, crying tears of hopeless frustration. I stood up; shook out my cold, cramped legs; and assumed the rest of the evening would unfold the way it had after other quarrels: later, back at the squat, when we had both cooled down, there would be an opportunity to make amends, to grovel or beg or do whatever it would take.

When I arrived back at the squat my hands were dirty after rummaging in the alley and I turned on the tap to wash them. Freezing water poured out but my fingers were so numb with cold that it felt almost warm. I went to our room. No Lukas. I was disappointed, and sat down on the bed to rest and to wait for him. I fell asleep, and woke in the middle of the night when I sensed movement on the mattress. *Thank heavens he's back.* I rolled toward him and opened my eyes, then recoiled in horror. Someone was lying next to me but it wasn't Lukas, or anyone I knew. It was a shivering, blue-skinned bag of bones and it was trying to climb under my coat.

I couldn't pack fast enough, gathering up our meager belongings with a single sweep of my arm. We had shared our room with two or three other people, sometimes four, but no one had ever crossed over to our corner, to our bed, not while Lukas was there.

With the temperature dropping and nowhere to go, I thought it best to keep on the move and found myself heading in the direction of Regent's Park, where the surrounding houses were bigger and more expensive. I felt a little safer there, however wrongheaded that was. Walking past the stucco facades of mansions, past the private driveways ringed with glossy black palings, I had the sensation of leaving behind my squalid life and crossing over into a fairy tale. There were, I realized, two versions of London: the one we had been living in, down below, grimy and impoverished, and another one, up above, that was glittering and rich.

The gates to the park were locked, but I found a section of the fence that was hidden by bushes and managed to climb it. Within the park grounds, surrounded by trees, under an open sky, I felt protected, at home. I had grown up in nature, and though this version had been clipped and tamed and the stars above were dimmer, it was comforting all the same. I wandered about, careful to stay in the shadows, and tried to make sense of the last six months. How had we sunk so low? The task of each day had become to get to the end of it without starving or getting mugged. We had lost sight of the future, of why we had come to London in the first place. For my part, I had been in denial, unable to admit the part my prediction had played in my leaving New Zealand. Not only had I deceived Lukas, but I had brought bad luck upon us by defying my fate. We weren't meant to be together, and nothing good would come of resisting what had been forecast.

But without Lukas by my side, I wasn't sure how to proceed. I had been carried along by his ambition, living his life, not mine, and before that, I had lived the life of the commune, a life that was shared with eight adults and six other kids. I had never made a decision for myself, and that night in Regent's Park was the very first I had ever spent entirely on my own. In two decades of life, I had never once gone to sleep without another person in the room.

To be suddenly independent was as terrifying as it was exhilarating, and with so many options, and no one to please but myself, I felt paralyzed.

White puffs of breath ballooned out in front of me, and a chill crept into my lungs. One minute I was fine, not even shivering, and the next, the ice of that February night had breached the perimeter of my heavy winter coat and every thin layer underneath. I felt my skin constrict with goose bumps and my teeth began to rattle. How long had I had been sitting under this tree, fatally still? I stood and stamped my feet, but the cold was inside me, in my blood.

A smooth grass table the size of a cricket pitch stretched out before me, the edges of it bordered by four neat rows of plane trees, bare but dignified. In front of my eyes, the grass turned silver, as though a wave was passing over, and I looked up and saw the moon was out. The lake rippled, drawing my gaze to the far side, where something between the plane trees moved. I thought it was an animal at first, a dog or a deer. But the movements were all wrong. It was a human, on the small side—a boy. He was very thin, wearing shorts, and running so fast his legs were cycling. He ran from one tree to another, hiding behind it for a moment before peeping out and sprinting on to the next. When he reached the end of the stand of trees, he hugged the last one, then peered out from behind the trunk—staring straight at me, daring me to stare back. He was playing a game.

The boy stepped out from behind the last tree and stood in front of it, staring in my direction for a moment before pushing off and sprinting diagonally across the field and straight toward me. He covered the distance quickly, almost gliding, his feet barely touching the ground.

I was already frozen, too numb to move, but as the boy got closer—so close that I could almost make out the expression on his darling familiar face—my heartbeat rose to a scattershot hammering. I didn't need to look twice to know who it was. I had known from his oddly galloping gait: one leg crooked, the other straight. But Fritz was dead—and he had died on the other side of the world. I had never been more certain that he wasn't alive, and even as I tried to lift my arms to embrace his ghost, my heart burst with grief. When he was less than six feet away, my eyelids grew heavy and then finally pitched shut. For a blissful few seconds, the image of my brother burned on my retinas, then it was gone.

CHAPTER 8

London
1984

I WOKE UP IN a hospital wrapped in stiff white sheets, a drip winding into my arm. No pain, just a heavy feeling, as though I had sunk to the bottom of a lake. Somewhere above me was the surface, but I couldn't swim to it, I could only wait in the depths where it was quiet and still.

The green curtains of my cubicle whisked open, and a nurse appeared. "Welcome back," she said, reaching for the clipboard at the end of the bed. "How do you feel?"

"Terrible," I wheezed. "What's wrong with me?"

"Pneumonia." She moved to the foot of the bed, lifted the sheet, and wiggled my toes, one after the other. "But no frostbite. You're lucky they found you when they did. It was minus five in the park. You were minutes away from hypothermia."

I assumed Lukas had found me and felt a surge of hope. "Is my boyfriend still here?"

The nurse shook her head. "You've not had any visitors. Would you like me to contact someone?"

The urge to see him was like a craving. "I don't know how to. I don't know where he is."

"Your accent," she said. "You're a long way from home, aren't you?"

My eyes welled up. "Yes."

The nurse smoothed down the sheet and tucked me in. "Well, if you work out how to contact him, or anyone else, let me know."

Her smile was caring but detached, reminding me of the way the mothers on the commune had tended to us, kindly and patiently but with something missing. I hated those memories, the way their faces blended to form the idea of a mother instead of a real one.

"There's no one else," I said, and the nurse patted my shoulder.

"I'm sorry, love."

I didn't want to leave the hospital. It was shabby, sure, with paint peeling off the walls, and they ran out of clean towels and syringes. But cooked meals of rubbery roast beef and mushy peas and stale Yorkshire pudding appeared on a tray in front of me, and I inhaled them and asked for more. I'd been hungry for so long that I'd forgotten what it was like to be full. But after six days, I was on the mend, getting plump, and the fluid had gone from my lungs. I was discharged. As I got dressed into the unclean clothes that had been folded and placed in a cupboard by the bed, the duty nurse took pity and gave me a plastic bag filled with stale bread rolls. "There's butter, too," she said. "I stole it from the canteen." In the bottom was the address of a women's shelter run by Catholic nuns.

On the steps outside the hospital, I wondered which way to go. Men and women scurried past, weaving around one another, so certain of their destination, and in such a hurry to get there. I set off in what I hoped was the direction of the squat, reluctant to go back but eager to find Lukas. I wasn't sure what I would say to him, only that I needed to see him.

The squat teemed with more lowlifes than ever, but Lukas wasn't there. Someone else had moved into our old corner, and all our belongings were gone. When I asked after Lukas, someone told me he had moved out. I felt hurt that he had abandoned me, even though I had no right to, and reminded myself, with a heavy heart, that no good could come of our staying together.

That night, I slept in the women's shelter. I took my allotted gray army blankets edged with red stitching to the basement and watched the stretchers around me fill up. In the morning, there was porridge for breakfast, just like on the commune. We had an hour's grace period to fold blankets and wash our faces before the nuns kindly but firmly kicked everyone out onto the street. It was nine A.M.

To keep warm and stay occupied, I went exploring. I walked toward Queensway and Notting Hill, then Shepherd's Bush, thinking all the time of Lukas, and then expending even more energy trying *not* to think about him. Still though, my loneliness was broken by small, unexpected waves of delight. The whole of London was mine to discover, and not just the parts where there might be bands playing. We had spent all our time in Camden because that's where we heard the happening music scene was, but I was never quite sure if we had found the up-and-coming bands or the ones that were on their way out. It always seemed to me that anything too easily found in London was for tourists, and the genuinely hip stuff was hidden from view.

No longer having to worry about any of that was bliss, especially since in the last few weeks, Lukas's commentary of other bands had become vicious. Not just "I could do better than that" but also "Those bands are so shit they deserve to die."

After a few solitary nights at the Catholic women's shelter, I met Fran. She had wobbled in late, sometime after midnight, gulped down four glasses of water, then claimed a vacant stretcher near mine. She was about my age and didn't look homeless, just wasted. There was a good reason why her stretcher, and mine, had been empty. The woman on the stretcher in between us smelled like she was decomposing, a stench so putrid that neither of us could sleep. We stood up at the same time to look for another spot. When there wasn't one, we ended up in the dining room, smoking cigarettes under a table. Fran told me she had often spent the night at the shelter after going out in the West End and missing the last train home. She thought I must be there for the same reason and was taken aback to hear I was genuinely homeless.

"Tomorrow," she said, "you're coming home with me to Tooting."

We hit it off immediately. Fran was bolshie, bold—an English version of Nelly—and not standoffish like most Londoners I had met. True to her word, the next day she took me home to Tooting. She lived with her mother, her stepfather, and his two sons from a previous marriage. It all struck me as outrageously exotic.

It was my first time in the suburbs. Fran lived on a long street of terraced houses that curved together like train tracks, each with a single bay window in the front. Some houses had been butchered, sprayed with pebbledash or had their windows ripped out and boarded over, but the gate Fran went through led to one that was perfectly preserved, very neat. At the front door, I hesitated. I was a long way from the city, in a place where Lukas wouldn't be able to find me. Then I remembered that he wasn't supposed to. This hadn't stopped me from keeping up a silent dialogue with him, telling him all day about my new friend and the novel things I was seeing, as if we were still together. The habit would be hard to break.

"This is my mum, Eileen," said Fran, introducing me to a short, round woman who was soft, like a pudding.

"Would you girls like a cuppa?" said Eileen. "I could heat up some leftovers." She didn't seem at all fazed that Fran had brought home a stray.

"Yes, please," I said, quite sure that even if I ate continuously for a whole week, it wouldn't make up for the months of living off scraps.

In the afternoon, we went to the pub. Fran liked to drink and took great pleasure in introducing me to her favorite concoction: cider and black.

"I can't believe you never had one," she said when I asked her what it was.

"Where I come from, there's beer or plonk, and I never drank much of either."

"Well, I've never left England," said Fran. "So we're even." She laughed. "My family tried to go to Scotland once but the car broke down so we ended up in Skegness—a big fat hole, in case you were wondering." Fran told me she was studying for a diploma in accounting at a polytechnic in the West End and worked a few shifts in a "posh caff" near there, but she wasn't sure what she wanted to do after her studies. "I know I don't want to be no one's secretary," she said. "Opening envelopes and typing bloody letters all day long."

"You're smart," I told her. "You could do anything."

"Nah," said Fran. "I didn't go to a toff university. Maybe where you come from that's possible but not here." She looked around the pub, then clinked her glass against mine, whispering conspiratorially. "But one thing I do want is to make loads of dosh."

I slept on a foldout trundle at the end of Fran's bed, hoping the thing wouldn't bounce shut while I was lying on it. Once or twice I woke in the night, heard breathing and thought for a moment I was back in our shared room on the commune. After I had been staying with Fran for a week, she came home one night excited because she had found me a temping job. It wasn't much more than a girl Friday position, but it was something. She had pestered one of the regular customers who came into her café, an elderly gentleman who worked for Beauchamp, Beauchamp & Beazley, a firm of chartered surveyors in Mayfair, and he had agreed to take me on. I started the next day, catching the rush-hour Tube from Tooting to Mayfair in a skirt and blouse borrowed from Fran.

The temporary job became a permanent one, and I was promoted from filing and tea making to the bottom of the secretarial pool. Fran, who had finished her studies and didn't want to work full time in the café, reluctantly took my old job, and the two of us moved into a bedsit in Fulham. Fran hated the tedious, repetitive tasks we were expected to do, but I loved the propriety of it all, the rituals and manners that ensured everything ran as inefficiently as possible. In the morning, we typed formal letters from scrawled notes or Dictaphone tapes. Then all afternoon, these letters went back and forth between the typing pool girls and the quantity surveyor men until they were absolutely perfect. A single mistake meant the entire letter had to be retyped. At a quarter past four, all completed letters were sealed in envelopes, stamped, and trotted down to the letterbox on the corner by one of us "gals." At five on the dot, and not a minute after, we abandoned our desks and filed out of the building to join hundreds of thousands of others on the long commute home. Months and months went by in this fashion before it occurred to me that I was contentedly working for "the man"—the very thing I'd been so vehemently warned against doing.

The summer of '84 was a riot. For the first time my life, I had money. Not a lot, but enough to keep Fran and me in hairspray and stilettos, and to be able to go out more nights than we stayed in. We went out to clubs to see up-and-coming bands, real ones, and it was so much more fun with Fran than it ever had been with Lukas. Once we had pulled apart the band's musical merits, and given them marks out of ten, we each had to say which band members we would most and least like to shag. Then Fran would set about trying to make it happen, while I diligently played the part of her wingman. Fran had decided that she wanted to one day manage a band and chalked all her conquests up to "research." She enjoyed the challenge, not minding if she failed or made a tit of herself. One night, after she had tried, and very nearly succeeded, in seducing the good-looking half of Deja Venus, a synth-pop duo from Putney, Fran finally asked me why I never went after anyone. "You only ever help me get laid."

"My ex-boyfriend was in a band," I told her. "I guess it put me off."

"How come you never told me about him?" asked Fran.

"Things ended badly."

"How badly?"

"He went back to New Zealand. We haven't spoken since." Talking about Lukas still felt raw, especially talking about him in the past tense, and even though Fran wanted to know more, I changed the subject.

No new surveyors had joined Beauchamp, Beauchamp & Beazley since the midseventies, but the property market was starting to boom, and with a great deal of self-importance, the company began to hire new staff. The first of these to start was Gavin Crawley, and he had been at work less than an hour before half the typing pool was after him, myself not included. They all fantasized about marrying him, after a short engagement, and settling down in a semi in the suburbs to breed. He was nothing special to look at, but he was at least twenty years younger than any of the other men who worked at B, B & B, and, it had been quickly noted from his bare ring finger, unmarried. These weren't the only things that set him apart, though. The older men had Etonian accents, wore pinstripe suits, and conducted business in an unhurried, jovial way, as though work was nothing more than a leisurely distraction. But Gavin walked into the office like a terrier let off its leash. He did twice as much work as the other partners, ten times as quickly, and still looked around for more. When the older men went off to the pub for a long boozy lunch, returning to the office shiny cheeked and red nosed, he stayed behind to make phone calls, send telexes, and pace up and down importantly. He never allowed letters to go through more than two drafts, and if correspondence was ready to be mailed by midmorning, he took it downstairs himself to make the midday post collection.

I enjoyed the spectacle of the other girls vying for his attention, and I was looking forward to seeing who would try to snog him at the office Christmas party. Fran had even started a sweepstakes in the weeks leading up to the event. It was a costume party, themed "Rule Britannia," a choice made by one of the partners, an old-fashioned patriotic bore.

On the appointed night, a flurry of sailors, wenches, and admirals made their way down steep limestone steps to a basement wine bar off Piccadilly. I had halfheartedly donned a pirate hat with my usual black taffeta dress and patent stilettos, and Fran went as Maggie Thatcher in a blue suit from a charity shop, her permed hair swept hideously back.

Her prop was a stiff black handbag, which she went around thumping people with.

The company hired a mobile disco—a fellow in a black tuxedo who came with dry ice, glitter ball, and strobe—and the DJ pumped out tunes to the empty room. Without enough of us to fill the space, we stood around the edges, nodding, smiling, drinking punch, the music too loud to have a conversation. At a quarter past seven, out of desperation, the DJ tried Frankie Goes to Hollywood, "Relax," but it was too early, and the randy lyrics, sent us further back into the shadows.

Fran and I were on the verge of leaving when, in a matter of sixty seconds, alcohol consumption reached a tipping point, and the party went from stiff and sober to a state of slurring, lurching snog-your-boss-under-the-mistletoe abandon. Roger, from accounts, was break-dancing to Michael Jackson, and a huddle of secretaries actually screamed when the Human League came on. "Jesus," said Fran, surveying the destruction. "It's barely eight o'clock." The only thing for it was to join in. "Wake Me Up Before You Go-Go," "Sweet Dreams (Are Made of This)," "99 Red Balloons." We sang and bopped to all the chart hits Lukas despised, and then, when a slow song came on, we rushed to the toilet to have a wee and change the Band-Aids on our stiletto-blistered feet.

I had forgotten all about Gavin, about the sweepstakes, but came out of the ladies' loo and there he was, standing with his back to me in a pool of dry ice. He had probably been at the party all night and I hadn't paid any attention to him—or his costume—but now, silhouetted like that, he stopped me in my tracks. On his head was a crown, and from his belt dangled a golden cardboard sword. He had on some kind of black britches and purple velvet cape, and he had come to the Christmas party dressed as a king. Despite all that, I still might have missed the significance of his costume were it not for the husky tones of Bonnie Tyler booming out "Total Eclipse of the Heart" across the empty dance floor behind him.

In a faraway land your true love waits . . .

No one took home the sweepstakes that night but a few days later in the tiny tearoom at B, B & B's, with a breeziness I didn't know I had in me, I invited Gavin to the movies the following weekend. Immediately afterward, my unexpected confidence vanished. I spent the next five days working myself up into a state of high anxiety, and by the time we stood in line outside the Odeon Marble Arch to buy tickets to see *Indiana Jones and the Temple of Doom,* I was awestruck, not because I was in awe of Gavin, the man, but because of the high expectations I had for our relationship. I was terrified of doing anything that would stop him falling in love with me and therefore jeopardize our destiny. I said everything I could think of to make him like me. I remembered Nelly's advice about flattery, which I followed to the letter, but also that you had to play it cool, which I tried to add to the mix.

Gavin, for his part, was inscrutable, and strangely quiet. I had expected him to get through our date with maximum efficiency and brio, the same way he answered the phone or replied to a telex, but instead he seemed distracted. After the movie, which I barely watched, he took me back to his

Westbourne Grove bedsit, where he opened a bottle of tart
Beaujolais nouveau before carefully unfolding his Japanese
futon and guiding me, wordlessly, toward its lumpy, button-
pocked surface. The sheet, where I sat down, was graying
and clammy and spiked with an off-putting sour odor, but I
pretended, with some effort, that I felt no disgust. He did not
smell as good as Lukas, I thought, before pushing that reflection to the back of my mind.

I did not feel romantic when Gavin placed his right hand
awkwardly on my shoulder and leaned over to kiss me, but I
did what I hoped was a good job of pretending. Making it
as far as the futon had been the sole focus of my efforts, but
now I was confronted with the reality of what had to happen
next. I had not prepared myself mentally for sex with someone other than Lukas, and everything about it came as an
affront to both my heart and my senses.

The sour smell of Gavin's sheets, I soon discovered,
came from him. He was not unclean—he also smelled of
soap—but the sourness never washed off. When he took off
his clothes, his flesh was the color of a porcelain sink. He
felt cold to the touch and while his breath wasn't bad, faintly
sweet, like peppermints or toothpaste, he tasted of a foreign
body, in a way Lukas never had. I tried not to make these
constant comparisons, but they kept coming to me, unbid-
den, almost as though Lukas was in bed with us, looking
over my shoulder.

Once I was naked, out of the blue, Gavin changed pace,
making love in a hurried frenzy, as though I was a lucrative
deal he wanted to close before lunchtime. His stroke was

swift and efficient, and after a few minutes, he came. My desire had not had time to ignite, or even spark, and when he rolled off me, I was still in the nervous, agitated state I had been in when I undressed. Gavin still had his socks on. I was disappointed, but in an optimistic, delusional way. This aspect of true love, I told myself, would improve as we got to know each other. We had the rest of our lives to work on it, after all.

But as time went on, what happened was exactly the same. I accepted the way he made love, and I adapted to his emotional distance. I even got used to playing the role of the person I was around him, to the point where it no longer took effort. I wasn't being myself but I reasoned that I was becoming a grown-up, and the main thing was, Gavin didn't seem to notice. He liked the fake me, lapped up my toadying and took as much control of the situation as I threw at him. Within six months, we were engaged, and in the summer of '85, he took me to meet his parents.

We went by train, late on a Saturday afternoon, to be there in time for dinner. They lived an hour south of London, in a village called Bletchingley, built in medieval times, when, judging by the size of the houses, humans must have been much smaller. The Crawleys' house was a newer addition at the end of a cul-de-sac that had been built to blend in with its neighbors. In front was a tidy lawn with a small round pond, bordered by a circle of obedient rose-bushes. Here and there, someone had hidden odd little statues of dwarves, and when I asked Gavin what they were, he said, "Gnomes," as though this explained everything, which it didn't, not to me. Frosted glass panels framed the front door, and as we walked through it, and were welcomed by Mr. and Mrs. Crawley, I had the immediate sensation of stepping onto hostile territory. Mrs. Crawley—"Call me Janet"—was very pleased to see her youngest son. So pleased that after they had embraced, her eyes remained rapturously fixed on him while I was being introduced. Greetings over, she steered him by the small of his back into the lounge for predinner drinks, and I drifted behind in their wake, feeling puzzled. The moment I had feared most was her appraisal, when she would give me the once-over, but it hadn't occurred to me that she would decline even to look in my direction.

Gavin's father, George, poured everyone a scotch, then guided us to the lounge suite, upholstered in moss-green velveteen. George positioned himself where he had the best view of the television set, tuned to a cricket match on mute. His cheeks and nose were ruddy, the scotch deeper in his glass than in ours, and as we settled into our places, the volume of the television crept up in tiny increments though George's hand, on the remote, had barely moved.

"Mark and Sophie are coming for lunch tomorrow with the children," announced Janet, "so I do hope it's a fine day." She glanced at me, for what seemed like the first time, then gestured to a china cabinet, the shelf crammed with miniature bugle-blowing shepherd boys perched on tiny porcelain hills. "Last time, we had a bit of a disaster, didn't we, Gavin?"

"They didn't mean to break anything, Mum."

Mark was Gavin's brother, but Gavin had never mentioned having nieces or nephews. There was a sister too, but she lived abroad. "How old are the children?" I asked. "Are they very young?"

"It isn't their age that's the problem," said Janet, casting meaningful glances at Gavin and her husband. "It's the way they've been brought up. No manners, and they're allowed to run wild." She lowered her voice. "Their mother doesn't believe in discipline."

"Oh," I said, at the same moment as Gavin and his father cheered at something that had happened on the television, which Gavin had been surreptitiously watching.

Janet frowned at her husband, a well-practiced expression. George switched off the television, cleared his throat, and then turned to his son. "I read in the paper about a house in South Kensington, by the park, that sold for three times what the couple paid for it. They only had it two years. Can you believe it?"

"Arabs, I expect," said Gavin. "They're buying up everything. Ripping out the insides and putting in gold taps, marble floors, Jacuzzis. Bit over-the-top but that's what they like. Shows the rest of us how much money they've got."

"More money than taste," added Janet.

I hadn't heard Gavin speak of other nationalities in this way, and I was appalled.

"What about you lot, though?" said George. "How are young couples meant to get a look in?"

"You don't need to worry about us. I've got shares. We can borrow the rest. The banks are giving away money— you can write your own check."

George looked worried, then smiled. "That's a lot to borrow."

"Dad, relax," said Gavin. "Everyone's doing it. No one saves anymore." He took my hand and squeezed it. "Anyway, that's enough shop talk. We've got some exciting news."

Oh shit, I thought, *he hasn't told them.*

George smiled expectantly, while Janet braced herself against the moss-green upholstery.

"Mum, Dad," said Gavin. "Poppy and I are getting married."

There was a moment of funereal silence, then George stood up and slapped his son on the back. "Congratulations!" he said warmly, and reached over to hug me.

"Thank you," I said, hugging him back, and turning to Janet, expecting the same.

"How lovely," she said, her smile rather wobbly. "We had no idea you two were so serious." She let me embrace her, enveloping us in lavender soap. When she pulled back, she had tears in her eyes. "My little boy," she said, turning to Gavin. "I can't believe you're getting married."

"Bloody hell, Mum, there's no need to panic," said Gavin. "We haven't set a date yet."

She wasn't panicking, but I was. Until this moment, the engagement hadn't felt real.

"Poppy, darling, are you all right?" Gavin looked at me with concern.

"Yes, I'm fine. Just . . . overwhelmed."

Janet had already left the room, something about putting on the brussels sprouts.

"Another scotch?" said George, proffering the bottle.

We had arrived on the Saturday afternoon and left the following Sunday evening but the time in between felt like a hundred years. There was no air in the house, nothing to do, and we were held captive in the lounge with the TV on while outside the rain came down in a deluge. The brother and sister-in-law canceled—one of the wild, undisciplined children had carelessly contracted chicken pox—but Janet insisted on a full Sunday roast regardless, and we sat around the dining table in stiff cooperation.

Janet had gone to considerable trouble with two types of meat and had set the table with crystal stemware, polished silver cutlery, and red cloth napkins folded to look like swans. There was a toast to us, the happy couple, with something sweet and fizzy from a green bottle with a gold label, and afterward, a long and awkward silence broken only by the scraping of silver on fine bone-china plates. I felt as though we were acting out a pantomime and I had failed to properly learn the part of ugly daughter-in-law. When George asked me what my father did, I veered from the script and made the mistake of answering truthfully.

"I don't really have a father, as such," I began. "But Hunter, the man who sired me, was the leader of the commune. He founded it with his wife, Elisabeth, who birthed me."

A forkful of roast beef and peas hovered at the entrance to Janet's mouth. "She did what?"

"She gave birth to me but I didn't think of her as my mother. I was raised in a group with all the other kids."

George leaned both elbows on the table, eyes wide, staring at me. Their horrified expressions seemed to egg me on, and suddenly I wanted to make my childhood sound even weirder than it already was.

"They didn't even tell us which of them were our parents until we were teenagers. They wanted us to grow up loving everyone the same."

"Poppy," said Gavin. "You didn't tell me any of that."

I hadn't told him any of that because he had never inquired. Throughout our courtship, Gavin had only ever asked the most perfunctory questions about my background, whether I had brothers and sisters, where I had gone to school, that sort of thing, and I had given him the sketchiest of answers, which seemed to be all he wanted. He much preferred to talk about the future, about the sort of giant house we would live in once he had made his fortune. His favorite topic was money. He could talk about that for hours.

"Do you mean," said Janet, "that you grew up on a commune?"

"I did."

"And you were raised by hippies?" Janet pronounced the word "hippies" with unbridled disgust—exactly the way Hunter would have.

"They weren't hippies. It was a sustainable community—a cooperative farm."

Janet's expression went from curdled to confused. She didn't have the foggiest what I was talking about. She looked to George for help while I continued to dig my hole.

"We grew all our own food without using pesticides or

heavy machinery. No one took acid or was into free love. In fact we weren't even allowed to drink."

Drugs! Free love! Booze! At the mere mention of these activities, Janet was outraged, no matter that I had been telling her they were prohibited.

"Well," said George. "That is an interesting way to grow up."

"You can say that again," said Gavin.

Janet didn't say anything, but later on, when I was clearing the dining table, I looked through to the kitchen and saw her locked in a passionate but whispered conversation with Gavin. They were trying to be quiet, but the discussion was getting more and more heated, and Janet was crying. When Gavin tried to comfort her, she pushed him away. "I can't," I heard her say. "I don't think I can tolerate any more savage grandchildren."

We got through dessert and a brandy in the lounge before Janet said she could feel a migraine coming on (Gavin had warned me that she often came down with one) and would we please excuse her? She retired to the bedroom with a pained expression on her face, and that was the last we saw of her. Gavin went upstairs to the bedroom we had slept in and came down with our bags. We said good-bye to George, who was well on his way to a brandy-induced coma, and then we left.

On the way back to London on the train, Gavin was sullen and withdrawn, and I was troubled by how badly the weekend had gone. I was certain I had failed to impress the Crawleys, including, possibly, Gavin himself. I was even more troubled by the way I felt about them. In Gavin's

childhood home, among the porcelain curios and servi-
ette swans, in the presence of his suffocating mother and
remote, booze-addled father, I had felt unable to breathe.
Part of that was my fault. I hadn't been honest with Gavin
about who I was or where I had come from. I had been foolish to think he would never find out, or that he wouldn't
be appalled when he did. But mostly what panicked me was
that I had spent the weekend in the bosom of the very sort of
nuclear family I had been brought up to disdain, and even if
I hated my upbringing more, I didn't know if I could pass as
one of their kind.

CHAPTER 9

London
1985

I F GAVIN WAS DISAPPOINTED to learn of my upbringing, he
chose not to talk about it, and within hours of returning to London, he acted as though the weekend had never
happened. We resumed our routine, spending five nights a
week at his bedsit and the remaining two apart, for no other
reason than habit, and during work hours, as was our cus-
tom, we continued the act of secretary and boss. But as the
weeks went by, I started to feel a tremendous pressure bearing down on my temples and I used this physical pain as an
excuse to skip one or two nights at his bedsit, spending them
instead in Fulham with Fran. When Fran asked me what was
going on, I told her about the headaches, and she nodded her
head and was thoughtful for a moment before suggesting
that maybe I had cold feet.

"About Gavin?"

"Yes, about Gavin. You got together with him so quickly
and a few months later—bang!—you were engaged."

"When the right one comes along, what's the point in waiting?"

"You think Gavin is the best you can do?" She was more amused than incredulous. "I mean, don't get me wrong, he's an okay guy and everything and probably good husband material—whatever that is—but I would never have picked out someone for you who was so fucking—" She stopped.

"So fucking what?"

"Boring. He's like the Morris Minor of guys."

I shook my head, refusing to consider the possibility. "We don't all go for unreliable jerks in tight pants and eyeliner, you know." I was well aware this was a low blow but I had been thinking it for a while, and it was good to get it off my chest. "Some of us prefer guys who don't have drug habits and who like to go out with one girl at a time."

Fran laughed. "Well, blow me. This whole time I thought I was just having fun, when it turns out I am a *fucked up* little slut." She stood up and adjusted her cleavage so that it was even more pronounced than it had been before. "Jesus, Poppy, I can't believe you grew up on a commune." She still wasn't pissed off—just animated. "You're the most uptight person I know."

"Uptight how?"

"As in *seriously* uptight. Like you need to be sodomized in a dark alley by a highwayman in tight leather knickerbockers."

"Knickerbockers?" I didn't want to, but I started laughing. "What are they?"

"They're old-fashioned pants that, you know, finish at the knee."

"Oh god," I said. "I think that's what Gavin was wearing the night of the Christmas party."

"He was?"

"Yes. He went as a king."

"Well, there's your problem," said Fran. "You were duped."

She was only stirring, but she had planted a seed of doubt, and from that night on I began to notice habits of Gavin's that I had willfully ignored. He ate the same thing for lunch every day (a plain ham sandwich on white bread from the greasy spoon on the corner) and for dinner, baked beans out of a can, without always warming them first. Under no circumstances would he try Indian, Lebanese, or Greek food, and once, when I had made him a chickpea curry, he had balked not only at the mild spices but because it was vegetarian. From then on, I had only ever cooked what I came to think of as English food: eggs, chips, sausages, peas and Spam. But the food thing was just the beginning. I was more and more bothered by that sour smell, and his businesslike attitude in bed. On the few occasions I had suggested he might want to slow things down a little, or maybe try a different position, he had given me the same refusal he had when I suggested we dine at the local Thai restaurant. Trying new things was not in his repertoire.

The strange part was, Gavin did not seem to notice my growing discontent. In fact, the more I started to feel withdrawn, the more attentive and certain of our future he was.

It was as though he had fixed upon the person he was going to marry, and as with his choice of food or sexual position, there was no going back. I was bound to him by his nature, by the very devotion I had cultivated in him, and most tightly of all by my prediction. Under pressure from Gavin, I agreed to set a date in the summer of 1988 for our wedding, far enough away—nearly three years away—that I could easily believe it might never happen.

In the meantime, I used the pattern of absence established by my headaches as a way to spend more time going out with Fran. Three or four nights a week, I played fiancée to Gavin, cooking beans in his bedsit, while he read quantity survey reports and listened to Phil Collins and I caught up on my sleep. The remaining nights, Fran and I went out to pubs and clubs and drank up the atmosphere of boomtown London. Throughout the whole of 1986, I don't think we paid for a single dry martini or flute of French champagne. Every establishment we went to was jammed with stockbroker bores who had so much cash to throw around it was falling out of their pockets. They made us feel as though we were doing them a favor by giving them someone to spend it on. Our usual routine was to start the night at a popular wine bar, then just as the night was getting interesting and we had drunk our fill, we would move on to the kinds of underground nightclubs we preferred. In our wide-shouldered suits and foxy black stilettos, with our frizzy little perms and eyes ringed with black, we thought we were so sophisticated. At least once a week, Fran went home with some good-looking ratbag, but I never did, and that was how I justified it to myself.

Sometime in 1987 I even bought a wedding dress. It was a huge white meringue made from taffeta and lace that Fran and I had picked out at Selfridges one hungover Saturday morning and that took up half the wardrobe in our increasingly crowded Fulham bedsit. The wedding was to take place in an Anglican church near Gavin's parents' house, with a small reception afterward at a local hotel. Fran was going to be my bridesmaid but I would have no family in attendance. I had considered inviting Nelly and the mothers and fathers from the commune, and had gone as far as writing a letter, but in the end I didn't see the point in sending it. None of them would be able to afford to fly over, and if they did, their presence would only embarrass the Crawleys. I was also terrified that someone from the commune would tell Lukas about my marriage. The thought of his ever finding out filled me with a terrible shame because he, of all people, would see through it.

A year out from the wedding, Fran and I upped our going out to four, sometimes five, nights a week, a schedule that Fran could chalk up to "research" but on my side was purely errant. I told Gavin that I was going to aerobics classes to look slimmer and more attractive in the meringue, and managed to sell the lie by dancing and drinking and not eating on the nights we went out.

One of our favorite haunts was Chelsea, which wasn't far from where we lived, making it easier to get home at three in the morning and still get up for work the next day. On one of these forays, Fran took me to a new club just off Fulham Road that was underneath what looked like an ordinary stucco house. She wanted me to see an unsigned band she had "discovered" and that she hoped was in need of a manager. "The lead singer is even hotter," she said, "than Morten Harket." She did not say much about their sound. The club had only just opened but was already hugely popular. We waited outside in a long queue of boys and girls in tight jeans and stringy T-shirts—even though it was January and freezing—all with such big bouffy hair that it was hard to tell them apart. It was a different scene than the one I was used to, and I had no idea what to expect when we got inside.

The first room we went into had mirrors all down one wall, making the space seem bigger than it was. There was nowhere to sit, just a bar on one side and sardines everywhere else. Fran pulled me through the sardines to the other room, the source of loud driving guitar music and screeching vocals. I held her hand tightly and we emerged into a wall of noise, eye to eye with a four-piece band shoved messily into an alcove, guitar cords and amp wires coiled like spaghetti at their feet.

The band resembled glam rock shipwreck survivors, all hair and tight, shredded pants and torn tank tops—the lead guitarist wore no shirt at all. He was whippet lean, tanned, and full of himself, more so than the apparently hot lead singer, whose face was hidden behind a cascade of blond, spiral-permed hair. To me they looked ridiculous—and sounded worse—and I questioned if this was the band Fran wanted to manage. But next to me, Fran had my arm in a vise grip and on her face was a look of intense determination.

Their performance *was* intense, ferocious, like animals

in heat, but it was also exaggerated, a pantomime of a rock band. At the end of the song, amid hysterical applause, the lead singer bent down to swig from a bottle of bourbon at his feet, then stood up and scooped the huge mane of hair out of his eyes, revealing his face.

For a few seconds I stared at him, convinced I was seeing things, maybe even hallucinating. He seemed different, skinnier and older, but there was no mistaking that the man under all that hair was Lukas. *My* Lukas. I hadn't seen him for four years, but it may as well have been four days, because everything that had happened in between fell away. All I wanted to do was run up and hold him and never let go.

Several rows of excitable teenagers stood between us and I hesitated long enough that the next song began and the rabble started pogoing again, making it impossible to get to him. I had hesitated, and into that gap flew reality. The best thing I could do would be to turn around and walk out of the club and pretend I hadn't seen him.

But when I tried to pull Fran in the direction of the exit, she mouthed "No!" along with a violent shaking of her head. She had locked her elbow through mine and dug the nails of her other hand into the flesh of my upper arm. I was captive.

Onstage, though I tried not to look, Lukas screeched out a slow number about the Cold War, of all things, his voice in a high register I didn't know he could reach. It was their torch song, and the girls and boys around us closed their eyes in rapture.

They played one more song, plus an encore—a replay

of the Cold War number—then put down their instruments and crab-walked off the stage, exiting sideways into a narrow, dingy corridor. The crowd dispersed, or tried to, then backflowed and settled into more or less the same position. Next to me, Fran burrowed frantically in her bag, surfacing with a pile of small neon-lettered cards. "This is it," she yelled. "The one I've been fucking waiting for."

"Are you sure this is the band?" I said.

Fran laughed, impatience sparking off her. "Of course I'm fucking sure." She shoved one of the little yellow cards in my hand. "Come with me."

I didn't have time to study it—Fran had grabbed me by the arm and was dragging me down the corridor and inexorably toward the door at the end of it.

"Stop!" I said, spinning her around to face me as forcefully as I could. "We can't go in there."

"Why not?"

"The singer—the singer in the band. It's Lukas."

Her eyes flickered with confusion. "Lukas—as in your ex?"

"Yes," I said urgently. "He can't know we're here. We have to leave."

Fran stared at me for a moment, weighing the situation, then turned and banged loudly on the door. "But that's so un-fucking-believably perfect," she said. "You can introduce us."

She didn't wait for a response, but pushed the door open into a small room with a low ceiling, lit by a single flickering tube. In the center of the room, a bunch of guys stood around a table with beers on it, and they turned around and stared at us. None of them was Lukas.

"Excuse me, ladies?" It was the guitarist. He had actually put his shirt back on and came and stood in front of Fran with his hands on his hips. "I know it's not the Albert Hall but it might have been decent to knock." He spoke with a toffy accent, totally at odds with his appearance.

"Easy, tiger," said Fran. "I'm not here to fuck you."

The guitarist turned to the other guys and laughed. "Then what do you want?"

"I'm here on business," she said, her sharp tone betraying nerves. "I'd like to talk to your manager."

The bass player, very pretty, smirked. He raised his eyebrows at the drummer, and the pair of them, at the same time, mouthed "Manager?"

The guitarist ran a hand through his black curly hair. "That's me."

"Yeah, that's what I thought," said Fran. She thrust one of her business cards into his hand. "I'm Frances, and this is Poppy, my assistant." *Her assistant?*

"Marlon," said the guitarist, taking the card and squinting to read it. "F-One Management?"

Fran nodded. "As in 'Formula One.'" She paused. "And 'Frances'—and all the other 'F' words you can think of."

"I get it," he said. "I just haven't heard of it."

"You will," said Fran. "At the same time everyone hears about your frickin' awesome band."

Marlon cocked his head to one side—she had his attention. Behind him, a sliding door opened, and Lukas appeared, silhouetted in the bright light of a bathroom stall. He had his head down and was trying to lace up the fly of his leather pants, and despite the resolve I'd had not to see him, there it was again, the impulse to throw myself at him as though no time had passed. He looked so different but all I could see was the boy I had grown up with, the same one I had teased and chased through orchards and shared a room with every night of my childhood. In the few seconds before he clocked me, I passed through every emotion from panic to joy to sadness and regret.

Then he saw me, and for a moment I knew what it felt like to be a ghost. He looked behind him into the bathroom and then again at me. "Poppy, is that you?"

I nodded. We held eye contact, and as we did so, a woman drifted into my sightline and stood next to him. She was tall and striking and leaned her arm on his shoulder. "And who do we have here?" she said, her accent posh, like Marlon's.

"Serena," said Lukas, turning to her. "This is Poppy."

"Poppy," she said, looking me over, until something registered. "You're the girl from the commune, aren't you?" Everything about her was so confident, so nonchalant, that I wanted to punch her lights out. I hadn't answered her question, and as the silence grew, Fran, Marlon, and the others turned expectantly and stared at us.

"Yes," I said eventually, mustering all my self-control. "Lukas and I grew up together."

Fran, never one to miss an opportunity for bluntness, said, "Wasn't it a bit more than that?"

Lukas said, "Yeah, it was," and Serena folded her arms,

not at all threatened, and added, "We thought you'd gone back to New Zealand."

"Well, it looks like I didn't."

"Poppy," said Fran, "I'm sure there'll be plenty of time for a reunion later but right now we need to talk business." It was her way of rescuing me, but also of bringing her agenda back on track.

"This chick wants to be our manager," said Marlon, addressing Lukas.

"Really?" he said, sounding genuinely amazed. He gave Fran a quick, appraising look and then smiled. "That's great. We bloody well need one."

Marlon softened. "We do." He studied Fran's card. "It takes F-One to know one," he said, and held out his hand in Fran's direction.

"You won't regret this," she said, taking the offered hand and shaking it firmly.

I worried they had jumped into things too quickly, but I kept my reservations to myself, more troubled by the momentous new turn in my personal life.

We sat down to toast the new venture, and I watched and listened with admiration as Fran plied her new charges with beer and whiskey and comprehensively mapped out the next five years of their career. She seemed to have it all worked out, from how to shape their image to what kind of sound they should develop to stay ahead of other bands. I wondered how she knew all this stuff, and then I realized how badly I had underestimated her. This whole time, she really had been researching the up-and-coming bands of London,

and not just sleeping with them. While Fran charmed everyone in the room, I played the part of her assistant, going to
the bar to fetch drinks and taking notes when she asked me
to, grateful to have something to do. For the past hour, I had
tried not to make eye contact with Lukas, but the second I
dared to glance in his direction he was already looking at me,
and our eyes locked on and everyone else vanished. I didn't
think Serena had noticed—she seemed so unflappable—but
then, after another one of my forays to the bar to fetch a
round of whiskey, I came back to the greenroom and she and
Lukas were arguing in the corner. They were trying to keep
their voices down, and when Lukas saw I had reappeared,
he tried to end their discussion. I didn't see what happened
next—I was busy handing out drinks—but when I looked
again, Serena was putting on her coat, and then she coolly
said good-bye to everyone and left.

I started drinking too much whiskey. I didn't know what
else to do. The meeting went on, and then at some point it
stopped being a meeting and started to be a party. And then
it was after three A.M. and everyone was drunk and standing on the pavement outside the club, deciding where to go
next. I had been avoiding so much as a sweep of the eye in
Lukas's direction, but now he put his arm around my waist
and pulled me to him and whispered in my ear: "How long
has it been since we fucked?"

"Excuse me?" I was genuinely offended, but elsewhere in
my body, something woke up that had been asleep for a very
long time. "Aren't you going to ask me where I've been for
the last four years?"

"Has it really been that long?" he said, leaning closer. "I'm pretty sure it was yesterday." He kissed me then, passionately, almost aggressively, and I was so taken aback that I went along with it. I could have been seventeen again, were it not for the overwhelming smell of hairspray and the strands of his mane that got in my mouth, leaving behind a metallic aftertaste. Coming up for air, I checked to see if anyone had caught our wild snogging, but the other guys were drunkenly loading gear into a battered-looking van. Fran was nowhere to be seen, and I remembered, vaguely, that she had taken her leave outside the club.

Still reeling from the kiss, I climbed into the van next to Lukas. The keyboard player drove, or rather swerved, clearly as plastered as we were. Apart from a few cabs, and the odd night bus, the London streets were deserted. At last we pulled into a cobbled lane, and the van idled next to a black garage door, then Marlon and Lukas and I climbed out before the others drove off. To the side of the garage door was another door that belonged in a stable. After Marlon had opened the top half, he had to reach inside to unlock the bottom. It opened into a garage the size of a barn, and in the middle of the garage was an enormous black car with a silver insignia and a bonnet that gleamed like an oil slick. I did not know a thing about cars, except that this one was expensive.

With a guitar in each hand, Marlon led us up a small staircase at the back of the garage and into a low-ceilinged apartment. Here it was made apparent why we had left all the rest of the band gear in the van: there was more of it here, a full drum kit and amps, microphone stands and wires trailing everywhere, enough to fill a recording studio. The rest of the room was taken up with the biggest lounge suite I had ever seen—a behemoth upholstered in orange and brown velvet. There was something odd about it, not just the size, but the way it was constructed, the squabs and cushions very plush, but at the edges, strips of exposed metal and plywood. Marlon must have seen me staring at it.

"It used to be a conversation pit," he explained. "Only now it's freestanding. No pit."

"Where did it come from?"

Marlon pointed behind him, beyond a small kitchen and a window with the blinds pulled. "The main house. Mother was renovating again."

So this wasn't the main house but an adjunct of some sort, which explained the presence of the giant, expensive car. I wished I had paid more attention to street names and borough signs on the ride here, but beyond pulling into a cobbled lane, I remembered nothing.

"It's an old wreck," said Marlon, plonking himself down next to Lukas. "But the terrific thing is it's basically four giant beds. There's always plenty of room for friends to crash." He put his arm around Lukas. "This guy's been here for years."

Lukas laughed. "I should probably start thinking about getting my own place."

"One day," said Marlon affectionately. "In the meantime, make yourselves at home."

After smoking a giant doobie, which he shared with Lukas but I declined, Marlon went upstairs to bed, leaving Lukas and me alone on the enormous velvet raft. No sooner had Marlon left than Lukas stretched out with his head in my lap and looked drunkenly up at me. "I can't get used to seeing you in all that makeup," he said. "Some women suit it but you look better without any."

I wondered if by "some women" he meant Serena. "At least I don't have hair like a poodle."

He laughed. "Thanks."

"Whose idea was it?"

"The hair?"

"Yes, the hair. You can't tell me you did that to yourself."

"Marlon's. It goes with our music. And Serena says girls love it too."

"Is she your . . . ?" I couldn't bring myself to say it.

"What do you think?" He leaned over and tweaked my nose, something he had done often in the old days.

"I think she's very pretty—and that she was in the bathroom with you."

"She was helping me take off my makeup."

"Then why was your fly undone?"

"You've obviously never worn lace-up leather pants." When I shook my head, Lukas smiled. "The fly on those things is always undone. That's the look."

Was he being serious or pulling my leg? "And you can't take off your own makeup?"

Lukas shrugged. "I could. But Serena does it better. She's very quick."

He wasn't going to admit it, which for some reason bothered me more than if he had just come straight out with a confession that he had been bonking Serena. I decided not to tell him about Gavin either, although honestly, it was the first time all evening I had even remembered I had a fiancé. I said, "I thought you went back to New Zealand."

"Really?"

"You said you were going to."

"I did?" Lukas was thoughtful for a moment, perhaps trying to remember. "Do you know I looked everywhere for you?"

"I didn't know that."

He nodded. "I even went to the police but when they found out we had been living in a squat, they basically told me to piss off. They can't file a missing persons report for someone with no fixed abode."

"So you gave up?"

"No," he said. "I went to the New Zealand embassy. They said they couldn't do anything unless you tried to leave the country."

"I was in the hospital," I said, choking up, because I had missed Lukas so much, and the news that he had searched so hard for me, when I hadn't looked for him at all, was painful to hear.

"Jesus," he said, "what were you doing there?"

When I told him, he was appalled.

"You could have died. It was about minus ten that night. I remember almost freezing to death in the squat without anyone to cuddle."

The thought that we had missed each other by a matter of hours, perhaps even minutes, made me feel sick. "You went back to the squat that night?"

"Eventually—after I had walked the streets of London calling you every name under the sun. There was a junkie in our bed. At first I thought it was you—then when I realized it wasn't, I beat the crap out of him."

"Did you really?"

"I kicked him out with my little finger."

We both smiled—mine watery, his wry.

"I was so fucking mad with you."

"I know."

Lukas cupped my chin, and I leaned into his hand, rubbing my cheek against his fingers. "But I would never have left you like that," he said. "Not without saying good-bye."

"I'm so sorry," I said, trying, and failing, not to sob.

"What for?"

Had he really forgotten why he had been so mad with me that night? I stared into his kind, familiar eyes, the eyes I had missed so much, and I suddenly didn't want to revisit the past, to risk what bringing it up again might do to us. "I should have tried harder to find you, that's all."

"How could you have?" he said. "You were in the hospital." There was nothing accusatory in his voice, only concern, and I realized that whether it was because he had forgotten or not, he wasn't going to bring up old wounds either. I was so grateful for his easy forgiveness that I leaned in to kiss him, and was relieved when he responded with tenderness.

What happened next seemed natural and inevitable, at least to begin with, as though we had never been apart, but then halfway through making love, once it was too late, along came my conscience, and I remembered that we were not boyfriend and girlfriend, not the innocent teenagers we had once been, and that what we were doing was hurting other people and would probably hurt us too in the end. Worst of all was a feeling of deep sadness that we couldn't turn the clock back to what we'd had, and had thrown away.

"Poppy, what's the matter?" said Lukas, pulling back. "Are you crying?"

I wiped my eyes and pretended not to be.

"You are. I can taste it." He dabbed at the skin around my eyes, then rolled onto his back and sighed. "I knew it."

A knot formed in my stomach. "Knew what?"

"That you still don't love me. You never really did."

"That's not true," I said, filled with passion. "I love you more than ever—but that's the problem."

"Why is that a problem?" said Lukas.

I tried to sound sober, serious. "Because we aren't meant to be together."

Lukas was quiet for a long time. "Please don't tell me that after all this time you still believe in that fucking prediction." There was a controlled anger in his voice.

When he put it like that, I wasn't sure I did believe in it, but I was so bone tired, worn out by the avalanche of feelings and booze. It was all too much. "Right now, I don't know what to think." I got up from where I had been lying with him, walked to the opposite side of the vast couch, and curled up on my own under a purple fake fur rug. "I really need to sleep."

After a few minutes, Lukas got up and came and kneeled

on the floor beside me, and put his head close to mine. "I'm sorry," he said. "I'm always such a jerk after a gig." He paused. "I was so happy to see you."

"I know. Me too."

"What are we going to do, Poppy?"

I turned around to face him. "I don't know."

He didn't move. "Poppy?"

"Yes?"

"Can I just sleep next to you?"

I wiggled over, made room for him, and he lay down beside me, one arm tucked under his head, the other wrapped around my waist, our bodies fitting together as though they had been hewn from the same piece of wood.

CHAPTER 10

London
1988

STREAKS OF SHARP SUNLIGHT woke me the next morning. I took in the strange surroundings and struggled to remember where I was. It was the weekend, I hoped, or else I'd have to go to work. My head was pounding but it was nothing a glass of water wouldn't fix. Then I saw Lukas in the tiny kitchen, spooning ground coffee into a white paper cone. He had his back to me, but I would have known his bare shoulders anywhere, the scoop of his spine, the wing-shaped mole at the top of his right hip. Only the hair, pulled up in a girlish knot, was new. To wake up and see him felt so right, as though every atom in the world was where it should be. But then I remembered it wasn't.

I still had my clothes on from the night before and wandered over to where he stood. "Good morning," I said, putting my arms around his waist and inhaling his scent. His hair wasn't so sticky this morning, and the toxic spray had worn off.

"Good morning," he said, twisting around to kiss me, his lips so soft and tender, his breath merging with mine. It was one of those moments where every inch of skin is charged with sensation and all modesty and reason fly away. We fell to the cold terra-cotta floor, ripped off any clothes that were in the way, and went at it. I was expecting just to fuck—that would have been enough—but less than a minute in, Lukas pushed his head down between my legs and found, first with his mouth, and then with his tongue, the hub that was driving it all. He had never done this before, not once, and just after I came with a force to lift the roof off, I rejoiced that he had finally found my clitoris, and then quailed because I hadn't been the one to show him where it was. In the three years we had been apart, he'd had an education, but from whom?

Lukas slipped into me and came almost immediately, and we lay in a heap on the kitchen floor, clutching each other and breathing heavily, and then a male voice called to us from upstairs. "Is it safe to come down yet?"

It was Marlon. *Dear god, has he been up there the whole time? Did he watch us having sex?*

"Yeah, man," said Lukas, rearranging my clothes in a way that was both loving and careless. "Just making coffee. You want some?"

"Love some."

I stood up, and pulled up my knickers, just as Marlon walked slowly down the stairs in his underpants, yawning. When he reached my level, he winked at me.

"Thought you'd never ask."

I had never met anyone like Marlon before. His confidence, the pantherlike way he moved—he was a different species. The only person he regarded as an equal was Lukas, and it made me think he was secretly in love with him. When he announced he was going up to what he called "the big house" for breakfast, I was relieved.

The second he had gone, I asked Lukas how they met.

"Well," he said, "it was only a couple of months after I lost you." He stared into the middle distance as if recounting a legend. "I was in a pub in Camden, feeling sorry for myself, as usual, when this joker came in. I could hear him talking with his mates on the other side of the room. He was very loud, very posh."

"Marlon?" I said impatiently.

"Yes." Lukas smiled at the memory. "He was looking for musicians to join his band, and he said he'd buy anyone a pint who could play something by Deep Purple."

"You played 'Smoke on the Water' and you got the pint—"

"And the rest is history. We started jamming that afternoon, right here, in this room, and we stayed up for about three days—with a bit of help, of course."

"Help from who?"

"From . . ." He paused. "From the BBC."

"You watched television?"

"Um, yeah, to stay awake."

I had a feeling that he wasn't telling the truth, but I didn't know what he was lying about, so I said nothing, and he continued to recall the legend of his meeting Marlon. For close

to a year, they had holed up together in the mews flat, performing for no one but each other, until they had developed
an almost telepathic way of playing. Along with musical
chemistry, they shared insatiable ambition. Alan, the drummer, and Vince, the keyboardist, were easy to recruit—they
were old boarding school "chums" of Marlon's.

"With Marlon," said Lukas, "I don't have to explain what
I'm trying to do. He just gets it and starts in—it's the same
when he starts playing something. I know exactly what to
add to make it better."

"I don't even know what you've called the band. I bet it's
something posh."

"The Communists."

"As in Russia, Vietnam, East Germany?"

"It's a double entendre," he said, trying to sound French.
"Marlon's a socialist, and I grew up on a commune."

I laughed. "Marlon, a socialist?"

"He can't help who his father is."

"Who *is* his father?"

"The Right Honorable Giles Andover—he's a QC or
something."

"Marlon should move out—live among the proles."

"He will," said Lukas. "When he turns twenty-one."

"What happens then?"

"Something matures—a trust, I think."

"Ha," I said. "Remember what Hunter said?"

"What?"

I lowered my voice. *"Beware the champagne socialist . . ."*

"Marlon isn't like that—he's genuinely passionate about

the cause. You heard our song—the one about the Cold War."

I had heard it but wished I hadn't. "Remind me how it goes."

"Frozen hearts," sang Lukas, "melting like ice . . . in the fire. Beating with one . . . true desire."

"Your musical style," I said, trying to keep a straight face. "It's really changed."

"Are you mocking me?"

"Would I do that?"

"Yes, you would. You bloody well would." Lukas leapt over to where I was sitting on the couch, and we wrestled, a little like we had in the old days, only this time it ended with what can only be described as quite rough sex. I didn't even feel guilty this time, although I did feel guilty, later, that I hadn't.

Showering, afterward, in the bathroom Lukas shared with Marlon, I noticed all their stuff—hairspray, razors, deodorant—was muddled together and appeared to be communal. Lukas had never spoken about any of his former bandmates the way he spoke about Marlon, and I understood this was different, that they were closer, more like lovers. Only the thing that held them together was stronger, in a way, than love, because in each other they saw how to get what they had always wanted: success. Lukas didn't have to tell me any of this. I could smell it on him. It was in the way he stood a little taller when Marlon was in the room. I had experienced the backdraft from it in the club the night before. While Lukas and Marlon had plotted world domination with Fran, the rest of us had become invisible.

A feeling of apprehension crept into my chest as I took a measure of the life I would be signing up for if Lukas and I got back together. Lukas and Marlon were a team, a club of two that I could never join. I could tag along all I liked, but I had to understand, from this day on, that what had happened last night in the greenroom would happen again. It might even become the norm. Was that the life I wanted? I had just had my first taste of independence, of surviving on my own outside of the commune. I had even had fun. Yet within hours of reuniting with Lukas, I was already contemplating a sidecar existence, my life attached to his once again.

And what about the prediction? Was I brave enough to go against it, to abandon Gavin? Even then I had the sensation of being pulled in the wrong direction but being too weak to go the other way.

Gray morning light filtered through the windows of the bathroom, which faced what appeared to be a brick garden wall, and I was abruptly curious to see what lay beyond it, the mansion Marlon had mentioned the night before. Wrapped in a towel, I went out to the kitchen and pulled up the blind and there it was, five or six stories high, and separated from the mews house by a decorative formal garden. Sun glinted off the building's slate roof, and in the middle of that, a winking dormer window, giving it the appearance of polished silverware. I couldn't be sure, but the house looked familiar somehow, as though I had seen it in a dream.

"There you are," said a voice close to my ear, and I startled as Lukas put his arms around my waist and nuzzled into my neck.

"Where are we?"

"Marlon's place."

"I mean where in London. What area?"

"The one rich people live in." He pointed up the garden to the big house. "On the other side of there is Regent's Park."

So that's why it was familiar. On the night I had almost caught hypothermia in the park, I had gazed at these buildings from the other side and wondered who lived here, thinking they couldn't possibly be real. "They're more than just rich," I said. "They're upper class."

Lukas shrugged. "I suppose so. But they're not snobby or anything."

We had been brought up to believe that living like this wasn't just ostentatious, it was morally wrong. All those lectures from Hunter about the evils of capitalism, elitism, and the moral bankruptcy of the Western world, and yet here we were, in the lap of it, enjoying the spoils. I opened the window to get a better look at the mansion and noticed a woman slowly making her way down the garden from the main house, careful to avoid any grass or puddles. "Is that Serena?"

Lukas peered over my shoulder. "She brings leftovers from breakfast, usually croissants. They get chucked out otherwise."

"She lives there?"

"Serena is Marlon's little sister."

I should have guessed. This information was both a relief, in that it explained Serena's presence regardless of her relationship to Lukas, and annoying, because it meant she would always be hanging around.

When she appeared in the kitchen, however, my dislike of her was as straightforward as it had been the night before. In her miniskirt and loafers, the scent of apples wafting off her glossy chestnut hair, she was just too perfect, too *aristocratic,* and I did not want her to get her hands on my man. I stood in front of her in a towel, defiantly clutching the clothes and underwear I'd had on the night before, and hoped she could smell on me the salty odor of semen.

If she shared any similarly hostile feelings toward me, she did a first-class job of hiding them.

"I've got the most terrific news," she said to Lukas, placing a small basket covered with a napkin on the kitchen counter. "I've been badgering Daddy for weeks, and I think I've finally made some headway."

Lukas mumbled something in response but hunger blocked my ears. Serena lifted the napkin, and a waft of yeast and sugar syrup hit my nose. These weren't croissants but five plump Danish pastries, bursting with apricots and blueberries.

"When did you last eat?" said Lukas, catching my wide-eyed stare.

"Oh," I said, trying not to drool. "I can't even remember."

He handed me a pastry, and I scoffed it, watched closely by Serena. At first I thought she was offended by my greediness until I realized she was staring at the pastry with intense longing, eating it vicariously through me. No wonder she brought us the leftovers—it removed the temptation of eating them herself. "Would you like one?" I said, jiggling the basket in her direction, and enjoying her look of repulsion.

"Made headway with what?" said Lukas, oblivious to the standoff.

The pastry had so mesmerized Serena that she had forgotten to tell him her news. "Daddy's agreed to pay for recording sessions," she said, coming back to earth.

"That's great," said Lukas. "Does Marlon know?"

"Yes, and he said he doesn't want Daddy's help."

"Fuck." Lukas threw back his head in frustration. "Most people would give their eyeteeth for that sort of leg up. Why can't he see it's so much worse to have all the advantages and to throw them away?"

"I agree," said Serena. "It makes no sense."

"Maybe he's afraid you won't have any credibility," I said.

Lukas was indignant. "With who?"

"I don't know. The music industry, fans, critics?"

"Bullshit," said Lukas. "They're going to love us—but if we don't record anything, no one will know we exist."

"Why don't you get Fran to try and convince him?"

"Fran! Of course." Lukas ran to the telephone to call her. "I forgot we had a manager."

On Sunday morning, after a second blissful night with Lukas, I went home to the grotty bedsit I shared with Fran and bawled my eyes out to her. "What am I going to do?" I said between sobs. "I can't break up with Gavin. We're . . . we're engaged." I still couldn't bring myself to tell her about the prediction, that I thought he was my destiny.

"You don't love him. Or you wouldn't have jumped into

bed with Lukas. Even I wouldn't cheat on someone I loved."

"You wouldn't?"

Fran thought about this for a moment. "It's an untested theory."

"You've never been in love?"

"I don't think so. I just don't see the point. It's messy. Too complicated."

I burst into tears again. "But I love him."

"Who?" said Fran. "Who the fuck do you love?"

"Lukas," I said. "I love him so much."

Fran smiled. "There, I bet that feels better—to finally admit it." She handed me another tissue. "Don't worry about Gavin. He'll get over it. He's too dull to stew on it for long."

"I hope you're right. I don't want to hurt his feelings—he's just so . . ." I tried hard to think of a complimentary word about Gavin. "He's just so decent."

"Decent?" said Fran. "For fuck's sake. Dump him now."

We had both laughed at that, but Gavin *was* decent, so decent that when, on Monday, I asked him to come to the greasy spoon with me for lunch, and told him that we had to call off the wedding, he said, "Is it because my parents didn't like you?"

"No," I said. "That's not the reason." And after a pause, "They really didn't like me?"

"I don't care what they think," he said. "I've told them we're getting married, and that's that."

"That's that?" Had he not heard me asking to call the whole thing off? "It isn't about your parents. It's about us."

"But the church is booked, and the reception, and"—he

took a deep breath—"I was going to keep this a surprise, but I've put down a deposit on a house in Croydon. Not far from where my parents live."

I was speechless.

"I was going to tell you after the wedding."

"Gavin," I said. "There isn't going to be a wedding."

"There is," he said. "It's all planned."

"I can't marry you."

"What?"

"I don't know if we can make our lives fit together. We're too different."

Gavin laughed. "I know about your funny upbringing and I don't care. That's all behind you—in the past. What matters is our future. The way we live now."

"You don't understand," I said. "I haven't been myself. I haven't been honest."

It was as though Gavin hadn't heard me. "Look," he said. "Take some time, think it over. The wedding isn't for another six months." He reached across the yellow-flecked Formica table and took my hand. "It's perfectly normal to get cold feet."

When I told Fran about our conversation, she thought it was the funniest thing she'd ever heard. "So let me get this straight. You tried to call off the wedding, but he wouldn't let you?"

"It was like he was deaf."

"But you didn't tell him about Lukas, did you?"

"I didn't want to hurt his feelings."

Fran snorted. "It's a bit late for that, darling."

In a very small voice, I said, "I know."

For five consecutive days that week, I tried to break off the engagement with Gavin, and each time he would not budge. Even when finally I told him there was someone else, he said it was normal to fantasize about sowing a few wild oats before settling down to have a family. In fact, he said, it was better to get that sort of thing out of your system before the big day than to have it destroy the marriage later on, when you had a family and things were more complicated.

On the sixth day, I gave Gavin back his engagement ring. I would have returned it earlier but because I never wore it, it had taken me a week to find the thing. "Well," he said, upon pocketing it, "I'm still not canceling the wedding."

"But I'm not going to come over to your flat anymore," I said, to which he shrugged, as though I had just told him I wasn't going to finish the rest of my sandwich. "And no more sex."

That's when I finally understood. His course was set; he was incapable of changing direction. Nothing I said would make any difference. It was why he couldn't eat Greek food, or fuck me from behind.

"As far as I'm concerned," I said, "we've broken up and it's okay to see other people." I didn't know how much clearer I could make it.

"The wedding's six months away," said Gavin. "You'll change your mind before then, I'm sure of it."

Is this what the prediction had meant by true love—a love that would stick to me like superglue?

I stayed with Lukas every night that week. When we

were together, I forgot about my other existence. I was intoxicated by our reunion and there was much going on that was exciting and distracting. Fran had worked her magic on Marlon, convincing him to accept the help offered by his father, and within weeks, the Communists had gone into the recording studio to cut a demo of "Frozen Hearts." Not just any studio, mind you, but Abbey Road. The Right Honorable Giles Andover QC was a huge Beatles fan, as well as a believer that if one was going to do something at all, one ought to do it properly. For three sessions that kicked off at the crack of dawn, when more famous bands were still asleep, he would have had to pull strings and fork out a considerable amount. The day before they went in, Lukas confessed he was terrified. He had done a bit of recording before, in New Zealand, but they'd only ever used shitty equipment and had never had enough time to get down anything decent. When the resulting record was awful, no one was dumbfounded, and there were plenty of factors on which to lay blame. This time, there would be no such scapegoats. If the record sucked it would be because the band sucked.

I was concerned the band did, in fact, suck but saying so would have been cruel. "You'll be brilliant," I reassured Lukas. "You guys are so tight. You saw everyone go nuts at that gig."

"But we won't be in front of an audience . . ." Lukas looked anxious. "It won't be the same vibe. The same energy."

"Isn't that what the producer's for? To give you that edge?"

"I hope so," Lukas said. "I bloody hope so."

While the Communists were recording, I went to work

as usual—when I saw Gavin, he acted as though nothing had changed. After work I caught a bus to the mews flat to wait for Lukas to finish. Neither Fran nor I had ever brought boyfriends back to the bedsit in Fulham. It was too small, just a room with two single beds, a kitchenette and shower cubicle, clothes strewn over the floor, and no privacy. Lukas had given me a key, and I let myself in and waited—and waited. I read a book, drank a glass of vinegary Beaujolais, watched *Dynasty,* ate leftover vindaloo, and then fell asleep on the velvet banquette. When I woke later on, Lukas still hadn't come home, and I figured they had skipped an evening off and gone straight into the next session. The following morning I went to work, where he rang me midafternoon. He was sorry he hadn't come home, they had recorded all night and crashed out in the studio, he couldn't talk for long, it was going well, much better than expected, the producer was a genius, and he was looking forward to seeing me later.

But later, the same thing happened. I waited and waited. Lukas didn't come home, and then I fell asleep. Not long after, I woke with a start. Someone was banging on the back door of the mews. I went to answer it, thinking it was Lukas, that he had forgotten his key. Only it wasn't him. Standing silhouetted in the moonlight was Serena. She had on an elaborate dressing gown, monogrammed at the breast with her initials, and she had put on gumboots to make the trek through the soggy garden. Her expression was improbably one of fear.

"Mummy and Daddy are away," she began. "My room is right at the top of the house and I . . . well, I can't stand being home alone at night."

"I thought you had a housekeeper—a maid of some sort?"

"She doesn't stay over."

I said nothing, wanting to make this hard for Serena.

"Look here," she said. "The thing is I'm scared to death. I thought I heard someone trying to break in."

"You can stay here," I offered. "In Marlon's room." I had tiptoed up there earlier, surveyed the disarray, and then retreated.

Serena screwed up her nose. "Eww, no. I couldn't possibly. I was rather hoping you'd come up to the house."

"Me?"

"You've been up there before, surely? Lukas has, many times." Was she gloating?

"No," I said. "I've never been invited."

Serena hovered in the doorway. I hadn't complied yet and I could see that it pained her to have to beg.

"Do you think you could stand it?" she said. "I'll make us breakfast in the morning—or rather, Aggie will. She comes in at seven."

Aggie, short for Agnes, was the housekeeper and cook, who had been with the family for decades. I had heard Marlon telling Lukas what a jolly good sport she was, especially for someone so ancient. Not that long ago, he had tried to bake hash cookies in the basement kitchen of the big house, and Aggie had come in halfway through his experiment and suggested an improvement to the recipe. When Marlon had asked if she would like to eat one, the old cook had laughed heartily at his mischievousness and told him she would take one home for her dog. I had never met a domestic servant before and was curious what one might be like, not to mention the fact that she would be serving me breakfast, an offer too glamorous to turn down.

"Okay," I said. "Let me get my things."

I followed Serena up a garden path bordered with pebbles, admiring the profusion of neatly clipped rose-bushes, each one a perfect globe. At this time of year, all the branches were bare, exposing all the thorns. A square pond had been dug into the lawn, and in the center of that stood a fountain, flowing for no one but the moon's benefit. There was a gazebo too, furnished with steamer chairs, and dozens of bulbous Grecian urns, carefully arranged to simulate disarray.

Serena guided me up a set of wide terra-cotta steps and through a heavy black door. Inside, the house was even more impressive than I'd imagined. First the kitchen, vast, with acres of counter space and a range, then wide stairs, the carpet so plush it purred under my feet. The ground-floor hallway was tiled in checkered black-and-white marble, and off it, a series of heavy paneled doors, thick with varnish and sporting ornate brass handles. A few of these were open, revealing large, lofty rooms and antique furniture, the polished surfaces glinting even in the dead of night. The carpet was an impractical ivory, pristine like fresh snow, its powder broken by thick Persian rugs. Weighty brocade and tassels adorned every window, and each wall was crowded with portraits of somber men and women in wigs and crinolines and breeches. "Who uses these rooms?" I asked.

Serena was puzzled. "What a strange question."

"It's just that everything's so old, so valuable—like it belongs in a museum. What if you broke something?"

"We never did," said Serena. "Even when we were children." I could tell she was proud of that fact.

"Where do you watch TV?"

She pointed upward. "In my room."

What she should have said was in her *suite,* for she had a bedroom and a bathroom and a dressing room all of her own. It was on the top floor, next to Marlon's abandoned teenage bedroom, which she showed me, still decorated with various medals and cricket cups and rugby shirts in frames on the wall.

"There," said Serena, pointing to a surprisingly small television set, bunny ears atop a neat black cube. "Marlon has one too."

"Television was banned from the commune," I said. "And we weren't allowed to make friends with children who had one, in case it corrupted us."

"We wouldn't have been friends then," said Serena, flopping down on one of two single beds in her room, both dressed up in doilies and covered with teddy bears and cutesy heart-shaped pillows—like a very young girl would have. Her walls were decorated with pony club rosettes. "Lukas told us about the commune. Was it really that awful?"

"Is that how he described it?"

"He likened it to being in prison."

"It wasn't that bad. We thought it was paradise when we were kids."

"Paradise," repeated Serena. "Lukas didn't use that word."

She pointed to the other single bed. "You can sleep there."

I had not brought anything with me to sleep in, and was wearing a going-out dress. "Can I borrow a T-shirt?"

Serena gave me a queer look. "Whatever for?"

"To sleep in."

"You mean a nightgown?"

"I guess so. I've never worn one." On the commune, boys and girls alike had worn T-shirts to bed.

"You've never worn a nightgown? That's so funny." Serena opened a few of the drawers in her dresser and held up something pink and frilly. "Hmm, I don't think this will fit you," she said. She rummaged some more and found a pair of silky pajamas. They looked about my size, but Serena said, "No, these won't either." She shut the drawer. "I don't seem to have anything. Sorry."

"So not even a T-shirt then?"

"Actually, there is this." She went over to another dresser and took out a folded black garment, which she carried over and threw, gauntletlike, onto the bed. "You probably recognize it."

Serena stood over me, waiting for my reaction.

I unfolded the T-shirt—it was one that had belonged to Lukas, a favorite from our Auckland days, bearing the logo of the Flying Nun record label. I had worn it myself once or twice, though Lukas had always asked for it back. We were strangely possessive of our clothes, the minute we had some of our own. "Thanks," I said, masking my disquiet. I did not want to get changed in front of Serena and asked if I could use her bathroom.

"Of course," she said, smiling. "Help yourself."

I went in and shut the door. The T-shirt seemed tainted, but I put it on anyway, noticing that it had been ironed, probably by Aggie. Had Lukas given it to Serena or had she "borrowed" it from her brother's flat? From the triumphant way she'd handed it to me, I guessed the former, but I tried not to let it get to me.

Quite why anyone needed her own exclusive bathroom was beyond me until I clocked the obscene amount of grooming paraphernalia she had: dozens of lipsticks, lids carelessly thrown aside; lip liners, eyeliners, pantiliners, and pencil sharpeners; eye shadows of every hue and texture; at least three hair dryers; a set of curling tongs and another hair tool whose metal teeth joined in a perfect zigzag line. There were skin creams and depilatory creams and hair pomades and razor blades, a dozen cans of hairspray, some lying on their sides, others with broken nozzles. And in among all this was a long flesh-colored plastic tube with a tapered end, the likes of which I had not encountered. I picked it up to take a closer look and found a switch on the side, which I flicked on at exactly the same moment as I began to have an inkling what it was. The thing hummed loudly in my hand, startling me, and I dropped it on the vanity unit, where it skittered among the lipsticks, its sound amplifying against the marble to a loud buzz.

Seconds later, I had switched the thing off, but when I came out of the bathroom, Serena was smirking.

"I see you found my vibrator," she said. "Did you have fun with it?"

For so many reasons, I was profoundly embarrassed. "I'm sorry. I didn't know that's what it was."

Serena laughed. "You're kidding, right?"

"I've seen . . . other ones," I lied. "But not one like that."

"Gosh," she said, "so Lukas wasn't making that up."

"Making what up?"

For a tantalizing moment, Serena looked like she was about to tell me, before changing her mind. "Nothing. Nothing at all."

I climbed into the bed opposite and pulled up the covers, her words whirring in my head as she turned out the light. What had Lukas told her that had to do with a vibrator? I wasn't sure we had ever talked about one, but then I began to see that was the point. One by one, and against my wishes, the pieces of a puzzle started dropping into place. However unlikely it seemed, had Lukas's education, the one I had already benefited from, been at the hands of this toffee-nosed little bitch?

I woke in the morning feeling sure of it, and would have skipped breakfast were it not for the intoxicating smell of freshly baked croissants.

Besides Aggie, I was the first to the kitchen, a room even more cavernous than it had seemed the night before, with marble counters and cupboards that went on for miles and were decorated with what looked like garden trellis but was only a painted effect. Aggie beetled around it in her starched white apron, her knotted legs as sturdy as tree trunks. The table was laid with croissants; a sharply angled pat of butter, just out of the fridge; and three types of marmalade and jam in fluted white ramekins. I had never stayed in a hotel, but this was what I had imagined breakfast in one to be like.

I said hello and introduced myself by name, and without asking anything more or ascertaining my right to be there, Aggie pulled out a chair for me at the table and reappeared seconds later with a fresh pot of tea and another of coffee. She then discreetly withdrew to the far recesses of the kitchen, where she seemed to be engaged in a flurry of baking and food preparation; I couldn't help wondering for whom.

I felt uneasy, sitting idly at the table while she bustled about, and wondered if I should get up to help. She was being paid, handsomely I hoped, to do what she was doing, but still it seemed wrong for a woman her age to be toiling so hard while I sipped coffee and gorged on croissants and jam. On the commune, the concept of one person waiting on another would have been considered immoral.

Presently, Serena floated into the kitchen, and Aggie was soon at her side, pulling out the chair. "Good morning, Miss Serena," she said chirpily. "Did you have good sleep?" Her English was less than perfect, in syntax more than accent.

"It was frightful," she replied. "I've so much to do. I simply don't know how I'm going to get through the day."

Aggie smiled. "You will have beauty nap."

Serena nibbled on a croissant but was already on her second cup of black coffee. "That reminds me, I shan't be needing lunch. I'm going out. But I've left a dress on my bed that needs dry-cleaning."

"For tomorrow?" said Aggie.

"Tonight. There's a party."

I was on my second croissant and thought I might help myself to another if Serena left the room. They were so delicious, all butter and air, not like the dense, earthy bread we had grown up on. When she did finally get up to leave, on her way out Serena turned to me from the doorway. "You don't need to come back upstairs, do you?"

"No," I said. "And I can't stay tonight, either."

"I don't need you to."

When Serena had left, Aggie came back to the table. "You are new friend?"

I didn't see the point in lying to her. "Not a friend, exactly, no."

"I think for myself you are not."

I laughed. "Is it that obvious?"

Aggie smiled, pushing the plate of croissants in my direction. "You like these? I make more. You take for lunch."

It was a Friday, the Communists' last day in the studio, but I spent it at work, avoiding Gavin, though I didn't know what for—he would never have alluded to our relationship while under the roof of B, B & B, and I had no intention of going anywhere else with him. Late in the evening, when I returned to the mews flat, Lukas finally appeared, eye sockets hollow, spirits high, perhaps too high. He was wired, a little absent, not himself, but I put that down to fatigue and sat around on the banquettes with the rest of the band, drinking wine, smoking cigarettes, trying to tune into their vibe. When they had relived, in exhaustive detail, the highlights of the recording session, they got out their guitars and noodled long into the small hours, making frequent trips to the bathroom, in groups of two or three, which at the time I thought odd, but for the wrong reasons. At around three or four in the morning they finally called it a night, and I lay on the behemoth with Lukas, comfortably drunk, and feeling content that I was at last alone with him. He passed out. The next morning, Lukas woke surprisingly early for someone who hadn't slept for three days. I was aware of his getting up off the couch before I was properly awake, and when I did surface, I had to go and look for him. The door to the bathroom was ajar, and I found him hunched over the sink, sucking crumbs of white powder up his nose with a rolled-up banknote.

"What are you doing? It's nine in the morning."

He stared at me, red-eyed, and held up a tiny, empty plastic bag. "There was only a bit left—I didn't want to throw it out."

"So you thought you'd have it for breakfast?"

Lukas sniffed, an ugly, phlegmy sound. "Sorry—it gets stuck in my nose."

He had dodged my question, and I didn't press it. "You must be exhausted."

"Actually I feel great."

"Because the demo's finished?"

"Yep, and it sounds fucking amazing."

A lot of things happened very quickly after that, as though our lives were on fast-forward. I would go off to work, then come back to the mews to find that several new developments had gone down while I was out. The demo of "Frozen Hearts" went out to record companies and while most were not interested, some guy in Manchester, of all places, drove all the way down to London to sign them the same day he heard it. Lukas described him as "just a really cool guy," and not at all what he imagined the owner of a record company to be like. His name was Spike, and, Lukas reported, the first thing he ordered the band to do was to change their name—the communist thing sent out the wrong message. "Get away from politics," he told them. "Hard rock is all about sex."

"You didn't change it, did you?"

"We had to or he wouldn't sign us."

I suddenly didn't want to hear the new band name—instinct told me it would be awful—and Lukas must have sensed my apprehension.

"We couldn't think of anything—so he kind of chose it for us."

"Just tell me what it is."

"Cheatah," said Lukas, a little sheepishly, "like the animal but with 'e' and 'a' at the beginning."

I had nothing to say. For so many reasons, it was dire.

"Do you get it?"

"Yeah, I get it. Cheatah, as in, 'He cheats on women.'"

He was so pleased he hugged me. "That's so cool you get it. Spike said everyone would—but I wasn't sure."

I worried that Lukas didn't know what he was getting himself into. I feared it would all end badly, but I didn't want to bring him down, so I kept those fears to myself. In any case, at that juncture, I was wrong. "Frozen Hearts" came out as a single and, after several weeks bobbing up and down in the low hundreds, went to number thirty-seven on the charts—a wild success for an unknown heavy metal band. They were invited onto *Top of the Pops,* as one of the novelty filler bands near the beginning, before the really big acts appear. Nevertheless, when we exited the back door of BBC Television Centre and walked across the parking lot to climb into the Bedford van, Lukas and Marlon and the boys were mobbed by squealing schoolgirls waving autograph books in the air. None of these girls knew who they were, but they did this to every band that came out of the stage door, capturing signatures and pop star sightings and stories to tell their friends back at school. "Bags the blond," I heard one of them say, and the girl next to her said, "Hands off, Tracy, he's mine."

After all the dead-end bands Lukas had been in, all the aborted concerts and recording sessions and bust-ups, he was about to experience overnight success. "Frozen Hearts" went to number twenty-eight on the charts, and they raced back into the studio to cut an album—paid for this time by the record label. At this point Fran, who had all this time been working as B, B & B's mail girl, decided to quit her job and become a full-time manager. She turned out to be very good at it—pushy but switched on enough to know when to pull back—and she didn't make the mistake other girls made of falling in love with someone in the band. She had even made sure to sleep with Marlon as early on as possible, she told me one night, to get it out of the way.

"When did you do that?"

"After *Top of the Pops.* You remember we all went to that club in Soho? The one with the posh toilets?"

"No! Not there." There'd been a cloakroom attendant,

lots of velvet, and heavy, wood-paneled doors. "How did he even . . . ?"

"I don't know. The long hair. Maybe she thought he was a girl?"

"But he's so tall."

"Yeah," said Fran. "That was awkward. Like trying to mount a penny-farthing."

"I thought maybe he was gay—he never brings home girls." I didn't add that I thought he was in love with Lukas.

"Shit, no," said Fran. "He's just a sneaky fucker. Doesn't like to spray in his own backyard."

"Before we got back together," I said, "I think Lukas was shagging Serena."

Fran shrugged. "Probably. But who's he shagging now?"

"Me."

"Just you?"

"I think so."

"Well, then," she said. "What's the problem?"

She was right. Much as I couldn't stomach the idea of Lukas and Serena together, he had dropped her the minute I had come back on the scene, and I couldn't ask for more than that—especially not when I hadn't told him about Gavin.

The following month was a haze of going out, getting plied with free drinks, meeting loads of people, forgetting who they were, going somewhere else, repeating the cycle, then coming home to Marlon's and falling asleep in the wrecked conversation pit, which Lukas and I had come to think of as our bedroom. Our worldly belongings were piled up on one wing of it, with another set aside for sleeping, and the third side left bare in case anyone else wanted to crash there. Once or twice we had woken up to find Marlon asleep with us, or had gone to bed with him there, only to find that someone else—Vince or Fran—had taken his place in the night. It was a while before I realized that Lukas and I were never alone, that we had replaced our pack of seven with another exactly like it: the guys in the band plus me and Fran and Serena.

Lukas noticed it too. "It's just like old times," he said one night, glancing around at everyone seated at the dining table of the mews flat and grinning. "Seven kids. No parents."

There used to be seven of us, I thought, but not anymore. "Don't you ever wonder what happened to Fritz?"

"I try not to think about it. But sometimes I do. That and all the other weird shit that went on."

"I can't believe you still hate the commune so much."

Lukas refilled his wineglass, spilling some over the sides. "I don't hate the commune—not the place itself. But I do hate the lunatics who brought us up. They had no right to experiment on us."

"They didn't experiment on us."

"The way we were raised. Not knowing who our parents were. Lying to us. Don't you think that counts as emotional abuse?"

"I don't know. In lots of ways, we were lucky."

"Poppy, it was a total head fuck." He was drunkenly serious. "Who does that shit? They fucking poisoned us. It was like Jonestown or the Manson family. That stuff makes you crazy."

"It was nothing like that. Nobody abused you or made you have sex with your mother."

"Well, you are kind of like my sister," said Lukas. "And sometimes I feel like I'm crazy—don't you?"

He was scaring me. "You're not crazy."

"You're right. I'm perfectly normal." He widened his eyes so that he really did look mental, then planted a kiss on my cheek. "I love you and you love me. There's nothing to discuss."

"But I *do* love you," I said.

He smiled. "Then relax."

Marlon had rolled a joint, lit it, and casually started smoking it as if it were a cigarette. He passed it around, and everyone toked on it except me.

"What I don't get," said Marlon, "is that if you chaps grew up on a commune, then how come Poppy's so straight? I can't even get her to share a joint, let alone sleep with me."

"Maybe I don't fancy you," I said, which wasn't wholly true. It would be impossible to meet Marlon and not think about sex, what it would be like with him. "It just wasn't that sort of commune. They were more into composting toilets and astrology."

Marlon pretended to yawn. "How utterly tedious."

"What about Shakti?" said Lukas. "Didn't she sleep with everyone?"

"Really?" I said. "Like who?"

"Shakti?" said Marlon. "Was she some kind of Indian deity?"

"Californian," I said, which made Marlon laugh out loud.

"Well, Hunter definitely had a crack," said Lukas. "But she preferred women, and, um"—he paused here and flushed slightly—"young boys."

"Oh yes," said Marlon. "I bet."

"She worked her way round everyone, even Elisabeth," continued Lukas. "Remember how they all used to visit her caravan to 'get their charts done'?" He laughed. "Charts, my arse."

"But she did do their charts. They told me about it."

Lukas raised his eyebrows. "Did you ever see one?"

I had to confess that I hadn't. "But that's how she decided what to put in the predictions."

"The *what*?" Ravenous curiosity flashed in Fran's eyes. "What the fuck were they?"

I said nothing, waiting to see how Lukas would answer.

"Poppy, you tell them," he said, grinning waggishly and nudging my elbow. "Tell them all about our rite-of-passage thing." He glanced at Marlon. "You'll love this, man. It's very *National Geographic*."

I hesitated. Talking about the predictions seemed like a perilous topic in light of the trouble they had caused between Lukas and myself—and yet he was the one who had made a joke of it. Perhaps it was safe to proceed.

"When we were sixteen or seventeen," I began carefully, "there was this ritual. Kind of like an initiation ceremony. Shakti took us all up to the top of a hill—there was some chanting, and she pricked our fingers and put the blood into a bowl. And then she made predictions about our future. She said they were based on our astrology charts, plus other stuff like palmistry and tarot. She predicted that I would . . ." The room had gone quiet, spellbound, as if I was telling a ghost story, and with everyone staring at me, waiting to hear my prediction, I lost my nerve. "She predicted I would go overseas."

"What?" said Fran. "Is that all?"

Serena said, "That isn't very interesting."

Lukas shook his head. He knew that I was covering—and why. "Come on, darling, don't be shy," he said. "Tell them about your destiny." His laugh was kindly, teasing, but there was an edge to it.

"It was nothing," I said. "A scribble on a piece of card, that's all."

"But what was the scribble?" demanded Fran. "You can't build it up like that and then *not* tell us."

"It was her true love—a knight in shining armor if I remember rightly." Lukas looked to me for confirmation but I shook my head, my face growing hot.

"No, it was a king."

"A king in knickerbockers?" Fran stared at me, unable to contain her amusement. "Are you serious?"

I shot her a genuinely mortified look, hoping she wouldn't say more, but it was Serena who saved me with a question that was even more horrible. She fixed me with her hard black eyes and said, "So what are you doing with Lukas if he isn't the one?"

I didn't answer.

Serena had been sipping burgundy and the teeth and lips of her victorious smile were stained red. Already bored with me, she turned to Lukas. "And what did you get?"

He laughed. "I can't even remember. I barely looked at it for a second."

"Bollocks," said Fran. "You must remember something."

Lukas closed his eyes and held his hands up to the ceiling. "It was a picture of a . . . hang on, it's coming to me . . . a giant—"

"Cock," said Marlon.

"Correct!" Lukas exclaimed. "It was a giant cock."

Everyone laughed, and I did too, from sheer relief, because the focus had shifted away from the embarrassment of my prediction and onto Lukas, but later, when I was finally alone with him, I said, "You told me you didn't look at your prediction."

"I did?"

"Straight after we got them. You told me you threw yours away without even looking at it—when really you *did* look at it."

Lukas sighed. "I might have glanced at it, okay?"

"But why did you pretend you hadn't?"

"Because I really didn't want you believing in mine as well as yours."

"Why not? Was it bad?"

"Poppy! This is exactly what I was afraid would happen."

"It *was* bad," I said. "And that's why you didn't want me to see it."

Lukas threw up his hands in frustration. "Bad. Good. Even if I trusted Shakti—which I don't—I wouldn't believe in it."

I remembered what he had said earlier, about her preferring young boys, and a penny that should have dropped long ago was finally shoved into place. "She tried to sleep with you, didn't she?"

Lukas was surprised that I had only just worked this out. "When I said 'everyone,' I meant everyone."

"But, when?"

"Not long after she arrived. She came on strong."

"And did you?"

"No way," said Lukas, emphatic. "I ran a mile."

"Thank heavens."

"And you?"

"What about me?"

"Did she try to sleep with you?"

"Of course not." To begin with, I was shocked he had even asked, but then I remembered the morning of nude yoga at the edge of the forest, and I wasn't so sure I had escaped her advances. "Actually, there was something weird that happened."

"And let me guess—you wouldn't put out?"

"It wasn't like that. Not exactly."

"Well," said Lukas, "now you know why I didn't look at my prediction."

"But you *did* look at it. You said you peeked."

"You still don't get it, do you?"

"Why can't you just tell me what was in it?"

"No." Lukas folded his arms and set his mouth in a stubborn line.

"Please?"

"Never. In fact, I've just remembered that I can't remember what it was."

"Fuck you."

"Okay," he said, "fine, I will," and set about ruthlessly seducing me, pinning my hips to the floor and working away on me until he had triumphed.

CHAPTER 11

London
1988

THE BAND HAD STARTED rehearsing for their first British tour. The album was coming out in May, and then in the summer of 1988, the same month Gavin thought I was marrying him, they would go on tour. In June, Gavin took me aside in the telex room, a level of intimacy he had never once attempted at work, and told me that much to everyone's relief, above all his own, he had managed to postpone the wedding.

"Postpone?" I said, taken aback. "You still haven't canceled it?"

He said, "I can't. I'll lose my deposit."

"Your deposit on what?"

"On the hotel ballroom. Where we're going to hold the reception."

I had never considered these details, as if the wedding had been organized by a magic spell. "Is it for a great deal, this deposit?"

"Yes," said Gavin, "a considerable amount."

This would be a sticking point—perhaps even the main sticking point—and I couldn't see a way around it. "How long will they hold it for?"

"A couple of months," he said.

OVER SEVEN LONG WEEKS that summer, Cheatah was booked to play in thirty-one university halls across Great Britain, starting in Aberdeen and ending in Southampton. I was joining them in Bristol, toward the end of the tour. They felt certain it would be a triumph. Everyone had high hopes for the future, discussing what types of cars they would buy, the places they would go on holiday once they were rich. Marlon and Serena had already driven Bentleys and Jaguars, and had vacationed with their parents in St. Barts, St. Tropez, St. Moritz, but they played along, bless them. The day the band left to go on tour, a Saturday morning, it was raining. It had been raining for weeks on end, and each day Lukas had wondered out loud if this would make more people go to the concerts or fewer. Ticket sales had been unpredictable. Good in some places, poor in others. A lot of students had already gone home for the holidays. Others were caught up in exams. Too late, someone suggested it would have been better to start the tour in early September, when all the students were back, instead of that being the end date. Packing to go, Lukas was in a melancholy mood, saying he would miss me too much and that he didn't want to go. Then, when the other guys in the band came to pick him up, and they started packing gear into the van—instruments galore plus a whole trunk of leather pants, studded belts, and cutaway vests—he caught their collective excitement, became overly jubilant, and was rushed and distracted during our farewell. "See you in Bristol, Pops," he'd called out, drumming on the roof of the car before he got in. "Miss you already!"

"Break a leg, guys!" I called to the revving car.

They drove off, tooting, and I opened the door to the mews flat and climbed the steep wooden stairs. Serena had drifted off to the big house to change before meeting her mother for lunch someplace she called "Harvey Nicks," and Fran had gone to her newly acquired office to sort out some promo. In the lounge, I opened the curtains, which had been drawn for so long that the mechanism was jammed, and the seedy wreckage of the last few months was thrown into harsh relief: discarded coats and shoes, empty wine bottles, ashtrays loaded with stubs. A full-length mirror stood by the coffee table, which had been used as a dumping ground for dug-out eye shadows and empty hairspray cans. Here and there the velvet couch cover had split, exposing its crumbling yellow foam innards. It resembled Parmesan cheese, in not just appearance but also smell. While the party had been raging, I hadn't noticed any of this ruin, but now it was hard to miss. I picked up one or two wineglasses and took them to the sink, a graveyard where every dish and vessel in the flat had gone to die. It would take hours to make a dent in the kitchen but the bathroom was worse, strewn with lipstick-smeared tissues, entrails of sticky blond and black hair, and towels so wet they would have to be wrung out. I could not

believe I had been using the toilet, which had been treated
for months like a urinal. Around the base was a tacky yellow
gunk, and at the sight of it I dry-heaved.

On the upstairs landing outside Marlon's uninhabit-
able bedroom, I found a small clear square of carpet and sat
down. The circus had rolled out of town, and I had been
left with the cleanup. Would this be my life from now on? I
couldn't even move back to the bedsit. We had disbanded it
and Fran had moved into a flat with other girls.

I tidied up just enough to make living in the flat bearable, but I couldn't get rid of the Parmesan stench that came
from the conversation pit and followed me around the
flat. The next day this odor tailed me to the Tube station,
boarded the train, and was still there at work, and the day
after that, the same thing happened. Paranoid, I sniffed at
my clothes, wondering if I was the source. I bought cans of
air freshener, scented candles, and the hippie cure, incense.
Nothing worked. The smell exhausted me, and at the same
time, made me hungry. In my lunch hour, and again at dinnertime, I went to the local café and ate crumpets and jam,
beans and eggs, sausages and chips. We had been so busy in
the last few months we had hardly eaten, but in the interval
between the first tour date in Aberdeen and the one in Bristol, where I would join them on the road, I more than made
up for it.

From what little information I could glean from Lukas,
the tour was a mixed bag. In some towns, such as Liverpool,
local metal fans came out in force to support them; in other
places—Glasgow was the worst—they were bottled off the

stage. Lukas was confused, at first, then depressed. He had started the tour by calling every day but as it went on his phone calls became more sporadic, his mood increasingly unpredictable.

One afternoon at work I picked up the phone to an apocalyptic drum solo and Lukas yelling over it, "Sorry, babe—in the middle of sound check. Just had to hear your voice!"

"Where are you?"

"Fucking York! Can you believe it? How the hell are you, babe?"

He sounded overexcited, maybe drunk, and when I replied, "I'm fine, you know, same as always," someone on his end of the line whooped so loudly it drowned me out.

He shouted, "Babe, are you there?"

"I said I'm great."

This was lost in a howl of guitar feedback.

I tried, "I love you."

"What?"

"I miss you!"

"Me too. Hey, I've got to go—they're testing the mics."

The next time he called, three or four days later, it was early morning and very quiet on his end of the line. He sounded as though he hadn't slept. When I asked how the gigs were going, he was irritable, as though he couldn't bear to revisit what had happened the night before. "Babe," he said, "I didn't ring up for an inquisition."

"I just hope you're okay."

"It's fucking tiring," he said, pausing to yawn down the phone. "We drive all day, arrive at some shitty venue, set up, go talk to some piss-awful student radio station, eat dinner, sink a few beers, then go onstage. By the time we get back to the pub or whatever shit-hole we're staying in, it's two or three in the morning. I'm sharing a room with Marlon, and he's an asshole. The next morning we get up and do it all over again." He yawned a second time. "Does that answer your question?"

"Yes, it does," I said, wondering why he had bothered to call me at all.

His mood swings took on a pattern. If he called before lunchtime, he was morose, reluctant to talk, but sometimes in need of reassurance. If he called later in the day, or in the evening, he was often so exuberant, so up, that it was like talking to a game-show host. As the time approached to join Lukas and the band on tour, I grew more and more apprehensive, particularly when, in the week leading up to the trip, he neglected to call me at all. Through Fran, I learned that he had laryngitis and had been sleeping it off during the day, under doctor's orders to avoid unnecessary conversation. Still, my apprehension grew. I was also worried, stupid as it was, that I had put on weight. I was never normally concerned about that kind of thing, and Lukas had never been critical of my appearance, but I had gone up a whole dress size, maybe two, and I figured he was bound to notice.

Fran left the tour and came back to London for a few days, and the plan was that I would travel cross-country with her to Bristol on the train. We met at Paddington at seven in the morning, an early start. I hadn't traveled much by train before and had terrible motion sickness from the moment we left the station. It was a dogged kind of nausea that came and went in gusts. "You just got up too early," said Fran, taking me to the dining car and forcing me to drink a cup of sugary tea. I bought an egg sandwich to go with it. Then another.

"I thought you were going to spew?" said Fran.

"So did I, but while the sandwich is in my mouth I feel okay."

The boys were staying near the station in an old Victorian hotel that went on for blocks and had once been white but was now various shades of gray. The interior was a riot of green and orange and red carpet from the seventies that had been dragged into the eighties and left there to rot.

We took the lift up to the third floor and knocked on a series of doors. No one answered. "They're probably still asleep," said Fran, producing a trio of keys on numbered tags. She consulted a piece of paper and gave me a room number and a key. "This one will get you into Lukas and Marlon's room. I'll go wake the others."

It was morning-tea time, not early anymore. In the last month, I had started measuring time not by the clock but by how close or far away the next meal was. The more weight I put on, the worse this compulsion became.

When I got to the right door, I knocked a few times but no one answered. I put the key into the lock and turned it, quietly, so as not to wake anyone who might be asleep in the room. Fran had booked the rooms and paid for them, so it was only fair that reception had given her the keys, but it still felt wrong somehow to let myself in unannounced.

I couldn't see much at first, just a pencil line of light around the edges of the curtains. This only served to intensify the range of smells that rose to meet me. Strongest was that of cigarette smoke and unwashed armpits, but there was also a swampy odor of liquor and something else that was sharper, more chemical. The combination made me gag, and I went straight to the bathroom and brought up all the sandwiches I had eaten on the train—not a good beginning to the reunion.

At the sink, I rinsed out my mouth with water. It had crossed my mind to borrow a toothbrush, or some toothpaste, but there was none, just an assortment of lighters, the ever-present hairspray cans, and a pile of rolled-up banknotes. Like an idiot, I clocked these items and thought, *Oh, how nice, they must be starting to make money.*

Light from the bathroom went a little way to illuminating the hotel room, and I made out the hump of a body passed out on each of the two double beds. Neither was under the bedclothes, but on closer inspection, one had his face buried under a pillow, and the other, with his face exposed, turned out to be Lukas. I sat on the bed next to him. He was fully clothed, with even his boots still on, but it was the appearance of his face that upset me. Even in shadow, I could see that his skin was ashen, and that he'd lost more weight than he could afford to.

"Lukas," I whispered, panicking suddenly that he might not wake up. I took him by the shoulders and shook him, feeling how easily he moved, his body so relaxed it was like jelly. "Lukas! Wake up."

He murmured something that sounded, at a pinch, like

my name and, without opening his eyes, pulled me force-fully to the bed and clamped his arm around me. For a liv-ing corpse, he was still very strong, but I wondered if he had actually registered my presence before grabbing me and sinking back into a coma, or if I was taking part in his dream.

Across from me, on the other bed, Marlon rolled over, still under the pillow, put his hand down his red leather pants and rearranged his tackle. I had grown up with four boys who did that kind of thing constantly, and his behavior didn't so much gross me out as remind me of life on the com-mune. There had been something so natural about living in close proximity to other people, as if that was how humans were meant to exist. We had never been cold, or lonely, or bored. And even if we didn't have proper parents, we always had each other. For the first time in ages, I yearned for my brothers and sisters, and wondered what they had been doing with their lives. I couldn't remember why or how we had lost touch, but I was pretty sure it was mostly self-centeredness. The last thing I noticed before falling asleep next to Lukas was that the table between the two beds was littered with minibar bottles, all of them empty.

I woke up a few hours later with a rod poking into my lower back and whiskey breath in my ear. In my relationship with Lukas I had grown familiar with the morning stiffy but I was flabbergasted when he pulled down my pants and began working it into me without so much as a hello.

"Hey, wait a minute," I said.

"So good to see you," mumbled Lukas.

"Are you okay? I've been worried."

"It's fucked," he said, pawing at my clothes. "Tell you about it later."

"Okay."

We kissed a little, but he tasted weird, like menthol cigarettes and chlorine, and I was self-conscious about my breath after puking. Better to just let him take me from behind, to get it over with, although once he was inside me, I started to enjoy the sex more than I had expected—not that it went on for long enough to really take me anywhere.

"Far out," whispered Lukas, collapsing on top of me. "I've missed you."

I'd had my eyes shut for most of it, and when I opened them, Marlon was staring straight at me from the other bed.

He let out a long wolf whistle. "Good morning, beautiful," he said, and rubbed the straining leather at his crotch. "How about you come over here and sit on this?"

"Fuck off, creep, the show's over."

"And it's lovely to see you too, darling. Especially your pink bits."

Behind me, Lukas snorted with laughter, while I gathered up my clothes and fled to the bathroom to die of shame. Regardless of how careless I had been in front of Marlon, I felt violated, as though the two of them had colluded against me to contrive the situation. On the other side of the door, I could hear them laughing and bantering as though nothing had happened. On and on they went, then silence. The door to the hotel room clicked open and shut. There was a knock on the bathroom door.

"I hope you haven't fallen in."

I opened the door but stayed inside, fiddling with the taps at the sink.

"Sorry about that," said Lukas. "Marlon does it all the time."

"Watches you have sex?" I was horrified. "With who?"

"No, shit. I mean he has sex in front of me. He doesn't care."

"How long has that been going on?"

"I don't know when it first happened. He came back to the hotel room with a girl . . . I was in the room, asleep or wasted, I can't even remember."

They had been sharing a room since the tour started in Aberdeen, over a month earlier. Did he really expect me to believe that Marlon had been rooting in front of him while he had been celibate?

"What happens on tour stays on tour. I know the drill."

"Believe me, you don't. Being on tour isn't like real life. It's horrible. Half the time you don't know what day it is, where you are, who you're talking to . . . Everything's a blur so you just kind of switch off."

"Is that supposed to be some kind of excuse?" Out of nowhere—or perhaps it had been building since I arrived in Bristol—I was filled with rage and unable to calm down. "You switch off—and the next thing you know you're fucking some groupie in Manchester or Newcastle or Leeds."

Lukas looked at me like I was crazy. I felt crazy. Instead of reassuring me I was wrong about the groupies, he said, "Are you okay?"

"Don't try to switch this back onto me. I know you're

lying—just like you lied about Serena—about what you two got up to in her room with her stuffed toys and her frilly pink bedspread. You even gave her your favorite T-shirt—the one you never let me wear. I know about the vibrator too—how she showed you her clitoris."

"Poppy?"

Lukas's eyes swarmed with secrets. I saw nothing else. I had lost it. "I should never have come on tour. This whole thing was a mistake."

"What whole thing? You mean us?"

"Do *you* think we're a mistake?"

"No, I . . ." Lukas hesitated. "I feel so shitty. I can't think straight. Can you wait while I take a shower?"

I said I could but after he had been in the shower a few minutes, I left. I had only planned on leaving the hotel to go for a short walk, but several blocks later, I was across the road from the railway station, and shortly after that, I was on a train.

Back in London, I didn't have anywhere to go except the mews flat, which now felt tainted. I managed to get hold of Fran and she said I could stay at her place while she was away, arranging for one of her roommates to let me in.

I had taken the week off work and passed it in solitude, moping around Fran's flat, going for long walks by the river and across the bridge in Battersea Park, in the shadow of the old power station. It was an unusually hot summer. Secretaries sunbathed on their lunch hours and clouds of dust and pollen circled the scorched pavements. I was tired all the time from the heat.

I regretted everything: joining the band on tour, the accusations I had hurled at Lukas, the way I'd walked out, and before that, the way I had thrown Gavin aside and generally behaved as though I was exempt from morality or consequences. Had I really expected that I could escape my fate simply by denying it? I had known nothing good would come of Lukas and me being together and yet I clung to him anyway, pretending things could work out. I had told myself it was because I loved him and he loved me when in fact I was plainly selfish. The words of my parents echoed in my head: *Loving just one person is selfish.* It was the flaw they had tried to breed out of us but it turned out they had failed.

As the week went on, I began to find what I thought was some clarity. If nothing good could come of being with Lukas and going against my fate, then surely my only shot at happiness was to follow my destiny and to be with Gavin. It felt like a trap, but I reasoned that any other path would result in disaster.

On Monday morning, I had it coming to me.

Armed with newfound resolve, I marched into the offices of B, B & B determined to throw myself upon Gavin's mercy.

"We need to have lunch," I said to him, in the telex room, pulling the ticker tape off a missive that was six feet long. "You were right. I've changed my mind."

Gavin looked nervous. "About what?"

"The wedding." To let him know I meant business, I planted a kiss next to his mouth—something I had never done in the office—and naturally, because we were at work, he recoiled.

"Not here," he said, glancing through the glass partition that separated the telex room from the typing pool. "Someone might see."

At lunchtime, we went to the greasy spoon on the corner. Gavin sat twitchily reading the paper while we waited for our sandwiches to arrive. When I told him I wanted to marry him after all, that he had been right all along, he wasn't as overjoyed at the news as I expected him to be.

"Crikey," he said. "This is very sudden."

He turned back to the paper. Our sandwiches arrived. His ham on white and my ham on brown; lately, I had adopted Gavin's plain stodgy diet as my own.

"Isn't it great?" I said, after a few mouthfuls. "You won't lose your deposit after all."

I had been attempting humor but Gavin's reply was grave.

"I have already taken steps to make sure that doesn't happen."

"Good for you," I said, then wondered if I had misconstrued his meaning. "What kind of steps?"

"*I'm* getting married," he said, looking past me and out the window.

"Yes, we are! I still have the dress."

"I'm getting married," said Gavin. "You're not."

A long, heavy interval passed before I understood he was marrying someone else.

"You didn't really expect me to wait, did you?" His tone was bitter, mocking—unlike anything I'd ever heard. "I mean, not after everything you put me through. The way you mucked me around. You led me on like a right little tart." He shook his head. "My mother was right. You can't trust a hippie."

"I'm not a hippie."

"Well, you're not like the rest of us. Decent." Gavin stuffed a triangle of sandwich into his mouth and chewed it to pieces. "If you want to know who I'm marrying, ask the girls in the office. They'll tell you. In fact, they were queuing up." He stood to leave. "One more thing. You're a fattie."

He swung out of the greasy spoon with a spring in his step, and I watched him go, feeling wretched, not because I had been wronged, but because I deserved every bit of scorn he had thrown my way. I probably deserved worse.

The napkins at the greasy spoon were rough, like sandpaper, and after I had dabbed at the area around my eyes and nose with about a dozen of the things, my face wasn't dry, it was raw. I had already eaten my sandwich, though I didn't remember doing so, and I was hungry again. I wasn't sure how long I had been sitting there, oblivious to the waning of my lunch hour, when a steaming hot mug of tea appeared on the table. "I know you didn't order a cuppa," said the waitress, "but you looked like you could use one. It's on the house."

"Thanks," I said, looking up into a face that was soft and kind. "Are you new here?"

"No, love, I've been working here for years." She perched on the seat opposite me. "You all right?"

The fact that she had bothered to ask, when I had never noticed her before, made me cry again. "I'm starving," I said. "All the time."

"I know just what you need," she said, and went up to

the counter, appearing soon after with a plate of toast and butter and strawberry jam, which she set down in front of me. She waited for me to tuck in, then leaned in close to my ear and whispered, "I got really sick with all my pregnancies. The trick is to make sure you never get hungry. Eat all day if you have to. It passes."

I listened politely to her advice, wondering who it was meant for, then realized it was for me. She thought *I* was pregnant. I didn't know what to say, but when she had gone back to the counter, I looked down at my swollen stomach and patted it, wondering if that was the culprit. I *had* put on weight, but that had happened before. It was no cause for panic.

When I tried to pay for the tea and extra toast, the waitress wouldn't let me. "I know the thought of having a baby is terrifying but I promise you'll never regret it. My kids are the best thing that ever happened to me."

"How many do you have?"

"Free."

"Free?"

"Terry, Lisa, and June."

In a nearby pharmacy, I bought a pregnancy test and buried it deep in the folds of my handbag. All afternoon it stayed there, a land mine waiting to explode. If it was positive, I didn't want to find out in one of the cubicles at work. It was bad enough that, all afternoon, I had to sit among the typing pool girls, pretending not to notice Joanna's fat finger was squeezed into my old engagement ring.

Lukas and I had been careless, caught up in the rock 'n' roll lifestyle, with no time for details such as contraception.

I was not even aware how much time had passed since my last period.

The test was positive, and the first person I rang was Fran. The tour diary said Cheatah was in Exeter, where they had a day off before the concert, so I called the hotel there and asked for her. I woke her up from a disco nap. She had spent the whole day corralling the band from one monosyllabic interview to the next, after driving the tour van from Cardiff to Exeter in the wee hours of the morning.

I regretted telling her almost immediately. The first thing she said was, "I thought you were on the pill."

"I forgot to take it."

"Well, it's easy enough to get rid of."

"You mean, an *abortion*?" I'd not said the word out loud before—it felt like swearing.

"Yeah, a friend of mine had one." She paused. "Actually I did."

"Really?"

"It was no big deal. Took half an hour. I'll give you the name of the clinic when I get back to London."

"I'm not sure I want to—"

"You haven't told Lukas, have you?"

"No. Not yet."

"Good, that's good," said Fran, adding, "Don't."

"Don't tell him?"

"Not until the tour's finished." There was a note of impatience in her voice that I wasn't accustomed to.

"But, Fran, he's the father."

"I know he is, sugar—but the last thing he needs to hear right now is more bad news."

CHAPTER 12

London
1988

MORE BAD NEWS. THAT'S all my pregnancy was to Fran: an inconvenience to the singer in her band. She had swapped allegiances. She was no longer my best friend but Cheatah's manager first and foremost. Yet despite her misgivings, and everything that had gone wrong between Lukas and myself, I didn't feel that way about the embryo in my womb—the same womb that had been forecast to bear only sorrow. I wanted what was in there to live.

There were still two or three days left of the tour, but I couldn't wait that long to tell Lukas. The next day, I called in sick and hopped on a train to Exeter. All the way there I felt buoyed. Carrying a human life in my belly made me feel important, and I had to stifle the urge to tell strangers so that they too would understand how important I was.

When I arrived I went straight to the hotel Lukas was staying at, marched purposefully to his room, and knocked on the door. Marlon opened it. He was half-dressed and half-asleep.

"Get out," I ordered. "I need to speak with Lukas in private."

"Yes, ma'am, tout de suite," Marlon said, sensing I meant business.

Lukas was sitting on the end of the bed, curled around a guitar, humming softly to himself. When he saw me he stopped playing and smiled, woozily, pleased to see me but not quite sure if I was real or a figment of his imagination.

"Hi," we both said, and with that one word, all the speeches I had prepared, of reproach and remorse, seemed irrelevant. Always, when I saw Lukas after being apart from him, I was struck by how easy it was to be in the same room as him, and how jarring it was, by comparison, to be with other people.

I went to the window and opened the curtains, flooding the room with light.

"I'm pregnant," I said, addressing the street below, where a newspaper seller called out headlines to passersby, loud enough that I could hear. "I think that's why I lost it. I haven't been myself. And look at me—I'm fat."

He didn't speak until he was by my side at the window.

"Is it mine?"

"Of course it's yours." I had spoken sharply, and was mentally preparing for combat, but when I turned to Lukas he was grinning. A goofy, ear-to-ear smile, the likes of which I'd not seen since we left New Zealand. "You're happy about this?"

"A child that's half you and half me? I can't think of anything more awesome."

I had hardly dared hope for this reaction. "Do you really think we can start afresh? Put everything behind us."

"We can try."

Before that could happen, I needed to come clean about Gavin. "While we were apart, I got engaged."

Lukas was incredulous. To a bloke with a sword?"

"Oh my god," I said. "Don't."

"Fine," he said. "But at least I can laugh about it."

"And Serena?"

"A fling." He paused. "For the record, I didn't sleep with any groupies."

"Why not? Don't they throw themselves at you?"

"It turns me off. I prefer women that are—"

"—unavailable?"

"Yes. How did you know?"

For the remaining handful of tour dates, Lukas didn't drink, and he came home a different man, more like his old self. He apologized for how out of control things had gotten on the tour and for turning into one of those rock star assholes that he had always steered clear of. As the tour had progressed, he said, he and Marlon had gone from casually smoking hash and drinking whiskey; to snorting a few lines here and there; to devouring a cocktail of cocaine, prescription painkillers, and whatever else they were offered each night. Things had reached a peak in Manchester, when Spike had taken them out to his mate's acid house club after the gig. The evening had been humiliating. When they arrived in full stage costume, everyone had laughed at them—and Lukas had coped with the situation by getting fucked up.

Someone gave him pills he had never tried before, and to his surprise, they started enjoying themselves. At least the rest of the guys did. The club had a swimming pool in the middle of it and people were throwing around beach balls, but Lukas had not been able to escape the uneasy feeling that Spike had taken them there to be mocked by his friends—a thought that escalated, under the influence of whatever he had taken, to how maybe Spike had signed Cheatah to his record label for the same reason: as a laugh, at their expense.

"You really think he would do that?"

"I don't know," said Lukas, "but we're the only metal act on his books. All his other bands play indie rock or acid house."

"Can you leave—sign with someone else?"

"No," said Lukas. "We're stuck with him for another two albums."

Stuck with Spike, stuck with spandex, stuck as Cheatah. I could see his dilemma, the pain it was causing him, but I felt disconnected from it, as though he was in a room that I had walked out of, and I was in another one that he couldn't enter. I was around three months pregnant, and even though the baby was only the size of a cashew nut, it was changing me from the inside out. I had stopped feeling queasy but in place of the awful fog of nausea was a whole new spectrum of emotions and anxiety. The baby was a living thing. A piece of me, but also separate. I began to imagine it was a girl, and then I dreamt about her. She was tiny, a talking doll with big blue eyes and tufts of soft yellow hair. I found that I already loved her, this being I had never met, and it wasn't like any love I had felt for Lukas or Fritz. It was boundless. But as this love grew so too did a corresponding fear. I kept harking back to my prediction, and the more I tried not to think about it, the more I thought about it. What did it mean, that my womb would bear only sorrow?

I shared none of my fears with Lukas and roughly six months into the pregnancy we were married in the registry office at Chelsea, with Marlon and Fran to witness. Getting hitched had been Lukas's idea, and I had gone along with it, unable to say no in my vulnerable state. Officials in the registry office had been concerned when they found out we already had the same last name, Harvest, like all of our brothers and sisters on the commune. Were we cousins or otherwise closely related? No, explained Lukas, we had grown up in a cult.

We moved into our own place, a small flat on the ground floor of a mansion block in Maida Vale, opposite a recreation ground, and I quit work to wait for the baby. Cheatah's first album had sold only modestly in England, but in Germany, Austria, Switzerland, Norway, the Netherlands—in fact across the whole of Northern Europe—fans couldn't get enough of *Hungry for Hell*. No one could explain the phenomenon, but as a result, real deutsche marks started rolling in. Every other weekend, Lukas jetted off to Düsseldorf, Helsinki, Vienna, Cologne, for gigs, TV appearances, rock festivals, and even to collect awards. A thirty-seven-date European tour was hastily planned for the spring.

As the tour approached, Lukas and I disagreed about whether or not I should go with him. He wanted me to, insisting my presence would keep him on the straight and narrow. I couldn't think of anything worse than being the beached whale on the tour bus, asking the driver to stop every five minutes so I could get out and find a restroom, so we had come up with the idea that I could jet in to meet him in various cities, only to be told by my doctor that I would be too far along to fly. We reached a compromise. My due date fell somewhere in the middle of the tour but I would accompany them on part of the first leg, through Austria and Germany, the most civilized part, then, when I had reached the limit of my endurance, catch a train back to London to fluff up the nest and wait for baby's arrival. At the last possible second, Lukas would fly home for the delivery.

I made it as far as Zurich. To get there I had suffered an overnight bus ride from Frankfurt, through the Black Forest, where, in desperation, I had climbed out of the tour bus and, unable to see my own feet, peed behind a tree at the side of the road. As the city lights of Zurich came into view, I thought, *No more.* I would never again put myself in such a compromised position. Straight after the concert, I would catch the first train home.

It was held in a huge discotheque that doubled as a concert arena in the heart of Zurich. From the minute we pulled into the car park at the back of the venue, exhausted after the long bus trip and a day spent dozing in the hotel, I wished I was somewhere else, a quiet place with no groupies or roadies or managers swarming around. I was sick of everyone staring at my huge stomach, or else ignoring me because they were too afraid to have a conversation with a pregnant woman in case it was catching. In the last three weeks, I had ballooned to the size of a house bus. I tried to behave like a normal person, to crack the same jokes, but no one could see past the bump. It canceled out my personality. Fran, in particular, seemed repelled by the thing that was growing in my belly. She had long ago stopped lending me her clothes or trying to style me, and once, near the middle of the pregnancy, when I had asked her if she thought I should wear a blue T-shirt of Lukas's or a green one, she had screwed up her nose and said, "To be honest, love, you don't look that flash in either. Have you thought about getting dungarees?" That same day I went to a department store in Knightsbridge—Lukas told me to splash out—and bought a selection of balloon-shaped dungarees and floral-patterned tents with Peter Pan collars. It was a relief to find something comfortable, but on tour with rock stars, I felt like Lady Di in an East End pub.

At the concert in Zurich I wore the pinkest of the tent dresses, the "smart" one, and wished that it really *was* a tent so I could zip it up and hide in it. The greenroom was behind the stage and up a flight of stairs so steep I'd had to stop for a rest halfway up. At the top was a large lounge area with dressing rooms off to one side and a big window that looked out over the stage on the other. In case we couldn't stand the noise, there was a selection of soundproof earmuffs. I still found it amusing that while everyone out front paid good money to hear the band at full throttle, everyone backstage blocked their ears.

Lukas fetched me an orange juice from the rider, then

apologized and said he had to go and run through the lyrics of a new song one more time before the show.

"I'll be fine," I said. "Serena's here, and lots of other people, if I need anything." At the sound of her name, Serena had glanced in my direction and held up her martini glass, which I answered with a nod of my slightly fizzy, off-tasting orange juice. Since last autumn, she had been going out with Vince, Cheatah's androgynous bass player, and though I was never sure if she loved him, or had simply hit on the best way to legitimately hang out with the band, it had made her slightly less insufferable.

Lukas stood at the darkened window overlooking the stage. "You should be able to watch the whole thing from up here. Save you going down those stairs."

"I'll have to go down at some point."

"Yes," he said, planting a kiss on my forehead—I was, in the late stages of pregnancy, treated more like an ailing pet than a lover. "But not without my help."

When he had gone, Serena plonked herself down next to me on the white leather couch. "Can't be long now," she said, gesturing toward my stomach with an olive speared by a cocktail stick. "You look ready to pop."

"To be honest, I'm not sure. The doctors tried to work out my due date but they weren't a hundred percent sure if it was this month or—"

In the middle of my sentence, Serena got up from the couch and wandered over to the window. "I think they're about to start playing," she said, cutting me off. "I'm going down. Want to come?"

"No thanks, I'll watch from up here."

Serena left the greenroom, her heels clanging on the treacherous metal staircase. Even in her able-bodied condition she was going slowly, taking her time. I was alone in the greenroom, everyone had gone downstairs, and I lumbered to the snack table to inspect the selection of meats and cheeses that had been backstage at all the German concerts, and that no one except me had ever touched. I nibbled on a few gherkins and a square of Emmentaler and poured myself another orange juice, this one fresher tasting. Then I sat back down to wait it out. Again.

Out in the arena, a huge cheer erupted, followed by galloping drums and howling guitar feedback. They were starting with "Autobahn Child," a song they had penned hastily to appeal to their German fans. The viewing window rattled, and I put on a pair of earmuffs. I thought about at least *watching* the band, but I had seen them play so many times before that I could already visualize the prancing and gyrating and posturing that went with each song. Besides, I did not think I had the strength to raise myself and the bowling ball once more off the couch.

At this end of the pregnancy, I often had heartburn, and the orange juice and gherkin were telling me they did not want to be together in my stomach. I had also drunk too much juice, too quickly, and needed to pee, but the only promising door was locked. I was going to have to go downstairs, and soon, before I was too desperate even to waddle.

I stood at the top of the staircase and looked down. The

descent did not seem as steep as I remembered, but the stairs went on forever, descending from high up in the roof of the arena to stage level far below. It was the kind of staircase that would normally have had a bend in the middle, but because of where it was, behind the stage, there was no room for a zigzag or a landing.

I took my time, feeling, in the metal handrail, the reverberating bass line from "Autobahn Child." It was one of my least favorite songs, all about a pretty, orphaned waif who lives underneath a motorway and grows up to be a hooker. The singer of the song is in love with her but before he can rescue her, she dies of an overdose. Total downer.

I had made it down a dozen steps, about a quarter of the way, when a clacking noise made me turn around and glance back up the stairs. I did not expect anyone to be there, and when I saw the figure of a woman silhouetted in the doorway, I got such a fright that I lost my footing.

The step went out from under me. As I thudded down the long staircase, my enormous, heavy body gathered a momentum I was unable to stop. When I landed, a burning sensation spread from the base of my groin, through my pelvis, and up into my spine. Hot liquid gushed out from between my legs, broken water, greenish black and slimy, the dregs of a duck pond.

I called out for help but my plea was swallowed up by my other least favorite song—a high-pitched power ballad about a childhood sweetheart with a taste for hard liquor and a tattoo of a rose on her arse. Between the stage and myself was a thick black curtain hemmed with lead. The floorboards underneath me vibrated. Even if I screamed, no one would hear me.

The woman who had startled me made her way down the stairs. She didn't want to fall, like I had, and held tight to the railing, her spiked heels wedging in the metal grating on every step. She took forever to get to me, and then forever went on and on, while she fetched Fran, who called an ambulance. Fran didn't want to stop the gig and I told her that was fine, that I didn't want to stop it either—to cause a fuss. "I'll send Lukas over the minute they come offstage," she said, adding, almost as an afterthought, "Do you need me to come with you?"

"Yes, please—would you? I don't want to go on my own." Then someone threw a blanket over me, I supposed to cover the mess.

The paramedics laid me on my side on the stretcher, and I put my hand on my stomach and tried to feel if the baby was still kicking. She wasn't moving, but sometimes she didn't for long periods of time and then she would wake up and nudge me in the ribs. Lately she had run out of room to do much except squirm.

Please, god, let her be okay. I turned to the paramedic. "Is she still alive? Will she make it?"

"We'll do everything we can," he said. "You had a bad fall."

"She was so close to being ready," I said, through sobs.

"That is not so good. Earlier in the pregnancy, there is more fluid to protect the baby. We will need to get her out as quickly as possible."

If he had passed me a sharp, cleanish knife, I would have

cut myself open. "What's wrong with this fucking ambulance? Why is it going so slowly?"

I lost consciousness for a few minutes and woke up in the hospital, feet in stirrups and hooked up to machines by a series of nodes on my stomach. "Is she okay?" I said to the nearest nurse, who didn't comprehend. "Is the baby alive?" My belly felt full, but deflated, not as tight.

The nurse went to get her supervisor, a woman who spoke English. "We're inducing labor," she said. "The fetus shows signs of distress."

"What kind of distress?"

"Rapid heartbeat. But you must not think of that. Labor is going to be very fast. We don't have time to do an epidural. It will hurt. Very much."

I thought I wouldn't mind the pain—that it couldn't be as bad as everyone said—but it was catastrophic, like being run over by a car and a lorry and a train, obliterating agony, then a few minutes of respite, long enough to catch my breath before bracing for the next juggernaut. When I thought I couldn't take it any longer, the gaps between contractions closed up, stranding me in a tunnel of pain. I began to imagine hellfire, and roaring, growling beasts, and the nurse gripped my arm and said, "You might want to put more effort into pushing—and less into making that noise."

"What noise?" I said, and she growled a little to demonstrate, as the roaring beast had done. Trapped in the tunnel, my thoughts turned bleak. I wondered if I was dying. A man stood by the bed, offering his hand, but I smacked him away and returned to the underworld, the trial by pain, to cross the river Styx and bring back my baby.

"Push!" said the nurse. "Push now!"

The bones of my pelvis creaked apart like the hinges on an old, rusty gate, and something vast, and wild, a rhinoceros, rammed against the wall of my backside. The pressure was immense, unstoppable, the pain ringed with tusks. And then, not a miracle at all but an indignity of the first order, I shat out the rhino, and was gored.

I opened my eyes. Lukas, in spandex tights, stood next to me, an elated look on his face.

"Jesus," he said. "I think you scalped me."

"Where is she?" I collapsed on the bed, spent but euphoric, the brutal goring already a lost memory, watching a surreal pantomime of doctors in white masks dancing around the bed, pulling machines off the wall and plugging others in. There was a single cry, the bleat of a lamb getting its throat cut.

"Was that her? Is she dying?" I looked at Lukas, alarmed.

"It's a boy," he said. "And he's alive all right."

A few seconds later something pink and fat and covered in blood and cream cheese landed on my chest. His face was puckered, as if he had just eaten a lemon, and the top of his head stretched out in a cone. He was beautiful, a warm, squirming wonder, and my heart grew in seconds to fill the whole room.

CHAPTER 13

Zurich
1989

A NURSE SHOWED ME what to do, shoving the baby at my breast and stuffing the nipple in his mouth. She made it look easy, but it wasn't. The baby wriggled, or wouldn't open his mouth, or clamped it shut on the wrong part of the breast. I tried so hard, but I couldn't get it right, and the baby screeched and thrashed, going from hungry to hysterical in a matter of seconds.

"If he won't settle, I will give him a bottle," said the nurse, and I remembered the women on the commune, how zealous they had been about breast-feeding. Once, Susie had snuck into a maternity ward pretending to be a midwife and stood over the hospital beds of petrified new mothers, railing against the evils of infant formula, until she was caught and thrown out. Her voice rang in my ear, and I felt like a failure. "I'd like to keep trying," I said, holding back tears. Everything to do with having a baby was so much harder than I had imagined.

Lukas wanted to call him Zurich, spelled "Zoorich," after the city he was born in, but I thought that was ludicrous, the sort of thing only a rock star off his tits would do.

"Imagine calling out his name in the playground. Or sending him off to school. He'd have to spell it out for the rest of his life."

We settled on Zachary, a regular name with the same initial.

The first night alone in the hospital with Zachary, I watched him breathing. *All night.* Too excited to sleep. When he woke up, bleating, I put him to my breast, then peered under the hospital gown at his little frog legs, curled up tight to his chest. When I tried to stretch one out, it pinged back into place, and his feet folded up against his shins. The skin on his tummy was so thin, and I could see his little organs, pumping underneath. I didn't know how to change his nappy, or even to tell if it was wet, so I pulled the nightgown back over his legs and wrapped him again in the blanket. He had woken up and suckled and turned away again and fallen asleep, all without opening his eyes. Was that normal? Was he just like all the other little babies in the hospital, or had I blinded him and given him brain damage when we fell down the stairs?

Your womb shall bear only sorrow.

In the morning, when the nurse asked if I had slept, and I said that I hadn't, she wanted to take Zachary away, so I could rest, but I wouldn't let her. What if something happened to him while I wasn't watching? What if he stopped breathing and I wasn't there?

"If you don't try to sleep we will take him to the nursery whether you like it or not," said the second nurse who came in and found me awake. "It is very important that you rest."

The next day, when I still hadn't obeyed orders, true to her promise, the nurse took Zachary away. Seeing his bassinet getting wheeled out into the hallway, I felt a dread so strong it was like a seizure and a second nurse had to restrain me. "Please rest, Mrs. Harvest. We will take good care of your baby."

She did not understand why I needed to be able to see Zachary at all times. It was to save his life. I was the only one who could keep him safe. When she had left the room, I put on a dressing gown and went out into the hall to look for him. For what felt like hours I wandered the corridors, lost and disoriented, continuing to search even when black dots swarmed in front of my eyes and I hallucinated that the walls of the maternity ward were melting.

Lukas found me staring through a window into a room filled with bassinets, each one cradling a baby wrapped in waffle blankets. They all looked the same and I was crying with despair because the labels were in German and I couldn't tell which one was Zachary.

"I've been looking everywhere for you," he said. "The nurse told me you went walkabout."

"Where is he? Where's Zachary?"

"In the crib, next to your bed."

"You're lying. He's not there. They took him."

"He's right there, I promise. We gave him a bottle."

"You did *what*?"

Lukas flinched and I realized I had screamed at him. "He was hungry."

"You've poisoned him," I said, bursting into tears. "You may as well have fed him arsenic."

Lukas took my arm and gently guided me down the corridor. "I really think you need to get some sleep, my love."

When we reached the ward, I made him sit and watch Zachary while I lay on the bed. "Whatever you do, don't fall asleep," I warned him. "You have to watch him like a hawk. *Like. A. Hawk.*"

I heard my voice, horrible and shrill, and for a fleeting moment understood that I was truly bonkers from not sleeping, before the blind came down and I lost all perspective on my own behavior and everything else for that matter. "I'm serious," I said. "He could stop breathing at any moment. Remember the prediction, what it said?"

Lukas didn't acknowledge my remark. While I tried to sleep, he watched Zachary, but not as closely as I would have, not like the hawk I had asked him to be.

Five days later, without Lukas, Zachary and I flew back to London, holed up in our flat, and remained inside, venturing no further than the front doorstep, for the next six weeks. Lukas stayed on in Europe to finish the tour (there were too many livelihoods at stake to cancel) and without him around I fell into a wormhole. Zachary did not sleep for more than two hours at a time, three at the most, which meant that by the time I had put him down and drifted off to sleep, I never managed more than an hour or two in one go. I lost whole weeks to this relentless cycle of feeding

and changing and putting the baby down and working out
whether or not it was worth trying to sleep in between Zachary's naps or to hold out, white knuckled, until the slightly
longer sleep he may or may not have at the end of the day.
When we'd been up all night, the new day starting without
the last one ending, I would sometimes just curl up on the
floor in my dressing gown and howl along with Zachary.

Often I would think about leaving the house, and mentally start making a list of all the items I would need to take
with us, and how long I might be able to stay out for, but the
effort of actually doing any of it was too great, and I would
sit down, exhausted, and stare at the front door in defeat.
Lukas had arranged for one of the PAs at his record company to deliver groceries twice a week, and each time she
came to the door, laden with bags, and asked to see the
baby, I carried him out to her so she wouldn't be able to see
how disgusting it was inside the flat.

When Lukas came home he was shocked, but I couldn't
explain to him what was going on because I was so deranged
with tiredness that I could no longer speak in whole sen-
tences. He tried to hire a nanny to give me a break but on her
first day with us I refused to let her anywhere near Zachary.
"What if he cries?" I had protested. "How will you soothe
him? What are your qualifications? Do you have a criminal
record?" At the end of the day, she had thrown up her hands
in frustration. "I give up."

One day Fran came around in an attempt to stage what
I supposed was a kind of intervention—as though motherhood was only a temporary condition that I could just be

snapped out of. She brought champagne, *Vogue* magazine, a gram of cocaine. "Since when did you start doing that stuff?" I said when she cut it up in front of me and casually did a line. It was eleven in the morning. I had gone from having no idea what time it was to obsessively watching the clock, waiting for nap time or waiting for Zachary to wake up, my days measured in portions of sleep. Fran reached for the Moët and expertly defoiled it. "Go on," she said. "Zachary's asleep. By the time he wakes up, you'll be sober."

"It doesn't work like that," I said, gesturing to my breasts. "The booze hangs around in the milk."

"Nonsense," said Fran, picking up my glass and clinking it with hers. "One sip of this and you'll forget you even have a baby."

Fran had lost weight, not just puppy fat but half of her breasts and hips and the filling that puffed out her cheeks. Next to her I felt like a living doughnut, soft and lardy and filled with cream. Since the baby was born, I had put on weight, not lost it. To please Fran, I took a sip of the champagne but it tasted like turpentine and I spat it back into the glass.

In the next room, Zachary whimpered, and I got up to check on him. He was so pure, so innocent, and I wished that Fran, and her drugs, would leave.

Lukas and I had been told by the doctor not to have sex for six weeks after Zachary's birth but that date came and went without either of us even considering it. He started sleeping in the spare room so as not to disturb us when he got home late at night after recording—Cheatah had gone straight into the studio to cut a second album—and when that had finished, in June, he didn't come back to our bedroom. After a while I couldn't remember what had instigated the separate rooms or who it was meant to benefit, but the arrangement had become a habit. Our lives collided for only a few short hours in the middle of the day. Lukas would crawl out of bed to lie on the floor with Zachary, staring in wonderment at his smiling, cooing son, until Zachary cried or shat his pants, at which point Lukas would hand him back to me. I had tried to show him how to change a nappy or settle Zachary with a gentle swaying and rocking motion, but too much time passed between practice runs, and he forgot, or lost confidence, and Zachary sensed his fear, his uncertainty, and mirrored it back to him with his bellowing.

Lukas thought the answer was to get me on my own, to take me away from Zachary for a few days so we could be a couple again, but I couldn't understand why he wanted to go back to the old configuration when we had become something new and wonderful, a family.

Our first official family outing after Lukas returned from touring—and the first time I had left the house in six weeks—was a disastrous trip to the park that I'd had to force him into. He couldn't see the point of walking around a pond in the middle of the day. "Since when do we hang out in Regent's Park?"

"We might see a squirrel. Zachary can feed the ducks."

He was too young to do anything but lie on his back and stare at the trees in astonishment, but I had packed a picnic and spent hours gathering up items we might need for the

outing—spare nappies, burping cloths, wet-wipes, a change
of clothes, baby powder, an extra blanket. The stroller was
so weighed down it needed a Sherpa.

"Are you sure you want to do this?" said Lukas, eyeing
the load.

"But I never leave the house," I said, hearing the petu-
lance in my voice. "You don't know what it's like to stay
home all day."

"That's why I hired a nanny, to give you a break."

"But I don't want a break from Zachary. I want us to
spend time together as a family."

Lukas shoved the stroller roughly out the front door, letting me know that he would go along with what I wanted
but only under sufferance. I stood on the top step, squinting
in the sunshine, blinded by it, overcome with fatigue after
packing all our gear, and wishing I hadn't bothered.

In the park, people stared at Lukas, but I didn't think it
was for the reason he thought, which was that he was famous.
There was plenty to stare at in an ordinary gobsmacked way:
the crocodile-print spandex pants, the waist-length cork-
screw perm, the fact that a guy dressed like that was pushing
a baby in a stroller. But just in case, he put on his sunglasses
and scowled from behind them at passersby to let them know
he was off duty and did not wish to be disturbed.

We fed the ducks by holding a piece of bread in Zachary's
hand, then launching it out for him to the waiting birds, a pretense that fooled no one and made the ducks charge aggressively at our ankles, trying to hurry us up. We spread out the
picnic a safe distance from them, ate a couple of fish-paste

sandwiches, then were pelted with rain at the same moment
Zachary chose to shit his already urine-soaked pants.

In the old days, or even six months before, we might
have laughed at the awfulness of the outing, what a farce it
had been, but that day we couldn't. I was too sleep-deprived
to find anything funny, and Lukas had his mind on a whole
other life.

At night, when I could have slept for a few hours, I lay
awake fretting over Zachary, consumed with anxiety. His
existence defied the prediction but at the back of my mind
was the thought: *What if it's only temporary? What if sorrow is
yet to come?* With each passing day, I loved him a bit more, and
had more to lose. Wide-awake, crazed with insomnia, brood-
ing, I would remember what we had been taught on the commune about the dangers of manifesting thoughts. We'd had
it drummed into us to be careful not to dwell on our fears or
we would make them a reality. But the harder I tried to expel
my dark thoughts, the more persistent they became.

I shared none of this with Lukas, partly because I knew
what his reaction would be, and largely because he was
never there.

In early summer, when the leaves on the plane trees outside our window were as green and crisp as Granny Smiths,
he came home early one morning and climbed into bed with
me, something he hadn't done for months. It was just starting to get light outside. I smelled whiskey on his breath.
"Darling," he said, low and urgent. "Wake up."

The first thing I thought of was Zachary. "What's wrong?
Is he okay?"

"He's fine. Guess what? It's finished!"

"What is?"

"The album!"

"Oh." I collapsed back onto the pillow. "What time is it?"

"I don't know. Six maybe?"

I had only just fallen asleep again after a three A.M. feed. "That's great, darling," I said, but with little enthusiasm.

He left the room, and a little while later, the front door slammed. The noise woke up Zachary. It wasn't even six—it was five forty-five.

Five hours later, midmorning to a normal person, Lukas came back, took a shower, made a pot of coffee. "You know, we're having a playback this afternoon of the new record," he said, a box of birds. "You should come."

"To the studio?"

"Yeah, bring Zachary, it'll be fun. Everyone will be there."

In my head I quickly tried to work out if I had anything decent to wear that still fit me that I could also breast-feed in if I had to, then I started on calculating how we would travel to the studio, how long it would take, whether it would interfere with Zachary's feed times or nap, and if it did, whether he would be able to hold it together, before getting on to whether the slight pleasure of listening to Cheatah's new album would outweigh the inconveniences. "I don't know, babe. Maybe you should go without us?"

"We could go to the park afterward. Or to a restaurant—we haven't done that for ages. Zachary can sit on my lap."

He had played on my weakness, the rascal. "Okay," I said reluctantly. "But if it all turns to custard, I might have to leave."

"Of course. Whatever you want."

A smooth black car, not quite a limo, picked us up at four in the afternoon. Zachary had woken late from his nap and I had rushed his feed, pulling him off before he was finished. In the back of the car, I lifted up my shirt and tried again, much to the delight of the driver, who spent more time glancing in the rearview mirror than he did looking at the road ahead.

"You're not going to do that in the studio, are you?" said Lukas, looking worried.

"No way. That's why I'm doing it now—to get it out of the way."

"I'm sure we can find somewhere private, if you really need to."

"Thanks."

The car swerved to avoid a pedestrian, throwing us across the slippery backseat. Zachary popped off the breast, yelped as though someone had stuck a pin in him, then searched again for the nipple and bit down hard on it. "Ouch! Fuck. Sorry," I said, and Zachary looked at me as if to say, *Don't even think about doing that again.*

"You know you don't have to come," said Lukas. "If you don't want to."

"Do you want us to be there?" My voice was harried, shrill.

"Of course. But I can get the driver to take you home again, if it's too stressful."

"Don't be silly," I said, brightly despairing. "I really want to hear the new record. Tell me what it's called."

"*Cover Me in Sugar.*"

"Cover you in sugar?"

"It's a reference to female ejaculation."

"Yeah, I think I get that."

By the time we arrived at the studio, Zachary was a human milkshake. In a flash of fatherly pride, Lukas insisted on carrying him in so he could present him to his friends, but even as we made our way across the lobby, a snail trail of white goo escaped from Zachary's mouth. He sucked it back in, miraculously, and we pressed on into the lift, which whooshed up to the eighteenth floor with rocketlike speed. It was so fast that my own stomach yawned, and I glanced at Zachary, who answered with a tiny burp. *Good—a burp is good. Air escaping.*

We were late. Marlon, Serena, Vince, Alan, and Fran, their expressions anxious, and some men in suits whom I didn't recognize and wasn't introduced to, were seated on long leather couches, waiting for us; Spike was there too, looking, as always, fidgety and smug.

Apart from Fran, no one had met Zachary yet, and I thought at least someone might be interested in meeting him now, but I was wrong. He was ignored, and so was I. If being pregnant had rendered me embarrassing, unfunny, mute, then having the baby had granted me the cloak of invisibility. Or maybe they were just nervous about the record. It stung to be overlooked, but I was also relieved. I had been worrying about what I would say to these people if they asked me how I was or what I had been doing all day.

I settled into the corner of the couch furthest away from the playback speakers with Zachary on my lap. He had started making the baby-lamb noise that led to his either falling asleep or working up to an almighty fuss.

We got through the first track okay, though I barely noticed the music coming from the speakers. When the track finished, instead of moving on to the next one, Marlon conferred with Lukas behind his hand, then walked over to the playback machine and switched it off. Lukas had his back to me, but I could see he was agitated, sweating. With no explanation, Marlon left the room, followed by Lukas. After they had gone, no one discussed the song we had just heard, but there was some discreet shrugging among the executives, and Zachary kept up his chorus. Then Fran and one of the executives started exchanging heated whispers, careful to keep their voices low so the rest of us wouldn't hear.

After about five minutes, Marlon and Lukas came back into the room, big smiles on their faces—too big—and the atmosphere in the studio lifted to match.

"Guys," said one of the suits, "we were just saying how fantastic the new stuff sounds. Love the direction you've taken it in. Really sharp, really fresh."

"Let's get on with it, shall we?" said Lukas.

When the next track started, I paid more attention, but I couldn't believe I was listening to the same thing as everyone else. Underneath the usual screeching guitars and driving bass was some kind of acid house beat. I didn't know rave music very well but I'd seen a news item on illegal dance parties and what reporters had been calling the Second Summer of Love. I listened more carefully, glancing at the drummer, Alan. He was staring at his shoes, looking shifty. Clearly, the acid house had not been his idea. Zachary didn't like it either. He curled up his fists, screwed up his face, and as the track reached what I supposed was the bridge, he opened his mouth, not to scream, but to let a torrent of curdled milk and saliva pour from his mouth. There was perhaps a cupful and it went all over him, all over me, all over the shiny red leather couch. When I tried to clean it up with the burp cloth, it came away in long, viscous threads.

No noise had accompanied the reflux but in a matter of seconds we switched from invisibility to the focus of everyone's horrified attention. Five or six adults jettisoned themselves off the couch to get away from us, away from the sick, while others checked their clothing for trails of white slime.

None of these adults helped us or followed us out of the studio, and we had made it down to the lobby and called a mini cab before even Lukas arrived at our side. "What just happened?" he said, looking flustered.

"You didn't see? Zachary spewed his guts out. I should never have fed him in the cab."

"You fed him in the cab?"

"Yes. You were there."

Lukas rubbed his cheek absentmindedly. He had been like that so often lately—present in body but not in mind, his brain down the road, having a pint.

I said, "Darling, what's wrong? Is it the record?"

"We worked so hard on this one." He looked down at his feet. "I really thought we had nailed it."

Rid of the milkshake, Zachary had fallen asleep in my arms, his head at a wonky angle, his cheek and mouth squashed together. Lukas was waiting for me to reassure him but all I could think of was that if Zachary slept now, in the cab, he wouldn't sleep later, at home, and I would spend the next four or five hours listening to him grizzling and squawking unhappily.

"It sounded great," I said, reaching for a compliment, and hopelessly paraphrasing one of the executives. "I love the new direction—it's so sharp, so fresh. I've never heard anything like it before." That last part, at least, was from the heart.

"I'm sure you're right," said Lukas, but I could tell that he didn't believe me, that he didn't trust my opinion.

The record came out three weeks later and it was an even bigger hit across Northern Europe than the last one. In West Germany it went straight to number one. Teenage girls queued up around the block the morning it was released, and some stores sold out within hours of opening. But in England, the album tanked. Not only that, the reviews were savage—so bad that I had to start hiding newspapers and magazines from Lukas, because each one plunged him into a cataclysmic funk. Even hard rock magazine *Kerrang!* had been unkind. The worst was in the *Guardian,* read by millions, not just music fans. Lukas got me to scan it first to see how terrible it was, and reading it in front of him, I felt sick.

When I got to the end of the column, I went back to the

beginning, hoping to find something positive. But the second read was worse. I had missed some of the sarcasm.

"Well?" said Lukas.

Was there anything I could say that wouldn't make it worse?

"The guy who wrote this is a jerk," I offered. "He's more interested in sounding clever than in reviewing your record. Don't even read it." I tossed the thing aside, to emphasize it wasn't worth the paper it was printed on.

Lukas retrieved it immediately, flipped straight to the review. I couldn't watch him read it and got up to make a coffee. When I came back, he was staring grimly ahead of him, eyes flickering with murderous thoughts.

He said, "Listen to this: 'If the Eurovision Song Contest had a Hair Metal Rave category, then this lot would take out the prize . . .'"

"Isn't that sort of a compliment?"

He continued. "' . . . but because it doesn't, it's hard to know what the audience is for this abomination of an album, which satisfies neither the appetite for destruction of the leather and lace set, nor the baggy trouser brigade's craving for beats without bombast.'"

There was nothing safe left to say, so I said nothing.

Lukas went into the bathroom, locked the door, punched it, cussed his head off, then fell silent. I thought about going in, trying to console him, but his anger frightened me. Wasn't it wiser to leave a rattlesnake alone? I would wait until he had cooled down. Besides, any minute, Zachary would wake from his morning nap, interrupting any headway I'd made with Lukas. I could already hear him bouncing his legs on the mattress and snuffling.

When Lukas came out of the bathroom ten minutes later, I was stuck in a chair, feeding the baby. He looked defeated, and hunted around for his keys and wallet, preparing to go out.

"Can you wait," I said, "until Zachary's finished?"

"I have to be somewhere," he said vaguely. "A photo shoot."

"When will you be home?"

"I don't know. Later."

When he left the flat, taking the tense atmosphere with him, part of me was glad. It was easier to focus on the needs of one human, not two. I gazed at Zachary, his tiny mouth slurping away, demanding nothing more from me than milk on tap and around-the-clock devotion.

For the first time since Zachary's birth, I thought about the way we had been brought up on the commune, passed from lap to lap, our parents giving up their rights to care for their own children. I didn't understand how they could have done that, how they could stand it, as though it was no more complicated than sharing clothes or food. The feelings I had toward Zachary were fiercely possessive and exclusive. I did not feel disposed to sharing him with anyone, not even Lukas.

Cheatah were booked to appear at the summer rock festivals across Europe—headlining the German ones, novelty side act in England—and the band had started rehearsing to play the new album live. Lukas was depressed about the whole enterprise. As the first tour date approached I saw less and less of him, and it was difficult to map the terrain of his moods. Sometimes he just seemed exhausted, physically wrung out from the effort of learning to play so many new songs. I would ask him a question—"How was rehearsal?" or "Do you think Zachary has put on weight?"—and he would carry on mouthing lyrics or practicing a pose in the mirror, unaware that I had spoken. As time went on, I got better at recognizing when he was distracted, and stopped trying to communicate with him. Whole days went by without a conversation between us, let alone hugs or kisses or any form of touch.

In high summer, something happened that brought us closer together, and for a few brief moments I had hope. It was a week or so before Lukas was due to go off on tour, and Zachary came down with a rogue fever, his temperature so high that the GP took one look at him and dispatched us to the hospital emergency room. His breathing was labored, a grunting noise, not babyish at all, and he alternated this with bouts of distressed, high-pitched screaming. He was admitted immediately, his symptoms closely monitored while they tried to work out what was wrong. Two or three baffled doctors examined him before one of them finally suggested a chest X-ray. I had called Lukas from a pay phone in the lobby, Zachary drooping from my hip. The phone receiver was warm and smelled of other people's spittle. I held it far from my ear, making it hard to hear Lukas on the other end. "Saint Mary's Hospital children's ward, third floor," I repeated, my voice loud and unhinged.

"Got that," said Lukas, or maybe, "What's that?" and I hung up. Zachary had started screaming again.

In the emergency ward, Zachary was placed in a cot with steel bars, a tiny jail cell. He looked small and forlorn and I picked him up, drawing him to my chest, where he whimpered, continuously, even in sleep. The doctors said I shouldn't hold him all the time—it would only raise his temperature—but I couldn't stand putting him down, letting go of him for even a few minutes. He wasn't hungry, wouldn't feed, and milk leaked from my breasts and pooled in the folds of my bra.

How long had we been waiting? I had lost all sense of time or of anything existing outside the hospital. Under my breath, I began praying, cutting deals with all the gods I did not normally believe in to please save my child. I was ready to trade anything to reverse the prediction, to avoid the sorrow that was heading our way.

Lukas, every bit as sick with worry as I was, arrived just as we were about to be taken in to have the X-ray. We clutched each other's hands for the first time in months, and when I met his gaze I saw, for a second, the old Lukas, *my* Lukas, the one I had grown up with, eager and warm and loving.

"He's going to be all right, isn't he?" I said, leaning my face against his.

"He survived a fall down the stairs—he's a fighter."

The nurse took Zachary and stripped off his clothes. Still in his nappy, she placed him in a plastic weighing bowl, where he curled up his legs and whined, trying to keep himself warm. Then she picked him up and placed him upright on a metal plate. He was too young to sit up on his own, and she had to prop him up while the doctor buckled him into a medieval torture device—two clear plastic plates that molded around his torso and the tops of his legs, and cupped the rolls of his chin. He squirmed and kicked to get out, and then when he couldn't he started screaming, a noise that was heart wrenching to listen to.

I lurched across the linoleum toward him but the nurse ordered me back behind the safety screen, where Lukas had to restrain me. "It breaks my heart too," he whispered, "but they're trying to help him."

I turned away and buried my head in Lukas's chest, finding some of the old warmth there. How long had it been since we had turned to each other for comfort?

In his plastic box, Zachary was wheeled into the X-ray machine and zapped, once, twice; green lightning lit up the room, and then it was over. He was wheeled back to us, unbuckled from the torture device, and handed over to me to soothe and dress. In my arms he was meek and droopy, his energy spent.

Back in the cubicle, waiting for the X-ray results, Lukas held on to Zachary and me as though his survival depended on it.

"From now on," he said, "I want us to be together."

"How?" I said. "You can't change what you do."

Zachary had fallen into a deep sleep, exhausted by his ordeal, and Lukas stroked his cheek. "I'd walk away from the band in a heartbeat, if I could."

"Really?"

"Every time we play, I'm up there onstage and I feel like the world is laughing at us." He pinged the spandex of his leopard-skin pants, which he wore even on his days off. "Look at me. I'm a joke. I'm in a fucking joke band."

I agreed with him, but I couldn't say it. "Why don't you just leave, if you hate it that much?"

"I don't know how to do anything else. And now I've got a family to support."

I hadn't thought about this consequence of having a baby, that it would end up contributing to Lukas's unhappiness.

The doctor arrived with a large manila envelope and took out an X-ray, which he held up to the light. "This lung," he said, pointing to one side of Zachary's tiny rib cage, "is perfectly clear. But this one on the right has spots of pneumonia."

"Pneumonia?" Just the day before, Zachary had been in bouncing good health. "How did he catch pneumonia in the middle of summer?"

"We can't tell if the infection started from bacteria or a virus, but we'll get him started on antibiotics, just in case."

"Does he need to stay overnight?"

"It isn't necessary," said the doctor. "But if you're nervous about taking him home, I can see if we've got a spare bed for you both."

Nervous? I had burned through so much adrenaline there was none left. I glanced at Lukas to see what he thought, and he just shrugged. "Up to you."

"I'd like to stay if we can," I said to the doctor. "I don't feel comfortable taking him home."

Zachary and I stayed in the children's ward overnight, even though his condition improved immediately, once the antibiotics kicked in. Watching his rapid recovery, I remembered how on the commune, when one of us was sick, the women had run through every remedy in a large, white book of natural healing before anyone was taken to the doctor. Most of the time, they were successful. We didn't get sick much; the commune was too isolated. But every now and then, someone came down with an illness that seemed to worsen with each herbal poultice or potion. When Meg was eight or nine she had cut her toe open on a piece of glass from a beer bottle that had washed up on the beach, and the skin around the wound turned shiny and red before her whole leg swelled up as though it might burst. After a night of vomiting and high fevers, she was bundled into the Land Rover and driven to Whitianga, where she was pronounced to be moments away from septicemia, which would have killed her, the doctor said. One helicopter ride later, she was in the children's hospital in Auckland, where she remained for a week. She had come home with mythical tales of rainbow Jell-O and vats of ice cream for dessert every night, and for months afterward, all of us kids had been on the lookout for broken beer bottles, in case we could catch a swollen leg and eat Jell-O and ice cream too.

When Zachary and I came home from the hospital in a taxi, Lukas wasn't there, but he had thoughtfully stocked the fridge with groceries and left flowers and a scribbled note on the table. The note said he was sorry but they were stepping up rehearsals ahead of the tour. He would try to be home for dinner. He hadn't made it home for dinner in months, so after Zachary had gone to sleep that night, I overlooked the word "try" and busied myself making a meal out of what Lukas had put in the fridge, a mismatched assortment of lettuce and parsnips, lamb chops and Camembert cheese. Chopping and dicing, sautéing and grilling, I felt a surge of optimism. If I made a good meal, if I was a better wife, more supportive, Lukas might come home more often and we could turn things around. As much as the band was to blame for taking Lukas away from us, I could see that I hadn't given him much of a reason to come home.

I set the table for dinner and put on what I hoped, in my doughy condition, was a sexy dress.

Eight in the evening came and went, and after it, nine and ten. The salad had dried out; the lamb was a Roman sandal. I ate my portion and covered Lukas's with tinfoil. I still thought he might come home to eat, but I was too tired to wait up any longer. Zachary had settled into something like a routine, waking once in the night for a feed and getting up at six A.M.—hardly restful—but there was still no guarantee that I would be able to sleep in between. I had gotten used to sleep deprivation, to spending my days in a fog, but every now and then, when I did get a good night's sleep, I felt so energetic, so *euphoric,* that I realized how rubbish I felt all the rest of the time.

The night of the uneaten dinner, I didn't hear Lukas come home, but when Zachary woke at two A.M. for a feed, he was in bed next to me, and I got a fright. He hadn't slept there in months. He was in such a deep sleep that he didn't even stir when Zachary chirped with elation all through his nappy change at six fifteen.

In the morning, *his* morning, which started much later than ours, Lukas found the dinner I had made. He felt so bad that he insisted on eating it for breakfast, a sweet gesture but one that was hard to carry through. The salad was brown, the lamb chops congealed with fat. I couldn't stand to watch.

"Please," I said. "You don't have to do that."

He forced down another mouthful. "But you went to so much trouble."

I took away the plate. "Why don't I make you something else?"

"Why don't I take you out for lunch? We could go somewhere flash—that place in Knightsbridge, what's it called?"

"Are you kidding?" I fast-forwarded to Zachary pulling silverware off white linen tablecloths, wailing between itsy-bitsy courses. The meal would be wasted on me. And why sit in a restaurant when you could be outdoors? Zachary had made a swift recovery, went my train of mad thoughts, but the fresh air would do him good. "Why don't we go to Richmond Park? Zachary would love the animals."

Lukas knifed his leftovers into the bin, put his plate by the sink, then came over and knelt beside me. "I don't have time for a day trip. Only lunch."

"We could go somewhere closer to home."

"Sorry, babe." He planted a kiss on my forehead. "They're expecting me in the studio. Another time?"

Zachary and I went to the park on our own, and I took off his terrycloth romper and nappy and let him lie on his back in the nude. Soft, dappled light played across his face as he gazed into the tree above him, blowing raspberries and warbling, each note as clear as birdsong. I wished Lukas was present to hear the lovely noise, but as with so many of the tiny marvels that had occurred since Zachary's birth, I was the only witness.

CHAPTER 14

London
1989

ON THE MORNING OF departure for the European tour, the suitcases were out, the cab was due in an hour, and Lukas couldn't find his passport anywhere. I had tried to be a good housewife, to make sure his eight or nine pairs of leather pants were dry-cleaned, and these he flung into three suitcases, along with armfuls of cropped tank tops, long fringed scarves, studded dog collars, high-heeled boots, fingerless lace gloves, chunky silver chains, and miniature fishnet vests. There was even a studded leather G-string that I hoped was not a costume for the stage. "Will you be warm enough?" I said, with wifely concern, when the last of these cases had been forcefully zipped up.

"Isn't that what bourbon's for?"

"Oh, darling, that's for cleaning your teeth."

He had been dreading the tour, the nightly humiliation, but now that it was about to begin, I could tell he was also a teeny bit excited. It was fun to hang out in a gang, to dress up in silly costumes, to travel all over Europe with your mates. That was one of the reasons I didn't want to go with him—the vibe when they were together was so clannish. But he wanted us to go. He begged us to go. He said if he knew Zachary and I were waiting for him back in his hotel room each night, he could stand it, the ordeal of performance. But each time he asked, I had come up with a new set of excuses. *You'll be too busy to spend time with us, and I don't fancy hanging out in a hotel room on my own with a baby. Zachary will take a few days to settle in each place and before he does, we'll move on. The change of time zones, the baby gear we'd have to take, I have nothing to wear. His routine would turn pear-shaped.* And the unspoken fear that if the hotel was a skyscraper, Zachary might fall out a window (there was no end to the sorrows my mind could invent). My reasons were so numerous and stubborn that I barely considered why Lukas was so adamant that we come—why maybe he *needed* us with him.

Just as Lukas found his passport, the cab arrived, and sat, idling, on the curb while we said our farewells. I had kept Zachary up past his usual nap time, and he sat on my hip, grizzling.

"Are you sure you won't come?" said Lukas. "Go on—you could meet us halfway through the tour. You could fly to Berlin with Zachary."

For a few seconds, I entertained the idea of jumping on a plane like the free-spirited Bohemian I was not and never would be. Underneath all my excuses was a layer of plain old terror. I thought if we stayed at home, I could at least keep Zachary safe. "I'll think about it," I said, to placate him.

"You will?"

"Sure. I'll talk to a travel agent on Monday."

He kissed me on the lips and fluffed the wisps on Zachary's head while the driver honked his horn. Lukas's hand was bony, veins showing through his skin. When had he lost so much weight? He was cold to the touch when we hugged, as though his pilot light had gone out, but his energy levels were high, and he took the stairs two at a time, as he always did, even when there was no rush. At the cab door, he turned around and saluted us good-bye.

"Good-bye," I said, waving back, and taking Zachary's fat, coiled fist and waving that at him too. "We'll miss you!"

The first week he was away, Lukas rang us every day without fail. The second week he skipped a call or two and on the occasions he did call, he sounded tired and distracted, and was hard to draw out, as though he was calling us out of habit when really he had nothing to say. I felt our connection slipping again and didn't know how to get it back. Lukas seemed to need my physical presence or he forgot I was there for him, forgot I was his wife. We were so different that way. If anything, I felt surer of my love for him when he was away. In absence I was clear that I loved him whereas he felt abandoned, as though I had left him, or he had lost me, and it wasn't just a temporary separation.

From time to time, if I hadn't heard from Lukas for longer than a few days, I would call one of the hotels on his itinerary and ask for him, or for Fran, if the band members were checked in under false names. In most places that wasn't necessary, but in certain cities—Düsseldorf, Cologne,

Zurich—they were superstars, and they'd had trouble with fans ringing the hotel and being put through to their rooms. Some had gone further, dressing up as hotel porters and trying to deliver room service.

On this particular date the band's itinerary said they were in West Berlin (fewer fans) and the hotel receptionist put me straight through. Lukas picked up the phone after two rings but didn't recognize my voice or know where he was. When I told him, he said, "No, it looks like Helsinki."

"But I just called the number for the Berlin hotel. The woman who answered spoke German."

"Well, if you know where I am, why did you ask?"

I took a breath. He wasn't trying to be mean, he was just tired. "How was the concert last night?"

"We had the night off."

"That's great. I bet you needed it."

"It's a waste of time. I'd rather play. Get this thing over with. Go home."

What could I say that would cheer him up? The baby would wake soon. We didn't have long. "Zachary put his foot in his mouth today."

Lukas didn't say anything. He was lighting a cigarette.

"One minute he was playing with it, the next he was chewing on his big toe."

"Cool."

"He was so pleased with himself."

"I miss him so much."

"He misses you too. We both do."

"He probably doesn't know who I am." He sounded so morose.

"Of course he does." In the next room, a bleat from Zachary, and my breasts needled, the milk letting down. Lukas muffled the receiver while he talked to someone who had come into his hotel room. When they left, he said, "Sorry, that was Fran. We've got a radio interview in ten minutes. I haven't even had a shower yet."

"You better find out where you are."

"Berlin," said Lukas. "You were right."

"I have to go, anyway. Zachary's up."

"What time is it there?"

"Two thirty."

"You should see a dentist about that."

"Har har. Very funny."

Tooth hurty was one of his favorite puns, and I felt reassured by it. "I love you," I said into the receiver, attached by plastic spiral wire to an old avocado-green rotary phone that we had inherited with the flat. I had been meaning to get one with push buttons that would be easier to dial when my hands were full. Lukas hadn't replied yet. Had the line gone dead? "Are you there, darling? I love you."

"I hope so," he said, then hung up.

The dial tone wasn't one I was used to, and even though Zachary's bleat rose quickly to an angry, high-pitched cry, I held the phone to my ear for a long time after Lukas had hung up, wondering why he had said that, and none of the reasons I came up with were good. When I tried calling him back, I couldn't get through.

I rang a travel agent and booked a flight to Cologne, leaving in three days' time. The next day, Lukas didn't call, and the day after that, someone else did—the receptionist at the record company. She was very young, her voice stuck in a chirpy register, no matter the news she delivered. For this reason, I took a while to take on board her message.

"Wait. Slow down. He did what?"

"He, um, overdosed!" she said, practically singing.

"What kind of overdose? Is he okay?"

"I don't know. They found him in his room."

"Where is he now?"

"I don't know. I just got told to give you this number." She had to repeat the number three times. My hand wouldn't write it down. Dialing it took another three shots. A German man answered. He spoke no English, but even if he had, he would not have understood my gibberish. He fetched his supervisor.

I finally got Fran on the line, but she had gone into public relations overdrive, and her answers were all smoke and mirrors. "Poppy, relax. He's fine. It isn't a real tour unless someone gets hospitalized with exhaustion. This time it was Lukas."

"Exhaustion? Is that what you call an overdose?"

"Who told you that?"

"The girl from the record company—Tina? Gina? I can't remember her name."

"Fucking Tina," said Fran. "She can't even send a fax without screwing it up."

"Fran," I said. "My husband's in the hospital. Don't lie to me."

"Don't have a cow, babe. He took one too many prescription tranquilizers—that's all."

"What was he taking those for?"

"All the guys do. It helps them wind down after a show." This was news to me.

"Who found him?"

"Marlon, Vincent, one of the guys—does it matter? The main thing is he's fine."

"It matters to me. Can I speak to him?"

"Not right now," she said. "He's sleeping."

"When he wakes up, tell him I'll be there tonight. That I'm on my way."

"I don't know if that's such a . . ." She paused. "Suit yourself. And by the way, if anyone asks, we're saying exhaustion, brought on by the laryngitis."

"Lukas had laryngitis?"

"No, it's just what you say."

The conversation left a bad taste. *What happens on tour stays on tour,* and I wasn't on the tour. To Fran, I was no better than the press, someone to be fobbed off and lied to.

The last flight to Cologne out of Heathrow left at midnight. Zachary was wired, his eyeballs on stalks, even after the plane took off and the narcotic hum of the aircraft set in. He stared at me, tripping on the unfamiliar surroundings, and I stared back, trying not to look as bleak as I felt.

We arrived at Cologne airport in the middle of the night and took a taxi to the hotel they were staying at, an austere L-shaped block of concrete and glass. In the lobby bar, a few of the band, plus roadies and hangers-on, swilled cocktails, their laughter raucous and loud. Fran was there too, in white-fringed boots, red leather hot pants, and a spangled boob tube, her bloodshot eyes ringed with black. When she saw us, she came over, while the others carried on drinking.

"It's been an absolute bloody nightmare," she said, slurring her words a little. "Reporters on the front step, following us everywhere. It couldn't have happened in a worse place. They're royalty here."

"How is he?"

"Oh, he's fine. Sleeping it off." She stubbed out her cigarette in a metal bowl filled with sand and her hands butterflied around for something else to do. She was thin and glossy, her makeup so thick you'd have had to take it off with a chisel. She had always been tough but now she was also hard. "I'll take you up to his room."

"Thanks. Do you know if the hotel has any cots? We'll need one."

"Shit," said Fran. "Are you all going to sleep in the same room?"

"Where else would we sleep?"

"It might not be such a good idea—not after what happened. Lukas needs to rest. They're playing tomorrow night."

"*Tomorrow* night? Lukas overdosed and he gets one day off?"

"Shhhh," said Fran. "Keep it down. It was laryngitis, remember?"

"Even if it was that he'd have to rest."

"Relax, it's not that serious."

When we reached the room, she came in with us and

fussed about, filling a glass of water by the bed, fluffing Lukas's pillow, checking supplies in the minibar—I wasn't sure what he'd need that for. He was dead to the world. Fran leaned against the wall, watching him, watching us settle in.

"I can take over now," I said. "Just tell me your room number. In case we need anything."

"I'm right next door. But I won't be there for a while."

"Will you be downstairs, in the bar?"

"We talked about going to a club."

"I'll call reception if we come unstuck."

"Sure," said Fran, finally heading for the door. After she had opened it, she turned and said, "Oh. One more thing."

"Yes?"

"If the phone rings, don't answer it." She lowered her voice. "*Reporters.*"

Zachary had been red faced and wailing for most of the plane trip but since touching down, perversely, he had conked out. He didn't even stir when the cot arrived and he was tucked into the stiff, unfamiliar sheets. He would wake in an hour or two, when he was hungry, but there was no use trying to feed him now.

I lay down on the bed, next to Lukas. He was in a deep, convalescent sleep, the sort that can go on for days and that you wake from in a sweat, feeling desolate. His hair was damp at the temples, his face pallid. I put my hand on his forehead to check his temperature. He felt cold, slightly clammy.

On the bedside table, next to the glass of water, were a host of prescription pill bottles. Most of the labels were in German, but I recognized the word "Valium." I had seen those in his toilet bag before, after a trip, and he had told me they helped him relax. Taking him at his word, I had said, "Just make sure to keep them out of Zachary's reach."

I climbed under the sheets and blanket, and wriggled closer to my husband, then closer still. His breath was stinky, as though he hadn't cleaned his teeth, even with bourbon, for a week. When I was near enough to hear his breathing, to hear if it stopped, I shut my eyes. If I managed a half-hour nap before Zachary woke up, I'd be lucky. I had been dozing for a few minutes, maybe ten at the most, when Lukas stirred. I had not been properly asleep and was instantly alert. "Hi," I said softly, near his ear.

He sighed, more asleep than awake, and said, "Where have you been?"

"I got here as quickly as I could but it took ages, I'm sorry."

"You were going to come straight back."

"I was?"

"Yeah. You said it wouldn't take long to get it."

"To get what?"

"Fran, babe, I'm too tired for this."

"Lukas?"

He opened his eyes and looked at me, and I could tell, in the few seconds before he spoke, that I was not the person he had been expecting to see—or the person he had thought he was talking to. "Poppy, my love, when did you get here?"

"Lukas—just before—you said 'Fran.'"

"Did I?"

"You thought I was Fran. You were waiting for her."

"I meant you," said Lukas. "I was waiting for *you*."

"Bullshit," I said, my head spinning with jet lag, confusion, and months of accumulated sleep deprivation. "You wanted her to come back to bed—not me."

"Poppy—don't do this. I don't even know what day it is."

"It's the middle of the night," I said, getting up from the bed and turning on the bedside lamp. "It's a Tuesday. You're in Cologne, you're fucking your manager, and just so you know, your band is so naff it's a crime against music."

Lukas winced. In the light, he looked worse, his lips chapped and skin yellow. He tried to sit up but he was too weak. "Don't go," he croaked. "I can explain."

But I had already gathered up my things, and now I reached into the cot for Zachary. He was in a deep sleep and had been sweating so profusely that even the outermost layer of his clothing was damp. I would change him in the lobby, or in the back of a cab. At the door of the hotel room, I hesitated. Was there any point in reminding Lukas that as a couple we were doomed? Turning to face him for what I imagined to be the last time, I said, "I thought we could outrun it but we can't."

PART III

CHAPTER 15

Gaialands
1989

WE CAUGHT THE FERRY to Coromandel from Auckland, bypassing the roads and landing on the wharf with the fishermen's catch. It was the beginning of September, that time of year when fierce sunshine can give way to squalls of freezing-cold rain in a matter of minutes. I had been forever removing layers of Zachary's clothing, then scrambling to put them back on, then taking them off, and so on. More than once, in the middle of one of these absurd costume changes, I had burst into tears, a reminder, in case I needed it, that I was barely holding it together. If anything, the crying jags had gotten worse since we had touched down in New Zealand, as if I had saved it all up until I reached home soil.

We had not dallied long in Auckland, half a day, and disembarking from the ferry in Coromandel, my first thought was that we had traveled back in time. The former gold-rush town, with its gabled storefronts and old-time saloons, had always been old fashioned. But now, after six years in London, I noticed how dilapidated it was, the once-quaint buildings falling apart and plastered with ugly signs for beer and fishing tackle. Everything was waterlogged, battened down against the weather, and above the settlement the green-black hills glowered with the threat of more rain.

In town, luck was on our side. Huddled in the Four Square supermarket with Zachary, trying to keep dry, I overheard a man in Swanndri and gumboots talking to the store owner about the state of the 309 Road, which he wanted to drive over.

"It's open," said the store owner, "but I'd take it easy on the corners if I were you, mate."

"No worries," said the man in gumboots. "That sounds about right."

I asked him if we could get a lift, and when he saw how young my baby was, he insisted on taking us all the way to the gate of Gaialands. He had heard of the commune, and even had a rough idea where it was.

"So it's still there then?"

"I expect so, love. Coromandel's the only place left for hippies."

The man said he was a farmer. He had come to Coromandel to pick up a part for his tractor. He cleared the passenger seat and buckled us in, renegade style, with Zachary strapped across my chest. The only other option would have been to sit in the tray with his dog.

The ute climbed the steep ridge of bush-covered hills that formed the backbone of the Coromandel Peninsula.

The gravel road was wet and slippery, and I wished we could turn back. I hadn't been in touch with anyone from the commune since we had taken off all those years ago, and my attempt to reach them from London had drawn a blank—no listing, no phone number. I had assumed they'd still be there, but what if they weren't?

Around the next bend, we came to a section of the road with a bite out of it, where a chunk of asphalt and concrete had crumbled off and washed down the hillside. The stretch of road that remained did not look wide enough to drive over but the farmer kept going, leaning forward in his seat to better see out the windscreen. As we inched along the narrow section of road, I made the mistake of looking down into the crevasse of dripping punga ferns, which ended somewhere far below in darkness and the roaring sound of water.

"Poor buggers in Te Aroha," said the farmer, wiping his brow once he had safely navigated the cutaway road. "House got washed away—and everyone in it. They found the six-year-old up in a tree. She was all right."

"And the others?"

"Still missing."

It was like this every year. Parts of the country took turns being victims of biblical flooding, or in really bad years, flooding and earthquakes. There had been a bad one in the Bay of Plenty while we were away—bad enough to make it to the English newspapers. This year, flooding only. At least the water tanks will be full, we would say.

We made it through the hills, and the landscape flattened out, shaggy fields interspersed with patches of knotty, unkempt bush. Here and there were clumps of beehives, the drawers painted in pastel colors to attract the bees.

Around another bend was the tiny shop that marked the entrance to Gaialands. At the sight of the wonky letterbox, the swinging wooden sign with its curly hand-painted letters, I nearly cried with relief. It was so familiar, so unchanged, exactly as I hoped it would be. On our way down the bumpy driveway, my heart expanded with anticipation.

We passed the workshop, where a man in silhouette—was it Paul?—tinkered on a tractor engine. He looked up as we drove past, but I couldn't see his face. The kitchen hut came into view, and a woman was out the back, hanging up washing. When we got closer, I saw it was Katrina. She had hacked off her long, auburn hair, except for a plaited wisp that ran down her back. She scowled at the approaching ute for a moment before her expression changed to one of pure joy.

By the time we had parked by the meetinghouse, in a patch of overgrown dandelions, she was running down to meet us. She pulled open the passenger door of the ute and leaned in.

"Poppy! It *is* you." She clocked Zachary and squealed with delight. "Oh my goodness! A grandchild!" She reached in and took the baby off me, holding him in the air so she could get a good look at him.

"Katrina, meet Zachary," I said.

She leaned over to kiss me on the cheek, then changed her mind and went for a full hug, squashing the baby between us. "Come here, girl. It's so good to see you."

One by one the adults appeared from the fields, orchards, and outbuildings and gathered in a little group around us. Susie, Hunter, Paul, Sigi, Tom, Loretta—they were all just as delighted to see us as Katrina had been. Zachary was passed around and marveled at, winning each heart with his bashful smile.

I was taken aback by how warm and open they all were, so different from the yuppies we had left behind in London. If they had ever been miffed about us all abandoning the commune, they didn't show it—just as I was confounded by how pleased I was to be back.

Once Zachary and I had been hugged by everyone and made to feel welcome beyond any doubt, we all went into the mess hut for herbal tea and a slice of the raw date loaf I had been told was cake as a child. It tasted worse than I remembered—a dense log of bark and brown goo.

I had prepared what to say, if they inquired about Lukas, but other than confirming Zachary was his son, they didn't pry, though there must have been so much they wanted to know. I was surprised to see them all enjoying downtime in the middle of the day—they had always been so busy, so industrious—but they were older now, and there weren't so many mouths to feed, so it made sense they had slowed down.

Zachary fell asleep on Katrina's lap. Sitting in the simple mess hut, with its worn wooden floor and wholesome smell of oats, I let go a little, and allowed myself to relax for the first time since he had been born.

I noticed, around this time, that I hadn't seen Elisabeth.

Of course she might have gone for the day, or been working in an outlying field, but I thought someone would have fetched her by now. And then there was the cake: she never would have made one *that* bad.

"Where's Elisabeth?" I asked. "Is she away?"

With apprehension, a few of them glanced at Hunter.

"Elisabeth left Gaialands," he said. "It was not long after the last of you children had gone."

"She left when we did? But—" I was going to add "But she didn't even like us," then stopped myself. "What happened?"

Hunter cleared his throat. "She had her reasons, I'm sure."

"Your poor father," said Katrina. "She left without a word. Just packed up and left in the middle of the night. A friend picked her up."

"Where did she go?"

"We don't know," said Loretta. "The city, maybe?"

"The worst of it," said Tom, "was that she took her bloody recipes with her." He held up a glob of cake. "No offense, ladies, but the grub round here hasn't been the same since."

"Feel free to step into the kitchen," said Susie, teasing. "There's plenty of room for one of you buggers."

"No, no," said Tom. "I know when to stay out of it. The last thing we need is to burn down the kitchen."

Everyone laughed, but underneath the friendly banter was a hint of tension that I did not remember being there before. In the old days, the women had known their place, which was in the nursery, laundry, or kitchen, and they had certainly never made jokes above or about their station. Perhaps it wasn't the women who had changed so much as Hunter. He had once been a bear of a man, fearsome to us kids, but since then he'd shrunk, or had the stuffing knocked out of him, and he seemed less intimidating, docile even. And hadn't Katrina openly referred to him as my father? That would never have happened before.

Susie patted Hunter's arm to get his attention. "I wonder if your girlfriend will visit this year?"

"She's not my girlfriend," said Hunter. "She's just a dear friend."

Susie winked at me. "Just a friend, eh? A dear friend who sleeps in your hut?"

The women laughed heartily, and Hunter stood up, clearing his throat and clumsily gathering up the dishes we had used. He would never have stood for being mocked in days gone by, and I waited for him to give the women a ticking off, but he didn't. When he had left, Susie leaned over and whispered in my ear. "Ever since Elisabeth left, he's had annual visits from Shakti. You remember her, don't you?"

"A little," I said, though the opposite was true.

"Turns out she isn't a dyke anymore," said Susie. "She converted."

"Now she comes to see Hunter," said Katrina. "Mostly in the summer but this year she dropped by in the winter too."

"We reckon she's trying to get knocked up," added Susie. "Happens to us all."

"Even I looked at men twice at that age." Katrina glanced apologetically at Loretta. "But of course I was happy to use the turkey baster."

"I should bloody hope so," said Susie, tickling Katrina at her waist.

"How old is Shakti?" In the past she had been only older than me, but now I wanted to know by how much.

"Over forty," said Sigi. "But she looks good for her age so it's hard to tell by how much."

"Better than the old boilers around here," said Loretta, and the women cackled, really cackled, like they did when no men were around.

Later in the day, after Loretta had taken me on a tour of the slightly damp vegetable gardens and the new and improved composting toilets, she and Susie started fussing about where Zachary and I would sleep that night. I said I didn't care, that I'd be happy on the woodpile, I was *that* tired, but the two women wouldn't hear of it. They went off in search of the most suitable place, while I went for a wander of my own, arriving after a time at the children's hut.

At the door, I hesitated. The two women were inside, in the midst of a heated discussion.

"It's too dirty," Loretta was saying. "Look at all the cobwebs. And over there—rat droppings."

"She grew up here," said Susie. "She won't mind."

"She's got a baby now," said Loretta. "And they're used to staying in fancy hotels."

"You don't know that."

"He's famous," said Loretta. "Of course they do."

"We didn't bring them up to have airs and graces. And besides, where else can they go?"

"They can have our place—mine and Tom's," said Loretta decisively. "It won't be as good as what she's used to, but at least there's no rat poo."

I had been on the verge of announcing my presence, and insisting that we sleep in the children's hut, when I realized how awkward it would be for the two women if they knew I had overheard their conversation. Instead I crept back to the mess hut, where Katrina had been minding Zachary. He had woken up crying and hungry, and I sat down on a pile of cushions to nurse him, watched closely by Katrina. After a time I noticed she wasn't just admiring Zachary but was staring at his mouth on my breast.

Zachary chomped on, oblivious, and half a minute later, Katrina snapped out of it and gazed wistfully at me. "Do you know?" she said. "Breast-feeding you kids was the happiest time of my life."

"Really? I find it kind of tiring. Especially in the middle of the night."

"Well, that's because you're the only one doing it."

I was curious. "Isn't that how everyone does it?"

"We ran it more like a co-op. When the babies were hungry, whoever was nearby fed them. At night, we took turns on duty, so everyone got a good sleep."

If I had ever known this, I had forgotten it. "You fed *all* the babies—not just your own?"

"You kids shared everything, including breast milk."

I looked down at Zachary and tried to imagine someone else feeding him. "I don't know if I could do that. It feels too intimate."

"Well, it is," said Katrina. "But that's why it was so wonderful. I felt so bonded with all you babies—not just the ones I had given birth to."

"And everyone went along with it?"

"Yes, in fact it was easier for the women, like Loretta, who couldn't breast-feed, and Elisabeth, who didn't enjoy it. They didn't have to do it." Katrina stared off dreamily into the distance, her eyes filling with tears. "It was the most magical time at Gaialands. We were one big happy family. There was so much love."

"I'm sorry, I didn't mean to make you cry."

Katrina smiled. "Don't worry, sweetheart, it doesn't take much at my age." She reached over and patted Zachary's head. "Just try to remember that saying: 'The days are long but the years are short.' Blink and your kids have grown up and left home."

I thought I knew what she meant, but I also couldn't wait for Zachary to grow up, so I could talk to him. The fun would really start then.

Susie and Loretta appeared in the doorway of the mess hut. "We're putting you in our cabin," said Loretta. "It'll be the most comfortable for you and the baby."

"Where will you sleep?" I asked.

"In the kids' hut," said Loretta. "Tom and I don't mind a bit of dust."

"I wouldn't mind it either," I said, hoping to disabuse them of the idea that I had come back from London posh. "You should have seen the squat we lived in. Besides, I feel bad about kicking you and Tom out of your beds."

"You won't change her mind," said Susie. "She's a stubborn old chook."

"That's right," said Loretta. "We've made up the beds and that's final."

Tom and Loretta's cabin was built around a set of stained glass windows salvaged from an old church. It was one of the last dwellings to be built at Gaialands, and for most of our childhood they had lived in a simple wooden shack. Then one day Tom had gone on a trip to Auckland and come home with the windows, which the men had propped up on large wooden joists, the two sets facing each other. Without working to a plan, they had built the rest of the cabin around these windows, using whatever lengths of wood they had to hand, as well as what they had salvaged from the old shack. The finished cabin had four walls, but no two were the same—or even completely straight. Atop the wooden structure was a tin roof, higher on one side than the other, and the outside walls were bright red, with white around the windows. It was straight out of a fairy tale, and like all the homemade buildings at Gaialands, it leaked. Over the long, wet winter months, Paul, the carpenter of the group, spent his days up a ladder, patching roofs.

Going to sleep in their cabin was a strange experience. As a kid I'd never really been allowed inside, especially not at night. Loretta had placed a sprig of wildflowers on the pillow of the double bed, and next to it was an old crib for Zachary, made up with pilled flannelette sheets. Loretta said they had been saving it, just in case one of us decided to come back to the commune to have babies. I was amazed when Zachary went straight down to sleep in it, but I shouldn't have been. I was learning that babies were nothing if not contrary.

When Zachary woke in the middle of the night to be fed, I wrapped a blanket around us both and went outside to sit on the veranda. It was a beautiful night, freezing cold, but so clear that when I looked up into the sky, it took my breath away. In between the usual array of stars were a million more, as though each one had exploded into glittering shards. A planet, too, pulsed bold and orange, amid streaks of white and purple space dust. Had it always been so dazzling? Underneath it, I felt very small, awed and lonely. I wondered what Lukas was doing. If leaving him had been the right thing to do, then why did I miss him so much? I kissed Zachary's face and held him close, trying to soak up his warmth, his contentment.

We went back to bed, Zachary in the crib, and me on Tom and Loretta's soft, doughy mattress; then later on, after he had refused, for hours, to sleep, Zachary tucked into the nook of my arm, and me, in the middle, afraid to do more than catnap in case I rolled on top of him or he fell out of the bed. A typical night all in all.

Not long after dawn, Zachary awoke, smiling and gurgling and eager to get on with the business of being alive, while I felt like someone had gouged my eyes out and replaced them with old worn cricket balls. We stalked the mess hall, waiting for food, company, signs of life, but the adults no longer seemed to get up with the birds. After what felt like hours, they arrived. Breakfast was porridge, gritty whole oats glued together and eaten in front of a group of eager, caring faces. How had I slept, how had Zachary slept, had there been mosquitoes, had we been woken too early by the rooster, was the bed comfortable, the porridge up to scratch?

"Yes, thank you," I said to everything, too knackered to elaborate.

After the breakfast bowls had been cleared away, Susie and Katrina asked if they could take Zachary for a stroll around the orchards and I was so grateful I wanted to kiss them.

Everyone else went off to do chores except Paul, who stayed behind and shyly presented me with a large cardboard folder tied with string.

"We collected all the clippings," he said. "You know, about *Chea-tah*." Paul pronounced the band name hesitantly, as though afraid to get it wrong. He opened the folder and began leafing through it. "There's some from Auckland too, from before you left, about the other bands he was in. And there's a review here somewhere . . ." He rifled through a few more pages until he found a dog-eared sheet of newsprint. "Here it is. Look, Poppy, there's your name."

He pointed to my byline, under the heading, "Rat Piss." It was a review of one of Lukas's more obnoxious bands, which I had tried to pass off as the next big thing. I quickly skimmed through it. *Oh dear.* That was the gig where the bass player had urinated into a bottle, onstage, and pretended to drink the contents, to prove what an authentic punk he was. Maybe he really had drunk the contents. He was a bit of a loose cannon. "Crikey," I said, putting it back. "I'd forgotten about that."

Paul chuckled. "We were glad when that phase was over."

The folder held dozens of pieces of carefully folded, yellowing newsprint, and more recent additions on thicker, glossier magazine paper. Paul kept up a running commentary, telling me which album had just come out and how it was doing in the charts. He was an expert, quoting statistics left and right, and I quickly realized that even though no one in New Zealand had known quite what to make of Cheatah, who'd not had any hits here, every step of their progress had been reported in the newspapers as a matter of slightly confused national pride. "I can't believe they got so much coverage here," I said. "Lukas is the only New Zealander in the band. The rest of them are English."

"But he's the lead singer," said Paul. "That's a big deal."

"Look at this story, though," I said, reading out a newspaper headline. " 'Cheatah's Second Album a Massive Flop in the UK.' Why would they report that?"

"I don't know," said Paul. "I guess they need an angle."

"The funny thing is, that's what Lukas feels like," I said. "A failure."

Paul was quiet for a moment, thinking. "I worried that might happen. He was always too ambitious for his own good."

"Too ambitious?"

"Yeah, if you want something that much, and you don't get it—or you get something else—it messes with your head."

"How do you know all that?"

Paul smiled wryly. "In my younger days I wanted to be an architect."

"But you built all the houses on the commune."

"Those are not houses," said Paul. "They are follies."

We both laughed.

"Well, you don't seem screwed up about it."

"I've got Sigi to thank for that. But there were some ropey years, while I came to terms with the fact that I'd never be Frank Lloyd Wright."

"You were aiming high."

"And so is our Lukas."

It hit me then why Paul had kept all these clippings, why he had been so eager to share them. He was tremendously proud of his son. In the last few years, he had probably shown this same folder to everyone who had passed through the commune. I felt guilty. Through all the years, we had not so much as sent a postcard. How would I feel, I wondered, if Zachary cut me off like that?

"I'm really sorry we didn't keep in touch," I said to Paul, gently touching his wrist. "We didn't think about what it would be like for you guys."

"Of course you bloody didn't," said Paul, eyebrows arched in surprise. "And I did the same to my parents. Couldn't wait to escape their clutches. Mum in her apron, always trying to feed me up, for what I was never sure, and Dad banging on about the rugby. Two years later, he was gone, and Mum was on her own, but do you think that made me visit her more often? Not a chance. I had just met Sigi and we were the only two people in the world that had ever fallen in love." He put his big, burly hand over mine and looked me in the eye. "So not another word about it, okay?"

I nodded. "Okay."

Before we had found out who our real fathers were, I had always hoped mine was Paul. He was kind, sensible, funny—all the qualities Lukas inherited. It made me happy to think that at least Paul was now my father-in-law—and the grandfather of my son. "Did you know Lukas and I got married?"

"Yup," said Paul. "We read about that."

"In the paper?"

"Yes."

"Sorry."

"Shhh, lass. What did I tell you?"

"I know. But that's awful."

"I'm sure it's here somewhere." Paul leafed through the folder, then read from a clipping. "'Expat Kiwi glam rocker Lukas Harvest married his childhood sweetheart in a registry office in Chelsea at the weekend. No details on whether or not the couple wore leather, but we heard a shotgun went off during the ceremony.'" Paul laughed. "Guess they knew about the baby."

"Let me see that." I wondered what kind of tabloid had run a story that dreadful. The cutting was tiny, taken from the In Brief column of a newspaper—the *Auckland Star*. Next to it, a postage-stamp-sized photo of Lukas and me in a night-club booth. My head was turned away from the camera and my hair was so big, so back-combed, that you could only see the tip of my nose. Further down, a low-cut top and cleavage, lots of cleavage, more than I had ever had in my wildest dreams, or even after Zachary was born. I looked again. *Not my cleavage, not my nose.* It could have been—even I had been nearly fooled—but it wasn't me. It was Fran.

I handed the clipping back to Paul and he held another page in front of me, but I couldn't focus on it. "Excuse me," I said, getting up from the bench. "I think I need a rest. The jet lag is catching up."

"Of course," said Paul. "You must be shattered."

In a daze, I walked to the orchard, looking for Zachary and the women, hoping the sight of him might cleanse the photo of Lukas and Fran from my mind. I started to panic. Where was he, my precious baby, and why had I let him so casually out of my sight? I walked through the orchard. The trees had bloomed and dropped a carpet of white petals on the ground.

"Poppy!" called a woman's voice. "Over here!"

Under a tree at the edge of the orchard, Susie and Katrina lay sprawled on the ground, and between them, Zachary, cycling his legs in the air.

"We've had such a lovely time," said Susie, tickling Zachary's tummy and making him giggle. "We were just saying how nice it was to have a baby here again."

"We've decided he looks like his dad," said Katrina. "Especially around the eyes and chin."

"He's got your mouth though," added Susie.

I scooped up Zachary. "He's hungry," I said, taking off with him clutched to my chest.

It was hard to find anywhere to be alone on the commune. I had forgotten that part. Even the huts, which in theory were private, had such thin walls and such drafty windows that it was more like being outside than in a house. In the old days, when I needed time to think or just wanted to be on my own, I had walked off into the forest, hid behind trees, ignored the call of my name.

Someone was calling it now, from the direction of the mess hut, where ten minutes earlier, the cowbell had rung for lunch. I wasn't hungry, nor did I want to have to explain to anyone why not. I just wanted to be left on my own to calm down.

I hid in Tom and Loretta's cabin, where I lay on the bed in fetal position, after settling Zachary in his crib. A few minutes later came a knock at the door.

"I brought you some lunch," said Sigi. "I'll bring it in, shall I?"

She bowled on in with the tray. I was lying with my back to the door, and she walked over to the bedside table, re-arranged whatever was on it, and set down the tray. "Chick-pea casserole," she whispered. "So much nicer when it's hot."

"Thanks," I mumbled, trying to sound half-asleep.

"Are you unwell?"

"No. Just tired."

"I'll fetch my herbs—make you a fortifying drink."

"Thank you but I'm fine."

I sensed Sigi hovering by the bed for a moment, then she went over to Zachary's crib, where she made clucking noises and rustled the sheets and blankets, probably trying to tuck him in. He had been sighing before that, drifting off to sleep, but now he roused himself and started cooing and gig-gling, wide awake. Not only would he not sleep now, but also because he hadn't napped, I wouldn't be able to either, and the pair of us would be grizzly and fractious all afternoon.

"Please leave him," I said irritably, sitting up and glaring at Sigi. She gave me a wounded look.

At dinner, the adults asked all the questions they had been too polite to ask the night before. Or maybe I was just in a bad mood, experiencing their loving inquiries as unwelcome intrusion. I wondered if they had started to suspect I was back at the commune because things had soured between Lukas and me. Perhaps they had guessed it the moment I showed up.

"Tell us where you live," asked Loretta. "Is it in a very posh part of London?"

"It's very small, a garden flat."

"And your neighbors, do they bother you?"

"We haven't met them. People keep to themselves."

Loretta's sigh was world weary. "They're used to seeing famous people in the neighborhood."

"I have no idea," I said.

"How long will you be here for?" asked Katrina. "You've come such a long way, you may as well stay for the summer."

I hadn't thought that far ahead. "Maybe."

"If you're here for the solstice," said Sigi, "we should celebrate. We could invite Nelly and her husband, track down some of the others."

"Do you think they would come?" said Loretta.

"They might," said Tom. "If we knew where to find them."

"Is Nelly still in Opua?"

"Yes," said Susie, her birth mother. "She's the only one who keeps in touch."

I thought of Nelly's prediction, swarming with offspring and love hearts. "How many kids does she have now?"

Susie chuckled. "At the last count, five. She told us Ned has one too. But we don't know who the mother is. We think he's still in Wellington."

"Is that where Meg is?" I looked to Sigi. She had tried so hard to make up for lost time with her daughter, once everything was out in the open. I hoped for her sake that Meg had stayed in touch.

With an unhappy look, Sigi said, "I don't know."

Katrina added, of Timon, "I don't know where my son is either."

The room fell into a gloomy silence. No wonder they had been so pleased to see us. I tried to remember everyone's predictions, as if they might hold clues to their whereabouts, but the only card I could recall with any degree of clarity had belonged to Fritz. No one, since I had been back, had mentioned him, and I wondered if they thought of him the same way they thought of the rest of us, as yet another kid who had left home and never come back.

"Did the police ever find out anything about what happened to Fritz?"

"No," said Loretta. "In fact, we've been thinking about holding a memorial. Not a funeral, as such, but something that means we can all get a bit of closure."

Paul nodded in agreement. "We ought to put that poor boy to rest."

Loretta glanced at Hunter, gauging his reaction, as she said, "It's been ten years now."

Hunter fidgeted a little in his seat but said nothing.

"We thought about asking one of the local *Kaumatua* for

a *karakia*," said Katrina. "To bless his spirit on the journey to the next world."

"Keep those old codgers out of it," said Hunter. "He wasn't a bloody Maori."

Tom raised his hand. "I'm with Hunter. The last time we got the elders involved, they told us this land was *tapu*."

"Maybe it is," said Susie. "Maybe we shouldn't be here."

"Nonsense," said Hunter. "When we bought this piece of land in 1961, there was nothing here. Now look at it—we've turned it into a slice of paradise."

"Open your eyes," said Katrina. "Your slice of paradise took one of our boys. Mother earth is angry!"

Hunter scoffed. "Gaia isn't angry with us! We look after her. Everything we take from her, we give back tenfold."

"Here we go again," said Susie. "The patriarchy claims to know what's best for mother earth!"

Several of the women laughed at Susie's put-down of Hunter. They didn't seem to put up with so much shit anymore but they certainly doled it out.

"What do you think, Poppy?" said Loretta. "Should we have a ceremony?"

"I don't know." I had been very quiet all evening but now everyone was looking in my direction, waiting for me to elaborate. "It would be nice to see the other kids—that is, if we could find them."

"There's a lot to consider, a lot to think about," said Susie. "So here's what we'll do." She put her fingers together to make a steeple and looked around the group to make sure she had everyone's attention. "In a week's time we'll hold a *hui* in the meetinghouse and try to reach a consensus."

In the old days, a meeting was a meeting, but now it was a *hui*, after the Maori word, which had been adopted by liberal Pakeha. Was Susie the new leader of the commune? She was acting like one, albeit in a different, less masculine style.

Rain spilled from the mess-hut roof in sheets, and I huddled under the eaves with Zachary, waiting for a break that was long enough to risk dashing across the field to our cabin. The rain showed no signs of easing up—if anything it was getting heavier, more persistent. There was no way around it. If we wanted to go anywhere, we would have to get soaked. I said my good night to the assembled adults and ran out with Zachary sheltered in the lee of my shoulder, covering the top of his head with my hand. In the cabin, I toweled him off and dressed him in dry clothes, while I stood shivering in my wet ones and dripping water on the sea-grass matting. I understood now why airplane safety cards instructed passengers to put on their own oxygen masks first. What they really meant by "passengers" was "mothers."

From the far corner of the room came the steady dripping of water on tin, and I noticed that someone had placed a pot underneath the leak in the roof. The cabin was lined with plywood, except that it wasn't really a lining, because it was the only layer separating us from the great outdoors. As a result it was just as soggy inside as out, and I longed to be back within the solid, dry brick walls of our London flat. But that life was over now. I had defied the prediction one too many times and my punishment had been Lukas's betrayal.

CHAPTER 16

Gaialands
1989

FOR THE NEXT SEVENTEEN days straight, the rain came down, sometimes by the bucket, other times in drizzle so fine that it hung in the air, too light to drop to the ground. On days of mild rain, it was better for the soul to pretend there was none, and to go about business as though it was fine, ignoring wet hair, dank skin, soggy clothes, clammy bedding. We had learned this trick as children to make long spells of bad weather more bearable, and I resorted to it, instinctively, on about day eight or nine. But by day thirteen, when I had run out of disposable nappies and the cloth ones wouldn't dry, and Zachary's bum was red and raw with diaper rash, his crib sheets spotted with mildew, I was having a hard time keeping up the pretense and had succumbed to the waterlogged blues.

On the eighteenth day, I awoke to the rattle of birdsong in the trees around the cabin, and opened my eyes to a world blanched in weak, milky sunlight, no drizzle. I dressed quickly and bundled Zachary into a makeshift sling, anxious to get out before the weather changed. I would feed him outdoors, where he could listen to the birds while he slurped. It was very early but a light was on in the kitchen. Someone was getting breakfast ready. I needed to borrow gumboots and slid my feet into the only pair on the porch. They were too big—my feet mooned around inside and rubber slapped my calves as I walked—but it was better than getting my feet wet or ruining my expensive London loafers.

I planned to cross the stream at the end of the orchard, then walk a little way up Mount Aroha to a clearing with a bench seat that caught the morning sun. But I got as far as the creek, which had swollen to a river, the trees at the edge of it submerged up to their lower boughs and netting driftwood and debris. Nothing remained of the little swing bridge that usually crossed the stream, not even the wooden platforms that bookended each side. I did not remember flooding like this, water licking the plum trees at the edge of the orchard.

Beyond the orchard, the newly hatched river flowed into the forest and through a gully where the banks on either side were steep and crisscrossed with bracken. There was a path through the forest that ran alongside it, but higher up, and that was the path I took with Zachary, stopping after about ten minutes to sit and feed him on a low, moss-covered log. Water from the log soaked into the backside of my pants, but I barely noticed it. I would have sat cross-legged in a puddle if that had been the only place available in which to feed him. Along with a lot of other things I swore I'd never be, I was becoming one of those mothers who took pride in her martyrdom.

After being cooped up for weeks in the various huts and shared spaces of the commune, it was nice to be alone, or at least alone with Zachary, who didn't mind if I stopped talking to him, so long as his tummy was full. For weeks, I had seethed privately with anger and confusion over the picture of Lukas and Fran, but over time those emotions had burned off, and what was left behind felt very much like grief.

Zachary bounced up and down in the sling as I walked. He seemed to like the motion, and his eyes slid drunkenly closed. We had come to the edge of the forest, to the clearing that fell away to the sea in scraggly grass-covered cliffs. It was a place of disagreeable memories: the humiliation of being made by Shakti to strip off, and that awful rising anguish when Fritz didn't come out of the forest after rotten egg. I did not wish to linger and soon found the still well-worn track that led down to the beach. As kids we had loved this bay, spending whole days here with little more than a bag of apples between us.

The geography of the beach was so altered as to be barely recognizable. Where normally the creek sputtered out across the sand in rivulets, a wide, rippling current flooded the paddocks bordering the beach and then lurched toward the sea. It cut the beach in half, making the far side of the bay inaccessible without wading across it. But the thing that caught my eye was pushed up against a tree in the swampy field in the middle of the bay. From this distance, it looked like a cubby house or a toolshed, though I didn't remember there ever being one down here, on the beach.

All morning, Zachary had been light in my arms but he was starting to feel like a dead weight, pulling down on my back and shoulders. Halfway to the shed, or whatever it was, I thought about turning back but I soldiered on. Something about it was intriguing, perhaps the way it listed to one side, or the fact that the closer I got, the more familiar it seemed. I had almost walked right up to it before I recognized what it was—not a shed but a caravan, Shakti's old caravan. The wheels had shorn off and it was buried up to its axis in clotted, buttery mud, but otherwise it was more or less intact, the moon and stars still painted down the side.

What the heck was it doing on the beach—and not in Auckland or wherever Shakti had taken it? It made no sense. The last time I had seen the caravan, Shakti and her friend Marcia, with the cloud of hair, had been towing it away from Gaialands behind a rusty beige station wagon. No one had thought they would get very far, but even in a four-wheel drive they would never have made it here. The beach was inaccessible by road. How else could it have got down here? The women had left Gaialands ten years ago at least, though apparently Shakti had been back to visit Hunter since then. All manner of things had been swept away in the recent floods—the bridge over the creek, for one—and debris littered the beach, including a few large trees. Had it washed up here on its own? The corners of it *did* look battered, as though it had been tossed about in a rough sea, then thumped in the side with what might have been an overhanging branch or two . . .

I gave up wondering how the caravan had arrived on the beach and focused instead on trying to open the door. It rattled a little but wouldn't budge. Either it was locked or wedged shut, so I went around the side of the caravan to look in one of the tiny windows. The glass had popped out but I peered inside, careful to avoid any jagged edges. My first impression was of wreckage: broken glass, smashed crockery, mud, and wet cloth. But slowly, the outlines of objects emerged: a bulbous orange pot with a wooden handle, a few damp books and candle stumps, a sprig of something that might once have been lavender. Considering how long it had been abandoned, and its possibly violent journey to the beach, it could have been in worse shape.

I tried the door again. It was locked, but on one side of the frame, a few hinges were coming loose, and I found a sturdy-looking branch to prize it open with. In his sling, Zachary mewled to signal he was waking up. A sour smell was coming from his nappy but it would have to wait until we got back. I hadn't anticipated we would roam this far, or be out this long, and hadn't brought anything to change him with. I chatted to him for a moment to soothe him, silly words that mothers say to their babies when no one else is around, and Zachary hummed and gurgled back in a code only I understood. I hadn't known before about this covert language, the way even the smallest baby could tell his mother, and only his mother, what was wrong.

Shakti had cleaned out most of her belongings at the time of abandoning the caravan; that much was clear when I stepped carefully inside. Everything that was left behind

had been drenched at one time or another and was now in
various stages of decay. There were ruined paintbrushes;
glass jars stained with paint; a china teapot that had split in
two, one half with a spout, the other with a handle. Nothing much was salvageable. Water puddled on the corkboard
floor.

Near one end of the caravan, where Shakti had slept
on a small platform behind batik curtains—now reduced
to matted, moldering rags—there was an upturned cardboard box with a pile of wet notebooks and paper spilling
out of it. Holding Zachary close, I made my way gingerly
toward it, testing each portion of the spongy floorboards
as I went. When I reached the platform, I sat down next to
the box and took off the sling, resting Zachary on a section
of the mattress that was relatively clean and dry. Released
from confinement, he flung up his arms, arched his back,
and pointed his toes, a comical routine that was an exaggerated version of someone stretching. When I grabbed his foot
and pretended to eat it, he giggled. "Ub-bub-bub-bub-bub,"
I said, and Zachary replied: "Oowaah oowaah," a noise that
denoted enthusiasm.

Most of the bits of paper inside the box were covered in
washed-out pencil sketches, not easily decipherable, but as I
flicked through them, I gradually started to recognize a few
of the motifs. Here were a man and woman holding hands,
drawn in a simple, childish style, and another showed a picture of a tree like the one that had been in Fritz's prediction.
My heart sank at the sight of it, and I reached into the box for
another sheaf of paper. There were drawings of a tiny little

crib, and another of a teeny tiny coffin. There was the word-
ing from my prediction, next to variations: *barren, childless,
infertile. A child that is born won't live.*

How many different versions could there be? I had
always thought Shakti was the deliverer of the predictions
and not their creator, but for the first time I considered the
possibility that she had made up their contents. Not only that,
but I saw how much deliberation had gone into her work, as
if she had been trying to achieve a particular outcome, or had
set out to manipulate our fate. But *why* she would interfere
like that was beyond me. As if in answer to my question, a
flash of light tore through the caravan, and from way off in
the distance came the long, low rumble of thunder, the storm
returning, in greater force. We would have to hurry back to
avoid getting soaked, or worse, getting struck by lightning.
I folded Zachary into the sling and hoisted it over my head,
took a moment to check he was settled comfortably, then
glanced around to make sure we hadn't left anything behind.
At the last possible second, my eye caught on something
hairy in the bottom of the box, a dead animal, a possum or
a bush rat. It was the color of sand, with darker and lighter
patches, pepper and salt, not an animal but—what was it? To
get a better look, I pulled aside the paper that covered it.

It wasn't hair-y—it *was* hair. Human hair. Swatches of
it, in different shades, separated in places by elastic bands
but mostly just mussed together. I had the odd sensation of
looking at something very familiar but not recognizing it,
and then, in the next moment, knowing exactly what it was.
I saw some of that hair every day. It was mine.

What was my hair doing in this box? I tried to make sense of it, and remembered long ago waking up in the children's hut to the sound of scissors, and then seeing Shakti, instrument in hand. *Shakti had cut off a chunk of my hair.* She had brought it to her caravan and tied it with an elastic band and then what had she done with it? I tried to stay calm, rational, but there was nothing rational about collecting people's hair. It was creepy, unhinged, the action of a psycho.

A gust of rain blew through the open window of the caravan, cold droplets that I didn't want to get caught in, not with Zachary. It was time to head off, but I was rooted to the spot, determined to find an explanation for the hair. I grabbed the nearest book—an astrology tome—and prized apart a few soggy pages. It was filled with finely printed charts, circular diagrams, zodiac symbols, weird equations, and maps of the constellations, but no witching spells or instructions for how to make a voodoo doll. The book underneath it held more of the same.

Lightning cracked the sky, followed by a roll of thunder, right above our heads this time. I scrambled for the door, forgetting, in my haste, to tread gently on the rotten corkboard, which gave way, under my gumboot, as though it was week-old Madeira cake. I sank past the knee into a dark, glutinous hole. By some miracle, my other leg had folded gracefully underneath me and I had put out my hands in front of me to stop the fall. I thought it was a lucky escape but then Zachary wailed, and my heart lurched wildly as I checked to see if he was okay. He appeared to be all right, not a scratch, but he was still crying and in my panic, I thought he was hurt, until I realized the pain I could feel was coming from my own leg. I looked down. I couldn't see anything. But then I slowly eased my leg out of the hole, and it came out minus the gumboot. I had scraped the skin off my kneecap, and the area was pooling with blood. I searched for something to dab it up with and grabbed a mildewed T-shirt out of a nearby plastic bag that was bursting with old damp clothes. On my knee, the cloth turned red, and when I lifted it up, I saw the cut was a proper gash, much deeper than it had at first seemed. But there was no time to worry about that. No one knew where we were or was coming to get us. The only way back was to walk. I tied the T-shirt around my leg and stood up. The gumboot was fairly well embedded, but after a couple of tugs it came out sloshing, and I tipped it upside down while a foul brown liquid trickled out.

It was raining pretty hard by now, and I had to walk hunched over to shelter the baby. I was worried about being out in the open, where lightning might strike us, but staying in the caravan, which had floated once and could float again, out to sea, didn't seem too sensible either. Zachary appeared to understand that things weren't going too well for us and added to the vibe with a constant high-pitched squawk. I tried not to think about the noise or the pain coming from my leg or the water that was dripping on us from all directions and focused instead on marching forward up the cliff, through the forest, through the orchard, across the paddock, one foot in front of the other until my gumboot hit the porch steps of our cabin.

Inside, I laid Zachary on the bed while I stripped off my

wet clothes. He was comparatively dry but shrieking with such intensity that anyone would think he was dying. In my underwear, shivering, I sat on the edge of the bed and jammed a breast into his mouth, cutting him off mid-shriek. Red faced and thrashing, he continued to grunt angrily even as he gulped down milk, letting me know how furious he was that he'd had to wait.

When he had settled down to a quiet, rhythmic slurp, I poked at the bloodied T-shirt, more of a tank top, that bandaged my knee. *Ouch.* I untied it and carefully unwrapped the wound, wincing when the fabric stuck to the raw skin underneath. Despite the pain, the shirt brought a smile to my face—it was an old one from the seventies, grass-green polyester, with a white number three on the back. We'd had one just like it in the communal clothing box. I hadn't worn it much but Fritz, he had worn it all the time. In fact he had been wearing it on the day he disappeared. I looked again at the shirt—the same shirt, it had to be. The cop had asked Nelly what sort of green it was, and she had said, *bright green, the color of new spring grass.*

CHAPTER 17

Gaialands
1989

THE GRASS-GREEN TANK TOP with a number three on
the back was soaked in my blood, the wrong person's
blood, and I wondered if I should wash it before handing
it over to the cops or if that would be seen as tampering
with evidence—though I supposed I had already done that
by using it as a tourniquet. What would happen after that,
I speculated—would the cops want to search Shakti's caravan? Would they find her and interrogate her and maybe
even arrest her? I was getting ahead of myself; and besides,
the cops were idiots. The general consensus was that they
had bungled the investigation. They had condescended to
us, not saying outright that we had been careless, that our
hippie lifestyle was to blame, but implying it. The tank top
had my blood on it. If we gave it to the cops, they might find
a way to pin the whole thing on us.

I was not thinking straight. I was freaked out, extrap-
olating, spinning conspiracies, all because of exhaustion,

a wounded knee, and not eating breakfast. I needed food, and then to talk it over with someone—not the whole commune, not in a bloody hui, but with someone who would know what to do. Paul was the most sensible, but he seemed wrong for this. Just the other night he had said it was time to put Fritz to rest. He might not be in favor of reopening the case. Hunter? He was Fritz's father, the person most devastated by his loss, even if he wouldn't admit it. I also still thought of him, out of habit, as the commune's leader, the person you went to with a problem.

It was difficult to get him alone. I tried to corner him at lunch, but Katrina and Susie were there, insisting on feeding Zachary a bowl of mashed avocado, even though I told them he wasn't ready for solid food, and their presence had seemed to scare Hunter away. In those first few days back on the commune, I hadn't noticed how strained relations were between Hunter and the two lesbians in particular, but now that I had been here a while, I was starting to wonder how much longer they could all go on living together. There was so much tension and so little trust.

All day, the rain had been coming down in curtains, and the wind had picked up, though there was no more thunder. Over dinner, Tom cautioned that it was going to get worse overnight. "A proper storm. Fifty-knot winds, according to the weather report, and more rain—as if we need it."

The commune dwellers were grim. Some of their seedlings, planted in early spring, had already washed away, and they couldn't plant more until the soil dried out. It was better to stagger planting, to put some crops in early and others in late, or else the produce ripened all at once and there was a terrible glut, so much wastage. Living off the land was perilous, each season a game of food roulette. Some winters the stores had been full and we'd eaten like kings; other years, we had subsisted on twenty-kilo bags of oats, rice, and lentils, sent over from Auckland as a last resort. At the end of those winters, the tough ones, there had always been talk of improving systems and of what had gone wrong, but no amount of planning could insure against a bad run of weather.

I waited until after dinner, until everyone had gone back to their cabins for the night, and then I bundled Zachary up and dashed through the rain and puddles to knock on Hunter's door. He was startled to see me, and embarrassed about the state of his cabin. He made us wait on the doorstep while he rushed about inside, straightening blankets and kicking underpants beneath the bed, none of which made much difference. Inside it smelled like the bottom of a laundry basket, of three-day-old socks and wet, graying towels. So this was what happened to men who lived on their own—they gave up.

Hunter cleared a space for Zachary and me on a window seat whose squabs had seen better days, or perhaps had always been wonky and tattered. "I'm sure the little fellow's grown since he got here," he said, running a huge, weather-beaten thumb over Zachary's cheek. He had spent so much time outdoors that he looked older than he was, his skin already creased and leathery. "He looks like you, you know."

"The women all think he looks like Lukas."

"No, he's got your eyes," he said. "Shy, and a bit worried."

"Is that how I look?"

"Yup," said Hunter. "Right now, you do."

I took out the tank top and gave it to him, explaining where I had found it and that the blood on it was mine—nothing more than that. Hunter studied the garment carefully, then buried his face in it and broke down in tears.

I had never seen him weep before, or even shed a tear, and it was deeply unsettling. To allow him time to recover, I walked Zachary to the window and pointed his chubby finger at the trees outside. The ones nearest the cabin were already bending madly, dripping water, ahead of the storm.

Behind me, Hunter spoke. "You're sure it's his?"

"We signed a statement to say that's what he was wearing when he disappeared."

"I know. But what if there's another shirt the same?"

"What are the odds of that?"

Hunter sank to the bed. "You're right."

"There was a whole bag of clothes—but I didn't look through the rest."

"Tomorrow," he said. "When the weather clears. I'll go and check out the caravan."

"Where do you think it was all these years?"

"I don't know," said Hunter. "We'll ask Shakti when she gets here."

"Shakti?" I thought she was the last person we should involve. "Don't you think we should tell the cops first? What if she's a suspect?"

"She's one of us."

"I don't trust her. Do you know she collected swatches of our hair?"

"That is odd," he said. "Maybe it was for that ritual—what did she call it? The prophecies?"

"The predictions."

"There you go." He laughed. "We were so caught up in the spirit of the times."

"Whatever happened to the Age of Aquarius? Wasn't there going to be a big shift in consciousness, and everyone would be enlightened or something?"

"We were young," he said. "We thought we could change the world."

"From a commune?"

"We hoped our ideas would spread. That once people found out about us, they would want to live the same way."

"Gee," I said. "Pretty much the opposite happened. You should see London. It's like the gold rush all over again."

"I am constantly astounded," said Hunter, "by man's inability not to act in his own best interests."

I could feel one of his lectures coming on. "The shirt," I said. "Should we hand it in to the cops?"

"I can take it in Thursday. I'm going to Whitianga for a meeting."

I was relieved I wouldn't have to do it myself. "Do you think we should wash it first?"

"Wash it?"

"The blood. They might think it's his."

"Oh, no," he said. "I'll explain."

I watched him roll the shirt into a small, tidy bundle,

then look around for somewhere to put it. There was a tall-boy next to his bed, bent out of shape, and he tried to open the middle drawer but it was stuck. The top drawer shunted open but only halfway, enough to shove it in. "We should probably keep this to ourselves," he said. "You know what those women are like, always gossiping." He laughed, to show he didn't really mean it, or maybe to cover that he did.

"Quite a bit has changed around here, hasn't it?"

"The women, you mean?"

"Yes, they act like they're in charge now. Are they?"

Hunter walked to the window and shoved his hands in his pockets. "It started when Elisabeth left." He stared out the window. "For a long time, I went to pieces. I wasn't myself. I spent all my time on the beach, going for long, mopey walks—all that sad-sack stuff. I let a few things slide. Maintenance, taxes, planting crops. Things got very chaotic. No one was in charge. The next thing I knew, Susie and Katrina had gone off to one of those women's conventions in Hamilton, and they came back saying it was all my fault."

"What was?"

"Everything and anything that pissed them off. From then on, they had a name for me." He paused, for emphasis. "Chief Bullshit Patriarchy—Chief B. P. for short."

"Did you think of leaving?"

"Why should I?" Hunter was defiant. "This is my home. I built Gaialands up from nothing. Broke in the land with my own bare hands. All the fruit trees—I planted those. I'm not like your mother. I can't just walk away from this place. It's my life's work."

Hunter had never called Elisabeth my mother before, and I still didn't think of her that way. "Why did Elisabeth up and leave? You must have some idea."

"I know exactly why she left," he said, suddenly fired up, his stance bullish, reminding me why we had all been so intimidated by him. "She thought we had fucked everything up. After Fritz went missing, and you kids all left, well, that was the proof she needed."

I had never heard Hunter swear before. "Proof of what?"

"That we had failed as parents."

I was indignant. "But she didn't even try to be my mother. When you told us who our parents were, some of the mothers, they tried to get close, but Elisabeth—she didn't do anything. She ignored me. Like she always had."

"Because she thought it was too late!"

"Too late for what?"

"To be your mother," said Hunter. "She didn't think it was possible to turn back the clock."

"Is that why you didn't start trying to be my father?"

"No," said Hunter. "I believed in what we were doing—in how we raised you. I still do. The mistake we made was that we didn't stick to our guns. After we told you who your siblings were, we should have carried on as normal—kept up a unified front. But not everyone felt the same way. Some of the parents wanted to see if they could try to have a special bond with their kids. I told them it wouldn't work, that it would only confuse you—and I was right. The second you were old enough—you all buggered off."

"We didn't just leave because of that."

"I know. Things were very difficult after Fritz . . ." His voice cracked, and he turned away for a moment. "But at that stage, I was delighted by how well you had all turned out. You were exactly how I hoped you would be."

"Which is how?"

"Liberated, freethinking."

"But Elisabeth didn't think so?"

I had pushed Hunter too far.

"Why don't you ask her yourself?" He went to the drawer he had hidden Fritz's shirt in and poked around until he came up with a folded piece of paper, which he shoved into my hand.

On it was an address, the suburb in Auckland, near where Lukas and I had lived.

"Go and see her," he said. "I'm sure she'll be over the moon to meet her grandson. Just don't bloody ask her to feed him!"

He had raised his voice, making Zachary cry. Outside, the rain was heavier than it had been all day, if that was possible. Our cabin wasn't far from Hunter's but we would get soaked. I was so tired of trying to keep Zachary dry. I started toward the door, shushing to soothe him, wondering if there was an equivalent noise that would calm Hunter down.

"Thanks for the address," I said. "I didn't know she kept in touch."

"She writes to me. About once a year. The others don't know."

"Maybe she still loves you?"

"Hardly—she does it because she's still angry with me for ruining her life."

I studied the address in my hand.

"And you think I should visit her?"

Hunter shrugged. "Up to you."

Zachary and I went back to our cabin, where we were buffeted all night by gusts of strong wind. The cabin was drafty at the best of times, but that night I feared it might take off across the fields. Zachary was oblivious to the racket, but I barely slept, and the little rest I did manage was disturbed by anxious dreams. In one, Shakti had caught me trespassing in her caravan, and I was running away from her, weighed down by Zachary, and bleeding profusely from my knee.

Susie and Katrina had been discussing a trip to Auckland they were going to make to join the protest against an antiabortion lobby group, and even though I didn't want to be a part of their political activities, I was desperate for a break from the commune. This lobby group, all Christian, had been picketing outside the women's hospital in rostered shifts for most of the year, but just in the last few days, the political had turned personal. The leader of the lobby group, a middle-aged white male, had launched a vicious attack on lesbians and feminists, saying they were pro-choice because they were trying to stop "normal women" from enjoying motherhood, and that if they had their way this would eventually lead to the extinction of the human race. Everyone had been discussing it nonstop at the dinner table ever since, and Susie, in particular, had been getting so fired up that I was scared she was going to take someone out. "How dare that man say that about us? He's made it personal—and I won't let him get away with it."

The day after the storm, when they finally set a date for the trip to Auckland, I realized it would also give me a chance to visit Elisabeth. "Is there room in the truck for me and Zachary?" I asked Katrina, over breakfast.

"Of course," she said. "The more the merrier."

Hunter wasn't at breakfast but in the afternoon, when I was helping to clean up debris with Zachary in a sling on my back, he came to find me. "This caravan of Shakti's," he said. "You're sure it was in the flooded paddock next to the beach?"

"It was up against a tree—right in the middle. You couldn't miss it."

"Well," said Hunter, "I did miss it. Either that or it's not there anymore."

"Are you sure?"

"There were a few trees down, and flooding right to the sea. I've never seen it like that before—the beach almost vanished. But no caravan."

"I wonder what happened to it."

"Those winds last night were gale force. Maybe it broke up, floated out to sea?"

"But it was so sturdy . . ."

"And very exposed, in the middle of the paddock like that."

I wasn't convinced. "I'm going to go and look for it—see for myself."

"I wouldn't if I were you," said Hunter. "It's not safe, there's land slips all over the place. I'm going to warn the others to stay off the beach."

"I'll be really careful."

"I know you will," said Hunter. "But I still don't think you should go."

Against his advice, I tried to get down to the beach. With Zachary in the sling, I got as far as the forest path, now washed out and crisscrossed with fallen tree trunks. The way ahead was even more treacherous than Hunter had warned, and I turned back to the commune, thwarted. We spent the rest of the day cleaning up, returning objects that had blown away to their right places and throwing out stuff that was broken. By the end of the day, I was beat, and went to bed early.

Sigi made sandwiches for the drive to Auckland. Hard, sour bread smeared with a thin layer of tahini and raw chopped garlic, so raw that it writhed in my mouth like a live thing. When we stopped in Pokeno to buy gas, I threw mine out and secretly bought a steak-and-cheese pie, the first meat I had eaten in weeks, scarfing it down in the ladies' loo, dropping crumbs and tomato sauce on Zachary's bald head.

Back in the truck, driving over the Bombay Hills, getting closer to Auckland, Susie and Katrina discussed tactics. They had been tipped off that the Christians would be out in force today, not just the usual hard core of picketers but a larger contingent of family members and supporters as well. There might be reporters, a television crew.

I had been cagey about my reasons for going to Auckland, and Susie and Katrina assumed I would join them in the protest. On the motorway, approaching the outskirts of the city, I tried to suggest that I didn't think attending the protest would be such a good idea, not with a baby in tow. They were miffed.

"It's a peaceful protest—if that's what you're worried about," said Katrina.

"I know, but even that might be too much for a baby."

"Don't you worry," said Susie. "If any of those bastards tries to lay a finger on him"—she pounded her fist into the palm of her hand—"boom! They're toast."

Exactly, I didn't say, *that's what I'm worried about.*

We pulled into the car park of National Women's Hospital, an ugly collection of imposing concrete tower blocks and a dozen unassuming, redbrick low-rises, the smallest of which was the day clinic where abortions took place. A handful of women were gathered on the front steps, all short haired and wearing army fatigues, all on "our" side. Over the next hour, this group swelled to number about three dozen, a motley collection of women and a few older children, teenagers, a couple of dogs. The day had started out soggy, overcast, but now it was warmer, almost muggy, and I had peeled off one or two layers of clothing. The plan was to wait for the Christians to arrive, then to form a blockade, linking arms in a line around the front of the clinic. We got into position. I had been sent to the end of the line, furthest from the clinic, while Susie and Katrina took the middle, ready for a fight, if there was one.

Late morning, someone sent word they were coming. A big group—singing hymns. To match their zeal, to keep up morale, we began to chant: "Not the church! Not the state! Women must decide their fate!" A few rounds of that and I was converted to the cause, shouting as loudly as any of the women. Strapped to my chest, Zachary gurgled his support.

A crocodile of men and women approached along Green Lane from the west. Some held placards; others flashed pictures of bloodied fetuses. A few held aloft pink plastic dolls, more fetuses, which looked out of place in their big adult hands. They sang a traditional hymn, very fundamentalist, then stopped in front of us, their expressions stern and self-righteous. Out of the corner of my eye, I noticed a police squad had arrived, but they hung back, assessing the situation, batons twitching.

For a few minutes, the Christians' singing and our chanting canceled each other out, then further down the line, toward Susie, the women started whispering. All eyes were on a white van that had just pulled up to the curb, a few blocks down from the clinic. A TV crew climbed out, led by a woman in an electric-blue suit, her red hair pulled sharply back in a ponytail. She marched toward us, pushing her way between the two groups, instructing the cameraman where to stand, where to point his lens, and then held up a cartoonish microphone.

The instant she started speaking—loudly, so she could be heard above the din—it was like someone had thrown a match among the protesters on both sides. The Christians surged forward, growing louder, jockeying for position, while the women linked arms, chanting with gusto and bracing for what—a Bible bashing? I tried to move back, to stand behind the line, and had almost managed it when

Susie appeared out of nowhere and started to wrestle Zachary out of his sling.

"What are you doing?"

"I need to borrow him," she said, tugging at the material. "It's only for a minute. Then I'll bring him back."

"No," I said, adamant. "He'll get hurt." I wrapped my arms around Zachary's tiny body, held him tightly to my chest. "He's just a baby."

Susie said, "I'll protect him," and began to prize him off me, using force. She was so robust, so strong, more—she would hate this—like a *man*. "Come on, Poppy—it's for a good cause," she said, untying the strap of the sling.

I was distracted for a moment by Zachary himself, who had started crying, and in this moment, Susie took advantage, gripping his body firmly with both hands.

"Please don't do anything stupid," I said, easing my hold so he wouldn't get ripped in two.

She took him from me and charged off in the direction of the TV camera, head down, shoulders squared, bulldog style, for battle. *Please don't hurt him,* I prayed, holding my breath, cursing myself for being weak and handing him over. I tried to follow, but the women on either side had taken hold of my arms and forced me back into the chain. "Hold fast!" they said. "Don't let the bastards in." I did as I was told for a minute or two, then saw my chance to break free. A skirmish had broken out near the TV anchor, and while the women craned their necks to see what was going on, I managed to wriggle out from their tightly clamped arms. I had lost sight of Susie and Zachary but fought my way through the crowd to where

I hoped they would be. Each step of the way, the crowd fought back. No one wanted to give up their hard-won position, and I was elbowed and heckled and abused by Christians and lesbians alike. I couldn't see Katrina anywhere.

In the distance, Susie appeared on the clinic steps, holding Zachary aloft like a trophy. His face was red, his little mouth open in a scream, but whatever sound he was making was lost in the far louder noise of the baying crowd.

"Over here!" shouted Susie. "Or I'll drop the baby!"

A few gasps rose from the ranks below her, but I had been traumatized into silence. Wielding her microphone like a machete, the TV reporter slashed her way up the steps to get to Susie, followed by the cameraman. When the microphone was within Susie's reach, she grabbed it off the reporter, holding Zachary in a football clutch under one arm. The TV reporter tried to wrest back the microphone, but Susie deftly held her at arm's length and nodded to the cameraman to start rolling. He obeyed, and the reporter signaled him: *I give up.*

"I'm a lesbian and a mother!" Susie bellowed at the assembled crowd, keeping one eye on the TV camera, to make sure it was filming. She maneuvered Zachary to hold him up in front of her. "And this is my grandson!" He obliged with a curdled scream. "We are not trying to stop other women becoming mothers. We are not driving the human race to extinction. We just want women to be in control of their own bodies!"

The women around her cheered, while, with equal passion, the Christians booed. The TV reporter snatched the microphone out of Susie's hand and turned to the camera to try to deliver her piece over the deafening furor. Susie remained by the reporter's side, leaning toward her trying to stay in the shot.

I plunged through the crowd, reaching Susie just as the reporter was signing off. She let go of Zachary easily, discarding a prop that she no longer needed. He was red faced and whimpering but unhurt. I, however, was livid. "How could you use him like that? How could you take him from his mother?"

Susie didn't register what I was saying, or even that I was mad with her. "That was fucking dynamite," she said, gazing beyond me at the crowd of cheering women. She raised her fist triumphantly, shouting, "Down with the patriarchy!" then rushed into their waiting arms.

I walked back to where the truck was parked, realized it was locked, then sat in the back tray to feed Zachary. All that crying had exhausted him, and halfway through, his sucking slowed, and his eyes drifted shut. His face was still blotchy, his hair damp, and I longed to share my outrage, to tell someone what had happened. A few people walked past, but most were preoccupied, doctors and nurses on their way to work, or patients caught up in their maladies. For the first time, I understood how vulnerable we were, what life as a single mother might be like. I could not protect Zachary physically, any more than I could provide for his material needs. I didn't want to stay on the commune indefinitely, but finding a house, getting a job, when he was so young, would be out of the question. My savings were running out and the only reason I *had* savings was that Lukas had paid for everything since I had finished work. There had been no discussion. He just did it. And in return for his generosity he had been pushed out of the circle. *I* had pushed him out. The intimacy that went on between mother and child, the obsessing and loving and fretting and all the minuscule routines that made up our day, was above all exclusive and didn't involve anyone else. Even if Lukas *had* been home more often, would that have made a difference, or would it just have been more obvious that he was shut out?

Over by the clinic, the protest had broken up, and the Christians and their placards drifted off in the direction from whence they had come. Katrina and Susie soon returned to the truck, their expressions victorious.

"We kept the clinic open," said Susie. "Every other time those nutters have shown up, they've had to close."

"How's the little guy?" asked Katrina, leaning over to pat his head.

"He's fine now, but he was pretty shaken up," I said with a look that was meant for Susie but went unnoticed by her.

CHAPTER 18

Auckland
1989

WE CLIMBED BACK INTO the truck and set off toward the city. The women were spending the afternoon with friends at a house in Ponsonby, and I was going to visit Elisabeth, who lived close by in Freemans Bay. I had been planning on sneaking off to see her without telling Susie and Katrina where I was going but at the last minute I decided to just be honest. I was tired of Susie's bullying, of tiptoeing around her in case she exploded. She and Katrina were surprised when I told them I had Elisabeth's address, even more so when I told them it was Hunter who had given it to me. "I knew we couldn't trust that bastard," said Susie. "Who knows what else he's kept from us?"

"I'm sick of his bullshit," said Katrina.

"Maybe it's time."

"Maybe it is."

I got out of the car. "See you later," I said, while the two women exchanged meaningful looks, absorbed in some drama of their own.

The car was parked outside their friends' villa, where I would meet them later. It wouldn't be hard to remember which one to go into. Painted on the roof was a giant black women's symbol. This was the area Lukas and I had lived in, and as I strolled down the gently sloping street crammed with run-down wooden villas, I was filled with nostalgia for how happy, even how poor, we had been. In the years since, some of the villas had been dolled up, their colonial trimmings fixed and painted in garish colors, and though there were still plenty of dilapidated houses like the one we'd lived in, with mushrooms growing in the basement, the neighborhood, as a whole, seemed less down-at-heel.

Elisabeth lived in the gully between Ponsonby and the city, in a block of flats next to a wide, sodden park and some tennis courts. The way the apartments were clustered reminded me of London welfare-housing estates. The front door was beveled glass, and I watched Elisabeth's shadow approach before it opened. *Too late to leave.* She opened the door and we stared at each other. I didn't recognize her to begin with; she had cut her hair from waist length to a short feathery style and she had on tons of makeup—blue eye shadow and frosted pink lipstick.

"Poppy!" she exclaimed, jumping forward for what I thought might be a hug but turned out to be a near miss. "Oh my goodness—is that a baby?"

"Yep," I said, tilting the sling so she could get a better look. "Meet Zachary. Your grandson."

She put her hand to her mouth, stunned. Were those tears in her eyes?

"I'm sorry. I should have told you we were coming."

"He's so . . ." She started to reach for him, then withdrew her hand. "I can't believe I have a grandson."

"Hunter told me where to find you. The others don't know where you live."

Elisabeth smiled, recovering her composure. "Even if they knew, they would never come to see me. I'm a deserter."

She invited us into her flat, small but sunny, with sliding glass doors opening out onto a patio covered with plants. The space was much lovelier than I expected. On the patio, shaded by a grove of large trees in the communal gardens beyond, she served tea, nervously spilling some on the table as she poured. Unlike the women on the commune, who had fondled and kissed Zachary like he was their own, Elisabeth had not asked to hold him, and I put this down to what I had always suspected about her, that she didn't like babies—or children of any age, for that matter. When she found out he was the father, we talked about Lukas, about his success, and then, when she asked why we weren't still together, I hesitated. How had she known we weren't?

"It's complicated," I said, reluctant to give too much away.

"Uh-huh," she said. "I'll bet."

After sleeping for so long against my skin, Zachary woke up hot and deranged with hunger, his little fists grabbing ineffectively at the fabric of my shirt. I took him inside to where I had seen a more comfortable lounge chair and Elisabeth followed me in, at first hovering nearby, tidying up, then standing quite still and openly staring.

"Ouch, that takes me back," she said, wincing in remembered pain. "Though I can see it doesn't hurt you."

"Katrina told me you didn't enjoy breast-feeding."

"Is that what she said?" Elisabeth shook her head. "I loved it, in fact, but breast-feeding didn't like me."

"So you gave up?"

"I had to. I was in so much pain that the milk dried up."

"It *was* painful at first," I agreed. "But I'm glad I persevered."

"And I'm glad I didn't," said Elisabeth. "Months and months of cracked, bleeding nipples—one infection after another. Have you ever had mastitis?"

I shook my head.

"Lucky you."

"It must have been a relief," I said, "when the other women took over."

"A relief?" she repeated, incredulous. "No. It was *not* a relief."

She got up, agitated, and went into the kitchen, while I worked out what I'd said to offend her. The kitchen was a galley, open to the lounge, and I watched her fill a glass of water at the sink. I thought she was going to drink it herself, but instead she brought it out and set it on the table next to me. "It's thirsty work," she said, trying to smile.

"I didn't mean to upset you—I'm sorry."

"Don't be. The other women thought they were doing me a favor too."

Zachary was full, and I sat him up and patted his back until he made a froglike noise that made us both laugh. Elisabeth reached out and timidly patted the top of his head, the downiest part, just beyond the soft, pulsing fontanel.

"Would you like to hold him?"

"I'd love that."

I stood up with the baby, and Elisabeth took my place on the lounge chair, settling in and smoothing her clothes to make way for Zachary. She formed a cradle with her arms, saying, "I was never very good at this."

Her hands, when I lowered Zachary into them, were trembling.

"He's so warm," she said, sitting very still, and staring, awestruck, at the human in front of her. Zachary stared back intently, then reached out to try to swat her face. She leaned a little closer, letting him touch her nose. He looked very serious for a moment, his little brow creased in a comic-book frown, then broke into a smile that was so ecstatic and so guileless that it made Elisabeth gasp with delight.

"He likes you."

Elisabeth nodded, and I noticed she really was crying this time.

"He's so much like you were at that age," she said, wiping her eyes. "It takes me back to those early days, holding you for the first time—before I realized I would have to share you."

"Didn't you *want* to share me?" Growing up, I couldn't remember a single time when Elisabeth had tried to hug me. Out of all the mothers, she was the least warm, the most detached. "I thought you all agreed to raise us in a group."

"It's what we agreed on before any of us were pregnant," said Elisabeth. "But once you were born, and I held you in my arms, I changed my mind. I felt so much love for you— and I couldn't bear to share you with anyone. Every bone in my body told me it was wrong. I thought we were making a terrible mistake, and I said so. But Hunter, and the others, they'd made up their minds and I had to go along with it—or leave the commune." She paused. "And maybe I would have done that if I'd been able to breast-feed."

"But you couldn't—so you stayed?"

Elisabeth looked wistfully at Zachary. "Once I stopped breast-feeding, I didn't know how to bond with you—or any of the other babies—and I suppose, after a while, I stopped trying. All that love—it had nowhere to go, so it dried up. When Fritz came along, I didn't even try to feed him. I just let the other women get on with it and pretended he wasn't *my* son." She smiled. "It was around that time I took over all the cooking. It kept me busy—kept my mind off you and Fritz."

"You couldn't love us the way you wanted to so you stopped loving us at all?"

"I know what it sounds like." Her voice cracked. "The other women seemed to be happy to love all of you to the same degree. Maybe feeding you created that bond. But I didn't feel like that. I loved you and Fritz with all my heart but I wasn't allowed to show that I preferred you to the other children. Whenever I comforted you, the other women told me off. 'You can't do that, it isn't your turn.' Of course, they were just keeping me to our pact. But I couldn't love you and share you at the same time. It tore me in half."

So that was Elisabeth who tried to comfort me when I fell off the fence post. "But growing up," I began, not knowing if I should continue, "I thought you didn't even like us."

"I regret that," said Elisabeth. "Deeply."

"And even after we knew who you were—you didn't try to get close like some of the other mothers."

"I saw how you looked at us. You didn't want that. Not anymore."

"And when Fritz disappeared . . . ?"

"I was broken. I am still." Elisabeth struggled to go on. "To lose my son when I had never been able to show him how much I loved him . . ." We sat for a few moments in silence. "It was the same for Hunter but he couldn't admit it to himself. He was a stubborn, bloody-minded fool. And then, when you all started leaving—well, I knew you hated us and hated the commune, because of what we'd done to you." She handed Zachary back to me. The sudden movement unsettled him, and he started to whimper. When she spoke again, she sounded annoyed.

"Do you know how I know that?"

I shook my head, listening to her and soothing Zachary at the same time.

"Because I hated the fucking commune too. I couldn't stand to be there. So I left."

"Except that I *don't* hate it."

"Well, you should," said Elisabeth. "After what we did to you."

"You didn't mean to hurt us." Only a few days earlier, I'd read in the newspaper about the leader of a commune, north of Auckland, who had been arrested and charged with molesting his own children, and worse. "You didn't abuse us or anything."

"But we did," said Elisabeth. "We emotionally abused you."

It was the same phrase Lukas had used.

"I don't feel abused."

"You probably don't know what you feel."

My first reaction was to refute her, followed by a jolt of recognition. She was right. And then I cried.

"I'm sorry," said Elisabeth. "I didn't mean to be cruel. I'm angry with us, not with you." She paused. "It's taken a lot of therapy for me to be able to say this to you but man, we were such fucking hypocrites."

I blew my nose on Zachary's burp cloth, a piece of damp, sour-smelling muslin that needed a damn good wash.

"You were?"

"Big-time. We all believed in free love—Hunter especially. It was why we started a commune. We tried it but we couldn't make it work. Everyone was consumed with jealousy, and before we put a stop to it, quite a few of us were badly hurt, myself included."

"You never told us that."

"It almost destroyed the commune. So we decided to stick with monogamy. But Hunter and some of the others got it into their heads that free love was the ideal, the way forward. He thought that if you children were raised outside the nuclear family—if you were taught from the beginning to love without being possessive—then you would grow up to be less selfish."

"He thought we would be better at free love than you were?"

"Yes."

"That's insane."

"I know." Elisabeth frowned. "Everyone has the same need for intimacy, to love and be loved, and I think all we did was destroy your trust—not just in us but in love itself."

A queasy feeling came over me and I felt sure I'd made a terrible mistake, but I didn't know what it was yet—only that it was bad.

"This whole time," I said, "I thought everything that went wrong between Lukas and me was happening because of my prediction."

"Your prediction?" Elisabeth was staggered. "That was another crazy thing we should have put a stop to."

"Why didn't you?"

"We were under Shakti's spell, I guess—and it was the seventies. There was nothing we wouldn't try. *Nothing.*"

Elisabeth cleared away the tea things and carried them into the kitchen, where she stood at the sink with her back to me, washing up. She wore pink rubber gloves, and jabbed at the dishes with jerky, irritable movements, like she wanted the task, and our visit, to be over with. I took it as a signal to leave, though it may not have been—she had always washed dishes like that, and hadn't I, after all, just learned that her behavior did not always reflect her thoughts? Even if she had not been allowed to show it, and had since forgotten how, it was comforting to know that the same all-consuming love I felt for Zachary, Elisabeth had once felt for me. I had been unaware until now of how badly, growing up, I had wanted to be loved by one mother exclusively, not passed around, but held close to her heart and cherished beyond reason.

CHAPTER 19

Auckland
1989

AFTER THE LIGHTNING VISIT with Elisabeth, Zachary and I drifted around the streets of Freemans Bay, resting awhile in a small park, drinking water from a fountain, until I started to feel like a homeless person. Somewhat reluctantly, we arrived on the front porch of the lesbian house, where a women's symbol, with a clenched fist inside it, had been woven into the doormat.

In the front door was a letter slot, and after I had knocked, the metal flap covering it swung open, and a pair of wary eyes peered out. Despite this initial caution, the owner of the eyes turned out to be a cheerful woman with a buzz cut, and after she had let us in, she ushered us into the hallway. I recognized her from the protest. "I'm Pat," she said, stepping out onto the porch and glancing up and down the street before bolting the door behind us. "There's only women in here, and we like to be safe." She pointed down a long, dingy corridor, crowded with cardboard boxes, piles of leaflets and posters stacked on top, a few suitcases too. "Susie and Katrina are in the kitchen."

At the back of the house was a narrow room with a sloped roof, not much more than a lean-to with walls. The carcass of an old coal range comprised the bulk of the kitchen, and the gappy wooden floorboards sloped ever so slightly toward the garden. A graying, emaciated woman stood at the sink, peeling a mountain of potatoes. "You made it!" exclaimed Susie, bounding over from the Formica dining table and peering into the sling at Zachary. "Ruddy hell, I am sorry about the protest. I got carried away. Pat and Linda gave me a right telling off when we got home."

"Technically, he isn't even your grandson," I said, chiding her, but smiling, so she would know I had forgiven her.

"I don't know about that," said Susie. "We love him like one. Same as we love you like a daughter." She pulled me into a no-nonsense hug. "How was Elisabeth? Does she miss us? Is she dying to come back?" She laughed—not wanting an answer, only to be facetious.

"She looked good. Didn't say anything about coming back . . ."

"Imagine it," said Katrina. "Elisabeth and Shakti in the same room. Hunter wouldn't know where to look."

"Is Shakti coming to the commune?"

"Apparently," said Katrina. "But her movements are always mysterious. She likes to keep Hunter guessing."

"When are we heading back?"

"Tonight," said Susie. "After a quick meeting." She turned

to the emaciated woman at the sink. "Linda? Do you mind taking care of my daughter and grandson?"

Linda put down her knife. "I'd be delighted." She had finished peeling the potatoes and was slicing them into thin, shiny ovals. "How old is the wee fella?"

"Nearly six months."

She came over and squeezed his cheek. "He's a bonny one, isn't he?" I had learned that "bonny" was the word people used to describe a baby with fat rolls and no neck. At his age, it was a compliment.

"He's got a big appetite, always hungry."

"Maybe he's ready for solids." Linda held up a teapot. "Chamomile, peppermint, or gumboot?"

"Gumboot, thanks."

The partition walls of the villa were thin, especially the one behind my head, which separated the kitchen from the lounge, where the women had gone to have their meeting. Through it I could hear Susie's voice, not muffled but clear as a whistle. I tried not to listen but when she mentioned Gaialands my ears pricked up. Linda had been giving me advice on how to start Zachary on solid food, but I was not much interested, and my ears kept tuning in to the meeting next door. They were definitely discussing the commune, something about there *being enough of us to reach a consensus.*

"Be careful mixing Farex and banana," said Linda. "It turns to concrete in their stomachs. Really bungs them up. When your little one gets constipation—boy do you know all about it!"

Thanks to Linda, I had missed the crucial part of the conversation next door. "Do you have children?" I asked Linda, trying to be friendly. She looked too thin, almost wizened, and it wasn't unusual for the childless to give screeds of advice.

"Four," she said. "All boys."

"Four?" I was so taken aback I forgot to censor my thoughts. "No wonder you ran away to a house full of dykes."

Linda smiled proudly. "They're all grown now. The youngest, Stephen, just finished school." She told me about each of them in turn, their accomplishments, her hopes for their future, but as I tried to listen, I was distracted by the increasingly impassioned conversation through the wall. I heard Hunter's name mentioned several times, then Paul's and Sigi's, before someone exclaimed, "After thirty years, they won't just pack up and leave, you know!"

I wondered if Linda had heard this too, but when I turned to look at her, she had gone back to arranging the potato slices in a roasting dish, still wearing the proud smile. The meeting in the next room fell silent for a moment, before starting up in a more muted way. Whatever they had been discussing, the heated part of it was over. A few minutes later, Susie appeared in the kitchen. Her face was flushed, but she gave nothing away about what had gone on in the room next door. "That smells great," she said to Linda, before asking if I needed a break from Zachary. "It's been a bloody long day. You must be knackered."

"Yeah, I am." I was grateful when she picked him up and dandled him sweetly on her knee. Susie was so unpredictable. Explosive one minute, kind and thoughtful the next.

Whatever Linda had made for dinner, we would not be

eating it. The women wanted to hit the road, and had procured hard-boiled egg and stringy Swiss-chard sandwiches to keep us going on the journey. A third woman had materialized at the house, and when I went out to the car with Zachary and my rucksack, she and Pat were already seated in the back.

"This is Barb," said Pat. "Want me to hold the baby while you climb in?"

"Sure." I handed Zachary to her, and she and Barb clucked over him. They were much younger than Susie and Katrina, perhaps in their early thirties. The boot, their laps, and every available leg space were crammed with crates and duffel bags and pillows, but the couple had left a small wedge of the backseat free. I slotted into it, molded by the gear all around us, and settled Zachary on my lap. We set off, Susie at the helm and Katrina in the front passenger seat. No one explained the presence of Pat and Barb, or their worldly belongings, and the first hour of the trip passed in near silence, as though everyone was holding their breath until we had left the city limits behind. A little way after the Thames turnoff, Susie loudly cleared her throat. "Pat and Barb are coming to live at Gaialands," she said, seeking eye contact with me in the rearview mirror. "The commune needs new blood. It's becoming like an old folks' home."

Katrina turned around in her seat to face me. "It's been heading that way since you kids left. No one under the age of fifty."

I could see her point, but I didn't know what to say.

"We've heard so much about the place," said Pat, who

seemed to be the spokesperson of the couple. "We can't wait." She laid a hand on Barb's stomach and beamed. "Barb's expecting."

I wondered how the news would go down with the others on the commune, not just the addition of two residents but in a few months' time, a third. Did they already know, or was it a surprise? I suspected the latter.

Susie shot me another glance, either daring me to say what I was thinking or warning me not to.

"I'm sure you'll love it there," I said, thinking what a shock they were in for if they had always lived in the city.

We still had a long way to go, and shortly afterward, Barb fell asleep on Pat's shoulder, and Pat tucked a pillow under her neck and leaned against the headrest. Katrina stared vacantly out the window, while Susie kept her eyes on the road. It was unusual for the two women not to chat. Something was up, that was obvious, but I had other things to worry about. Since the visit to Elisabeth, I had been thinking a lot about Lukas, about our relationship and what it would take to save it. I could see very clearly how we had arrived at this point, the fracture, and faults on both sides, but I was less clear about whether, going forward, we could make it work. Would Lukas always wonder if I loved him enough, and could I ever prove to him that I did? What if Elisabeth was right and we were too damaged? The prediction, in its way, had been a far simpler obstacle than this.

On the winding road from Thames to Tairua, I dozed off once or twice, though with Zachary rolling around in my lap, I could not fall properly to sleep. I had tried, with the seat belt, to tether him to me, but it wasn't an especially safe or reliable setup. We made a toilet stop at a service station in Tairua, then wished we hadn't. Getting out of the car had displaced all our gear, and we could not fit comfortably back in. For the rest of the journey—still another three-quarters of an hour—Pat's guitar case was jammed into my leg, and a renegade suitcase kept nudging me in the head, threatening to escape from the boot.

For the last twenty minutes of the journey, with no clue how close to our destination we were, Zachary thrashed his little arms and legs and screeched about being cooped up in the car for so long, giving voice to how we all felt. I had tried to put him on the breast, but the car was bouncing too much to get a proper latch. It was dark when we arrived at Gaialands and we parked up by the chook house and got out and stretched our legs. I didn't realize how cramped, airless, and downright stinky it had been in the car until I got out and breathed the virgin night air, pure and fragrant. I had forgotten how vital this place smelled.

The lights in the mess hut were on, and through the window we could see everyone was still around the table, waiting for us to get back. "Let's go and introduce you—and see if there's any food left," said Susie. "We'll unload the car later."

A long trestle table ran the length of the mess hall, but the adults only took up one end of it. Since we kids had left, they had never had a full table. They would have finished eating hours before and were now deep in conversation. They fell silent when we came in, all eyes on the newcomers, Pat and Barb.

"We brought a couple of mates back with us," said Susie. "They needed a break from the city." She introduced the women, and hands were dutifully shaken, though with none of the warmth I had received at my homecoming. "I thought we could put them in the children's hut."

"Oh," said Loretta. "Tom and I have been sleeping in there." She looked at Tom, and then at Zachary and me. "Just while Poppy's here."

"Good thing there's so many bunks," said Susie. "You don't mind sharing, do you?"

"Not really," said Loretta, looking peeved. "The more the merrier, I suppose."

Easygoing Tom smiled. "No skin off my nose."

I waited for someone to ask how long Pat and Barb planned to stay, but no one did, and the women themselves didn't mention it, leaving me to wonder whether Susie had overlooked this information or left it out on purpose. Instead, she told Pat and Barb to take a seat, and began passing bowls of food in their direction. It was the commune way to share what we had, no questions asked, but even so, a few of the men gazed sadly at Pat and Barb's plates, what would have been tomorrow's lunch.

I noticed the seat next to Hunter was vacant but that someone had been sitting there and left behind an empty plate. I searched the room for Shakti, half expecting her to materialize, but she did not seem to be around. I was suddenly very tired, and immensely relieved when Paul offered to carry Zachary and our bags to the cabin.

Zachary, bless him, chose that night to sleep through for

the first time—a feat he did not feel compelled to repeat—and I hardly knew myself when I woke up the next morning. My head was bracingly clear, as though someone had got in there with a bucket of ice water and sluiced it out. On waking, I had risen from the bed and checked, with no little anxiety, to make sure Zachary was breathing, rejoiced that he was *still* asleep, then gone outside to listen to the birdsong on my own, a rare treat. So high was I on that eight-hour block of sleep that I wanted to sing too, or dance, or take up karate, but I was not the only one up. Far away across the still dewy field, a lone figure practiced yoga. She was no more than the brushstroke of a straight back in downward dog, but that was enough to accelerate my pulse. *Shakti.* After all this time, would I be able to stand up to her?

I was in the mess hut, eating breakfast, when she walked in, bold as anything, and sat down next to Hunter, kissed him, and slid her arm around his waist, as if he was her property. "Hello, Poppy," she said, digging in to the bowl of porridge that Hunter had obediently fetched for her. "I hear you've got a little one. What a lovely surprise."

Was she already toying with me—alluding to the fact that I had bucked her prediction? The animosity I felt toward her was difficult to hide. "His name is Zachary," I said, checking to see the baby was indeed where I had left him, over by the window in Katrina's arms. "He's very robust."

"Well, he is truly a blessing," said Shakti, smiling with what was either genuine appreciation or audacious shit-kicking smugness. "I can't wait to get to know him."

I could not finish my breakfast.

"Excuse me," I said, and walked out to the porch of the mess hut, where I struggled to control my emotions. I pulled on the first pair of gumboots I found, paced to the edge of the paddock, burst into tears, told myself to get it together, grow a spine, *harden the fuck up,* then sniffed like a drainpipe, wiped my face on my sleeve, and marched back to the mess hut to face my nemesis.

She was every bit as beautiful, damn it. Older but still the exotically plumed creature plucked out of a fantasy world and stranded on earth among dull and clumsy oafs. Around her I had always felt so ugly, so inadequately feminine, and nothing had changed. She still had the power to dazzle me.

I wasn't the only one. When I looked over at Hunter he was awestruck.

Pat and Barb arrived in the mess hall looking tired and disheveled. They eyed the vat of gray, lumpen porridge warily, as if it wasn't quite the whole-food smorgasbord they had hoped for. *Yes,* I felt like saying, *we really do eat that stuff three hundred sixty-five days of the year, even on Christmas morning; do you still want to stay?* I wondered what they had made of the long drop, not as monstrous as it had once been, but still dire enough, most mornings, to make your underpants retreat up your legs.

Pat slid onto the bench seat next to me, and Barb shunted close to her side, bowls of porridge in hand. They had both drowned it in molasses, a rookie mistake, and I watched them take a big mouthful, thinking it was golden syrup, then gag.

Pat sniffed the contents of her spoon. "Well, that was an interesting flavor."

"Molasses," I said. "You'll get used to it"

She grimaced. "Really? I find that hard to believe."

"It's packed with iron." I nodded at pregnant Barb. "You'll need that. There's no meat within a hundred miles of this place."

Barb swallowed it down, bravely, while Pat spooned hers off to one side. "Crikey, we had a rough night," she said. "Barb found a weta in her bed, and being the gentlewoman that I am, I had to see it off the premises."

"It was huge," said Barb, speaking for possibly the first time in two days.

"Poor Barb almost crapped her pants," added Pat.

Barb nodded agreement while Pat used her spoon as a ruler to demonstrate how big the weta was—the length of the handle—and how she had flicked it off the bed with her bare hands. I struggled to remember a night of my child-hood when my sleep hadn't been disturbed by one critter or another: slugs, centipedes, cockroaches, daddy longlegs, and the occasional white-tail spider. Often put there by one of the boys but not always.

From across the table, Hunter and Shakti watched this exchange—he with amusement, she more like a cat when it picks up the scent of a nearby dog. It wasn't just Pat's tale that was turning Shakti off but her whole demeanor, so forth-right that it was obvious, from even this small interaction, that Pat alone, out of all the humans in the world, would be immune to Shakti's charms. Sure enough, after a few minutes, Shakti got up and left, Hunter's gaze tracking her. If I had thought he was docile before, with Shakti around he was ten times worse.

"Hunter," I said. "The cabin I'm staying in—I think there's a problem with the roof. Would you mind taking a look?"

"Sure," he said, still in a dream world. "How about later?"

"I was hoping we could look at it now—while Zachary is with Katrina."

I wasn't sure what I was going to show Hunter at the cabin. A number of things were broken or falling off it, but I suspected they had been that way for years. There had been a roof leak, but Paul had patched it up a few days earlier. Halfway across the still-soggy field, with Hunter in tow, I remembered the rotten floorboard on the veranda that I had almost put my foot through. I showed it to him, and he agreed it was dangerous and needed to be seen to. "I'll ask Paul to fix it right away."

"How did it go in Whitianga?" I said, training my eyes on Hunter so as not to miss an iota of his reaction. "Did you hand over the shirt?"

For a moment he was blank. "The shirt?"

"The tank top Fritz wore. You were going to give it to the cops in Whitianga."

"They said they would look into it."

"That's all? They didn't ask where you found it?"

"I told them, and they said they'd look into that too."

I suspected he was bullshitting, that he hadn't handed in the tank top at all. Of course he hadn't. He was too besotted with Shakti, and she had likely encouraged him not to. "Did you tell Shakti about it?"

"She didn't know how it got there."

So he had told her. "What about the caravan? How did that end up in the estuary?"

"She doesn't know. She said she abandoned it at the side of the road. This is years ago. Right after she left here. She and her friend—Margie, Margot—"

"Marcia. Her girlfriend."

"We don't know that's what they were." Hunter's cheeks reddened. "Anyway, they drove here in that old rust bucket to pick up the caravan. Shakti said they hadn't got very far up the road when the tow bar snapped. The caravan rolled off into a ditch, and they left it there."

"They just left it there?"

"You know what Shakti's like—she doesn't care for material possessions. She's more in tune with the spiritual side of life."

I was speechless.

"Poppy, look, I can understand why you might find it hard to see me with another woman but what she and I have—"

"Believe me," I said, dreading what he might say. "It's not that."

"I was going to say," he continued, "that she has a pure soul. She's incapable of doing something that would deliberately harm another person."

Talking to him was a lost cause. He was so cunt-struck he was seeing fairies. If Shakti had anything to do with Fritz's disappearance, I would have to confront her about it myself.

"Are you coming to the hui?" asked Hunter.

"Is that today?"

He nodded. "Susie wants us all to be there. It's about the memorial for Fritz."

A hui would mean hours and hours of talking, discussion that went around in circles, everyone getting a chance to be heard, even if they had nothing to say—then thrashing it out to reach a consensus that pleased no one but infuriated the least number of people. We had covered the process, exhaustively, in women's studies. I could think of nothing worse. "Do you think we should have one? A memorial."

"How can we?" said Hunter. "We don't know where he is."

"But you think he's still alive?"

"I don't know," said Hunter. "Nobody does."

When I went back to the mess hut, Katrina and Zachary weren't there, and no one seemed to know where they had gone. Even though I knew he was with an adult, and theoretically should be safe, I felt anxious, a sensation that came over me whenever I had been separated from him for even a short time. I searched all the obvious places: Susie and Katrina's cabin, the chapel, the orchard, and the schoolhouse, now used as a library. Then, with a rising sense of panic, I looked in all the places I hoped they would never have ventured: down by the river, so swollen it would be treacherous even to look at; anywhere near the toilet block, where each long drop was a six-feet-deep, shit-filled grave. I was still getting used to the way my maternal instincts went rogue, always calculating the potential for fatality in nearby hazards, even if the baby was safely tucked up in bed. But Zachary wasn't tucked up in bed—I didn't know where he was. By the time I arrived at the door of Hunter's cabin, the only one I hadn't yet investigated, Zachary had met with a dozen violent and catastrophic ends, and my nerves were completely shot.

On my way up the front steps, I heard a sound that was music to my ears: Zachary bleating with the first signs of hunger. Or perhaps someone was sticking him with a pin. I didn't care—he was alive. With some urgency, I pushed open the door, strode into the cabin, and then froze at the grotesque pantomime before me. Relief turned to bewilderment, horror, as I stared and stared, trying to make sense of it.

Seated with legs crossed on the end of the bed was Katrina. She was smiling and nodding encouragement to another woman, also seated on the bed but at the head of it, against the wall. This other woman had no clothes on. She was propped up with pillows, her long, muscular limbs a glossy nutmeg brown, ill matched to the pink, squirming baby in her arms. The anatomy of it was easy to understand. The woman was Shakti, the baby was Zachary, but what was she doing to him? She had cupped her hand around the back of his head and was pushing his mouth toward her bare breast. When he got close to the nipple, he thrashed his head from side to side, kicked his legs, and complained, but Shakti ignored his protests and pressed on, trying to maneuver her breast in the direction of his mouth. "Suckle," she was saying, "please, just once."

I had entered the room without knocking or announcing my presence, but the two women were so absorbed in their task, Katrina murmuring encouragement, and Shakti concentrating on Zachary, that they hadn't noticed I was there.

I managed to call out "What on earth are you doing?" before charging for Zachary and trying to wrestle him away from Shakti.

I got as far as the bed. Katrina grabbed me around the waist from behind, stopping me in my tracks. "You don't need to worry," she said. "What's happening is natural."

"No, it's not," I said, trying to push her off. "He doesn't like it."

Deranged with concentration, Shakti folded Zachary more securely in her arms and while he screamed into her chest, his hands white and curled into fists, his body rigid with distress, she tried once more to ram her breast down his throat.

I escaped from Katrina and put my hand in between Shakti's breast and Zachary's mouth, shushing to calm him down, at the same time working to free him from Shakti's arms, devilishly strong after a lifetime of yoga. "Please," she said, in a plaintive register. "He almost took it."

Zachary had switched from screaming to the really desperate cries that make no sound.

I felt Katrina's hand on my shoulder, squeezing it. "Let her have one more try."

"For fuck's sake, can't you see how upset he is?" To be taken seriously, I'd had to yell.

Shakti released her grip, finally, and I lifted the baby from her. Letting go of him, in a pathetic voice she said, "I just wanted to know what it feels like to nurse."

"Shakti can't have children," said Katrina. "That scar she showed us, on her cervix—the botched operation." She lowered her voice to a whisper: "She thinks they damaged her uterus."

I recalled Shakti's self-examination, how she had urged us to take back our bodies from the medical profession. No wonder she didn't trust anyone with a scalpel. That doctor really had butchered her. And then, I remembered my prediction.

"You're the one that's infertile?" I said unkindly. "*You're the one with the womb that shall bear only sorrow?*"

Shakti sobbed—something I had not known she was capable of. "To be a mother," she said. "It's all I ever wanted."

With the better part of me, I felt for her. To be denied the one thing in life she wanted was cruel. But in the end I couldn't forgive her for yoking me to her misfortune. "Did it make you feel better," I said, "to share your misery?"

"That's not why I did it," pleaded Shakti. "I was trying to help you. The way you were brought up . . . I was worried what would happen if you ever had children."

"As you can see, we're doing just fine." I had been holding Zachary to my chest, comforting him, but he was still naked, and now he peed on me. The warm liquid seeped through every layer of my clothing, the last clean lot I had. I felt no disgust, his urine was comprised of fluid from my own body, but Zachary was wet, and shivered with cold.

"Why did you take all his clothes off?" I said, looking around for something to wrap him in.

"Skin to skin," said Katrina, handing me a terrycloth jumpsuit. "Such a beautiful way to bond."

"With your own baby," I said, for myself but also for Elisabeth. "Not with mine."

CHAPTER 20

Gaialands
1989

THE HUI WAS IN an hour's time. I did not want to go. I did not wish to face the strange adults who had raised me, or the woman who had turned her sorrow into mine. But for the sake of Fritz, to honor his memory if nothing else, I had to go. There was also the matter of the tank top. I had meant to confront Shakti about it, but in the confusion—the horror—of seeing her trying to breast-feed my baby, I had forgotten about it entirely. Before I did anything else, I wanted to know if Hunter had taken the T-shirt to the police or if, as I suspected, he had hung on to it, done nothing—either to protect Shakti, or because he had taken her at her word.

I waited until the last possible minute to carry out my plan, when I knew Hunter and everyone would be assembled in the chapel, waiting for the hui to begin. Then, with Zachary stowed in the sling, I took a roundabout route through a grove of lemon trees to Hunter's cabin, which he had been sharing of late with Shakti. The door was unlocked, just as it had been for the last twenty-five years. "If I wanted to lock my door at night, I'd move to the city," was one of Hunter's favorite maxims.

Sure enough, the tank top I was looking for was exactly where I had expected to find it: in the drawer Hunter had shoved it in, still near the top. The blood on the tank top had dried to an orange crust, and when I tried to unfold it, the most saturated areas of fabric stayed glued together in a lump. Unsure if it would prove anything, or be of any use, I stashed it in the sling under Zachary's sleeping body.

A few minutes later, I slipped into a pew in the back row of the chapel. Paul glanced behind to wink at me, but the others stayed facing the front, where Susie was perched on a small podium. Her seating position, her manner, was that of someone who wanted to lead the meeting without appearing as though they were. In the front pew to her right, Katrina sat next to Barb and Pat. In the pew behind them sat Loretta and Tom, he with his arm around her. Sometime in the last week, perhaps while I had been in Auckland, Loretta had chopped off all her hair.

Across the aisle, as though they were wedding guests from the groom's side of the family, sat Hunter and Shakti, and behind them, Paul and Sigi, her hair long and flowing, like Shakti's. Everyone talked among themselves, waiting for the meeting to start. Susie chewed on her nails. She appeared to be gathering her thoughts, running through a speech in her mind. I had seen Hunter doing the same thing before one of his long diatribes and wondered what it was she had rehearsed to say.

Zachary stirred, and I remembered the tank top, stashed in his sling. Now that I had it in my possession, I wasn't sure what I was going to do with it. I hadn't thought this through at all.

Susie stood up and cleared her throat. "We're here to reach a decision about Fritz, whether it's time to have a memorial." She gulped, and her voice, when she started speaking again, was shaky. "He's been gone ten years, and the majority of us think the time has come to mourn him. We need to close the wound."

From the pew to her right, where Katrina and Loretta and the lesbians sat, came murmurs of assent. From the other side: silence. I had expected Hunter to protest but he didn't.

"Does anyone want to get the ball rolling?"

No one said anything.

I put up my hand. Everyone turned to look at me.

"Yes, Poppy?"

I had been about to show everyone the tank top, then chickened out. "We could put it to a vote?"

"We could do that," said Susie, "but I'd prefer to reach a consensus."

Someone in the left-hand pew, I think it was Paul, groaned. A consensus could take weeks.

In the middle of this exchange, Shakti had leaned to whisper something in Hunter's ear, and when she was finished, he had turned and whispered back. This went on, back and forth, loud enough that we could hear the swish-wish-wish of their whispering, but not a word they were saying, until Susie rapped her knuckles on the side of the podium.

"For goddess's sake. Don't just sit there whispering like a couple of schoolboys. If you've got something to say, spit it out."

Hunter and Shakti turned to face her, then Hunter glanced one last time at Shakti before he stood up.

"We can't have a memorial for Fritz because we don't know that he's dead."

Moans of frustration emanated from the right-hand pew. "You're living in cloud cuckoo land," said Katrina, getting to her feet. "And it's not fair on the rest of us. We've been in limbo for ten years. He was our son. We all loved him but it's time we accepted he's gone." Her voice faltered. "I just can't do this any longer." She sat down, in tears.

"Katrina's right," said Tom. "We all miss him but it's time to face facts."

"And what exactly are they?" said Hunter.

"Mate, he's dead," said Tom. "Fifteen-year-olds don't just disappear into the forest, never to be heard of again."

"Fritz did." Shakti tried to stop Hunter from saying anything else, to pull him back down to seated, but he was rigid with frustration, and wouldn't budge.

Susie eyed the pair quizzically.

"Hunter, Shakti, do you know something we don't?"

Hunter gave Shakti a pleading look. She shook her head.

"No," he said. "I don't."

"Then stop wasting our time," called Tom, across the aisle. "Sit down."

Hunter sat. Susie waited for the unrest to subside. "Well,

if no one has any other suggestions, I propose we kick things off with a show of hands."

"Just call it a bloody vote," said Paul. "We all want to get some sleep tonight."

"Do we all?" said Susie. "Or by 'we' do you mean the men?"

Paul sighed. "Oh for fuck's sake, can you leave gender out of it, just this once?"

"No, I can't," said Susie. "Women have been oppressed for thousands of years, and we cannot just leave it out."

"Excuse me," I said.

While they were arguing, I had wiggled out of my pew and made my way to the front, standing in the space between the two aisles, on what I hoped was neutral ground. I held the tank top aloft, pinching each of the shoulder seams between thumb and forefinger. There were audible gasps when everyone saw it. I spoke at full volume so everyone could hear.

"This is the shirt Fritz was wearing on the day he disappeared." More gasps, and someone drew our attention to the blood. "That's mine," I reassured them. "I found the shirt in Shakti's old caravan, and used it to bandage my leg. I don't know what it was doing there but I think Shakti does."

I turned to look at Shakti, and so did everyone else, while she stared straight ahead, determined not to meet anyone's gaze. From her profile, I tried to read her expression. It wasn't neutral, but nor was it the face of a person who has just been found guilty of committing a heinous crime. If anything she looked vaguely self-satisfied.

"Do you have an explanation for this?" said Susie, stationing herself in a wide-legged stance, arms folded, in front of Shakti.

Shakti didn't respond but Hunter stood up and squeezed his temples in exasperation.

"You've got it all wrong!" he said. "You're jumping to conclusions. Shakti didn't do away with Fritz, she—"

He was stopped by Shakti, who gripped his arm and vehemently shook her head.

"You've got to tell them," he pleaded with her. "Otherwise they'll think you've done something awful."

"Tell us what?" said Susie, turning to Hunter. "This is exactly the kind of bullshit we've had to put up with from you for years."

"Hear, hear!" said Pat, even though she had been at the commune for all of five minutes.

"Yes, Shakti, what is it?" said Sigi, trying to sound reasonable, calm. "If you have some information about Fritz, you must share it with us."

Finally, Shakti stood up. The smug look had gone from her face, and she seemed, for her, to be nervous, at a loss for what to do with her hands.

"I have to go back to the beginning," she said, hesitating. "Otherwise you won't understand."

"Try us," said Susie, bristling.

Shakti scanned the faces of the small gathering, then reached for Hunter's hand. "When I first came to Gaialands, I could see there was a lot of suffering."

A few people murmured their dissent.

"Suffering?" said Susie. "What do you mean by that?"

"I'm talking about the way the children were brought up, not knowing who their parents were."

Dissent became hostile silence.

"I think you all knew by then that your experiment had failed, but you couldn't admit the effect it was having on the children." She appealed to the gathering with a smile but was met with cold stares. "I did what I could to try and put things right. First, with a healing ritual, the ceremony I called the Predictions, and then"—she pointed at the soiled green tank top, now hanging limply at my side—"I helped Fritz to start a new life."

"You did *what*?" said Susie, incredulous.

Shakti looked to Hunter for reassurance, but he wouldn't acknowledge her.

"Fritz wanted to run away," she said. "So I helped him."

No one breathed. Our collective disbelief leached the air from the room. But Shakti seemed to take this as a sign we were captivated. She continued, more confident than before.

"The plan came together so serendipitously—as though the universe wanted it to happen. Fritz met some friends of mine at Nambassa who had a yacht. They needed a deckhand from Auckland to Australia. We arranged for me to pick Fritz up on the road outside Gaialands and take him to meet Johannes. I had hoped to pick up my caravan as well, but Fritz and I found it at the bottom of a gully—the old girl wasn't going anywhere. I gave Fritz new clothes so he wouldn't be recognized, and we left his old ones there. To be honest, I thought you'd find it sooner." Here, Shakti paused, and tried to make eye contact with someone, but none of us would look at her. "Anyway," she continued. "The good news is, Fritz isn't dead. This whole time, he's been living in Australia. In Sydney, I think."

Shakti stood before us, smiling, awaiting a positive response, cheering or applause, then—*thwack!*—out of nowhere came a fist powered by a decade of wasted parental grief and centuries of patriarchal oppression, a fist so righteous that when it socked Shakti on the jaw, she folded to the ground as if the puppeteer above her had cut her strings.

Susie recoiled, as shocked as anyone that she had knocked Shakti to the ground, cradling her fist as though it had betrayed her, as if she was ashamed of it. But she had nothing to be ashamed of. When Tom patted her on the back, muttering, "Good job, Suze," he put into words what we had all been thinking. Any one of us could have punched Shakti. She deserved it.

Hunter helped Shakti to her feet. On her face, even a split lip was fetching, the blood congealed in a single, perfect droplet, like a beauty spot. She did not try to fight back, but cowered behind her hands, playing the consummate victim, after playing the reluctant hero.

Around them the gathering stood in traumatized silence, each person processing the news in his or her own way. Katrina wept, her tears profuse but making no noise, while Loretta buried her head in her hands, and was comforted by Tom, moist eyed but holding his emotion in check. I sobbed too, for the years I'd lost with my brother, and wished with all my heart that Lukas could be here.

There was a lull in which no one said anything, then everyone reacted all at once, showering Shakti with pent-up abuse.

"How could you?" said Paul. "We loved him."

"I cried every night for five years," said Katrina. "All that grief—all that suffering."

"How long have you known?" said Tom, addressing Hunter.

"Not long," he said. "I swear." Throughout all this, Hunter stood at Shakti's side, shielding her with his arm, while his face told a different story. "You know I grieved with the rest of you."

Paul glanced at Shakti. "And yet you can forgive her?"

Hunter said nothing, nor looked at anyone.

When the hubbub had died down, and it was quiet enough that she would be heard, Susie instructed Shakti to "Pack up your things, leave tonight, and don't ever think about coming back to Gaialands."

Upon hearing this, Shakti straightened her spine and defiantly addressed Susie. "This place could have been paradise on earth but you ruined it for yourselves." Then, with as much dignity as she could muster, she walked regally out of the chapel, followed, to the door, by Hunter, her loyal, if chastened, lapdog. But in the doorway, after Shakti had already walked out, he hesitated, then turned and spoke to the assembled group.

"If she goes," he said, "then I go too."

"Hunter," said Paul, "think it over. Don't throw away your life's work—at least not for her."

"I have thought it over," said Hunter. "And there's no longer a place for me here."

"Bullshit." Paul shook his head. He had always been Hunter's right-hand man. His ally. "There's always a place for you here, brother. You made Gaialands what it is."

"That's right," said Hunter. "I poisoned it."

"He's made his choice," said Susie. "No one's forcing him to go."

"Aren't they?" Paul glanced around at the assembled group. With the addition of Pat and Barb, women now outnumbered men two to one. "Isn't that what you've been trying to do all along—to get rid of us jokers?"

For once, Susie was lost for words. She looked to Katrina for backup.

"Not all the men," said Katrina. "We still need a few of you."

"Yeah, right" said Paul. "To fix the bloody tractors."

"Actually," said Pat, "I'm a qualified mechanic."

"And the latrines? Who's going to dig those in the middle of the winter when the ground's like concrete and the shit's frozen solid?"

"We're strong," said Susie. "I'm sure that between us we can dig a hole."

"Sure you can," said Paul. "But up until now you haven't wanted to. You can bitch all you like about how hard it is to be a woman, how the likes of me and Hunter here have held you back, but not one of you has ever put your hand up to help us shovel your shit."

"Well," said Loretta, "the same goes for your dirty

underpants. Who do you think scrubs the skids out of those?"

"Skids?" said Paul. "What skids?"

But quiet Loretta wasn't finished. "Or the toilet seats. They don't clean themselves. Nor does the shower block. You get three hot meals a day, thanks to us"—she looked at the other women, who nodded—"and then we do all the dishes." Loretta had shaken off Tom's embrace, and he stood by her side, dumbfounded. "Has it never occurred to you we might not like cooking and cleaning—that we might want to have a go at something else?"

I could scarcely believe she was voicing the exact same ideas that Shakti had planted in her head all those years ago.

"You can have a go at shoveling shit," said Paul. "All you have to do is ask."

"Good as gold," said Loretta. "And you can scrub your own undies."

I couldn't help it. After all the tension, I let out a snort of laughter. I tried covering it with a cough, but everyone had heard, and turned to look at me.

"Strewth," said Paul, shaking his head and grinning. "Poppy's right. We just found out Fritz is alive and all we can do is stand here bloody arguing."

"It's a bit of a shock, to be honest," said Susie. "All this time, well, I thought you blokes were to blame."

"Us?" Hunter glanced from Tom to Paul. "How?"

"I thought Gaia had cursed us. That she wanted us to destroy the commune and start afresh." She shook her head. "Grief makes you think crazy things."

"That wasn't all grief," Hunter said. "We did a few things wrong, here and there. I've had a long time to see the error of our . . . of my ways."

They stood for a moment in silence, and then Katrina exclaimed, "Which one of us is going to look for him?" She threw her arms in the air and whooped for joy. "Our darling boy Fritz is alive!"

At last, the dour mood lifted. One by one, each member of the group broke into smiles, as though finally the news had set in.

"We'll all go," said Paul. "We'll comb the streets until we find him. Then we'll bring him home to Gaialands where he belongs." To Hunter, asking far more than if he was coming to Sydney to find Fritz, he said, "Sport, are you in?"

Hunter gazed out the door through which Shakti had disappeared and then turned back to his comrades. "You bet."

A cheer went around the parents, the sound of reuniting over shared love for a lost son, and I realized how badly they'd needed to find him, that they had been waiting for something that would bring them back together.

The noise woke up Zachary, and he looked to me for the reassurance only I could give him. It was one of those moments when I felt very keenly that his life was in my hands, just as mine had been in the hands of my parents, and theirs in the hands of their parents before them, a chain of loving but sometimes incompetent responsibility that stretched back to eternity. For the first time in my life, I felt compassion for the adults. All parenting was an experiment, and however wrongheadedly theirs was conceived, they had

carried it out with the best of intentions. Behind every mis-
guided step had been love.

I had carried Zachary over to the window, where it was
quieter, and glanced out when something colorful in the distance caught my eye. Some fifty feet away, at the end of a
row of sleeping huts, where there was a partly covered area
we called the loggia, though it was no more than a lean-to
held up with sticks, a woman struggled with a large bundle of what looked to be clothing or textiles. The bundle
obscured the woman's head, but I didn't need to see her face
to know that it was Shakti. She came to the end of the loggia
and paused. Her car was parked not far off but between it
and her was a stretch of sticky mud that had been all winter in the making. This mud cropped up in the same place
each year, and I had stood in that same spot where she now
hesitated, deciding whether to take the long, sensible way
around or to risk walking through it. Never one to retreat,
Shakti adjusted her load, hitching it high on her shoulder,
and stepped, barefoot, into the bog. The first couple of paces
seemed to go okay, but roughly a third of the way across,
the bundle of clothing came unbalanced, and in an effort
to right it, Shakti overreached, striding where she ought to
have tiptoed. Her legs went out from under her, and the bundle swayed violently to one side before coming undone in a
cascade of multicolored silk. Shakti landed, ungracefully, on
her backside, the fabric spread out across a nice, wide area.

Up until this point, I had been passively transfixed, as
though watching a nature program on television, but now
I wondered if I ought to go to her aid. I was next to use-

less with Zachary in my arms and the adults were still in a huddle at the other end of the chapel. "Hunter," I called out, "come quickly."

He came to the window and stared out at Shakti, now extricating her saris one by one from the mud, and scratched his head, unsure what to do.

Presently, Paul came and joined us. "Looks like she needs a hand."

Hunter turned to his mate. "You reckon I should give her one?"

"Your call," said Paul.

With undisguised eagerness, we crowded in front of the glass to watch the show. In gumboots and shorts, his year-round uniform, Hunter strode purposefully in Shakti's direction, then, when he was still some way off, called out to her. "Do you need a hand?"

She stopped what she was doing and glared at him. Mud streaked one side of her face, and the look in her eye was feral, almost crazed.

Louder this time, and more for our benefit than Shakti's, Hunter repeated, "I said, 'Do you need a hand?'"

Shakti looked past him in the direction of the chapel, fixing her gaze on the window where the rest of us stood crowded at the glass. "Fuck you!" she yelled, at the top of her lungs, adding, for good measure, the fingers. "And fuck your lousy commune!"

CHAPTER 21

Gaialands
1989

A FEW DAYS LATER, a letter arrived, postmarked London. It had been so long since I had seen his handwriting on anything that I had opened it and started reading before I realized whom it was from.

Dearest Poppy, it began, *I am so sorry for everything.*

A landslide of emotion hit me, but I read on.

When you found me in Cologne, I was the most out of it I have ever been—not just from the overdose, but far away from the man I want to be for you, the man I am. I have loved you since I was ten years old, maybe even since before that, when we were four or five, and the adults started to leave us kids alone in the huts at night. Whenever I woke up and it was too dark or I was having a nightmare, you were the first person I thought of and wanted to be near. I guess other people get comfort from having their parents around (I don't know) but the only person I get that feeling from is you.

I had to stop reading and find a tissue to blow my nose. I felt exactly the same way about Lukas—that he alone *comforted* me from the trials of the world—but I had never been able to put it into words. Of course we meant more to each other than lovers. We hadn't been able to rely on our parents so we had relied on each other for everything, since we were kids.

The next part of the letter was about how he had started going to rehab. No one had forced him to go—he had rung up the clinic himself and booked in for rehabilitation treatment for addiction to alcohol and narcotics. He honestly hadn't realized he was addicted, he wrote, until he took the overdose in Cologne, even though he should have seen the writing on the wall months before that. Marlon had introduced him to everything initially but the ongoing problem was that it was all too easy to get whatever he wanted, whenever he wanted it. He didn't have to go out and buy the drugs on the street from a dealer; Fran did all that. She had contacts in every city. He thought that was how she fed her own habit—by taxing whatever she procured for the band. He wasn't trying to blame her for the mess he was in, but she had enabled him to a level that he would not have been able to reach on his own. *Even that wasn't her fault,* he wrote. *We were the first band she ever managed, and none of us knew what we were doing. We made every rookie mistake in the book.*

I read that part again, struggling to remember the conversation I'd had with Lukas before I walked out of his hotel room. He'd said he was waiting for Fran, that she hadn't come back, and I had assumed it was because they were having an affair. I'd assumed the same thing from the photograph Paul had shown me but on its own, there was nothing suspicious about a singer and his manager snapped together in a bar. A manager's job was to be with her band all the time and photos were taken wherever they went. And Lukas had been waiting for Fran to come to his room that night, not because he was sleeping with her, but because she was his supplier.

I didn't waste time writing him a letter back. I packed up Zachary and my things and the next day Paul drove us to the international airport in Auckland. I had just enough in my savings account to pay for our airfare, and once I had booked it I rang Lukas and told him when to meet us at Heathrow at the other end.

"Did you get my letter?" he said, sounding worried that I hadn't.

"Yes, I got your letter. It made me cry."

"You're not mad with me about the drugs?"

"Not at all," I said. "I thought you were shagging your manager."

"Dude," said Lukas. "The first rule of rock 'n' roll is don't screw the crew."

"I don't think she follows that code."

"Oh, everyone's slept with Marlon. That doesn't count."

Heathrow Airport was jam-packed with the endless variety of nationalities and colors and social groups that did not exist anywhere outside of London, but even among that crowd, Lukas stood out. It was one of the only times in our life—the other was when I came across him performing in that basement bar in Chelsea—that I had ever gotten a true first impression, seeing him as a stranger would, not as a member of my immediate family. The ridiculous curls were gone. He had put on weight, had cut his hair short, and wore normal clothes. He

looked once again like the boy I loved, and had done for as far
back as I could remember.

Approaching him, I suffered a sudden bout of shyness, a
fear that someone like him, someone *famous,* couldn't possibly love an ordinary girl like me, and it was the first time I
knew to call it that, and not to mask it with a trick or a prediction that would keep him at a distance.

Lukas's expression had been neutral but the minute he
saw us it bloomed with love. I had not seen him look like
that for a very long time, not on the day we were married,
not in the hospital when Zachary had pneumonia, perhaps not even on the day our son was born. The real Lukas,
I realized, had been absent for a very long time. He smiled
his goofy smile, mirroring mine, and we wrapped our arms
around each other and sandwiched Zachary in the middle,
the heart of our little family.

"What have you been feeding him?" he said, squeezing
the fat rolls on Zachary's arm. "He looks like a pudding."

"So do you," I said, patting his stomach. "Maybe not a
pudding but a champagne socialist."

"I don't fit my leather pants anymore. If Marlon finds
out, he'll fire me."

"He can't fire you. You're his muse."

We walked hand in hand down the causeway to the car
park building, where Lukas had trouble finding the car he
had borrowed from a friend, an old yellow Renault Five. It
was rusted on the outside and filled with apple cores and
parking tickets and squashed polystyrene cups, but Lukas
wouldn't mention the car's shabby appearance because he

knew I didn't care. We had been brought up not to mind that sort of thing, and we still didn't mind it, nor did we have to explain.

"You'll never guess who came back to Gaialands while I was there," I said, remembering that I hadn't told him yet about any of the insane stuff that had happened.

"Who?"

"Shakti."

"That crazy witch?"

"You were right about her."

I told him of Shakti's deception, how she had helped Fritz run away to Sydney, and that Elisabeth, when I rang her up and told her, had immediately set off to find him, not caring if it interfered with anyone else's plans.

"Wow," he said, incredulous. "That's some heavy shit."

"I know. They want to find him and bring him home to the commune, but I'm not sure he'll want to go back."

"I'm surprised you didn't go straight to Sydney to look for him."

"I wanted to," I said to Lukas. "But I wanted to see you more."

"You really mean that?"

"With all my heart," I said, resting my hand on his knee, then feeling self-conscious about it being there. "I never want to be apart from you again."

Lukas drove on in silence, studying the oncoming cars, and then I lost my nerve and withdrew my hand.

"I liked it there. Put it back."

When I did as I was told, he moved my hand a little

closer to his crotch, before turning to me and grinning. "I guess it's safe, now that you don't believe in it, to tell you what was in my prediction."

"I *knew* it, you dick. I knew you were only pretending you didn't look."

"Of course I looked." He stared straight ahead at the road, teasing out the moment, a smirk playing at the edges of his mouth.

"And?"

"It was nothing."

"What do you mean 'nothing'?"

"There was literally nothing in my prediction. It was a blank piece of card."

"She left it blank?" Of all the things it could have been, I had not expected that. "And that's why you thought it was bullshit?"

Lukas laughed. "Finally! My wife sees the light."

I laughed along with him, mainly to mask my incredulity, but then, when I thought about it, I wondered if he'd waited so long to tell me his prediction because it *had* meant something to him once. If he had really always thought it was bullshit, knowing Lukas, at every available opportunity he would have used the contents, or lack of it, as ammunition against me. But he hadn't. When it came to us, he had been insecure, and I didn't think that was all down to how much stock I'd held in *my* prediction. Had he been under the influence too? Was it in the way he'd lost his nerve when we first got to London, and later on, in the way he'd hit self-destruct? Perhaps underneath all that striving had been the fear he'd amount to nothing. "That blank card," I said. "Are you sure it didn't scare the crap out of you?"

"What makes you say that?"

"It would have scared me."

"You'd have let it."

I dropped the subject. If I had stumbled on the truth, Lukas wasn't ready to admit it. And maybe he was right not to. I had given my prediction too much power, and irrespective of how false it turned out to be, through that one act of stupidity, I had very nearly lost the love of my life.

"I'm so sorry for everything I put us through." The words sounded so inadequate, barely hinting at how immensely at fault I had been, and I supposed I would find myself repeating them many times in the years to come. "I've been such a fool."

"There's nothing to forgive," Lukas said. "I've been foolish, you've been foolish—we both got taken for a ride by a filthy, rotten hippie—but it doesn't matter because we found our way back to each other."

Lukas's description of Shakti made me smile, and Zachary chose this moment to pipe up from the backseat with a deliriously enthusiastic "Ooowah" of his own, as if he had been listening to our conversation and had something to add. When we both turned to look at him at the same time, he was so pleased to have drawn our attention that an ecstatic grin spread over his entire face, crinkling his eyes and shooting drool down his chin. He had put so much effort into the exclamation and the smile that afterward I thought he would collapse from exhaustion. I loved him so much it brought a lump to my throat.

"And we've got him," said Lukas, beaming in my direction.

I took a deep breath, the first since we had landed at Heathrow, and made sure to measure our good fortune. We had money, health, brick walls to keep out the rain. We had Zachary. We had each other. We had left the commune far behind but it was the glue that held us together.

ACKNOWLEDGMENTS

For your long-distance loyalty, dedication, and enthusiasm, thank you, Lisa Grubka. For patience, encouragement, and incisive editing, Katherine Nintzel and Margaux Weisman. Thank you also to everyone at William Morrow, Fletcher & Company, and Foundry who helped *The Predictions* on its journey.

The author gratefully acknowledges the generous support of Creative New Zealand during the researching and writing of this book. ARTS COUNCIL NEW ZEALAND TOI AOTEAROA creative nz

I am indebted to Grimshaw & Co. and the Sargeson Trust for enabling me to finish it.

Thank you to my early readers and helpers: Martha Dewey, Marian Evans, Janis Freegard, Penny Hammond, Rachael King, Sarah Laing, Jonathan Lane, Peter Roberts, and Stephen Stratford.

Likewise to my colleagues and students at Auckland University of Technology, and to Dizengoff café for letting me scribble in the corner.

It takes a village to write a novel when you have young children. My most sincere thanks to all the friends and family who minded the babies, especially Azedear, Chris, and Lesley, who often looked after me as well. Matthew—I couldn't ask for a more loving and supportive husband. To share a life with you, Rafael, and Hector is my good fortune.

About the author

2 Meet Bianca Zander

About the book

3 Reading Group Guide

Read on

5 Excerpt from *The Girl Below*

Insights,
Interviews
& More . . .

Meet Bianca Zander

© Jane Ussher

BIANCA ZANDER is British-born but has lived in New Zealand for the past two decades. Her first novel, *The Girl Below*, was a finalist for the VCU Cabell First Novelist Award, and she is the recipient of the Creative New Zealand Louis Johnson New Writers' Bursary and the Grimshaw Sargeson Fellowship, recognizing her as one of New Zealand's eminent writers. She is a lecturer in creative writing at the Auckland University of Technology. ᷒

Reading Group Guide

1. *The Predictions* begins with
   the narrator's assertion that at
   Gaialands she was raised "to believe
   in freedom—personal, societal,
   spiritual." But this freedom is not
   always easily won. Can you think of
   some ways in which Gaialands is not
   a particularly "free" place?

2. Have you known a person like
   Shakti in your life? What causes
   some people to be so influential and
   charismatic? Do you think Shakti
   was a positive or negative influence
   on the children?

3. Lukas and Poppy's relationship
   has significant ups and downs.
   At times he seems extremely toxic,
   but then he often redeems himself.
   Ultimately, do you think Lukas is a
   good fit for Poppy? Why or why not?

4. How could Poppy's life have been
   different if she'd never received
   her prediction? Can you think of a
   moment in your own life that ended
   up changing the course of things
   irrevocably?

5. Poppy's impression of Gaialands
   when she returns with her own
   son is very different from that of
   her childhood. What are some of
   the most significant shifts in her
   feelings and opinions about the place
   and the way of life? ▶

Reading Group Guide *(continued)*

6. The novel's narrative follows its characters through many years of fads, fashions, and musical styles. How does the author use these changing trends to reflect the characters' actions and states of mind?

7. The author raises many interesting questions about fate and free will. Do you believe in fate? Why or why not? Can free will overcome destiny? ∾

Excerpt from
The Girl Below

London, 2003

IT WAS ONLY MAY, but the streets flared
golden like they do in high summer, and
all around me the neighborhood sighed
with so much privilege that I felt shut
out—a stranger on the block where my
childhood took place. In the twenty
years since we had moved away, Notting
Hill had changed beyond recognition,
become a kind of joke suburb—part
tourist bauble, part film set—and a
ludicrous place to say you were from.
Of course I'd changed too in that time,
but not so much that I was ready to
accept the slight. Instead, for the last
ten minutes, I had been glued to the
doorstep of our old building, staring
at a familiar name on the buzzer, too
shy to press it but feeling aggrieved that
I couldn't get in.

On the other side of a spiked black
railing, the basement flat was oblivious
to my injury, and bore no trace of our
having lived there. Fresh paint slicked
the iron bars that guarded the front
windows, and behind them our homely
green and orange curtains had been
replaced with stiff white venetian blinds.
Shorn long ago of my mother's pink
and red potted geraniums, the patio
was bald, and had been industrially
water-blasted to remove any residue of
dirt or character. Fleetingly, the lemony
scent of geranium leaves spiked my ▶

5

Excerpt from *The Girl Below* (*continued*)

nostrils and I saw my mother, hovering over her plants, trimming rogue stems and plucking off blooms that had died.

I had been right, in one way at least, about coming back to London: everything here reminded me of her. She had left behind a trail of crumbs, a dusting of sugar to guide me through the woods.

That day was only my second in London, but already the optimism I had been fizzing with was beginning to seem false. On the long flight over from New Zealand, I had imagined a triumphant homecoming: streamers and banners above a red carpet the length of Kensington Park Road, or at least an easy transition back to my old life. I had been out of the country for ten years, living in Auckland for most of that time, but I had thought that the old life would be waiting for me, that if you were born in a place and had grown up there, you were one of its citizens and it would always take you back.

Other places maybe, but not London. At the Heathrow arrivals gate, no one had been there to meet me. On the way into London on the tube, I had tried smiling at people, projecting a sunny attitude, but I had been met with frowns, and some had turned away. Getting off the tube at Willesden Green, I had gone into a newsagent's to buy a packet of wine gums, had excitedly told the cashier that you couldn't buy them in New Zealand, and he had silently—no, scornfully—handed me my change. Still feeling upbeat, I had walked from the tube station to my friend Belinda's flat only to discover no one was there. Belinda had left a note, and a key, and I had let myself in and sat down on my suitcase—stuffed to the zipper with all I owned—and that's when deflation began. I had come back to London without any plan besides entitlement, and staring at the two-seater couch in front of me that was about to become my bed, I realized what a fool I had been.

The name that had caught my attention on the buzzer of our old building was Peggy Wright: our former upstairs neighbor, a force of nature, someone to be reckoned with, older than my parents but ageless. I remembered her well—her high, cackling laugh, her lipstick-stained teeth—but wasn't sure if she'd remember me, at least not in my present incarnation. At the time we left the neighborhood, I was a scrawny eight-year-old waif in glasses so thick that no one—including me—knew what I looked like behind them. Since then, I had grown tall and robust and switched to contact lenses, but along with those things had come caution, and that's what hindered me now.

From the front stairs, I surveyed the altered street. The most obvious thing missing was Katy's, the junk shop that had doubled as a grocery store, and the first shop I had been allowed to visit on my own—pound note clutched in sticky hand—to buy bread and milk and liquorice allsorts. There was no signage over the door, just a blank awning, but everyone knew the old lady who owned it and referred to the shop by her name. Katy would have been well into her eighties or even nineties back then, and walked with the aid of a Zimmer frame, but she had the smile of a schoolgirl and ran her shop like she was one. Sliced bread and newspapers were her staples, but she sold these alongside a gargantuan pile of moth-eaten trash: lace doilies, books, curios, plates, petticoats, brooches, hats. How any of it got there, nobody knew, but if you spotted something in the junk pile you wanted to buy, Katy would examine it in her shaking hands as though she had no idea how it got there either. She would mutter that she just had to check with her daughter to see how much it was worth. And that would be the last you saw of it. Katy's daughter ran a stall in the Portobello Market arcade, and once alerted to the desirability of certain objects in her mother's junk shop, she whisked them away, polished them up, and rebirthed them as exorbitantly priced antiques. Now in place of Katy's there was a boutique for "hommes" with a solitary, art-directed sneaker displayed in its long, gleaming window—nothing else—and I wondered if it was progress or absurdity that Katy's path of excessive bric-a-brac had culminated, decades later, in a store for one-footed Frenchmen.

In front of me, the buzzer beckoned. What did I have to lose? Even if Peggy didn't recognize me, surely she'd remember my parents and that would at least get me a cup of tea and a biscuit. We could talk about Peggy's children, Harold and Pippa, who would be grown, with kids of their own by now. When I was a child, they were teenagers, old enough for Pippa to trip ▶

downstairs in her New Romantic get-up and impersonate a babysitter. Her brother, Harold, had been more of a rumor, a floppy-fringed sulker who'd gone away first to boarding school and then to Cambridge University, from where he'd come back arrogant and spoiled (or so my father was fond of saying). Harold did nothing to quash the impression of aloofness, hovering at the edge of Peggy's soirees, shunning endless games of charades, and never lowering his gaze to the level of grasshoppers such as myself.

Pippa, on the other hand, had been my idol, and being looked after by her had been an event. She always arrived in a cloud of hair spray and kohl, armed with secrets from the teenage frontline, and I'd looked forward to the nights my parents went to parties as much as if I too was going out. She would demonstrate the latest dance moves—mostly jerky, New Wave stuff—and if I hounded her, she tossed me a few scraps of advice about snogging and other unbelievable acts. "Don't put on too much lippy or it'll rub off on his face," and, "Never tell a guy you love him straight after you've bonked." She had magnificent boobs, quite the biggest I'd ever seen, and together we'd raided my mother's wardrobe and tried on all her clothes. Unlike her brother, she had not been sent to boarding school, but had made do with the local comprehensive and a hairdressing course at a third-rate polytechnic. My mother, who had gone without haircuts (and many other things) to send me to private school, thought Peggy had done her daughter a great disservice, but anyone who had ever met Harold could tell you that was not necessarily the case. Spurred on by such memories, I pressed Peggy's buzzer and felt the click of a small electric shock. A brisk voice hissed over the intercom, "Peggy Wright's residence. Can I help you?" She sounded formal, like a receptionist.

"I've come to see Peggy. I'm an old friend." The woman didn't reply but let me in, and I heaved open the front door, which slammed behind me on a spring. Since we'd lived there, the lobby had undergone a makeover. Instead of letters stacked on the radiator and piled haphazardly on the doormat, each apartment now had its own brass-numbered pigeonhole.

The smell was different too, no longer boiled cabbage and

mildew, but fresh paint and carpet shampoo. And Harold's bicycle, which had leaned permanently against the bottom staircase, someone had finally moved that too.

I bounded up the first five flights of stairs, eager to see Peggy, but with three still to go I was gasping for breath and had to stop for a rest. Each landing was more or less identical, so it was hard to be absolutely sure, but I thought this floor had belonged to Jimmy, the bogeyman of the building. I had not even known his last name, only feared him, and I'd never stopped on his landing in case he jumped out and threw a sack over my head. When I tried to recall his appearance now, all I could remember was a shadowy, retreating figure, his face a caved-in slab.

Peggy's front door was already open, sweet disinfectant vapors leaking out into the hall. I crossed the threshold, prepared for renovations, but none had been made: the black-lacquered walls, chessboard floor tiles, and accents of orange were, shockingly, identical to how I'd remembered them. So too was the ornamental birdcage, its perches wired with a colony of faded stuffed canaries. Not so much furniture as props, stage dressing for a farce set in 1970s Bohemia. So unchanged was the interior that when I looked in the hall mirror, I was surprised to see an adult face staring back at me.

The brisk woman appeared from the kitchen in white slacks and a white smock, an efficient spring in her white-plimsolled step. "She's just had her afternoon dose," she said. "So I expect she'll be rather groggy."

Too late, I noticed the dim lighting, the hushed, churchlike atmosphere, and regretted my impulsive visit. To arrive unannounced was so terribly un-English.

After ten years in the colonies, I had forgotten my manners. Not only that, but something was clearly wrong with Peggy, wrong enough that she required the services of a live-in nurse.

"I'll come back another time," I said. "I'd hate to disturb her." "It's probably best to see her while you still can," said the nurse, directing me across the hallway. "She's quite weak today but it always cheers her up to have visitors." Peggy had been moved into Pippa's old bedroom, close to the kitchen, closer to the front door if she needed to check out. The room was dark and cool, with ▸

Excerpt from *The Girl Below* (continued)

blinds at half-mast and thick net curtains obscuring the warm summer sun. It took a few seconds to locate Peggy, and much longer to recognize her. She was on a trolley bed, wrapped in a cocoon of crisp hospital sheets, the pillows tilted to cradle her piplike head. From her left arm, a drip trailed, and her skin spread like tracing paper over a map of her bones. Most of her hair had fallen out; what remained was aubergine fluff. But she still had her stenciled eyebrows, arched in permanent surprise, and I realized with an odd sting of pity that they must be tattooed on.

Trying not to wake her, I shuffled toward the bed, but a floorboard creaked under my shifting weight and her eyelids flickered open. She had trouble focusing, and looked blurrily up at the ceiling.

"Hello, Peggy," I said, softly. "It's Suki. Suki Piper." At the sound of my voice she started, and I picked up her dry, weightless hand and squeezed it to reassure her. "We used to live downstairs in the basement flat. I'm Hillary's daughter." My words did not register.

"We moved away a long time ago and I haven't seen you since—at least, I don't think I have. For some of that time, I've been living in New Zealand. My father, Ludo, went to live there when my parents separated. I think you saw Hillary a few times after that but she . . ." The end of the sentence got stuck in my throat.

Peggy blinked. "Hillary," she croaked, her lips sticking together at the corners. "Darling Hillary."

I tried to give her a drink of water, but most of it rolled down her chin, and I gave up, resting the glass on a side table next to a half-empty bottle of scotch. Alongside it sat a plastic measuring cup with a sticky brown residue on the rim. When I picked up Peggy's hand again, she pulled on mine, and her eyes danced a little, like they used to. "Lovely Hillary," she said. "How wonderful to see you!"

"I'm not Hillary. I'm her daughter, Suki."

"And how is Suki?" With great effort, Peggy lifted her hands to her face and made ring shapes around her eyes. "Pink glasses!" she exclaimed. "Always dancing. Wet the bed when she came to stay with us."

After this, she collapsed, closed her eyes, and began to snore. Mistaking me for Hillary meant Peggy didn't know, or had forgotten, that my mother was no longer alive. When people forgot I often couldn't bring myself to correct them. Sometimes they started reminiscing about Hillary's beauty, the way she'd lit up a room with her grace, or her legendary abilities to sew and cook, and by the time they asked the appalling but inevitable question, "How is she, your dear mother, Hillary?" the weight of their admiration bore down on me so hard I told them what they wanted to hear. "She moved to Scotland to look after Grandma," I'd explained to one old acquaintance, telling another that she'd gone to India in the midnineties to find herself and was still there on an ashram. Lousy fibs but much kinder on us all. Everyone had loved my mother—no one more so than I—and if I never said out loud that she'd died, then I sometimes believed that she hadn't.

While Peggy dozed, I stroked her hand and took an inventory of her daughter's old room. The dresser where Pippa had teased her hair and kohled her eyes for hours was in the same place, and so was the antique Victorian dollhouse, over in the corner by the window. Pippa had outgrown the dollhouse years before I came on the scene, but she'd remained proprietary of it, and had only begrudgingly tolerated my sticky fingers on its tiny antiques. Though the dollhouse was now dusty and faded, I had never encountered its equal, and I finally understood why she hadn't wanted to part with it. Really, it belonged in a museum—or here in this flat that was so much like one.

I let go of Peggy's hand and walked to the window, curious to see if our old terrace was visible from up here. Our basement flat had gone through from front to back, with a set of French doors opening out onto a patio. At first, I didn't recognize the chalk paths and lavender pots—it had been remodeled in ersatz French Provincial—and then one or two features stood out as familiar: the way the patio was on two levels, the white gate that led out to the communal garden. But what I couldn't locate—what I was, abruptly, desperate to see—was the pitted iron plate that marked the entrance to the air-raid shelter. This shelter was a relic from the Blitz, a deep concrete bunker where families had gone to sit ▶

Excerpt from *The Girl Below* (*continued*)

out the bombings during World War II. My family had gone down there too—only once—but the experience had been so awful, so chilling, that the bunker had quickly come to represent the most terrifying thing in my world. Even now, I shivered to recall the narrow stone stairs that descended into the chamber, how frigid the air had been so far under the earth, how we had not been able to get out.

Once more I scanned the terrace, looking for the trapdoor. Had I lost my bearings or was the air-raid shelter no longer there? Searching again, I found no trace of it, and surmised that it had been filled in or concreted over to prevent anyone's falling in. Good job, I thought with immense relief, for a death trap such as that had no business being in a garden. Peggy had stopped snoring, and her breathing was weak but regular. When I picked up her hand, she didn't stir. The room had become stuffy, claustrophobic, and I decided I had been there long enough.

Out in the hallway, trying to remember my way to the bathroom, I felt drugged, disoriented, as though Peggy's medication had leaked out through her skin. On the wall next to the phone was a list of emergency numbers, one of which was Pippa's, and I wrote it down on a dog-eared receipt from my pocket. Many of the rooms between Peggy's and the bathroom had been closed up, sealed off, but the door to one of the bedrooms was open, and I saw a mess of books and boxes spilling out. That must have been Harold's old room. How careless and wasteful, I thought, to have so many disused rooms in such a nice flat, when all I needed was one.

It was passing back through the drawing room that I saw her, and froze immediately with the rigid fear of a five-year-old.

How could I have missed her on the way to the bathroom? The statue of a young girl kneeling where she'd always knelt, on a dais between two faded velvet chaise longues that had once been cherry red. The dais was varnished mahogany, but the girl's skin was the color of dirty cement. She was rough-hewn, abstract: her smooth granite eyes had no irises. Her tiny hands were folded in her lap, and her hair was in a bowl cut. She wore an old-fashioned smocked dress with a round pansy collar. Peggy had called her Madeline—referring to her by name, affectionately and often, as though she were her daughter or a little friend.

She had been real to me too, though not in such a benign way. As a child, I had refused to be left alone with her, and even in a room full of adults, Madeline could freak me out. It was partly the blankness of her stare, a gaze that nevertheless followed me wherever I went in the room. And partly, it was that she was the same age as me but was stuck being that age and would never grow up. It made me think that inside her was a thwarted adult, who had grown evil over time because she was trapped in a noose of perpetual childhood.

Once, at one of Peggy's especially raucous parties, there'd been dozens of adults in the drawing room, dancing, drinking, laughing, and I was there too, up past my bedtime, and giddily lost in the forest of their legs. For a brief moment, those limbs had cleared, and there was Madeline, motionless but hunting me through the trees. My screams had been so hysterical that I had been taken home immediately—the party over for me and my parents.

On the sofa opposite Madeline's dais, I sat down to observe her from a safe distance. I was curious to know if she'd still have any power over me at twenty-eight years old.

To begin with I was fine, in control, but then outside, clouds passed overhead, casting Madeline's features into shadow. She had not moved, but my first thought was that it was Madeline who had taken all the light out of the room, and before I could reason against it, a sensation of quickening vertigo came over me. When I stood up to move away from her, I felt dizzy and also that I was physically shrinking. Around me, the room seemed to waver, but in a way that was too subtle to grasp. I looked down at my scuffed and ill-fitting trainers, bought in a size too big because I'd meant to use them for jogging but never had. The shoes appeared familiar, but I was sure that the feet inside them weren't mine—that these feet were tiny impostors. I held my hands out in front of my face, spread the fingers and wiggled them, but even these looked counterfeit, rogue hands on the ends of absurdly slender limbs. My perspective had shifted lower down, and for a few seconds, I was a child ▶

again—a child who was pensive and scared.

I bit down hard on my tongue, and one by one, the walls of Peggy's drawing room regained their density, and the weight of my adult feet sank into my shoes. Once more, I stood on solid ground, in a London apartment I had not been in for almost twenty years. An apartment so like a museum that briefly, I rationalized, it had pulled me back with it into the past. That I'd imagined the whole thing was plausible but that didn't change how unsettled I felt—especially when I turned to leave the drawing room and had the uncanny sensation that I was being watched.

Too late, I realized I had turned my back on Madeline, and when I swiveled round to face her, I fancied she was gloating. This amounted to nothing more than a dead-eyed stare—but then again, it never had. The year after next I'd turn thirty, but Madeline still had it over me. Her power was intact, had perhaps even grown. In the old, cowering way, I turned and walked out backward, hoping to catch the very last rays of that untimely summer evening. ❧